ELUSION

C.G. BLAINE

ISBN-13: 978-1-950847-01-3

To J,
for trying and failing to be cool.

"I hope for nothing. I fear nothing. I am free."
-Nikos Kazantzakis

A drum literally receives a beating anytime someone uses it, but hurl it into one concrete wall, and the shell cracks. This severe design flaw continues to run through my head while I run through the courtyard. I secure the towel around my waist and survey the students walking to class for any new faces.

Rusty's standing on the roof above me, watching my time tick away on his phone. We're closing in on the two-minute warning that he'll all too happily yell out. Excited for me to walk home in a lime-green thong, he wants me to fail, but the joke will be on him when he has to drive me to the hospital for hypothermia. My extremities are already aching and turning red.

This punishment system is archaic. We need a better method for settling shit between bandmates—at least during the winter. Even without a cold front dropping the temperature to sixteen degrees, February's not the month to run around sans clothes.

"Two minutes," he shouts, enjoying himself. "Pick it up, dude."

I sprint around the building where I hope to find an ample number of people, one of whom wants to act as savior to a random guy in a towel. First up, a petite blonde in a sleek black jacket with one of those saggy hats.

I skid to a stop in front of her and, for the eighth time, deliver my line. "Can I kiss you?"

She smiles, and my luck changes the moment her gaze lowers. She'll say yes.

I glance up to ensure Rusty's witnessing my impending victory. He flips me off. For someone who spends so much time without a shirt on, he should know better than to discount the power of a toned chest and abs.

My eyes move back toward the blonde but stop just short of their destination when a bright flash of color enters my field of vision. A red coat stands out against the white snow, dull gray buildings, and all-around lackluster surroundings of campus. The stark contrast draws me in, but the brunette wearing the coat makes my damn eyes refuse to look away.

"You want to kiss me?"

"What?" I ask, my stare hovering over the blonde's shoulder.

Her gaze follows mine straight to the beautiful girl in the red coat. When her head turns back around, she's no longer smiling. Understandable, considering she caught me checking out another girl at the same time I was trying to convince her to kiss me. She folds her arms across her chest, and I don't bother waiting for her no before running off.

Since she cost me a sure thing, my sights set—or reset—on Red Coat. On my way over, I only see one other person in the area other than her and her friend. *Shit, where is everyone?* Any other day, coeds are crawling all over this place.

By the time I reach her, I've entered full-blown panic mode. "Can I kiss you?"

Wide blue eyes give nothing away. Lips show no hint of a smile. She offers no indication of a yes. Nothing. *Damn.*

I reluctantly direct my tenth attempt at the bundled-up friend. "Can I kiss *you*?"

My new target looks at my original target, who shrugs, indifferent. Then my new target examines her feet and blushes through her freckles. So, a no from her.

I'm tempted to stay longer to convince Red Coat to overlook the towel, but my last shot walks some twenty yards away, and in a few seconds—

"A minute-thirty."

"Not helpful, Rusty," I shout as I dash away.

He laughs, and from three stories off the ground, he begins flirting with the two girls I left behind.

Really not helpful.

This blonde, in a drab brown coat, appears unamused when I saunter up. If ever there's a time for my confidence to save me, this is it. I take a breath, smile, and attempt a calmer tactic. "Hi, my name's—"

"Jordan," she says.

Shit. Do I know her?

A scowl on her face says I know her, but I don't know how I know her.

"Two weeks ago?"

My mind blanks.

"After your gig downtown?"

An absolute void.

"One minute ten seconds." Rusty's reminder further increases the awkwardness.

She sighs. "Samantha?"

"Of course. So glad I ran into you." I continue smiling even with zero recollection of her. "Can I kiss you?"

Her eyes widen, and she plants her back foot. I brace for her to slap me, which will be a fair ending to my morning. But she huffs and walks off, sparing me at the last second. At least she's permanently ingrained her name in my mind.

I drop my head back and try to massage away the tension in my forehead. My resource pool has dried up with one minute left.

I jerk my head back up when I get a glimpse of Red Coat. She peers at me over her shoulder. One minute's plenty of time for a last-ditch effort, and she's just given me an opening if I ever saw one.

My muscles are sluggish, but I manage a burst of speed in their direction and come to a stop in front of them. "Ladies, I apologize for earlier. I understand the oddity of my behavior and will gladly explain—"

"Forty seconds."

I flip off Rusty for interrupting my Hail Mary pass. "My name's Jordan. I love dogs, tolerate cats. I have a weird affinity for late eighties slash early nineties music." I glance between them. "Is this getting me anywhere?"

"Thirty. You're screwed, man."

"Shit, uh…" I rub my hands together as the cold compresses my nervous system. I'm shivering more and more, my fingers are gaining a blue tint, the brief surge of energy fades. I can't even think straight. Not to mention my poor dick and how far my balls have crawled up.

Screwed is right.

"What happens if time runs out?"

My eyes snap to the girl. "What?"

"When his countdown ends, what happens?"

"I lose the towel and am down to a G-string." I tack on a grin, aiming to win her over.

She shakes her head, but I can't gauge her response beyond that. Does she find me funny? Charismatic? Deserving of sympathy? Creepy enough to call campus security?

"Fifteen … fourteen…" Rusty continues counting down to my defeat as another uncontrollable shudder rolls through me.

She rolls her eyes. "I have a strict policy against weirdness before coffee, but kissing you wins out over seeing you in a thong, so…"

Wait, what?

"Five … four…"

She steps forward, and holy shit, she's going to kiss me. I lean down, still in disbelief she's going through with it until her warm lips press against mine. They burn in an incredible way, reigniting my dulled senses. Profanities rain down on us from Rusty, but his voice fades out when my body feels the heat coming from her.

So warm.

Primal survival instinct takes over.

I need her close.

One hand finds her lower back, pulling her to me. The other slides underneath her scarf, seeking the warmth of her skin. Our extreme temperature difference scorches the tips of my fingers. It makes her break the kiss, jerking back from me, and I'm colder than before, my mind slowing.

"Here." She unravels her fluffy purple scarf and drags off her vibrant pink hat. "Keep them. I don't want you to die of hypothermia."

Not my usual style, but I don't hesitate to accept. Once I wrap the scarf around my neck and pull the hat on, she fights off a smile. Even in a state of half-shutdown, I am confident in my ability to pull off such a ludicrous outfit and manage a grin. She responds, not close to how I expect, with the most abrupt exit I've ever witnessed. The friend has to rush to catch up with her, saying Red Coat's name, but my teeth chatter so loud that I miss it.

I consider following after them, but they're walking in the opposite direction of my clothes—my warm clothes in a warm bathroom a few warm buildings over. The anticipation of thermostat-controlled air hitting me when I open the door moves my feet before my brain issues any instructions. I almost start running again, and the more my muscles work, the more my mind clears.

I forgot to thank her.

Once inside, I offer a tight-lipped smile to the disapproving stares as I cruise through the hallway. Everyone acts like they've never seen anyone wander through the science hall in only a towel, scarf, and the boldest hat imaginable.

Rusty's laughter spills out when I push the door open to the men's room. "The dude is introducing himself, telling them he likes cats and shit. Totally worth the broken tom."

"Which I already paid for," I shout to whoever he's talking to on the phone.

I slam the button on the hand dryer. The heat burns my stiff fingers, and even the mostly room-temp air hitting my feet stings. After finger function improves, I'll need to double-check the symptoms of frostbite.

"Hey, Jordan." Rusty snaps a picture when I raise my head.

Perfect.

I rip off the hat and scarf and toss them on the counter by the sink. He digs my phone, wallet, and keys out of his pocket while I swipe my T-shirt and jeans off the counter. Socks and boxers are noticeably absent, but I accept this. My punishment could have been far worse, given the gravity of my offense.

A few weeks earlier, when Rusty dropped Gavin's bass guitar, Gavin made him jump into the lake and refused to let him bring a change of clothes. The poor guy formed icicles on the walk back to the van. I like to think the experience softened him to my benefit, if only slightly.

As I use a mirror to tame the dark mess on my head into its proper level of disorder, a security guard steps in. He closely monitors us as he checks for feet under the stalls. Rusty threatens to laugh, so I shoot him a warning glare. I'm not about to go down for his choice of punishment. Any trouble with the university would disrupt my parents' plans for my future, and I prefer not to deal with them.

"You boys see anyone come in here with a towel on?" he asks.

I move in front of the one on the counter and nudge it into the sink behind me. We both shake our heads, Rusty overplaying his hand with a shoulder shrug. The security guard leers a few seconds longer before leaving. The door swings shut, and Rusty's hysterics resonate through the stalls.

When we step into the cold air again, we head toward the parking lot. Heat pours from the vents in my Jeep, the engine still warm after my ten-minute excursion into the land of public indecency. An ache creeps into my toes as sensation returns.

"This picture of you should be all over Easton's campus by this afternoon. Maybe we can use it as the band's new flyer."

Rusty's comment reminds me of the hat and scarf in my coat pocket. I pull them out, and the front seat fills with the scent of … coconut maybe? No non-creepy way exists to smell someone else's clothing, so I commit and press my nose to the hat. Still not sure.

"Dude, smell this." I shove the hat in Rusty's face. "Coconut?"

"Hell if I know, but it smells good." He snatches the scarf from my hand and sniffs. "I detect a hint of eucalyptus."

I'm not even going to tread on why he knows that.

With the scarf about halfway to my nose, I become conscious of the lady eyeing us from her parked car. I drop the scarf and throw the gear shifter in reverse before she calls campus security, and they search the vehicle for a body.

Shit. I missed her name. Haley? Molly? Who kisses someone without asking for their name?

Now that my brain is working outside of survival mode, I want to find her. At least to return her things and thank her. Maybe explain I'm not a nudist or apologize for kissing her longer than appropriate. But between the warmth radiating off her and those soft lips, I blocked out the unusual circumstances.

"Did you recognize those girls?"

Rusty grunts a no, helpful as always.

This part of campus includes the science building and freshmen dorms. Neither offers much information to go on. Freshmen females plus girls enrolled in science classes equals, you tool, why didn't you ask for her name?

The answer's obvious; I never think further ahead than five minutes.

I remember she mentioned coffee and flip on the blinker to turn right toward a new coffee shop on Anna Street. Rusty's phone stops him from noticing our change of direction. He'll carefully monitor the response to the picture for the rest of the day. Beta Void has a few gigs on the horizon that the guys have wanted to draw more attention to. So glad I could provide for them.

"You want anything?" I ask, parking across from Java Quest.

Another no grunt answers me.

Such an articulate individual, but his tattooed bad-boy persona more than makes up for it with the ladies. None of them care if he can put his emotions into eloquent words when he wails on the drums, shirtless, with a cigarette hanging out of his mouth.

I leave the keys and stick the hat and scarf back in my pocket. Crossing the street, I have no clue what I'm doing. I kissed a random girl, bloodhound-smelled her clothing, and tracked her across campus. Hi, Jordan Waters, creepy stalker, sounds like a pretty accurate description of me at this point.

The place is crowded for so early on a Monday, almost every seat with a body in it. I scan the tables up front without luck. A few more steps in, and my eyes catch on a red coat slung over an empty chair in the back. I would bet my life a pair of blue eyes accompanies the brunette one seat over.

I take advantage of a lull at the counter and mull over opening lines while the barista fetches my order. At a gig, meeting girls requires minimal output on my part—eye contact, a slight nod, smile as I set down my guitar, and then I walk past her and wait for her to find me. Foolproof. Any work outside of that, and I bail.

"Hey, Jordan, love the winter wear."

A nod thanks the person following the band's social media. A few more peek up from their tables as I breeze through.

Yeah, that's me wearing a towel.

I recognize the friend with her red hair pulled back from a young face. Eighteen, nineteen at most.

The perfect line hits me, and I slide into the last empty chair at their high-top table. "The wildest thing happened to me this morning, let me tell you."

I sip my coffee and watch the girl over the top of the lid. Dark layers frame her face as vivid blue eyes focus on her cup. She looks older than the friend, more mature. Her lips press together, suppressing a smile. A challenge I accept.

"So, as I was saying…" I turn in my chair to talk to the friend. "My temper got the best of me over the weekend, and I broke something that wasn't mine. Even though I replaced the drum, my buddy chose to punish me. Which is how I ended up running around campus, wearing a towel, trying to find someone to kiss me in under five minutes."

Out of the corner of my eye, I check on her but only find pretty eyes blinking. Damn, she roughs up the ego. The friend, on the other hand, giggles and gives the reaction my performance deserves.

"See, Callie? I told you there was a good reason."

I have a name. Callie. Unreadable, beautiful Callie.

The friend is my in.

"Officially, I'm Jordan Waters. And you are?"

"Felicia. Felicia Gibson," she says. "This is Callie Henders."

I look back to Callie and present her with the hat and scarf from my pocket. "I believe these belong to you."

"Thank you." She tucks them in her coat.

"Thank you for not letting me die of hypothermia."

A polite smile is her only response, and she returns to staring at her cup. She wants nothing to do with me, so it's time to retreat and lick my wounds. I scrape the chair over the linoleum, loudly announcing my exit. Everyone in the vicinity grimaces at the sound with one exception. Callie rewards me with a real smile.

Mission accomplished. Even though it only lasts a second.

"Ladies." I pause next to her, and she looks up. "I want you to know that I plan on being fully clothed for all future encounters."

A catcall and three fist bumps from strangers later, I push out the door.

Rusty remains unmoved, eyes on his phone when I return to the Jeep. "Pic has been reposted, shared, liked, hearted, and made into a meme. This chick and her coconut hat added a hundred followers in twenty minutes."

"Callie," I say.

"What?"

"Her name."

"Well then, Callie, wherever you are, sweetheart, thank you." He jerks his head around, confused. "Where the hell are *we*?"

I chuckle, pulling into the street, and chance a glance out the window, toward the coffee shop.

No hat.

No blue eyes.

No idea how I'm going to get her out of my head.

What type of person has no social media presence? Serial killers? Cult leaders? Beautiful girls who want nothing to do with me? Despite an extensive search last night, I search her name again.

Nothing.

Again.

I flop back on my bed and stare at the ceiling, thinking about her. This adds to the two days' worth of classes and most of the night I've already spent wondering why she would kiss me and then not want to talk to me. If I made an asshole comment or maybe, off the top of my head, checked out another girl in front of her, I would understand.

The door opens without a knock, and Benji waltzes in. He goes straight to my dresser, checks his blond bun in the mirror, and nods at me on his way out.

What the hell?

I attribute his strange behavior to him being Benji. He's a fantastic front man and singer but a peculiar guy nonetheless. Also, the best friend a person can find.

My thoughts drift to later and the frat party we're set to play. With Gavin a member at one of the houses, we receive plenty of invites to parties, along with opportunities to play shows. A gig's a gig, but I wish we'd quit playing college keggers. We should perform at more clubs and bars. Several feature live music on the weekends, one of which I want to check out when we go out for my twenty-first birthday.

The door opens without a knock, and Benji waltzes in—wait, this seems familiar. This time, he plops down on the bed, leans back against the headboard, crosses his ankles, and rests his hands behind his head. "You're welcome."

This guy.

I sit up on the edge of the bed and turn toward him. "What did you do for me?"

"Vanessa was downstairs, looking for you, so I checked your room to see if you were here. You weren't."

"Thank you," I say, and I mean it.

Vanessa plays a role polar opposite to the one of Callie Henders. She won't stop talking to me after we hooked-up over winter break. It's been over a week since she last asked me to call her. It's also been over two weeks since I deleted her number.

In comes Rusty, and without hesitation, he stretches out on the bed between Benji and me. Fresh out of the shower, he's ready for tonight with his black hair spiked down the middle, holes in his jeans, and a white button-down he'll only keep on through our first song.

I'm struggling to remember when exactly I enacted an open-door policy to my room. "Can I help you?"

"Was Vanessa here?"

"Apparently." I scoot further down my suddenly crowded mattress.

Benji tugs on his lip piercings. "She's shown up twice now. Jordan needs to find a better way of getting his point across."

"Or get his *point* across her sweet ass one more time," Rusty says, ever the charmer. "Unless you're still in a mood."

"It's not a mood," I snap, doing nothing to help my case.

"What's not a mood?" Gavin asks on his way in.

"We're talking about Jordan's mood the last two days." Rusty shifts closer to Benji to make space for him.

"Oh, yeah. What's up with that?" Gavin sits down and reclines into a similar position to Benji's.

He rubs a hand over his buzzed hair. We're still adjusting to the new look, and Rusty reaches over to touch his head, too.

So weird. It feels like I'm hosting a damn sleepover for a bunch of preteen girls.

"It's not a mood," I repeat.

"I think he's bored," Gavin says.

"Why would he be bored?" Rusty asks. "The dude does whatever the hell he wants."

Benji gets in on it, shaking his head. "That's exactly the problem, man. He's not being challenged."

Oh, great. Here they go.

"He needs to do something new."

"Or someone new."

"No, he does that every week."

"Maybe he needs a hobby."

"Something he commits to for once would be good."

"Let's not get carried away, boys. We're talking about Jordan here."

Jesus. Throw a blonde wig on Gavin and add a few comments about how I'm a disappointment, and we're at a family dinner at my parents' house.

I get to my feet and go to the door. "Can you guys decide what I need in my life in any other room of this house?"

They stare at me for a second before picking up their conversation again. I walk out and down the stairs to the living room. The merry band of misfits has successfully driven me out of my own room. They do this—talk about me like I'm not there and sort through all the parts of my life they deem need fixing. I collapse on the couch to wait them out.

A new addition to our wardrobe for the night sits on the coffee table. The color shows through the translucent plastic bag, catching my eye. I reach in and pull out a pink hat. And another. And another. And one more. All are identical to Callie's, but none smell like coconut. Three of them go back in the bag, but I stick the fourth down in the couch cushions. I'm over the color pink, hats, and beautiful cult-leading serial killers who want nothing to do with me. More importantly, I'm done letting it put me in a mood.

Once my roommates recommend that I buy a pet rabbit to solve all my problems, we load up Gavin's van and drive over to the frat house. We carry in our equipment and start setting up on a small stage in the corner of the living room. Most of the time, we perform on the floor, so an actual performance space impresses me.

Gavin brings over one of my cables. "What will it take for you to finish setting up for me?"

I think it over for a second and say, "You tear down for me."

"Done." He jumps off the stage, sights set on two girls giggling in a corner.

One of them came by the house over the weekend. A hard-to-get woman who insists on getting to know him before she sleeps with him. He spent an hour complaining about her the other night and swore up and down that he was done with her. Not so much.

Sound check goes quick, and Rusty's shirt peels off earlier than expected. He entertains a group at the keg while we all get a beer. The only set of long legs in combat boots strikes up a conversation with Benji. She "really digs" his neck tattoo but refers to it as a quarter note instead of an eighth note, so he loses interest fast.

When the four of us reconvene on the stage, they groan over my sabotage of the cute group costume. I ignore them. They don't need me to participate. Dozens of other people are walking around the party, wearing pink hats. The damn things are unavoidable.

Benji gives his introduction, and Rusty counts us in to start our first of two sets. Gavin's chick hovers near the corner of the stage, and his focus stays on her. During the second song, Rusty stands up to get a better view of his options. He smirks, sitting back down once he picks out which coed he wants. Soon after, a black skirt and green jacket gain Benji's attention.

I concentrate on the music for a few more minutes before I spot a petite blonde. Not *a* petite blonde. *The* petite blonde whose eyes said yes the other day until I blew it. She smiles, indicating forgiveness. Man, am I glad she's not wearing a pink hat.

Eye contact? Check. Head nod? Check. Now, I just need to entertain her until I put my guitar down.

All of us make better performers when we show off for someone. Benji exercises more range with his vocals. I throw a little creativity into my riffs. Stick tosses become a part of Rusty's routine. Gavin does … well, whatever the hell a bass player does to look more impressive.

Petite Blonde moves farther back in the crowd with a friend, and I reposition onstage to see her. When I find her, my gaze wanders right over her head to the red coat walking into the house.

Callie.

Petite Blonde who?

The friend, Felicia, grabs Callie's hand and leads her up the stairs. A few minutes later, they bounce down with another girl in tow and quickly disappear into the kitchen. They return with red beer cups, and when they stop in the middle of the room, Callie looks to the stage.

My eyes drop to the fretboard on my guitar. Why? I have no excuse other than she surprised me. She must not frequent frat parties or I would have noticed her before now. Especially if she'd worn a tight top and ass-hugging jeans like she is tonight. By the time I casually glance up, she is no longer standing where I left her. Her blue sweater moves toward the front door, and then out she goes. Since she doesn't take her coat, I don't worry about her leaving for long.

Over the next two songs, I practice what to say when I accidentally bump into her later. It's Callie, right? What are you doing here? Are you stalking me?

Questions only. Anything to keep her talking.

She comes back inside, almost causing me to miss the transition to our next song.

Two more to go.

Not staying anywhere long, she wanders around the party. It makes tracking her a full-time job. On her way past, her eyes finally connect with mine. I nod, completing both steps one and two. As she rounds the corner and heads up the stairs, we start our last song. The same song we're playing when she descends and walks out the door, wearing her coat.

Shit.

The remaining two minutes of the set might as well last an hour. I cut the final note short, rip off my strap, and lean my guitar against my amp. Benji says something, but I jump off the stage and push my way through the people.

I stop short when someone steps in front of me. Petite Blonde, who I forgot about until now.

"I thought I recognized you yesterday," she says.

"Uh." I wonder how many people would notice if I shoved her out of my way. Too many probably. "You know, I should really—"

"Well, if you ask me again, I won't say no."

Persistent—one of my favorite qualities in a woman … until this very second.

"Oh, well, that was just a friendly reminder to always stay aware of your surroundings when walking alone." I have no idea what the hell I'm prattling on about, but it sounds legitimate. "Anytime someone you don't know approaches you, please be prepared to use pepper spray, a whistle, or to utilize self-defense."

My security speech wraps up as Rusty turns on music to play during our break. The pounding bass provides a distraction, and I slip around a now-confused blonde.

The door swings open when I bolt out, banging against the house and back shut. Callie only has a few minutes on me. A cab takes longer, and she wouldn't have made it far on foot. I stop at the end of the sidewalk, clasping my hands behind my head, and scan up and down the street.

Nothing. Nowhere. Gone.

I let out my frustrations through multiple syllables' worth of obscenities. Once again, the girl has derailed me. My arms drop to my sides on my way back to the porch, but the disappointment only lasts until I reach the steps. A body leans over the banister—big, round eyes watching me.

"Callie Henders," I say with a smile.

So much for my questions-only tactic.

"Too many clothes on to enjoy a run?" she asks.

At least she's talking this time. Better yet, she's asking questions, which require answers and guarantee a more extensive conversation.

"Actually, I spotted a red coat leaving and hoped to catch it."

"No redcoats," she says, not missing a beat. "But Paul Revere rode through a few minutes ago."

"Clever girl."

I hop up onto the banister, close enough to her that I catch the scent of coconut. She doesn't move away when my thigh brushes her arm. A positive sign.

"Shouldn't you match the rest of your band with a pink hat?" She's so much better at questions than I am.

"I've experienced the real thing. A cheap replica will never do it for me now."

"I told you to keep it." She hands me her hat from her coat pocket, and I brush my fingertips over her hand while taking it. "It's the least I can do, considering the picture."

I jump down, pulling it on, and lean next to her. "I think you owe me something else, too." The comment sounds more suggestive than I intended, and she raises her eyebrows.

"Which do you prefer, dogs or cats?"

She relaxes back on the banister, realizing what I meant. "I'm also more of a dog person, but I like some cats."

"Music preference?"

I wait for the standard answer of *I like everything*, but she asks, "General or specific?"

"The more specific, the better."

"Eighties hair bands, nineties grunge, late-nineties alt-rock." She pauses, really thinking it over before adding, "With a guilty pleasure of anything two-thousands pop."

"Where have you been all my life?" I ask.

I expect a flirty response or maybe even a blush, but the same fake smile from the coffee shop appears. She straightens, and without another word, she tries to step around me. Damn it. I keep going in the wrong direction with her.

"Hold on, we're not going back to this." I sidestep to place myself between her and any potential exit. "The polite-smile-and-not-talking thing. I've invested too much time to go back to that."

She laughs once, clearly annoyed. "Too much time? We've had maybe seven minutes of interaction."

"Interaction, yes. But I spent time yesterday morning tracking you down at the coffee shop. I spaced out through classes both yesterday and today, trying to figure out why you wouldn't talk to me." I tick off the interruptions to my life on my fingers. "I scoured social media last night, trying to track you down." A little earlier, too, but she doesn't need to know *everything*. "A complete failure, by the way. And since you walked in tonight, I've been practicing talking to you in my head."

She stares at me, not giving off any clues to what she's thinking. It drives me mad that I can't read her, and I'm about to ask, but music floods out of the house. She looks at whoever steps out behind me.

"Ready, Jordan?" Rusty asks.

"Really not a good time, Rustin," I say, not taking my eyes off her.

"Yeah, we don't care. Oh … hey, Callie."

As the noise dampens, her attention shifts to me. "You told your friend my name?"

"No," I lie. A smile plays on her lips, and I need more time with her. "Can I borrow your scarf?"

She hands it over without any questions. Hoarding all her winter wear lowers the chances of her disappearing while I play the rest of the show. Not a solid plan, but it's better than nothing.

"We have another thirty-minute set before I'm finished for the night. Then I'm going to win you over." I slowly back toward the door and push it open. "Drink. Stay. Good Callie."

"You're going to win me over?" she asks.

"Yeah, you don't want to miss it." I step into the house and wink at her before shutting the door.

I need a new strategy. An idea that doesn't rely on my no-longer-foolproof system. I glance around the party for inspiration, but instead, I find Benji.

He shoulders into me as he walks by. "You finally decide to lean in?"

"What the hell does that even mean?"

"The hat." He gestures to my head with his beer cup. "You decided to stop fighting it and lean in. Make it work for you."

Brilliant.

I grab his face in my hands, the purple scarf rubbing against his cheek. "Benji, you fucking genius."

* * *

Yesterday's degenerate stares back at me in the mirror. Thankfully, pink emphasizes my green eyes because, for the second time in two days, I'm in a towel, a frilly scarf, and the now-iconic hat. At least I'm wearing my own underwear this time. I imagine the grand finale will include someone ripping off the towel since my friends are obnoxious. But to be fair, I would do the exact same thing to any one of them.

"All right, Waters. Let's go make her smile."

I burst through the bathroom door and dash down the stairs. The crowd parts, and I barrel-roll onto the stage to cheers and laughter. As I throw the guitar strap over my head, I scan over the faces. No sign of Callie. If she doesn't walk through that door, then all this is for nothing.

Rusty counts us in, and I check my finger position. With the first strum, my eyes lock on her coming back inside. I'm still in the game. I keep a vigilant watch on the stairs, waiting for her to come down. Lucky for everyone in attendance, I can play our set comatose because anything happening anywhere other than the base of the stairs fails to register at all.

At the end of our first song, her hugging-in-all-the-right-places sweater rematerializes. She looks everywhere but the stage while she maneuvers through the room. Damn it, woman. I'm playing up here without clothes on for her, and she still manages to evade me.

After pushing through the crowd, she reaches the best weapon in my arsenal. The friend. Felicia grasps Callie's chin, twisting it in my direction. I put on what Gavin calls my *get some* smirk and zero in on her. It takes a second, but she smiles. Real. Incredible. No joke, I develop tunnel vision. She demands my attention, and I have no idea why. All I know is she needs to smile again.

My next idea for Mission Make Her Smile develops toward the end of our set. Benji agrees when I shout my request in his ear. We play this song all the time for the hell of it, and it just so happens to perfectly fit.

On the last note of our final song, I hold the whammy bar longer than necessary because, well, I'm that guy. Callie's on the couch off to the side of the room in perfect view.

Listen up, beautiful.

Benji nods to me and calls out the song for the other two. Rusty tosses his head back, chuckling. He loves this song as much as I do. A perplexed Gavin shrugs his shoulders, wondering what the hell I'm doing. Yeah, I can't recall ever working this hard in my life to get laid.

"Unfortunately, guys and gals and non-binary pals, our evening with you has come to an end." Benji rattles off his spiel into the microphone, the crowd groaning in response. "I know. I know. But lucky for you, Jordan, in all his scantily clad glory, has made one final song request."

They roar to life again at the opening notes for Guns N' Roses "Sweet Child o' Mine." Late eighties hair metal? Check. For the verses, I join Benji at the mic, serenading the girl with the smile and the bluest eyes. I kill my solo, unsurprisingly, and as I hit the last note of the song, Benji rips off my towel. His disappointment is obvious when he sees my boxers. Like I said, they're obnoxious. After a dramatic bow, I set down my guitar, leap offstage, and sprint upstairs.

Now, *that's* what it looks like to win someone over.

The bathroom's occupied, making me glad I didn't leave my clothes in there. I dress in a room lit by the light of the hallway. Coats cover the bed. Callie's sticks out among the multiple black jackets, so I tuck her hat and scarf in the pocket. Thanks for the loan, and I hope never to wear them again.

"So much for being fully clothed for all future encounters." Her reflection watches me in the mirror when I look up.

"A senseless thing to say." I turn around for a better view, not disappointed by what I get. "I meant, all future encounters in public. I guess I failed on that front as well."

She wanders the edge of the room, touching every object on the shelves as she passes. "An interesting song choice."

"What can I say?" I sidestep into her path, hip-checking the dresser in the process. It fucking hurts, but I work through the pain. "Inspiration struck."

She stops in front of me, and the scent of her fogs my brain. Her eyes only momentarily distract me from my target. Her pouty lips. Mindful of how she spooks and reverts to being polite, I move slow. She lets me tuck her hair behind her ear and seems wanting as my hand lingers on her cheek.

Execute, Waters.

I lean down and press my lips to hers. It's the same sensation as the first time I kissed her, but this time, the heat has nothing to do with a temperature difference. My fingers curl around the back of her neck, pulling her closer. She runs her hands up my chest and parts her lips. My tongue dives in, stroking hers, and then—

She's three steps away and once again a challenge to my ego.

"Sorry." She touches her lips where mine belong. "I'm unsure about this..." She looks at the door when someone laughs in the hall.

"If you put your tongue in my mouth unsure, I'm dying to see where you put it when you're certain."

It's a shitty joke in my head and sounds much worse out loud. I internally cringe as shock widens her eyes. Then they narrow.

"I am so sorry, Callie. Sometimes, the asshole falls out of my mouth."

She grabs her coat out of the pile, not even looking at me anymore. "I was going to say, I'm unsure about this being the best place, considering everyone's coats are in here."

On her way by, I touch her arm, and she whirls around, wearing a scowl for the history books.

"Do not touch me. I was right the first time."

Out the door she goes.

Two steps into following her, I stop.

What am I doing? I do not pursue girls. But my life has consisted of very little else since meeting this one. Every time she does something unexpected, I rack my brain to figure her out. My fascination comes from the chase. It's the challenge tempting me, not the girl. Maybe refusing to run after her will counteract whatever power she holds over me. I should let this bring our little adventure to an end.

Sound reasoning, yet my urge to go after her decreases zero percent.

I make it almost three steps and circle back, cursing my inability to let this go—to let her go. She is, without a doubt, uninterested. Why waste my time? A ticking clock hangs over my freedom. The parental unit laid out our deal in unmistakable terms: use these years to get everything out of my system before settling in for a mindless existence full of responsibility—not in those exact words. They used terms like law school, prestigious attorney, and high-profile law firm, but the outcome remains the same. I won't waste a single second to pursue one girl for one night. Especially one I've so royally screwed up with already.

This time, my argument defeats the overwhelming impulse to race after her. She'll be fine. I'll be fine. I just need to not think about her.

My resolve lasts about another three seconds.

Shit.

I tear out of the house so fast that I jump over someone sitting on the stairs.

———

My stupid ass keeps a twenty-foot distance between us as we walk the blistering cold, snow-covered sidewalks back to her dorm. Dead phone. No coat. Number one contender for this year's polar dip right here, folks.

I consider trying to catch up, but the last time, Callie warned me about the pepper spray on her keychain, and the time before, she threatened to call the cops. Someone has apparently already given her a random campus security speech on what to do if a stranger approaches.

After a car drives by with a drunk loser yelling at her out the passenger window, I once again attempt to cross the great divide. She ignores me but at least lets me walk next to her. I stay quiet, not willing to push my luck. Blocks pass without so much as a blink in my direction. Then, out of nowhere, she takes off her gloves and hands them to me. Any chivalry that would stop me from accepting the offer froze and fell off blocks ago.

It appears that braving subzero temperatures garners her sympathies. Good to know, except I don't seek her sympathy. I just want to make sure she reaches the dorms without issue since she stubbornly refused to let me drive her or wait for a ride. Granted, chasing her down the street made the situation worse; therefore, I accept partial responsibility for my current predicament. A twenty-eighty split with her shouldering the brunt of the load. But I couldn't let her walk alone.

She catches me staring at her and rolls her eyes. God, her sass is strong and the allure undeniable. It reels me back in, and I want to figure her out more than ever.

Maybe she's a virgin. Sex tends to carry more emotional weight for the inexperienced ones, and my shit joke offended her. Plausible.

Maybe she has a boyfriend. Colleges on opposite sides of the country forced them apart, but she remains determined to keep her promises. Admirable.

Maybe she's hiding a deep, dark secret, like a Mafia boss father. She wants to keep him from putting a hit out on me, which he does to everyone with a dick that comes near her. Dangerous.

Maybe—

Oh shit, we're at her building.

I follow her inside, planning to apologize when she stops to dig out her keys. Only the key turns in the lock before I think of anything to say. She walks in but leaves the door open. Quite the symbolism.

Freshmen dorm suites. A common living space with two separate rooms attached. I do not miss these.

On the couch sits two girls. Their jaws slacken as I come in from the hall. Given the reaction, I gather Callie doesn't frequently bring dudes back. It oddly supports all three of my theories: a virgin with a boyfriend in California and a don for a father.

Somehow, I want her more.

"Jess, Cam, this is Jordan." She motions over her shoulder in my vicinity without pausing.

I give an awkward head nod while the one with light-brown hair undresses me with her eyes. The other, a dark blonde, shakes her head and returns her attention to the TV.

Callie hangs up her coat on her way to her room. I continue to shadow her because—might as well admit it—I'm nothing more than a hopeless puppy dog in the girl's wake.

Above her bed on the wall hangs a bulletin board featuring a calendar with numbers written in the center of each day. Being after midnight, today's one sixty-eight. She plans that far in advance, and I don't know what I'm doing from one minute to the next.

On the nightstand, there's a picture of her with a boy and girl. Siblings. The young girl resembles her, and the teenage boy shares both her hair color and high cheekbones. They appear to be a happy family, smiling, arms around each other.

"Call a ride," she says, taking her gloves from my hand.

"Phone's dead."

She tosses me her unlocked phone.

I tap the browser and search the number for a cab but lose all motor function when she lifts her sweater over her head. The flawless skin on her back displays a single freckle on her shoulder blade, next to her purple bra strap.

My virgin theory takes on water as she slips her jeans down over her hips and steps out, not caring I'm in the room. The purple lace panties grip the curves of her ass, but my attention slides back north the second she unhooks her bra. Chivalry still lost to the frigid night, I watch her slide the straps down her arms and drop it on the floor. Callie reaches for a tank top, spinning around before she pulls it all the way on. The clear view of her perfect tits produces the appropriate biological response, and I'm hard.

She looks up, and my eyes fly back to the screen.

"I'll be right back." She smirks on her way past me, well aware of her effect. "Oh, and I really hope you enjoyed the show because I'm *certain* you won't receive another one."

The door shuts behind her, and my mouth falls open. *Holy shit.* She just gave me a payback erection for my dick comment. One I have to adjust before remembering to call for a cab.

While on hold, I pace the small room. Under normal circumstances, I'd cut my losses and walk away without a second thought. But I'm starting to view Callie as a unique case. Something about her messes with my head.

Benji's advice from earlier might apply. Instead of fighting the chase, maybe I lean in. Like steering into a skid to regain control. The guys think I need a fresh challenge or new experience or something to commit to. What if I dedicate some time to decipher the enigma of her and knock out all three? Trying to fuck a hot puzzle sounds far more practical than their solution of a pet. Also a hell of a lot more fun.

By the end of the call, I've decided on a never-before-taken course of action. I'm going to spend some time on her and see what happens.

I close my eyes and point at her calendar. Shit, I landed on my birthday. I pick again but land on the same date. Very well. I have until a week from Friday to screw her. Then, win or lose, I'll walk away from Callie Henders.

Here everyone thinks the apocalypse needs to occur for me to make a plan. All it really takes is two hypothermal events and a chick throwing down the gauntlet. Of course, this is about as well thought out as everything else in my life. Not at all.

I swipe through her contacts and grab a pen from the desk to write Felicia's number on my palm. She'll give me an advantage if I play my cards right. Curiosity gets the best of me, so I also flip through her calendar for the reason behind her countdown. A giant red circle surrounds July 23 with the number nineteen in the middle. Birthday.

When I hear footsteps returning, I lie down on the bed to look inconspicuous. Not my brightest idea, but better than her catching me going through her shit. As Callie slips in, unfortunately wearing shorts, a text message from a Connor vibrates her phone.

California lover?

"Cab will be here in ten," I say, holding out her phone. "Someone texted."

She laughs at the screen.

"Boyfriend?"

She reaches between the bed and nightstand for her phone charger, brushing my arm on the way. "It's my little brother."

The answer doesn't clarify whether she has a boyfriend. If I plan on spending the next week-plus trying to get with her, I should double-check a few things.

I sit up on the edge of her bed. "Do you know anyone between the ages of eighteen and twenty-two on the West Coast?"

Her head tilts to the side. "That's an oddly specific question, but no, I can't think of anyone."

Two theories down. One to go.

"What does your father do?"

She rolls her eyes. "Factory worker."

Mental note of the reaction.

"Are you Italian?"

"Not to my knowledge."

"Any ties to the Mafia?"

Smooth, Waters.

"No?" she asks rather than tells.

"Would you honestly tell me if you had ties to the Mafia? Is that, like, a rule or something?"

"What are you talking about?"

"Nothing." I lick my lips, questioning the legitimacy of her Mafia answers but decide to focus on a more important point. "I'm incredibly sorry for what I said earlier. I meant it as a joke, but after that, I might refrain from making any jokes ever again."

She gives her polite, half-assed smile. "Apology accepted. And I'm sorry about my retaliation. It was childish."

But hot.

"Great. We're both sorry and both forgiven." I stand up, ready to move on to the main event. "Now, back to winning you over."

She crosses the room to a desk and sorts a stack of textbooks into new piles. "Don't waste your time."

I chuckle. "Oh no." I tried that logic. It didn't work. "We're far beyond that argument."

Callie stops with the books and turns toward me, her eyes soft and kind. I use the same look anytime I let someone down easy.

"Look, between school and everything else, my life is complicated enough. I can't handle anything else right now."

"Your life's complicated..." I repeat.

An interesting yet vague deterrent—also an excuse I used until last year when it backfired. Sweet Leah took it upon herself to help me in overcoming my "complicated life." She wanted to help me study and run errands for me. It took weeks to get rid of her.

Well, Callie's met her Leah.

"So, you need someone to make your life easier."

"Yeah," she says dryly, "because it's that simple."

What makes an eighteen-year-old freshman's life difficult? An overwhelming class load? Poor time management? A dislike of the food on a meal plan? She underestimates my abilities if she doesn't think I can help with all those.

"I accept this challenge."

She frowns. "What challenge?"

"You need someone to make your life easier. I can help. When you end up finding me irresistible along the way, we can work something out."

"Actually, I'm saying—"

"You already find me irresistible?"

"No," she says.

I shrug, stepping toward her. "You will."

She stares at me, and I swear, her lips twitch while she fights a smile.

"I'm not going to find you irresistible," she says.

"Of course." I overemphasize a wink. "All right, beautiful, as much as I'd love to stay and chat about you falling for me, my cab should be here any minute. I'll see you tomorrow."

Confusion washes over her face, and to throw her further off-balance, I kiss her forehead on my way out of her room. I bid farewell to the ladies on the couch, who seem more curious about my short stay than my original entrance. The one's stare tracks me across the room, only falling away when our eyes meet.

I have the cab take me home instead of to the party. I need to charge my phone and strategize. With the challenge in place, I'm willing to admit, I was bored. But not anymore.

Once back at the house, I take the stairs three at a time to my room. I plug in my phone, and as soon as it powers on, I text Felicia.

If Jordan wanted to find himself in Callie's good graces, how might he go about it?

Her number flashes on my screen within a few seconds.

"Felicia," I answer.

"Coffee," she says. "Lots and lots of coffee."

A morning person once told me, "Everyone has the capability of being a morning person."

That fucker lied.

Hard.

I work on draining the last drops of my coffee as Felicia answers the door—perky and bright-eyed. I hate her. She ushers me in, and without waiting for an invite, I sink onto their couch.

"Please tell me this is her only early morning class."

Felicia giggles and joins me, but in a less dramatic fashion. "The only day that starts before nine. She has a project due, and her partner wants to meet before class."

I offer her one of the two remaining coffees. "Extra points for an extra shot, right?"

"Right," she says, "but I think you need it more than I do."

On this, we agree. I lean forward to place them both on the table in front of us when Callie's door opens. She stops short at the sight of me.

Showtime. I wink at Felicia and hop up.

I channel her annoying pep, carrying one cup to Callie. "Felicia told me how you like it. I also added an extra shot."

I smile at her while she glares. Clearly, she's not a morning person either. She's dressed in a pair of gray sweats and a maroon hoodie, and she has her espresso hair knotted in a disaster of a bun on the top of her head. Damn does she pull it off.

"How?" She rips the cup from my hand and takes a sip.

"How did she tell me?" I ask. She raises her eyebrows in response, and I tell her, "I texted and asked."

I wait for the dots to connect. Me. Phone. Unsupervised.

"Did you hijack my number, too?" she asks.

"No, but you'll give it to me."

"I told you," she says, "I'm not worth wasting your time."

"And I said, we're beyond that. Mission Win Callie Over has already commenced."

Her eyes narrow. "I don't have time for Mission Win Over—"

"Mission Win Callie Over. I'm thinking of having T-shirts made." I smile, proud of my improv skills.

There goes her eye roll. She walks away and holds up the coffee. "Thanks."

"If you need a ride, I could—"

The door slams, and she's gone.

Felicia snorts out a laugh, falling over on the couch.

"Well," I say, sitting down next to her, "I can't imagine how that could have gone any better."

She gasps for air. "T-shirts?"

I shove her off the couch.

⸻

For my second attempt of the day, I wait for Callie outside of her class, coffee in hand. She emerges, pulling on her coat, and I jog over.

"Hey. You need a ride?"

She Mr. Cellophanes me. Looks right through me, walks right by me, and only acknowledges my existence enough to take the coffee out of my hand. I think that's it until she peeks over her shoulder, and our eyes meet. Maybe I'm not so invisible after all.

I go to class but leave early when Felicia texts. She meets me at their suite, and I toss a sandwich in the mini fridge for Callie. On our way out, I scribble a note, sure to let her know of the alliance between Felicia and me.

Lunch in the fridge. —Team Jordan

Felicia attaches tape to the top and slaps it on the outside of their door. She leaves me when we reach the parking lot to go to class. For the next twenty minutes, I finish the reading for my class that begins in thirty. The alarm sounds on my phone, and I hustle inside for another shot.

Callie steps into the hall, her still-wet hair in a high ponytail. The *just fell out of bed* look from earlier she's replaced with leggings and a top that outlines the curves I got familiar with last night. A lot of effort goes into looking her in the eyes.

"Do you need a ride to class?" I ask.

"No, I don't. You really should stop wasting your time. I have a car. If I wanted to drive, I would." She steps inside and shuts the door but opens it right back up. "Thank you for lunch," she says, begrudgingly.

"Anytime, beautiful."

The door closes again.

Since waiting outside in the dark for Callie after her study group might send the wrong message, I sit in her well-lit hallway instead. I'm on my phone, not paying attention, when she's suddenly stepping over my outstretched legs. There's not even enough time to stand up before she disappears inside.

Another round to Henders.

I head back down the hall, worried I might be pushing this whole thing too far. A shout stops both my train of thought and my body before I reach the bottom of the stairway.

Felicia bounds down after me. "Come tell her good night."

"I don't know. I—"

"Trust me," she says, grabbing my arm.

Before I can further protest, she drags me back up, not letting go until we're in front of Callie's bedroom. I sigh and knock.

No response.

When I turn around, Felicia's giving me the most encouraging smile. It's this type of behavior that makes for an excellent sidekick.

The suitemate who can't keep her eyes to herself, Jess, is studying on the floor in front of the couch. I crouch next to her and steal the pen from her hand along with a piece of notebook paper. She leans in closer than necessary to watch me write, *Need anything? Water? Snack? Company? - J.*

"All the above," Jess says, raising an eyebrow.

Less than subtle but easy enough to ignore.

I fold up the note and slide it under Callie's door. This time, when I knock, a shadow appears in the strip of light at the bottom, followed by the crinkle of paper. I watch the shadow, expecting her to shout an answer, but the note reappears instead.

No.

Then, from the other side of the door, "But thank you."

Always so polite.

"All right, beautiful," I say, flipping the paper over. I use the wall to write down my number before slipping it under the crack again but only partway. "If you change your mind, let me know. I'll see you tomorrow."

The note disappears, and after a few seconds, so does the shadow.

"See?" Felicia hooks her arm through mine as she walks me out. "You'll get her tomorrow, champ."

Right. Tomorrow.

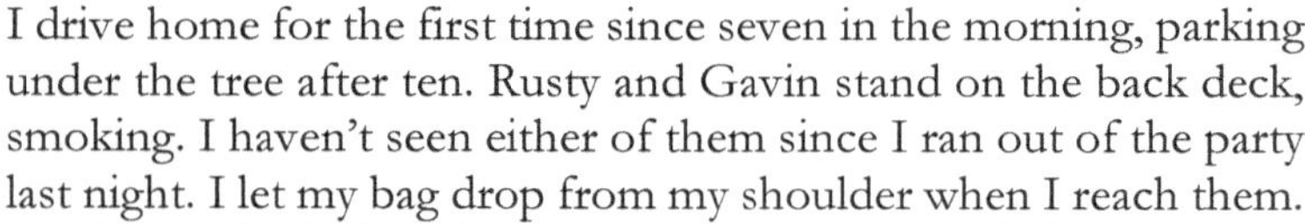

I drive home for the first time since seven in the morning, parking under the tree after ten. Rusty and Gavin stand on the back deck, smoking. I haven't seen either of them since I ran out of the party last night. I let my bag drop from my shoulder when I reach them.

Rusty checks his phone. "We thought you'd died."

"Negative." I sit on the top step of the deck and fall back, putting an arm over my face to block out the porch light. "I'm trying to hook up with Callie."

"Who?" Gavin asks.

"Coconut chick," Rusty says. "I'm confused by your use of the word *trying*. As in you're making an effort to fuck her?"

"Fuck who?"

I move my arm to see Benji staring down at me.

"Callie." I sit up, yawning. "I'm leaning in, asshole."

Propped against the side of the house, Benji shakes his head. "Explain."

"He's playing the long game." Gavin lights another cigarette. "It's like what I'm doing with Tara. Or what I was doing. She put out last night, and I got out this morning. Thirteen days from start to finish."

I get to my feet and pick up my bag. "Callie only has until next Friday."

"No other girls in the meantime?" Rusty stares at me like he's witnessing a car wreck in slow motion. Shocked and not sure what the hell he can do to stop it.

By committing time to a single woman, I apparently shatter his perception of reality.

"It'll be okay, little guy." I tap his cheek on my way past. "In nine days, the world will return to normal, and we'll go hit a sorority. My treat."

Benji follows me in and up to my room. He hovers in the doorway while I unload my bag and has yet to move when I head for a shower. I turn around in my bathroom to find him still there, deep in thought.

The guy has two modes: candid and cryptic. At the moment, he's choosing to exercise the latter.

"Benj, say what you want to say."

He leans against the doorframe, arms crossed over his chest. "Not yet, man."

"Why not?"

"You're not ready to hear it yet."

I rub the back of my neck. "Is this a red or blue pill thing where you either point out a harsh truth or let me continue on in blissful ignorance?"

He shrugs. "Which one would you choose?"

"The blue," I say. Then I shut the door before he tries to force feed me the red.

I wake up late.

I skip half the stairs, running down, yank on my hoodie, and drag an ice-scraper over my windshield. The engine finally warms after I arrive at the coffee shop, providing heat by the time I return with Callie's coffee. At the dorms, I hurry into the building, up the stairs, around the corner, and down the hall.

Felicia answers with a grin. "You came back."

"Was I not supposed to?"

"Of course you were." She moves aside to let me in. "Callie bet you wouldn't. So, thanks for winning me ten bucks."

"You're welcome," I say.

She pushes the door to Callie's room open. "Jordan's here." She scrunches her nose at me and crosses the suite to the other bedroom. "Good luck, my friend."

I knock and wait in the doorway. Callie comes over, her mood not yet established.

"Back for more ego-shrinking?"

Banter—I can work with that.

I hand her the cup. "Hopefully you do a better job today. Yesterday wasn't that impressive."

A smile appears for a second before she neutralizes the expression. Her finger taps the side of the cup as she studies me, sizing me up. "You owe Felicia ten dollars," she says.

"*You* owe Felicia ten dollars. You should never bet against me."

"Fine." She bends over to pick up her bag, and the bottom of her pink fitted top slides up. My attention bounces between the exposed skin and her ass. Once she straightens up, she stares me down. "I'll find time between classes and studying to get her money. You're doing a superb job of making my life *less* complicated."

I know she's playing me, but she makes a solid point. I hold her gaze, fishing out my wallet. My eyes lower long enough to find a ten and return to hers. She tries snatching it from my hand, but I pull it away and hold it over my shoulder out of her reach.

"Do you need a ride to class?"

"No." She looks up through her lashes. "I also don't need a ride after class. Thank you for the coffee and settling my bet, but you shouldn't waste your time."

She slowly leans in and almost has me until her eyes dart to my hand.

So close, beautiful.

She grabs for the money again. This time, I let her, using the distraction to kiss her on the forehead.

"See you after class," I say, walking away.

Before leaving, I detour to properly introduce myself to Cam on the couch. According to the Calliepedia—Felicia—Cam's girlfriend lives off-campus. She stays with her a majority of the time, which gives Callie the room to herself. We exchange the small talk and realize Gavin and her brother are members of the same fraternity.

My alliances continue to grow.

As I pull out of the parking lot, I see Felicia walking to class. Unlike some people, she accepts my offer for a ride. I drop her off and pick up soup she recommends for Callie's lunch from a deli downtown. I swing by for another coffee and park in the lot near Callie's class.

My first lecture starts in ten minutes, but if she turns down my offer for a ride, like I anticipate, I'll make it on time.

Students flow out of the building as I wait for her. A few minutes pass and still no Callie. A double-check of the schedule Felicia sent me confirms I'm in the right place at the right time. That's when I spot her through the glass door, walking out on the opposite side.

Rather than going through, I jog around the building.

"Callie," I say when I see her.

She glances back and then picks up speed. Shit, she's trying to ditch me. With her damn cup in my hand, I take off at full speed after her.

"I brought coffee," I shout.

This revelation brings her to an immediate halt, and she turns around. Once I catch up, I bend over and rest my free hand on my knee, pretending to catch my breath. If she wants to make me work this hard, she can at least feel sorry for it.

Nope, she couldn't care less. I half-expect her to tap her foot in annoyance. So, I change strategies and drink half her coffee. Over the cup, I watch her working hard not to smile. A small victory, but I count it.

"Here." I shove the cup at her. "Do you need a ride?"

"No." She walks backward, holding up the mostly empty drink. "Thanks for the coffee … kinda."

"See you later, beautiful."

"We'll see." She spins around and hollers back, "I might get better at hiding from you."

When I drop off Callie's lunch later, I attempt to give her some space. I set the soup outside the door, knock, and walk away. I even resist the urge to look when she calls down the hallway after me.

"Thank you, but you should stop wasting your time."

I smile, rounding the corner.

With a few hours of downtime, I pick up a sandwich and head for the campus library. Physical books help me connect with the material when writing philosophy papers, one of which I have due tomorrow. I focus better with all the text in front of me at once instead of clicking around between windows and tabs. Plus, public spaces prevent me from pacing and ranting—a terrible habit of mine.

The paper writes itself after I get going. School has never been a challenge, and I easily skate through. But graduating next year summa cum laude requires a little effort. And I *will* graduate summa cum laude.

For all my avoidance of responsibility and commitment, only my brother understands why I consider graduating with highest honors so important. Competition between the two of us has existed as far back as I can remember. Whether we have an interest in what the other does matters not. The only goal is, do it better. He learned to ride a bike at six; I learned at five. I beat his SAT scores; his pompous ass retook the test to show me up.

Well, two years ago, Dustin graduated, missing the top tier by a tenth of a point. It presented me with an opportunity I couldn't pass up, which means I've maintained a perfect GPA with no intentions of letting it lower.

I round the corner with a book in hand, checking if I remember a quote correctly. When I look up, I stop. Callie's walking in the main entrance.

What the hell is she doing here?

I hang back, watching her settle into a chair and pull a book out of her bag to read.

Unbelievable. She played me with the bet and tried to ditch me after class, and now the frustrating woman's actually attempting to go into hiding. Chuckling to myself, I return to my table. She's set herself up for quite the surprise in a little while.

Within the hour, I've finished my paper and returned all of my books. Before submitting it, I'll go over it once more, but first, I need to talk to a beautiful girl.

Callie doesn't look up when I approach. I sit on the arm of a leather chair across from her and wait until it becomes apparent that she either doesn't notice me or doesn't care.

I clear my throat, and wide eyes slowly rise from her book.

"A safe house is a much better choice when going underground," I say, a smirk forming.

"Are you…" She checks around for witnesses.

"Following you?" I finish for her. "Absolutely not. I only show up where I already know you'll be. There's a difference."

She tilts her head to the side, dubious of my distinction. I understand why, but the truth is the truth.

I hold up my laptop. "I have a paper due tomorrow."

"Oh." She relaxes in her chair.

"Do you need a ride to class?" I ask.

Her attention returns to her book. "No."

"You would make all of this a lot easier if you would just—"

"Spread my legs for you?"

"Not what I was going to say, but we can do it your way. I'm only trying to make your life easier. You should consider leaning in."

She tries to ignore me, but her lips purse, suppressing a smile. I've never known anyone who works as hard as her to conceal their emotions. I, on the other hand, stand and let out a loud, dramatic sigh, which draws the attention of everyone around us. Everyone, except for Callie. She doesn't bother looking up from her book.

Who suggested we stop at the music shop where Rusty works, I can't remember, but we've been here for half an hour. A majority of our visits turn into expensive ones, but we're all adamant about not buying anything this time.

Gavin plugs in a bass and sits down on a stool, while Benji and I finish our discussion about a wah pedal in a glass case. We move on to playing with a drum machine, re-creating a beat from one of our songs. Behind the counter, Rusty hears us joking about replacing him. Luckily, helping a customer stops him from any retaliation other than discreetly flipping us off.

After a few minutes, Benji wanders toward two full-size electric keyboards set up to face one another. He gestures to them, standing behind one of the benches. I position myself behind the other, and we bow before taking a seat. His shoulders shrug a few times. He lifts his hands to the keys.

"Rondo in C Major," he says.

I crack my knuckles, mirror his position, and nod.

His fingers flit up and down the keys. At times, his eyes close with a peaceful expression on his face. Notes go from staccato to legato and back again. A third of the way through, he lifts his hands and waves flippantly in my direction.

Very well then.

Picking up where he left off, my fingers glide over the keys. A crescendo moves us from the lighthearted theme to darker chords. Each note becomes a little louder than the last, reaching forte, and then descends to piano again.

Six years of lessons, all so I can play Beethoven from memory in the middle of a store on a Thursday night. Money well spent. My parents required well-rounded children, which included learning one instrument. They then expected us to abandon the training and focus on more important things, like networking. Dustin had no problem giving up the cello, but I couldn't let go so easily.

I complete the next third before letting Benji finish out the piece. We've always shared music as a solid connection. The two of us read and write music, play a few instruments, and enjoy conversations using proper terminology. Gavin and Rusty understand how to make sounds with their respective instruments, but their knowledge ends there. Respectable all the same.

Once he's done, we perform a quick rendition of "Chopsticks" and then unplug Gavin. We're traveling dangerously close to purchasing two keyboards and a bass guitar and need to leave. The three of us pile into the Jeep, heading for home, but on a whim, I turn into the dorm parking lot. Gavin sighs in the back. Benji shakes his head in the front. It'll only take a few minutes to tell Callie good night. They'll survive.

A girl's pushing open the glass door on my way in. She smiles when I grab the handle and hold it for her. She pauses, half-in and half-out, her eyes on me. She's seriously misinterpreting my polite gesture. I'm being a gentleman, not proposing marriage. She finally accepts my lack of interest and releases me from door duty.

Felicia answers my knock with a grin. Happy-all-the-time people really exist—at least one anyway. She invites me in and returns to her blanket on the couch. I'm getting used to finding Callie in her room and almost miss her curled up on the opposite end of the cushions. The sight of me triggers an eye roll, and she presses a button on the remote to resume whatever they're watching on the TV.

"I was driving by and thought—"

The volume on the TV increases until it drowns out my voice. Callie raises her hand to her ear, indicating she can't hear me.

Cute.

I try again, raising my voice louder only for her to crank the volume more.

She mouths, *What?*

The girl has jokes, but if she thinks this will deter me, she's dead wrong. It only fuels my desire to win. I walk over to her end of the couch and lean down in front of her. In a normal voice, I recite the alphabet. Her eyebrows pull in as she studies my lips, trying to read them.

"Mary Had a Little Lamb" comes next.

It takes until midway through "Humpty Dumpty" for her finger to hit the button and pause the TV. Hearing my nursery rhyme, she smiles the most amazing smile. She reins it in, fighting off the rogue facial expression within a few seconds, but it's too late. My work's already done.

"Do you need anything?" I ask, still eye-level with her.

She shakes her head, unbothered by our proximity. My gaze drops to her sexy lips. Shit. I really want to kiss her. I force myself to straighten up. I've made progress, and I am not about to get slapped.

"All right, beautiful, I'll see you tomorrow."

"Come prepared," she says. "Felicia and I bet double or nothing."

Of course they did.

I sigh, pulling out my wallet. "Here. Take my money now."

Felicia quickly relieves me of the twenty in my hand. Callie presses her lips together. She knows how to play the game. And me, which is a somewhat unnerving thought.

Screw it. If she wants to keep taking my money, then I'll keep kissing her on the damn forehead. Her eyes widen when I lean down again and press my lips to her skin. When I pull away, she rolls her eyes. I roll mine back but more dramatically. As soon as her mouth starts to turn up at the corners, I head for the door. I've earned a new all-time high score for smiles.

A record I plan on breaking tomorrow.

"Bacon ciabatta and two large coffees, both with an extra shot."

A kid at the counter of the coffee place grimaces. "We're out of those."

Shit. I forgot a backup plan. "Do you have anything like it?"

"We have one that's basically the same."

"Yes!" I'm entirely too enthusiastic over a breakfast sandwich.

"It's turkey sausage though. It's also on a bagel with different cheese."

"Do they taste similar?" I ask.

"Turkey and bacon?"

"Fair point. Do the turkey sausage one then."

He shuffles away but circles right back. "I guess we have a bacon one."

"Great. I want that one."

"Along with the turkey sausage?"

I blink the slowest blink in existence, hoping for him to disappear in the time it takes for my eyes to reopen. *Nope.* "Just the bacon one," I say. "And the two coffees." I massage my forehead after riding an emotional roller coaster. "For the love of God, don't forget the extra shots."

My face hides in the crook of my arm as it rests on the counter. One of the reasons I never commit to anything? This. Is.

Exhausting. Conflicts between our schedules mean I'm running all over campus, and the early morning shit's for old people and birds.

The guys still think I'm insane for pouring my time into a girl who may or may not sleep with me in the end, and I'm starting to agree. Even if she does, will it really be worth all this effort?

A sack rustles next to my head—that kid watching me. I grab the bag and beverage carrier and give him a quick salute on my way to the door.

The clock on the dash is kind enough to inform me my two-and-a-half-hour philosophy lecture begins in four minutes. Callie's first class won't start for an hour-and-a-half. If she says yes to a ride, it doesn't make sense for me to even show up for my class.

I rap on the suite door.

Jess answers, greeting my dick with her big brown eyes. "Good morning, Jordan."

I nod and slip past her. "Jessica."

Felicia zooms around me with a friendly smile. My godsend full of tips and tricks. I owe her for the breakfast sandwich idea and the salad I add to the fridge for later.

Outside of her and Callie, I can't recall the last time I spent so much time hanging around women who keep their clothes on. Of course, I'm planning for Callie to lose hers again soon enough. Felicia, though, I never want to see naked. Not because she's unattractive, but it would be well past weird at this point.

The door to Callie's room sits ajar while she puts her books in her bag. Instead of a tight top, like she's worn the other days— excluding Wednesday morning—she sports a baggy T-shirt. Her jeans are also a more relaxed fit, not hugging her ass. A braid hangs down her back in place of loose waves. The whole vibe seems different, and she looks much younger than I've ever seen her.

I knock, gaining her attention.

"Hello, handsome," she says, taking the cup from my hand.

As much as I'd love to flatter myself, I know better. "You're talking to the coffee?"

She nods, and her eyes widen. "Is that a bacon ciabatta?"

I hand her the sack, and she barely removes the paper before taking a bite. Her eyes flutter shut as she moans. Fuck, it's hot. My cock twitches at the sexy sound and again at the mental images I conjure up of her coming on it. Those doubts about the potential payoff of my experiment? They cease to exist.

I clear my throat and think of Nana Waters, which, as always, does the trick. "Do you need a ride this morning?"

She goes to her bed. "No, Jordan. I also don't need a ride after class or later. Thank you for the sandwich and the coffee, but you shouldn't waste your time."

"So I've heard." I lean down and kiss her on the forehead. "See you after class, beautiful."

Her lips twitch, almost losing out to a smile. I saunter through the living area and out to the hall in case she watches. But as soon as the door latches, I sprint to my Jeep and speed across campus.

The professor hesitates when I crash through the door but carries on. Whatever he's lecturing on, he knows I'll follow, late or not. I'm one of his best students. Philosophy just makes sense to me. For a person who floats through life without a sense of purpose, sitting around and searching for the meaning of it all is an easy enough task, I guess.

Ah, he's discussing Sartre's *Being and Nothingness*. I read the book last year. Humans are condemned to be free. Our past has no bearing on our choices. I pull up my hood, and my head lands on my forearm.

Someone shoves my shoulder, disrupting one hell of a nap. I open my eyes and discover that I'm the focal point of the entire lecture hall with Dr. Miller down front, arms crossed.

"Should I repeat the question, Mr. Waters?" he asks.

Considering I've been asleep for at least forty minutes, yes, he probably should.

"What are we looking for…" a dude whispers beside me. "The meaning."

Thank you, random classmate.

I recline in my seat and relax with my hands on the back of my head. "What an absurd question."

A few students shift uncomfortably in their seats, and one laughs. But Dr. Miller just shakes his head with an amused look. "Enlighten the rest of the class with your response."

With his permission, I launch into an insane man's rant about absurdist philosophy. The conflict between our search for meaning in a meaningless universe, and even if meaning exists, the amount of knowledge the universe encompasses would be impossible for man to grasp. The only escape routes from the madness are suicide, finding religion, or accepting the absurdity of it all. Of course, while inherent meaning might not exist, one can potentially discover their own meaning as long as they accept the absurd along with it.

Eventually, Dr. Miller raises his hands in the air in defeat. "Mr. Waters, please continue your nap."

"Thank you, sir." I lay my head down and sleep for the rest of the lecture.

My final class of the day runs over, leaving three minutes until the end of Callie's. I turn the key in the ignition and notice the line of cars waiting to exit the parking lot. The only way to make it is to run. Cue my internal screaming as I grab my coat.

When I get there, an empty room waits for me. I check the halls and reach for my phone—the one still sitting in the cupholder of my Jeep. But the location of my phone is irrelevant because Callie never gave me her number.

"No, but you'll give it to me." God, I acted cocky. No, Jordan. No, she will not.

I sulk in my defeat for a few seconds before dashing out the door, hoping to catch up with her. I make it all the way to the dorms without spotting any red coats or pink hats.

Felicia answers, surprised to see me.

"I missed her after lit," I say, dropping onto their couch. "Is she back yet?"

She winces. "No, and she won't be until Sunday."

"What?" I'm back on my feet.

"She drove to her last class and went back home as soon as it finished. She didn't tell you?"

I start to pace. No Callie for two days? She's not coming around at all if she didn't tell me about abandoning campus for the weekend. Why the hell even bother with her? I drag the heel of my hand over the tension forming in my forehead.

"Are you okay?" Felicia asks. "Do you want her number?"

I sigh and stop. "No. She might actually kill you, and I've grown rather fond of you, Gibson." I attempt a smile and tell her goodbye.

The trek to my Jeep feels colder, probably because I'm walking instead of running. I can't let go of the fact that she didn't tell me she planned on leaving. The way she smiled at the coffee and breakfast sandwich earlier replays in my head along with the tug of her lips after I kissed her forehead.

Pull it together, Waters. Two days without Callie means no early morning trips for coffee or nearly killing myself, hauling ass across campus in unreasonable timeframes. This gives me a chance to reclaim my freedom. I can go out with the guys over the weekend, maybe find a new distraction. Chances are, by the time she returns, the infatuation will have passed, and I'll call it quits early.

When I reach for the shifter, my eyes land on my phone. A missed call from my brother shows up. Dustin wants to confirm plans for spring break, but I'm reluctant to agree. In his second year of law school at the University of Pennsylvania, he and his buddies define fun as going on a coke bender and hiring escorts. It made for an eventful winter break. Even though he snorts lines off stripper tits on the regular, he still manages to win the Most Outstanding Son award with our parents. Add that to the list of shit I'll never understand.

Other than a text from Rusty about band practice later, I only have one other message from an unknown number.

Sorry. I waited as long as I could. Gone until Monday.

Callie. She must have finally used my number off the note. Now, if only I could have seen her face when she realized she'd had it this entire time because I added myself to her contacts after the party. The girl should have never left me alone with her phone.

I reply, *No worries. I'll be waiting.*

Band practice runs smoothly, and we agree to work on new songs over the next few weeks. Benji and I, with my guitar, plan to focus on melodies and lyrics. The other two will help in small ways, but we all know the most magic happens when the two of us lock ourselves in the soundproof garage without interruptions.

Hopefully, he'll wait until everything with Callie wraps up. I can't handle anything else right now—and the irony is not lost on me.

As on most Friday nights, everyone decides to go to the bar. My new schedule has me yawning by eleven, but I'll go along for wingman duty. While I wait for the guys to primp, I sit on the couch, staring at my phone for far too long.

Callie's only other message came when I asked if she'd made it safe, and she replied, *Yes.*

I send her one more text to end our day the same as the last three, allowing for one minor adjustment.

> *All right, beautiful, I wish I were seeing you tomorrow.*

She answers right away.

> *Goodnight, Jordan.*

Wow. Not snarky or sarcastic or ego-shattering.

The feel of their eyes on me causes my gaze to slowly lift from my phone. All three of my roommates are staring down at me. That's when I notice my smile. I stand up, wiping the expression from my face.

When none of them move, I ask, "What?"

In unison, they simulate cracking a whip. "*Whaahh-pssh!*"

I push through them as they pantomime riding horses, and they gallop out the door behind me.

Obnoxious.

Our night wound down around three, but my eyes open at eight. I thought it took weeks for a body to adjust to a new sleep cycle. What the fuck do people do this early on a Saturday morning?

I roll out of bed and take a shower. A long one.

Once dressed, I head downstairs. A foot hangs over the end of the couch, toenails painted purple. Fantastic. Not wanting to wake Sleeping Beauty, I make toast and retreat to my room.

I eat at my desk while rifling through papers and come across an unopened letter from my father. I rip it open and find information to register for the LSAT along with a list of contacts and phone numbers. My elbow nudges the envelope over the edge of the desk, and contents and all fall into the trash can.

One major drawback of acting impulsively based on what I currently want is I fail to consider what it could mean in the long-term. Case-in-point: my agreement to go to law school.

At seventeen, it was so far in the future. Who cared about what happened in four years if I could do whatever the hell I wanted until then? Well, let me tell my even cockier asshole younger self who cares.

Me.

I do.

The right-now Jordan who faces the decision of being miserable for the rest of my life or once again letting down my parents. Not that it's difficult for me to disappoint them. Regardless of my achievements growing up, I always fell short with them. Unlike my brother. If Dustin were to fetch a stick like a dog, they would deem it the most glorious fetching in history.

Years of constantly seeking approval turned me into a high-strung twelve-year-old with stress ulcers. I'll never forget the day I snapped. I stood in the middle of the sixth-grade classroom and ripped up my math test. It was the most liberating moment of my short life. Right then, I vowed to live for me and not give a shit about other people's expectations. A resolve further strengthened when I went home. My parents gave me the same lecture they had the one time I brought home an A-minus. Word for word. An A-minus was equivalent to an F in their eyes.

I melted into hysterics. Full-on rolling around on the sitting-room floor, tears in my eyes, couldn't-breathe laughter. I accepted them as impossible to please after that, and my mindset changed. Life became fun, including my rivalry with Dustin. Instead of feeling like I *needed* to beat him in the hopes of earning praise from our parents, I *wanted* to beat him to prove to myself that I could. Every win, award, and accomplishment since has been all mine, and no one can take them away from me.

Over time, though, my parents and I have struck a balance. Our relationship's like a game. I love playing the role of disappointing child because, in actuality, I don't come close. But it will change if I don't go to law school.

Everything up to now has shaped me for the path they chose for Dustin and me when we were children. One I agreed to go down. Not following through will be viewed as the ultimate act of defiance. Again, I'll feel like a disappointment, and I'm not ready for that yet.

I pick the papers out of the trash can and leave them on my desk to deal with another day.

With the start of my morning heavier than a hungover Saturday should ever be, I return downstairs. I open the basement door and proceed down to Rusty's room. I grant him the same courtesy everyone in the house does me and let myself in without knocking. He's asleep on his floor, naked, and I nudge him with my foot.

"Dude. The house guest yours?"

He grunts and sticks his arm in the air, giving me a thumbs-up.

"Do I need to take her home?"

He grunts again, and his thumb stays in place.

Perfect.

I rouse our couch surfer, make sure she's wearing all her clothes, and find her a coat to wear on our drive. Based on her confusion and blushing, she doesn't remember much of anything from last night, which explains why she slept on the couch. We might be a house full of horny college dudes, but none of us would ever cross the line of hooking up with a girl that out of it.

She looks awful, so I swing through a drive-through and buy her breakfast.

Our verbal exchange remains limited to directions and a, "Thanks," when she returns Gavin's jacket.

Once she disappears into the building, I declare her someone else's problem. People who get wasted enough to forget what they did confound me. I always wonder if what they want to escape from is really that bad or if they just don't know how else to cope with the everyday shit in their lives.

When I arrive back at the house, Rusty's cooking bacon and eggs. I sit at the kitchen island and snag his plate as he turns around.

"I'm not a taxi service."

He shrugs, returning to the stove to restart his breakfast. "I figured her not seeing me this morning would make her feel less awkward. She couldn't even walk down the stairs last night."

I pick up a piece of bacon while checking my phone. It's almost eleven, and since most people are awake by now, I text Callie.

Good morning, beautiful.

She doesn't reply by the time I finish my second breakfast of the day. Or after I've restrung my acoustic guitar. Still nothing when I wrap up my in-depth playlist organization session. Shit. Last night's text might have been a fluke. Her sanity suffered a momentary lapse. I chance another message.

I said, good morning, beautiful.

This time, I receive a response.

Hi.

Short, to the point, and very Callie. But then another message pops up.

I'm Cate.

Her little sister maybe? The picture in her room had a little girl in it, and her name starts with a C, like Callie and Connor. I have no idea how to estimate the age of a child, but she didn't look more than five. Can five-year-olds text?

How old are you? I ask.

Six.

Can you even read? How are you texting?

Yes. The phone helps.

I scroll through the settings on my phone. She must use the voice-to-text function and the setting that reads messages. The wonders of the modern age are all around us.

Cate sends, *What are you doing?*

Talking to a six-year-old.

Connor's playing basketball. I'm bored.

Gavin has claimed one of the couches in the living room as a napping spot, so I stretch out on the other. I wonder if Callie's a sports fan. I could leverage my lacrosse days.

Cate continues to send messages. She's funny. And as she makes known multiple times, bored. After a while, a picture pops up from her. Her eyes are wide, and she has a maniacal grin. Cute kid. I imagine Callie looked exactly like her at that age. I do what any mature adult would do and send an equally ridiculous picture with my cheeks puffed out and eyes crossed.

We exchange a few of those before I ask her if Callie knows how to make funny faces. Less than a minute later, she sends me a picture. I stare at the beautiful—no, stunning—girl on my screen. If I thought the rare glimpses of Callie's smile were impressive, then consider me blown away by the real thing. Her entire face lights up, her eyes shining the most brilliant blue.

Another picture replaces the first. Callie pouts with her bottom lip stuck out and her forehead scrunched. I laugh as the images continue coming, revealing a new side of her. One where she doesn't hold back her emotions even if she exaggerates them for the sake of entertaining a six-year-old.

I start noticing things about her. On her left temple, she has a small indentation, similar to a chicken pox scar. Darker blue rings encompass her pupils. Her bottom lip appears slightly fuller than her top.

Callie's name pops up on the screen, and I already know what to expect when I answer.

"Jordan," a small voice says through a burst of giggling, "this is a very important call from the doctor."

I gasp. "Oh no, Dr. Cate. Whatever is the problem?"

Gavin sits straight up on the couch, a concerned look on his face. "Doctor?"

I dismissively shake my head and go to the kitchen, so I don't further disturb his nap. A thorough explanation of my diagnosis ensues. Luckily, I'll make a full recovery because Sad Feet is curable with lots of rest and a blue slushie. Once I know I'll live, we move on to the important stuff, like her classroom's new seating arrangement. Life as a first grader is both thrilling and taxing, and between school and her friends, the poor thing barely keeps up.

After a while, she starts talking about being forced to attend her brother's basketball tournament. About the third mention of Cal, I realize she's referring to Callie. According to Cate, she's been reading a big book forever, and she is finally putting it down.

"What is she doing now?" I ask.

"Nothing. She looks bored."

"Would you do me a favor?"

"Maybe," she says.

"Will you tell her she looks beautiful and give her a kiss on the forehead for me?"

The phone rustles as she grants my request. Callie gushes over her cuteness and thanks her. But when Cate reports back, she realizes she kissed Callie's cheek instead of the forehead. She goes to correct her mistake, and a shrill whine comes through the speaker.

"Jordan?"

Oh shit.

"Callie?"

"What the hell are you doing, talking to my sister?"

"Uh … we were tired of texting?"

"What?" she shrieks, her voice getting farther away.

Why didn't it occur to me that talking to her little sister might upset her? If she doesn't want me bothering her, obviously, her family is off-limits. I'm thinking I've royally screwed up, but then she laughs. God, she has an amazing laugh.

"Does this mean you aren't mad?"

"Oh, I want to be furious," she says. "But you distracted her long enough that I finished my assignment for Monday."

Point for Waters.

I grin, proud of my victory. "Sounds like you enjoyed a rather uncomplicated afternoon then."

She's quiet for a few seconds, and in my mind, she's smiling. "Thank you," she says, her voice soft.

"Anytime, beautiful."

Cate squeals, and then she's back on the other end. "So, Jordan, I think we should talk about what happened on the playground last week."

Which we do—until she grows tired of me and gives the phone to Callie.

I receive a quick, "Bye, Jordan," before the call ends.

I don't care, though, because there was a smile in her voice.

The rest of my day remains, as my new companion loves to say, boring. I accompany Rusty for a touch-up on a tattoo and grab supper with Gavin. By ten, my creative side is seeking an outlet. I pull on a hoodie and make my way out back to the garage, my guitar calling.

Benji's on a stool in the middle of the space, writing in a notebook.

"This going to bother you?" I ask, plugging in my guitar cable.

He tosses his notebook on the floor. "Play me something pretty."

I try to think of a piece to fit his request but end up playing "Raining Blood" by Slayer. We both thrash around and headbang. He plays Rusty's cymbals for a few measures. I shred. By the end, I collapse on the floor and finish out, lying on my back. Being a heavy metal rocker is an exhausting life.

Benji returns to his stool and resumes whatever he's been working on in his notebook. Other than my sweating and Rusty's drumsticks sitting an inch farther to the left, no one would ever be the wiser about our impromptu concert.

My mind wanders off on its own while I play through scales.

At the end of next year, the four of us will go our separate ways. Gavin and I are both looking at a few more years in school if I cave on the lawyer front. Benji never discusses his plans. Rusty, well, shit, he'll impress all of us if he manages to stay out of jail.

Not sure why I keep worrying about the future all of a sudden, I pull out my phone for a distraction. Callie's number will only stay in my contacts for another week, but I set her contact picture to the one of her smiling anyway.

All right, beautiful. I'll see you tomorrow.

Callie: *Goodnight, Jordan. Monday.*

She wants to put me off, but the sooner I see her, the sooner I can gauge whether two days away has lost me any ground.

Tomorrow, I shoot back.

Monday.

As stubborn as ever.
"You texting the girl?" Benji asks.
I nod, pushing off the floor.
He shakes his head. "You coming out tonight?"
"Sure am." I unplug my guitar and place it on the stand. Heading out the door, I send one more message.

Tomorrow. Stop arguing.

She doesn't respond, and I smile. If she can't disagree with me, she won't answer. I don't think she even knows how to stop challenging me. Hell, I don't think I want her to—not for the next few days at least. I'm having too much fun at the moment.

Sunday night. One guy. Two girls. A couch.

A Disney movie?

No, the last one won't work.

I let out an exasperated sigh and roll my head toward the two young ladies sitting next to me on the couch. Neither Felicia nor Jess respond. Soon enough—if not already—they'll regret telling me to stay.

Felicia claimed Callie usually returns by nine, but we're at nine-thirty and still no Callie. I offered to leave and come back, but they insisted I wait with them. So now, they can deal with the consequences.

"Someone in this suite has to have decent taste in movies," I say.

I've never been a good guest. I'm much more the type of person who shows up and forces my way into the family. They might as well consider me an honorary roommate of suite six; I do.

I hold out my hand for the remote until Felicia gives it up.

Victory.

It takes no time at all to find a replacement to whatever junk they want me to watch. I stop on *Hot Rod* which elicits a groan from Jess.

"Suck it up, buttercup." I fling a pillow at her.

Felicia giggles as I hit play on the remote. "Callie made us watch this movie last week."

I'm not surprised Callie likes this classic.

The entire hour-and-a-half passes without interruption. Not even one from Callie walking in the door. It seems inappropriate for me to hold an opinion on her not being back yet. I mean, who am I to dictate a curfew, but when does her not showing up become a concern?

Felicia must read my mind because, when I turn to ask, she shrugs. "This happens sometimes. I'm not entirely sure of the story."

"I thought you knew everything about her," I say, only half-joking.

She shakes her head. "I know a lot about a small part of her. Anything that happens away from here is a mystery."

The Callie Henders enigma continues to grow. Bad news, considering my dwindling timeframe. "Well, I'll get out of here then."

I start to stand, only for Felicia to drag me down again by the arm.

"She won't be much longer. I'm sure of it. Stay and be here when she gets back."

A pang of guilt settles in my chest as Felicia's hazel eyes meet mine. I'm almost positive Callie knows my *challenge* to make her life easier is a veiled attempt to fuck her. Hell, other than bringing her coffee and the random luck with Cate, I have done nothing remotely helpful. But I'm not convinced Felicia knows. She might be acting as my accomplice with the notion that I want to *date* Callie.

"Do I get to pick the next movie?" she asks.

I force a smile. "Just no girlie shit."

Felicia claps and grabs for the remote.

I shake off the unsettling feeling and check my phone. Almost eleven. Well, if for some reason Callie doesn't make it back, I'm not going to miss keeping our little ritual intact.

All right, beautiful, I text her, *in case I miss you, I'll see you tomorrow.*

Jess tells us goodnight, her eyes lingering on me before she goes to her and Felicia's room. There's a looming possibility of her jumping me one of these days. Either she knows better than to think I want to date Callie or she's a genuinely awful friend.

With her gone and Felicia going to charge her phone, I take advantage of the full length of the couch. I grab the pillow and stretch out. Felicia comes back and doesn't hesitate to plop on my legs until I pull them out of her way. This is another new one—I'm alone with a chick on a couch, watching a movie with no temptation to do anything else. Something I haven't done since middle school. These women are ruining me.

The screen lights up, and I groan. A movie about animated puppies.

Ruining me.

———

Coconuts and Callie. The threat of light makes it hard for me to open my eyes, but I sense her close to me.

A hand reaches out, and I stroke her hair. "Good morning, beautiful."

"Hey, Jordan," Jess says.

I jerk upright to see her hungry eyes gazing at me. She's on the floor in front of me. Confused, I search around. The dorms. I fell asleep on the couch, waiting for Callie. Who's nowhere in sight. The blanket on my lap normally sits on her bed, explaining the scent.

"Sorry, I thought you were Callie."

"Sure you did." She twists back around to finish eating her bagel.

I swipe my phone off the table. Callie texted at midnight, saying goodnight. Then I see the time. *Shit.* Her first class starts in fifteen minutes. In no scenario will I make it to the coffee shop and back in time. Then Felicia—the miraculous angel she is—walks in the door, carrying three coffees. I drop to my knees in front of her to grovel.

"Stop being so dramatic," she says. She hands me two cups and disappears into her room.

Two days without seeing Callie has me standing in front of her door, hesitant. Sweaty palms. Uptick in my heartbeat. Add a suit, and I might as well be in the coat closet with Cecelia Buckley at Philip Weston's thirteenth birthday party again.

When I knock, she swings the door open, holding the phone to her ear. "Yes, for the morning classes," she says. "Just feeling a little under the weather" She listens. "Right, rest and fluids. Thank you, Mrs. Rodriguez." And then, "You too." She tosses her phone on the bed and slips the coffee out of my hand without looking at me. "Good morning, Jordan."

A warmer welcome than all of last week.

Given the phone conversation, I almost ask her if she feels all right, but she looks fantastic. She's in a sexy sweater and tight jeans with her hair in loose waves.

"Good morning, beautiful."

On the second delivery of the line this morning, it receives the right reaction. An eye roll.

"Please don't make a habit out of sleeping on our couch." One side of her mouth turns up on her way past me. "The blanket needs to be folded and put back on the bed." She leaves but pops right back in. "No, I don't need a ride, but thank you for the coffee."

I shake my head and complete my chore. Bossy Callie—I like her.

The rest of the day goes smoothly. Well, as smoothly as it can with her refusing me every step of the way. But whether she admits it or not, I'm winning her over. One exhausting day at a time.

Felicia asks if I want to go with them to a party. Not wanting to push Callie too far, I say no. Our last experience at one isn't something to relive. Plus, Beta Void has band practice.

A starting time of eight means we congregate in the garage by nine. Musician stereotypes each and every one of us—self-absorbed and flakey. Fortunately, the chance to play in front of an adoring crowd keeps us reliable for gigs.

Benji throws a stick between Rusty and Gavin to break up their conversation, and we finally begin running through our set list. Only an hour and ten minutes late.

We're working through the third song when Brooke walks in. On a Monday night, she's sporting five-inch heels and an entire makeup counter. Even from across the room, her perfume overpowers Rusty's cigarette. A little much to crash band practice.

He stops mid-song to greet her, but she beelines for me. She struts by, dragging a fingernail across my chest. A few times on my dick, and she thinks she owns me. Under that logic, she owns all of us.

"Need a tambourine player?" she asks. "Maybe the triangle?"

Already sick of her shit, I shake my head. "We're done. Everybody out."

"Everyone but Brooke?" This time, her finger trails down and hooks in a belt loop on my jeans.

Jesus.

"Wasting your time, sweetheart," Rusty says. "Our Jordan's already spoken for."

I step away from her and flip him off. I'm not spoken for— I'm just in the middle of something.

"Who's the lucky girl?" Brooke cocks her head to the side.

"Not you." I unplug my guitar and throw the cord on the ground. "Benji, are we writing tonight or not?"

It's slightly melodramatic, but everyone disperses. Benji and I stay in the garage while Rusty and Gavin take Brooke into the house. I'd let Jess ogle me every day if it meant never dealing with Brooke again. Not only has she made the rounds through my friends, she's awful to every other chick that comes near her.

A bad mood from sleeping on a couch catches up with me— an extremely bad mood. On top of that, Rusty's comment is grating on my nerves. He should be supporting me in my endeavor, not acting like an ass.

My brother texts.

Tomorrow. Coffee. Nonnegotiable. 2:30.

Now, it's a fucking trifecta.

I growl out my frustration. Callie's class lets out at two forty-five. Unless Dustin tags along to meet her—not at all an option—

someone is attending the dance without a date. Unless I send an alternate dance partner…

"Hey, can you do me a favor?"

Benji swivels around on his stool. "We don't do favors for each other."

Right, tit for tat around our house. "Okay, can we make a deal? I need someone to pick up Callie from class tomorrow afternoon."

He smirks. "I want your room for six months."

"Fuck off. I'm not giving you my bedroom."

He shrugs and rotates back around. Without offering any alternatives, he shuts me down. No spin and grin and *Just messing, man.* Nothing.

I could push coffee with Dustin. *Wait, what am I doing?* Callie won't care if I'm there. I've offered her a ride to and from each class every day, and she's never once accepted. When tomorrow rolls around and she says no, then I'll be an asshole for skipping coffee with my brother for the girl I'm wooing.

Wooing?

That's it. I'm in over my head, and I need to stop. The whole thing has gone on for far too long.

Mission officially aborted.

I'm ending it.

How exactly does one end a fake challenge set up as a scheme to get a girl to have sex with you? I ask myself this when I take Callie coffee in the morning. Again, when I show up to offer her a ride after class. Once more, knocking on her door fifteen minutes before her afternoon class. The one I won't be waiting outside of when she comes out.

"Right on time, Jordan," she says.

I stare at her, waiting for the answer to come.

When I don't respond, her eyebrows pull together. "This is where you say, 'Do you need a ride to class, beautiful?' Then I say, 'No, Jordan, I don't, but thank you.'"

I half-smile because I'm supposed to, but I have no idea what to say. How do I let her know I won't be bothering her anymore? Maybe I don't. Maybe I just stop bothering her.

She tilts her head to the side, studying me. "Are you okay?"

Snap out of it, Waters.

I slap on a more *me* grin, forcing out an answer. "Of course I am. I just forgot my lines. Thanks for reminding me."

A split second of a smile precedes an eye roll. "Whatever. I'll see you later."

The door shuts, and she's gone. It's over. The end.

I walk to my Jeep. No more trips to the coffee shop or running around campus. I drive home. I won't see Callie anymore or Felicia or Jess or Cam. I park under the tree. When's the last time I committed to something this wholly and failed? Not even failed. Gave up.

I go inside and up the stairs. How long will she wait for me when she comes out of class? Will she? Or will she return to life as usual, grateful I finally moved on?

I pace the length of my room. My big, beautiful bedroom with an en suite bathroom and more closet space than I can fill.

Most of the time, she doesn't act like she gives a shit about my presence. Then she mind-ninjas me with smiles or questions about my well-being or says she'll see me later. Why would she say that? Of all the days. The one time she will without a doubt *not* see me later.

Goddamn it.

I head down the hall and kick open Benji's half-ajar door the rest of the way.

"Benj, I—" I stop at the sight of his room. His teeny-tiny, already-packed up room. Boxes on the floor. Dresser drawers empty. Even his mattress is propped up against the wall for easy removal.

"Well, well, well," he says from behind me, "look who's standing at my door, ready to fold."

My chin lowers to my chest as I once again question what the hell I'm doing.

"Six months, and we trade back?" I turn around, and he meets me with the most irritatingly cocky grin—and that means something, coming from me.

He nods and extends his hand. "Deal?"

Dustin flirts with a coed the next table over. I love my brother, but wow. If I act anything like him with women, I'll need to reevaluate. He stares directly at her breasts, and his hand finds her knee within five seconds of introducing himself. Thigh by twenty. And he's whispering in her ear just under the one-minute mark.

Other than his short blond hair, his approach to girls and recreational habits are the most glaring differences between us. We both sport the same green eyes and our father's strong jaw. Trait-wise, we share the overly competitive nature and a tendency for the dramatic. He strikes an odd balance between being the least restrained person and most motivating force in my life.

I can't bear to witness more of his surprisingly effective methods, so I check my phone. My eyebrows shoot up when I see a message from Callie.

I like Benji.

He check out your rack? I text.

Immediately.

Sorry.

I set down my phone, thinking she won't respond, but she does.

He drives your Jeep like a madman.

You rode with him?

She replies, *Why wouldn't I?*

Challenging woman.

I smile at the screen like an idiot. It's our longest text exchange yet, and she initiated. Other than the first time, she has only responded, and then she keeps to the point. I would have introduced her to Benji on day one had I known the effect. He's my personal Callie whisperer.

"Bro, no." Dustin's returned his attention to me as his girl exits. "We don't do that."

"Do what?"

He swipes the phone from my hand. I reach for it, but he pulls it away. Flashbacks from childhood commence. His head shakes as he scrolls through my messages. "We don't text girls and then gaze all starry-eyed and shit at their response." He tosses my phone back, setting his sights on another conquest. "Excuse me…"

Jackass. He insisted we meet and then spends the entire time talking up women, only to stop long enough to give me shit about something he doesn't understand. Of course, neither do I anymore. I'm living in a shoebox of a room for the next six months and refer to my pursuit of Callie as wooing.

I'm an uncharted Waters.

I roll my shoulders to relieve a building tension—a residual effect from my lingering mood further amplified by everything else from the day.

Girl three loses Dustin's interest in record time, and he twists around in his chair. "She talks too much." He dazzles the waitress with a grin as she returns his credit card and receipt to our table.

Shameless.

I chuck part of a muffin at him. "Why am I here?"

"Mom and Dad want you to meet with Dad's buddy, Stan. His recommendation goes a long way with admissions officers."

"What if I don't want to go to law school?"

He chokes on his coffee. "What?"

My brother and I rarely discuss topics of a serious nature, but I have no one else to bounce my concerns off of. "I've been thinking about it a lot lately, and—"

"No," he cuts me off and straightens up in his chair. "You made the same deal I did. An all-expenses paid trip through undergrad in exchange for law school. What else could you possibly want to do?"

I shrug. A million things carry more appeal than what they have planned for me. "What if I take a real shot with my music? Or get a master's degree in philosophy?"

He laughs and leans back again. "Who do you think you are? Kant? Law school is the plan. You follow the plan."

"What if I come up with a different plan?"

His brows pull in, morphing his face from one of mocking to one of alarm. "You're serious about this?"

I shrug again, unsure of what I want. A common theme found in my life all of a sudden.

Callie sends, *You like a challenge, remember?*

A well-timed reminder makes me smile. Yes, but I prefer the challenge to deal with beautiful women and not decisions that will potentially affect the rest of my life.

"Romeo." Dustin kicks me under the table. "If you're set against law school, you need to come up with an alternative. Not a whim. A solid plan. Commit to what you want to do with your life and present it to the parents." He smirks. "They might die from shock, seeing you put forth an effort, but that would also get you out of going."

His advice helps—not something I ever thought would happen. He's introducing a previously unseen scenario. One where I don't go to law school, yet my parents don't view me as a complete failure.

"Let me have Stan's number," I tell him. "I need to think about it."

He texts it to me, confirming the visit was to make sure I agreed to use it. I add the contact under *SDog* and listen to him detail the trip to Tijuana for spring break. He's doing little to persuade me to jump onboard, throwing around the words *hooker* and *donkey* way too often to pique my interest.

Benji strolls through the doors of the coffee shop a few minutes later. A quick dangle presents my keys before he drops them on the table. This guy flips a chair around from another table and makes himself comfortable. His legs extend, and his hands rest on the back of his head. Then he says, "Your girl's cool, man."

I cringe in anticipation of the words about to come out of Dustin's gaping mouth.

"*His* girl?" His eyes dart to me. "I should have read those text messages closer. I just saw it was *a* girl." He chuckles. "No wonder you're suffering from an existential crisis."

"Don't be a dick," Benji says. He shoves my shoulder. "Let's go."

Apparently Benji's left his cryptic pants at home, and his bluntness saves the day. We all stand, and Dustin hugs me, slapping my back much harder than necessary. I reciprocate by pounding between his shoulder blades. He gives me another reminder about Stan and tells me to hurry up and book my ticket for spring break. A few steps out the door, I decide not to go. The entire trip sounds like an infection waiting to happen.

A ride with Benji rarely winds up peaceful with him being a chatty type. Yet, on our way to the house, he's preoccupied. Up in his head about something. Since their time together, both he and Callie have been acting odd. I dismiss a half-developed notion of something happening between them. Shit, I feel guilty for even considering it. Benji's loyalty never falters. I know better than to ever question it.

A few blocks from the house, he mutes the music. "You should invite Calico and her friend to that gig next week."

"Calico?" I chuckle. He has a nickname for her, and she won't even accept a ride from me. "She might say yes if you ask her. She likes you."

His eyebrow arches. "You want me to ask her to our gig next week?"

I shrug, not seeing any harm. "Sure. It might help me out."

Benji props his foot up on the dash. "Five … four … three…"

I glance over to see his asshole smirk. "What's with the countdown?"

He stares out the window, not answering. I stand corrected; he's wearing his cryptic pants. I pull into the driveway but keep the engine running. A swing by to see if Callie needs anything is in order. I turn to tell Benji to get out, but he's already smiling at me.

Then his mind bomb detonates.

"Next week I won't be talking to Callie."

"Nope," he says. "Your little nail-and-bail experiment ends on Friday."

I see what he's trying to do. "Benji, get out."

"Tell Calico hi from me, man." He whacks me in the chest before climbing out.

Walking into the dorms, I'm already predicting the upcoming exchange. Callie will answer, roll her eyes, tell me she doesn't need anything, and then say, *"Goodbye, Jordan."*

A ten-minute car ride both ways that I willingly make, all for this maddening woman to deny me.

The door opens.

"Hey," she says casually. "My other class for the day was canceled."

Then she returns to the couch where her books cover the coffee table. I stay in the doorway, fully convinced this is a trap. She's setting me up for something. But trap or not, it's an opening, and I need to take advantage.

"Good," I say on my way over to join her. "You have plenty of time to explain yourself. I bust my ass for you, and Benji reaps the rewards?" I settle in, close enough to feel her without physically touching her. "The world is cruel enough without you adding to it."

She shrugs. "He had a compelling argument."

"What was that?"

"He wasn't you," she shoots back.

"Ouch," I say, feigning offense. "You're breaking my heart, beautiful."

She stacks up her books and relaxes beside me again. "So, where were you?"

I'm still waiting for the other shoe when I say, "My brother was in town, so we met up for coffee."

"Older brother?" she asks.

"By three years." I sound distracted, trying to decide if she's closer now. "He's in law school at UPenn."

"That's the same age difference as Connor and me."

"Dustin's a complete asshole," I tell her.

Her head tips to the side. "You two get along then?"

I chuckle at the dig and run a hand over my jaw. "Most of the time, yeah. What about you and Connor?"

"He's one of the best parts of my life." The corners of her mouth turn up a little. "Do you have class this afternoon?"

"No," I tell her. "Tuesdays, I have a class at ten and one right after lunch."

She pulls her legs up, facing me with her bent knee on my leg. "A class at ten?" She sets her jaw and glares when I nod. "If you have a class at ten, why were you at my door earlier, offering to take me to my ten-fifteen class?"

I grimace, realizing my mistake. "I mean—"

"Pull up your schedule right now," she commands.

The return of Bossy Callie equals fucking hot. I quickly find it and hand her my phone even though she might come at me swinging once she sees all the conflicts between our classes. She shakes her head, scanning my schedule, and when her mouth opens, I safely assume she sees Friday's conflicts—the entire day.

"You're not doing this anymore."

Before I can argue that one, she leans over to the coffee table. She tears a piece of paper from a notebook and begins writing. Now and then, she huffs to remind me how frustrating she finds me. Seriously, what did Benji do to her?

She finishes and shoves the paper at me. "These are the only times you can *help* from now on."

I read through her proposal. With Friday as an end date, her way allows me to see her four more times. Not enough. I slide the pen from her hand and use her thigh to write on to add more. She doesn't pull away, so I write slowly to further stretch out our contract contact, my knuckles skimming up the inseam of her jeans whenever I shift the paper.

I fold the paper in half and hold it up, not letting go until she forcefully tugs it.

Our negotiations continue after she refuses my amendments. She leans over to cross out a few of my suggestions, and her hair falls between us. I stop myself from reaching out to tuck it back, not wanting to ruin whatever the hell is happening.

She resubmits a counterproposal stricter than the first.

I scoff and rip up the paper. "Nope. I reject your proposition and end our mediation."

In a dramatic display, I toss the paper in the air, and the pieces rain down on us.

Her lips twitch. "You realize you're picking up all this, right?"

"Yes, ma'am."

I collect the scraps scattered all over the couch and notice a piece on her shoulder. As I grab it, she casts her eyes up to mine and smiles. Genuine and without any attempt to hide it.

And then I feel it. Everything. Shifts. A millimeter at most but undeniable, nonetheless. Callie's different or I'm different or we're different, and maybe in a few minutes or hours or days or eventually, everything will gain a clearer meaning, but right now, I have no explanation other than something has changed.

Callie's smile fades, her brows dipping. "Can I ask you something?"

I let my hand fall and nod. "Go for it."

Her eyes bounce between mine and then she asks, "Are you still doing all this just to prove you can sleep with me?"

Fuck.

I knew she knew, but it knocks me further off-balance to hear her voice it. Up until this moment, I expected to lie and feign offense if she straight out asked, continue whatever game this has turned into between us. Now, Callie's inches away with a genuine question in her gorgeous blue eyes and spouting a bullshit line at her seems inconceivable. She waits for an answer I lack. Expects honesty when I'm not even sure of the truth anymore. Of all the times for my confidence to waver.

I finally respond with the only word that fits, "Unknown."

Those two syllables make her face fall, and I want to crawl into traffic for being the reason.

Her chest rises with a deep breath. "Five seconds," she says, exhaling. After a beat, she leans forward for a book. "I really should study."

It's a polite hint for me to leave, and I can't blame her.

I stand up, not wanting to do any more damage. "I'll stop distracting you."

Halfway to the door, something hits me in the back. When I turn around, a pen lies on the floor by my shoe.

"You forgot something," she says. Then she fucking points to her forehead.

I attempt to mask my disbelief and pick up the pen on my way back. My knee hits the cushion as I dip down, and my gaze snags on her mouth. So. Fucking. Tempting. Before I kiss her the way I want to, I tuck that section of hair behind her ear and press my lips to her hairline.

I only pull back enough to see her blinking up at me. "See you later, beautiful."

Sans eye roll, she takes the pen. "See you later."

Callie smiles at me as I back to the door.

Just like that, the walls come crumbling down. She texts, invites me in, shows concern, and reprimands me for not kissing her goodbye. Instead of unraveling the mystery of Callie Henders, I'm only more tangled—less clear on what I'm doing now than when I walked into the coffee shop a week ago.

***

A theory exists involving multiple universes, an infinite number of alternate realities. Each holds different versions of people where every possible event can occur. Various alt Jordans all exactly like me, except they're right-handed or blue-eyed. One enjoys the pressure of commitment; another has proud parents.

I appear to have stumbled into one where Callie smiles when she greets me in the morning, grabs her bag, and asks if I want to give her a ride. A parallel dimension where she invites me to stay after her class, so I won't need to drive across campus later in the afternoon for my own. It's in this world I am studying on the floor while she lies on the couch behind me, reading a novel for her lit class.

My eyes scan over the material on being, existence, and reality. Questions regarding what it means to exist swirl in my mind. What does it mean to be? Is existence a characteristic? Can something stop existing?

"Pen," Callie says, dragging me out of my thoughts.

The pen I started lightly tapping against the page, I'm now beating against my metaphysics book. I warned her that I'm a pain to study with. Earlier, I lost myself in an idea and circled her couch, raving like a lunatic.

I reach over my shoulder, handing her the pen. "Sorry, I thought tapping would be less distracting than pacing."

Her fingers graze mine as she removes the pen. The burning questions fade, and my attention diverts to her. I stay facing forward, but I'm hyperaware of her breathing, each minute movement, the touch of her arm resting between her body and my back.

I take a deep breath and refocus on my book. Over and over again, I read the same line, making every effort to absorb the information and not think about her, inches away. My finger drums out a beat under the single line of text my mind refuses to take in.

"Jordan."

Shit.

I reach my hand back. "Better take it. It's the only way to stop me."

She smiles when I check over my shoulder, and any chance of me studying vanishes.

I slam shut my useless book and twist around. "Now *you're* distracting *me*."

Her book rests on her chest, and she intently watches me. Bright blue eyes compelling enough to drive me mad, never giving away her thoughts. I still have trouble reading her other than when she smiles. And those are not something she gives away freely, but damn, when one appears, it's thrilling to know I'm the reason. Second only to a laugh. *God*, that laugh.

My eyes drift over the rest of her features, taking advantage of the opportunity to study her up close and in person. Again, I notice the small scar on her temple, superficial with uneven edges. A small freckle just under her eye, only one.

"What are you thinking?" she asks, interrupting me.

"Would you like the smooth answer or the real one?"

"Both," she says. "Smooth answer first."

"Very well." I pause for effect. "You are the most beautiful creature in existence."

Her eyes start to roll but stop. "What's the real one?"

Not hesitating this time, I tell her, "You are the most beautiful creature in existence."

She smiles and laughs, and I love a double victory. Except it reminds me of the fast-approaching deadline, which, right now, looks like it might come down to the wire.

"Come out with us Friday night." I brush my knuckles over the smooth skin of her cheek. It's the first time I've done it, but she lets me. "It's my birthday, and the guys are taking me somewhere."

Her eyebrows draw in. "Your birthday is on Friday? On Valentine's Day?"

Oh.

"Does that make asking you weird?" I ask, but of course it does. I really didn't think this plan through.

Finally, emotions flash through her eyes, only they cycle too fast for me to identify. I steel myself for a giant leap backward. I pushed her too far.

"I have to leave after my last class to go home. Otherwise, I would," she says. "I'm sorry."

A record scratch has my knuckles freezing on her skin. "You're…" I pause, not loving the feeling coursing through me. "You're leaving Friday afternoon?"

She nods.

Fuck any subtlety. My head falls forward, and I shove the heels of my hands to my forehead to relieve the instant tension. "Worse. So much worse," I mumble my thoughts before reining them in.

Her leaving again is worse than a setback. It means, I only have the rest of the day, tomorrow, and part of Friday left.

I need more time.

As if mocking me, the alarm on my phone goes off for class. I get up off the floor and take a deep breath to get my shit together. "What are you doing to me, beautiful?"

She stares up at me, no doubt wondering the reason for my dramatics. I lean down and kiss her forehead. "I'll see you later."

I walk out the door, defeated. No, anxious. No—hell, I don't know. Conflicted.

So very conflicted.

With my adjusted timeline, I begrudgingly agree to go to band practice instead of driving Callie to her study group. A mistake. Physically, I play through our set list in the garage, but mentally, I'm running scenarios on how to speed up my progress with her.

I check the clock hanging on the wall and miss a key change. A groan comes from someone over the music, but I don't bother checking for the source. My fingers speed up, forcing Rusty to up his tempo.

A cymbal crashes, and I dodge his stick.

"What the fuck, Waters?"

I lift a hand in submission. "Sorry."

Gavin drags the strap of his bass over his head. "Should we even bother practicing until after Friday?"

I wait for Benji to chime in so they can gang up on me with one of their focus groups dedicated to figuring out what's wrong with me and my life. Instead, he puts his mouth close to the microphone and grins. "I'm hungry. Practice over."

It's all I need to unplug and sprint out the door. I drive over, eager to try a new strategy—push. Instead of worrying about spooking her, just go for it. She won't hesitate to let me know if I've crossed a line.

I walk into the suite without knocking. Unfazed by my entrance, Felicia pauses the TV and waits for me to plop down on the couch with her.

"Good," she says. "I didn't want to watch this by myself."

"What are we watching?"

"You'll see," she says, pressing play.

See I do. Why Felicia decides to traumatize us, I never have the chance to ask. I'm too busy wrapping my head around the atrocities on the screen. Chickens confined to tiny cages where they lay eggs like machines. Male chicks being thrown into a grinder merely because they're male. Chicks grow so huge, so fast, that they can't even bear their weight before being slaughtered.

Callie comes in during a cutaway to the slaughterhouse. I grimace, and Felicia cries again. To protect her from what happens next, I drag her over and she buries her face against my chest.

"Documentary about chicken farms. Worst. Thing. Ever." I wince and force my eyes to Callie, a welcome fucking sight after the horror show. "Do you know how they make chicken nuggets?"

Felicia wails into my shirt, something about the evils of capitalist culture.

Callie rushes to shut off the TV. "Why would you keep watching it?"

"Uh, to learn how the world works, Callie. Duh."

She's not impressed by my response. Felicia straightens up, smearing tears across her face with the heel of her hand. I grab her a tissue and make sure she calms down. When I glance up, Callie's disappeared to her room.

"Gibson," I say, "can we never finish this?"

Tears fall as she nods. Bringing the tissues with, I help the poor girl to her room. The most pathetic attempt at a smile forms as I hand the box to her. I wait for her to shut the door before setting my sights on the other bedroom.

This is it. Time to make it happen.

Callie is sitting on her bed, back against the wall. I knock on my way in, but she doesn't look up from her phone.

"I sent the mess to bed. She cannot handle the harsh realities of our world." I lie down on the bed and use her lap for a pillow. "Do you want me to describe the particulars? The images are etched into my mind for eternity."

She shakes her head, still distracted. "No, I'm good, thanks."

"Thank God. Now, soothe me. I'm very upset."

Without looking, she trails her fingers through my hair. And she needs to never stop. I close my eyes, not sure if I've gone too long without this type of physical contact or if it's her. Every move of her hand relaxes my body while amping up my cock.

I search Callie's face for any hint at what has her so focused because she's not here with me. She stares off, eyes vacant and a blank expression. Her hand stalls out then.

"You stopped," I say after several seconds.

She blinks a few times, coming back from wherever she went. The light returns to her eyes when she gazes down at me, and she flashes a grin. "I'm not sitting here all night, stroking your hair."

"Not a problem." I roll out of bed to my feet and nod to her pillow. "Lie down."

"What? Jordan, I'm not—"

I grasp her ankles and tug her toward the opposite end of the bed. She shrieks and laughs.

"Okay." After a glare, she scoots the rest of the way and lies on her side with her back to the wall.

I crawl in, sure to brush my body against hers as much as possible. They line up so perfectly that I have to fight the urge to push her onto her back. I end up as close as I dare get for my sanity, not quite touching her with my arm tucked under my head.

I drag her hand to the back of my neck.

"See, easy solution," I tell her.

Callie doesn't even hesitate, her fingers threading through my hair. I bury a groan and slide my hand over her hip, flexing my fingers against the temptation of pulling her against me. The space between us lessens anyway until the tip of my nose touches hers.

When my gaze lowers to her mouth, she licks her lips and her breathing accelerates, not a damn sign of stopping me. Eight days, a dozen-plus coffees, who knows how many noes, and we've finally arrived. Callie Henders wants me to kiss her. Given the way her fingers tighten in my hair and the heat in her eyes, that's not all she wants.

It all plays out in my mind. I'll cup her face in my hand, sweeping my thumb over her cheek, and bring my lips to hers. My heart will pound while I slip off her shirt and see those gorgeous curves, touch what she taunted me with last week. A smile or a laugh when one of us fumbles while undressing the other. Her thighs clenching while I make her come with my tongue. Those eyes staring up at me as I finally push inside her. Anticipation, excitement, pleasure, and then I'll walk out the door, and it'll be all over. Life will return to normal without the random, beautiful, perplexing woman who's taken over.

But when my palm reaches her cheek, a lump forms in my throat. I skim my thumb over her soft skin, and my stomach fucking knots. Callie's gaze is locked on mine as she waits for what we both want.

And I can't do it.

I can't fucking do it.

My lips press to her forehead, lingering and still against her skin when I say, "Goodnight, beautiful."

———

A moment of clarity rips me from my sleep, my eyes opening.

The light from the parking lot glows through the window and highlights Callie's face, tucked against my chest. I swallow, looking down at her before I ease my arm out from under her. I leave the weight of my hands on the mattress to keep the bed from moving as I climb out. She stirs but stays asleep. I toss the blanket from the end of her bed over her and make a quiet exit.

It's almost four in the morning. I speed home through the empty streets, and when I get there, I unlock the garage and shut myself in. My feet walk me in a large square over and over while my mind sorts through the realization that woke me up.

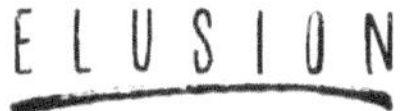

"No more Callie," I repeat the words a dozen times at least and turn imaginary corners.

But it doesn't matter how many times I say it.

I can't even imagine a world without her anymore. Barely over a week has passed since I existed in that reality, but I hate the possibility of ever going back. No more Callie stopped being an option the moment she smiled, and her eyes met mine. Hell, it probably happened further back than that.

I drop onto the floor and stare up at the rafters of an unfinished ceiling while accepting my fate. I want to be with a girl—*the* girl—and not just for a night or two. I want Callie Henders for weeks or months or some other indefinite amount of time.

Now comes the real challenge. I have to tell her I want to be with her and hope she doesn't think I'm full of shit.

Somehow, I function around Callie for the day. On the inside, I'm a whole lot of nerves with anxiety as my new best friend. To avoid a coronary, I decide to wait until tonight for any proclamations. It helps … to an extent.

Our last classes of the day end at the same time. She insists I stay for the entire lecture, which proves almost more than my patience can endure. I'm the first one out the door and almost hit a full sprint on the way to the Jeep. Once I drop her off at the dorms, I only need to get through band practice. After that, I can focus solely on her.

She is waiting for me in the parking lot when I get there. The simple sight of her almost has me blurting it all out, but I keep my shit together. I turn up the music to avoid further temptation on our drive. A Nirvana song plays from the *Impress Callie* mix I created the first night after the party.

Maybe in hindsight, I was fucked from the beginning.

"May I?" She looks at my phone.

I nod and smile, knowing she'll see the name of the playlist.

She picks it up and immediately shakes her head. "Do you put this much effort into everything you do?"

I choke back a laugh. "Not in the slightest."

"Then why all the effort with me?" She sets my phone down, turning to face me.

"Because you, Callie Henders, are my muse."

She sighs. "That's the smooth answer. What's the real one?"

Honesty without bearing my soul—a tap dance. "I don't have one. Not a solid one anyway. I could make up some bullshit filled with half-truths, but you deserve better." I make my last turn into the dorm parking lot. "I have band practice tonight, but can I come by later?"

"Not if you make me stroke your hair," she says.

I almost offer my dick to stroke, but settle on, "Pssh. You loved running your fingers through my luscious locks."

When I glance over, she squints with an adorable wrinkle in her nose.

I park at the curb near the door. Her head rests on the headrest, and I call her over with my finger. She leans over the center console. Her lips beckon me, but I stick to the plan and kiss her cheek. "I'll see you later, beautiful."

She starts to get out but comes to a hard stop, facing forward. All color disappears from her face, a void to her expression similar to last night. I follow the blank gaze, but she stares straight ahead at the rust spot on a truck parked ahead of us.

"Callie?" She doesn't respond, so I graze my knuckles down her pale cheek. "Hey, where'd you go, beautiful?"

She blinks and looks over.

"Are you okay?" I ask.

Callie flashes a smile that never reaches her eyes, but then she says, "Yeah, I'm fine. I'll see you later." She climbs out and gives me a little wave through the window before heading to the building.

Now, just to get through practice.

***

Our run-through goes without a hitch. We wrap up after a quick change to our set list and a minor tweak to the bass part on a song. Our gig next week should go flawlessly. Benji and I toss around the idea of writing over the weekend while Gavin runs through his adjusted parts on the bass a few more times.

When we finish, Rusty offers me a beer.

"No, I'm heading to Callie's."

He lights his cigarette and twists the top off his bottle. "You gonna keep lying to us about her?"

I'm not lying to them. They just haven't asked about her since my middle-of-the-night realization.

"What do you want to know?" I ask.

Benji steps between us to get to the fridge. "Gentlemen."

Rusty flicks his cigarette, the ashes landing on the concrete. "She still just pussy, and you're done after tomorrow?"

"Don't fucking call her that," I warn.

"We'll both kick your ass for that one, and of course he's not done." Benji smirks as he pulls up a stool between us. "Calico's sticking around. I might beat the shit out of him if he fucks this up."

"You met her once and for, like, a minute," Gavin says.

"Sometimes it only takes five seconds." Benji lifts a brow at me like I'm supposed to have any idea what he's talking about.

The garage erupts then, the Jordan's Life Committee convening without giving me a chance to respond. No need for *my* opinion about *my* life with such a worthy group of experts on hand.

"Fifty bucks says he jumps ship tomorrow."

"I'll take that action. He's going to fuck and run tonight."

"You're both wrong. The dude's fallen for her."

"Must I always be the one to remind you? We're talking about Jordan here."

"He does tend to lose interest rather fast."

"The kid can't even commit to hair products."

"Once he gets his dick wet, he'll be over it."

"No reason to deny his nature."

"Yeah, there's no shame in enjoying your freedom, dude."

"Shut the fuck up," I shout over them.

They stop, but the words are already chipping away at me. Way too much of what they said holds truth, and I fucking hate the doubt creeping in from the edges.

I grab my hoodie and start for the door, turning around before leaving. "You guys"—I search for the right word—"blow."

Not my best, but I commit, slamming the door behind me. It does little to muffle their laughter and even less to minimize the damage coursing its way through my conscience. What if I screw this up? What if everything I told myself about not being a disappointment is just something a disappointment tells himself to feel better about what a complete failure he is? What if I'm being impulsive and not thinking shit through again? What if the challenge ends, and so does my interest in Callie?

I drive around for a long time, incapable of heading toward the dorms without thinking about lacrosse. For years, I put everything into it. Training camps, two-a-day practices, giving up valuable social time for conditioning, even during the off-season. Then they chose me as captain junior year. A first for the team and a year earlier than Dustin, who'd captained the team as a senior. The very next day, I hit snooze on my alarm and skipped practice. All my passion for the game I'd thought I loved had vanished overnight. Later that day, I dropped off my uniform. I quit. Just walked away. I beat Dustin, my entire reason for playing, so why bother anymore?

Now, here I am again, about to be named captain. Every interaction with Callie inches me closer to my original goal, only now I'm dreading the possibility of achieving it. I can't lacrosse her, which means the stupid fucking deadline needs to come and go before anything happens between us. It's the only way I can guarantee my feelings for her aren't just tied up in the chase. For the first time in my life, I want to lose.

Hell, I need to.

I approach her suite's door with an entirely new focus—don't touch Callie until she comes back after the weekend.

Jess answers, and her eyes travel down to my crotch. The only part of my body she ever addresses directly. "Jordan."

I slink around her when she refuses to move. One day, she will unleash a whole new level of awkward. She returns to the books on the floor, stealing one last glance as I go to Callie's room.

More nervous than before, I lift my hand to knock, but before my knuckles meet wood, Felicia grabs my arm and hauls me across the common area. She unleashes some freakish strength to shove me into her and Jess's room.

"The fuck," I say, rubbing my bicep. "How are you so strong?"

Arms crossed, she glares at me. Pissed-off Felicia—not someone I want to fuck with, apparently.

"Tell me what the fuck you did to Callie," she demands.

I shake my head. "Nothing."

She steps forward, stabbing a finger into my chest. "Ever since you dropped her off, she's been acting weird. She's barely left her room, and when I try to talk to her, she spaces out. It's like she's only half here."

My stomach drops as I remember what happened in the Jeep. "Vacant?"

Felicia nods, her finger falling away.

"Shit." I drag a hand through my hair. "She seemed upset for a second earlier, but then she was fine. I can't think of anything I would have done though, I swear."

Her stance loosens, a bit of nice Felicia breaking through. "It must be something else going on with her then. Sorry. I release you." She steps aside to let me leave. "Don't make me regret being on your side."

I half-smile, and the last of the tension leaves her face. She trusts me, adding another person to the list of people I risk letting down. No pressure or anything, ladies.

In a few seconds, I'm standing in front of Callie's door. I let myself in after a rapid knock. My eyes fight to adjust to the darkness, so I fish out my phone and use the backlight.

What has the unpredictable girl done now?

I navigate my way toward the two stripped beds, a tent of blankets built between them. Muffled voices come from beneath the fabric. They stop, and Callie peeks her head out of a slit, looking up at me. "Shoes off."

She says nothing else before disappearing inside. I snort and slip off my sneakers. Two hours away from turning twenty-one, I prepare to enter a pillow fort. I crawl in, examining her handiwork. Two desk chairs and the beds keep the structure erect. Pillows from her and Cam's beds cover the floor along with extra blankets. Seven-year-old Jordan would have approved of her clear experience in the art of fort construction.

With her back against her bed, Callie's in shorts and a tank top, holding her phone, dark hair cascading over her shoulders. I drop beside her, and without a word, she resumes a movie. Anyone else, and I'd complain about the rom-com, but for her, I'll watch a chick ride through traffic in a taxi while a guy chases her ass down. They talk and kiss, and thank God the end credits roll within five minutes.

She closes the app and stares straight ahead, not entirely focused on anything. She seems more here than earlier, but I still proceed with caution. "May I ask why we're hiding under a pile of blankets?"

"Nothing bad can happen under the blankets." She says it as if it were the truest statement ever made.

Her head falls onto my shoulder, and she sighs. I rest my cheek in her hair. The fort falls dark when her phone's screen shuts off, and we just sit. It feels like where I'm supposed to be. With her in this blanket tent. If only I could trust myself to feel the same way after tomorrow.

"I'm in a very bad mood," she finally says.

"Does Very Bad Mood Callie like to talk?" I lift my head when she moves.

"No." She illuminates the space with the flashlight on her phone and sets it in the corner. A trace of a smile crosses her lips when she looks at me. "She also doesn't like to be around anyone."

I remove my keys, phone, and wallet from my sweatpants pocket and toss them next to her phone. "My presence is nonnegotiable." I sprawl out on the pillows and make myself comfortable.

Bad mood or not, I have no intention of spending my night anywhere else. If she argues, I plan on playing the almost-birthday card. But she drags my arm away from my body and flops down in the newly created space. My priorities shift from keeping my hands off her to comforting her. All other shit I cast to the wayside as I pull her closer. Now, if only we could stay like this for the next twenty-six hours with her head on my shoulder and a hand on my chest.

"Do you like your parents?" she asks after a while.

I mull over a response, not sure anyone has ever asked before. "I think I like them as people, but not as parents."

"Elaborate?"

I skim my fingers over her hair. "I come from a family of firstborns. Simply by being the second child I began a lifetime of disappointing my parents. My brother either does everything first or someone else does better. Win a science fair? Dustin already won two. Graduate second in my class? Elsa Parker's kid was valedictorian. I accepted it as a losing battle not worth fighting a long time ago."

"A perfect GPA isn't you trying to prove something to them?"

"Nah, that's a compulsive need to outshine Dustin at every turn. Our parents think he can do no wrong, so it's my job to keep his ass grounded." I rethink her question and ask, "How do you know my GPA?"

"Have you met Felicia? That girl knows everything about everyone."

Almost everyone, I want to correct. One particular person's story in this tent continues to elude her, to elude me.

"Does she keep a file on me?" I ask.

Callie shrugs. "It's entirely possible. She spent the entire day of that party trying to tell me every detail she could dig up about you."

Fuckin' Gibson. She planted herself in my corner before I even started playing the game. The chick deserves a Christmas card every year for the rest of my life or something else along the lines of repayment.

"What all did she tell you?"

"Not nearly as much as she wanted to," she says. "Your major, age, but she didn't know your future plans."

Who does?

"Hmm, well, unless I can convince my parents to let me do anything else with my life, I'll be attending law school after graduation. Another battle I've probably already lost." My hand trails up the length of her bare arm, and she shifts even closer, her palm drifting lower. It stops halfway down my abs, so not helping me out here.

I swallow. "So, now you know about my overly competitive rivalry with my douchebag brother and my status as constant disappointment to my parents. What about you? Do you like your parents?"

"No."

If the tone wasn't enough, the way her muscles tense make it clear I've stumbled upon the root cause of her bad mood. Despite my curiosity, I decide to steer clear.

I stroke her hair again, thinking of a topic change. "Who was your first childhood crush?"

She immediately relaxes back into me. "Pete Daniels in preschool. You?"

"Maggie Larsen, our babysitter." I ask, "What about your first kiss?"

"Pete Daniels." Callie lifts her head to look at me. "Just to save time, he was also my first date and first boyfriend."

I shake my head, realizing I chose a shitty line of questioning. "Pete needs to die," I sigh out.

A ghost of a smile appears, and she turns it back on me. "First kiss?"

I don't even hesitate. "Maggie Larsen."

A spark returns to her light eyes when her smile fully develops. Callie's back.

"Really?"

"No, Callie." I push her head back onto my chest. "She was fifteen, and I was five. Shockingly she wasn't into me."

She laughs, snuggling into me. "A real ladies' man would have sealed that deal."

Her mood exponentially improves as I aim to distract. We cover from our least favorite movies to most embarrassing moments. Every time she laughs or smiles, I swear a world outside of the makeshift tent ceases to exist. Even the concept of time folds and warps around us, losing all meaning. At least it seems to until my phone starts buzzing. The messages ruin the illusion of us being the only two people in existence.

I switch it off and toss it back in the corner, not the least bit interested in anything but her. Fuck, that feels true.

Callie sits up, bracing on a palm as she stares down at me. "You can't possibly want to start your twenty-first year on the planet in a blanket fort with a bitchy girl who won't put out."

"You're right." I reach up and trace the curve of her bottom lip. "My birthday wish included a bitchy girl who *will* put out. Do you think Jess knows how to build a decent fort?"

"You could go ask," she says coolly. "If not, you two can borrow this one."

"Celibacy sounds preferable. Now come back down here."

She lowers onto her side, facing me, and I turn my head, sliding my arm under hers. Her eyes search mine, the question already there before she says it. "Is this still just to screw me?"

The urge to answer her nearly wins out, but my recently discovered self-control stops me. I can't risk even the slightest chance of it being about meeting a challenge. She deserves certainty, and I need to prove to myself it's more.

I roll toward her, my thumb skimming up her jaw. "Ask me on Saturday."

"I won't be here on Saturday," she whispers.

I'm focused on her mouth, my resolve slipping with it so close. Needing to feel my lips on her, I lean in and kiss her forehead, then the tip of her nose. It's not enough, but I won't stop if I go any further. "Just do as you're told, you maddening woman."

She holds my gaze, the space between us harder to maintain. All of a sudden, she drops onto her back and lets out a loud sigh. The dramatics suggest she's spending too much time around me.

"This is the longest five seconds in the history of the world," she says.

"Five seconds?" The choice of number snags my attention, and with the way her lips twitch, I know it holds significance. "Why do you and Benji both keep mentioning five seconds?"

Ignoring my question, she grabs her phone from above our heads. "Less than a minute to midnight. Should we start a countdown?"

I swipe her phone away and toss it away. "Yeah, let's start one at five seconds. Until then, you can explain the relevance."

Callie shrugs and smirks. "Ask me on Saturday."

She amazes me, and I have every intention to do exactly that.

Holy hell.

If given the option, I would walk over hot coals rather than sleep on a floor again.

Callie's already gone, which leaves me rather disappointed. The light blinds me as I emerge from the blanket fort. I turn on my phone, and once it finishes alerting me of missed messages, I check the time. Class starts in an hour, giving me plenty of time to fetch coffee. I slip on my shoes and comb my hands through my hair. The marvel of a messy-hair look is, no one notices the rare days of rolling out of bed without styling it. I flip up my hood anyway.

Felicia leaps off the couch. "Happy birthday!"

"Thank you. But I believe the proper greeting on this particular birthday is a shot."

"I did you one better." She tosses me a travel-sized bottle of mouthwash. "Multipurpose."

"Bottoms up." I empty the bottle and swish, and she giggles when I spit the blue liquid back in. "Thanks, Gibs."

I drop the container in the trash on my way to the door. But as I reach for the knob, it opens.

Callie smiles on her way around me, carrying coffee. "Good morning, beautiful."

"You steal my line and my move on my birthday? Have you no shame?"

Felicia retrieves the tray of cups, and Callie delivers me one. "I think you'll find my coffee delivery service adds an extra pep to your step." She winks, hanging up her coat on the way to her room.

I chance a sip. The whiskey blends well with the coffee; of course she can mix a drink. I'm starting to believe her ability to surprise me knows no bounds.

Within minutes, we return the pillows and blankets to their rightful places and remove all evidence of her return to childhood. She packs a bag for her weekend trip. I quickly dismiss the thought of asking her to stay. Her off-the-shoulder top will lead to my undoing when mixed with alcohol.

From the other room, Felicia loudly clears her throat, and it sounds painful.

"Time to go, Jordan." Callie grabs my hand.

I brush my thumb over her skin while she leads me out of her room. "You can't kick me out on my birthday."

She pulls her hand from mine and opens the door. "I'll see you this afternoon."

"No, you'll see me after—"

Out of nowhere comes Felicia, fully hulked out and throwing me out into the hall. Seriously, scientists need to study She-Ra in a lab. The door shuts before I turn around. Confused about what the hell just happened, I stand there for a second, drinking my coffee. Erratic women have overrun my life.

I'm almost to the main entrance when Callie calls my name. She bounces down the stairs and comes to a stop in front of me with expectant eyes. "Say it," she commands.

I smile and gladly do as I was told. "I'll see you later, beautiful."

She pulls my face down until my lips meet her forehead. When she tries to pull away, I grab the back of her neck to stop her. I let her go after a second, and she steps back, taking my coffee cup from me.

"You're done with this, right?"

Well, since she runs up the steps with it in hand, I am.

By the time I reach the parking lot, I'm still wondering whether to take offense to them kicking me out. She's out of her mind if she thinks I won't see her after class. If I had my way, I'd spend the entire day in the cozy world of blankets, pillows, and Callie. My favorite world so far.

Music blasts from the speakers when I turn the key, and I slam the knob to kill the sound. I was distracted on the drive over here last night, but I don't recall deafening myself on the way. Movement in the backseat brings my attention to the rearview mirror.

Gavin rises from under my coat. "Hello, Jordan."

Oh, shit.

Both passenger-side doors open in sync, and Benji and Rusty climb in.

"Fancy a trip to the casino?" Rusty lights a cigarette beside me. "Don't bother answering. We're going either way."

The pieces of my odd morning align.

I'm being abducted.

Several hours and a vehicle change later, Benji's station wagon—recalled in the nineties—barrels down the road. The engine sputters, and the brakes squeal as he slows. Gavin pushes me out of the still-moving vehicle. Somehow I stay upright, taking a few uneasy steps until I gain my balance.

Assholes.

Callie slides off the hood of her black Prius. "Day drunk?"

"Day buzzed," I correct with a drunk grin.

"I need to go," she says as we meet at the back of the car.

The thought of burying my face in her neck and breathing her in crosses my mind. And with the reaction time of my brain slowed, I do exactly that. With a twist. I slide my hands through the opening of her coat and down to her ass. She gasps when I yank her flush against me, and I shove my nose against her neck and feel her skin against mine, but then she links her hands behind my neck.

Fuck, she feels good. Too good. I kiss her neck, fingers flexing. We're so close. Right there.

"Tell me it's not about sex," she says, dragging me back into the right mindset.

I pull back enough to meet her gaze and shift my hold to her hips. She deserves for there to be no doubt about my motives. For all of this to be about her and not some stupid challenge. I kiss her cheek before trailing my lips farther down and pressing them to the corner of her mouth. "Tomorrow."

Her hands slip down my arms as she steps back. "Goodbye, Jordan."

"I'll talk to you tomorrow, beautiful."

Before she get in, she glances at me once more. I sigh, relieved, because the next time she sees me, nothing will hold me back. No more games or deadlines—just us.

I hope.

———

Around five o'clock, it becomes clear that a drunk Jordan has no qualms with pouring his heart out to Callie. So, I alternate between water and drinks. Food also helps my resolve return, and by the time we arrive at the bar a few hours later, I'm confident enough in my chill to make it through the rest of the night without calling her—just as long as my phone stays in my pocket.

A table clears out in the corner, and we settle in. Rusty quickly removes the red heart centerpiece from the middle. Courtesy of Valentine's Day, my three chaperones dodge everything woman. Watching them provides more entertainment than drinking ever could. Each one's terrified to maintain eye contact with someone for too long and let them mistake it as interest. God forbid any of them take someone home on this holiday.

People come and go from our table. Some stop to buy me a drink, whereas others join us for longer. Once the shots start stacking up, I find it harder to pace myself. I take a few in a row and switch back to beer. The remainder I hand off to Gavin and Rusty to divvy up.

The bar comes to life with loud music and shoulder-to-shoulder warm bodies. We lose Benji to the crowd at some point, and Rusty appears one drink away from losing an article of clothing. Despite all the noise and everything around me, I can't stop thinking about Callie. Even the near disaster when Gavin forgets his no-chick rule fails to distract me for long.

After a while, Benji reemerges from the throng of people with a body slung over his shoulder. The grin on his face alone should clue me in, but he catches me off guard, dropping Callie into the chair next to me.

"Don't say I never gave you anything," he says.

Ecstatic that I conjured her, I smile before remembering why she needs to be anywhere else. My expression disappears along with my composure. "What are you doing here?"

She tilts her head to the side, her face falling. "You invited me."

"I just didn't think I was seeing you until Sunday." Panic wreaks havoc in my mind as I process how this changes the rest of my night. Our night. All I have to do is maintain for a few more hours, so no more drinking. I slide my beer in front of her. "You can have this one."

Her eyes narrow. "Thanks."

Not a very positive start.

Felicia materializes out of nowhere—well, obviously from somewhere, but until now, I've forgotten about every other person in the place. She lands on Callie's lap and hands me a shot. "Happy birthday—the right way."

"Thank you, Gibson." I set it down. "I'm pacing myself."

She shrugs and wanders off.

Every thought cycling through my head involves my inability to follow through. How I'll let Callie down. I look over and notice the concern on her face. Shit. She probably thinks I'm mad at her for crashing. Not that she has. She's right. I invited her. But she said she wasn't coming, and now she's here. I have no idea what to do.

My chest hurts.

Should my chest hurt?

Gavin interrupts what ramps up to be one hell of an anxiety attack to introduce himself to Callie. I force a few breaths and focus on anything else. From the other side of the table, Jess is staring at me. A tight-lipped smile seems like a safe response.

Shirtless, Rusty appears behind her and mouths, *Can I hit this?*

I shoot him a *fuck no* look. The night's already messy. I really don't need to add him banging Callie's friend to the list of complications.

Gavin's finishing up his meet-and-greet when I look over. He gives me an approval nod. For some reason, his acknowledgment of how hot the woman I'm working desperately not to screw things up with doesn't help my current situation.

Aware that any attempt to talk to Callie will lead to incoherency, I concentrate on my water glass. Conversations occur around me, and I engage only when necessary. All my focus centers on not gawking at the beautiful girl sitting next to me.

The ice cubes melt. I check the time. A quarter to ten. Almost there.

Benji kicks the chair next to me before plopping down. His arm hooks around my neck and jerks me closer, his expression anything but friendly. "Let's go talk or kick your ass or whatever."

At first, I'm not sure what he means, but then my eyes dart to Callie, her jaw set, looking like she wants to be anywhere but here. With me. Fuck. How long has she been upset with me? Benji doesn't give me time to find out before removing me from the chair. He, less than gently, escorts me through the crowd to the hall leading to the men's room.

He pushes me in and slams my shoulders against a wall. "I remember warning you that I'd kick your ass if you fucked this up."

I shake my head at how severely he's misreading the situation, but he's not done yet.

"Birthday or not. Drunk or not. I'm not letting you treat Calico like this."

I shove him off. "I'm far from drunk." He lifts a brow at that, so I spread my feet shoulder-width apart and extend my arm out before touching my nose. The grout lines on the tile help me further prove my point, and I walk heel to toe to the opposite wall and back. "See? Sober as a questionable judge."

"Then I really see no reason not to kick your ass. What the hell are you doing?"

"I don't know," I admit.

"Well, figure it out. She bailed on whatever she had going on to be here."

"That's the problem. I need her to *not* be here. I want her here, but I can't be with her. Not until tomorrow…" I give up, my rambling impossible to follow.

Benji slaps his hands on my shoulders and surprises me when he jostles me around. "When did you hit zero, man?" His question only adds to my confusion, and he chuckles. "The other day, on the drive home, Calico said all this was to prove you could fuck her."

"She what?"

"I told her it might have started out that way, but you were about five seconds away from admitting you wanted to be with her."

"You what?"

The longest five seconds in the history of the world. Callie's question about whether I want more. Both she and Benji knew the answer before I figured it out. She's been waiting for me to catch up, and then I act like she doesn't matter when she shows up.

Tool of the Year Award goes to Jordan Waters.

Thank you for coming, everyone. Please drive safe.

"Yeah, Benj, I screwed up." I drag a hand through my hair. "I convinced myself, if I tell her how I feel before the deadline, I'll change my mind about wanting to be with her and bail."

Benji grips my jaw with one hand, squeezing my cheeks together. "Why does this chick have more faith in you than you do in yourself?"

"Because I always sheem tolet eryone down and uin errhing."

Benji's still smashing my face, but he seems to get the point. "Then do better." He tosses my head to the side and taps my cheek. "It's time to man up, son."

The guy has found his calling as a life coach or something. I nod as he walks away and take a deep, centering inhale. It does nothing to prepare me for what I need to do now—trust myself—but it's time to do it anyway.

Callie's nowhere around when I return. I glance around the bar for her.

"Waters," Rusty shouts over the noise from the other side of the table. "Did you tell your girl what I said about her ass or what?"

I shake my head, remembering I need to fuck him up later for that.

"Well, you must have done something." Gavin offers me a beer, but I push it away. "She left."

"What?" My eyes snap to the empty chair-back, previously occupied by Callie's coat.

Felicia's apologetic shrug further confirms. Before I can even think, someone throws my coat at me. I push my way through the crowd toward the door. I need to find her and fix this.

Again.

Searching around the front of the building, I call Callie. It goes straight to voicemail. *Shit. Shit. Shit.* I pull on my coat on my way through the parking lot. Déjà vu hits as I look up and down the street. No sign of her anywhere. The campus is three miles away. She wouldn't walk that far on a Friday night. She probably found a ride or had brought her car. The chances of her letting me in the suite are abysmal, so I guess I'll need to beg for Felicia's help one more time.

On my way back toward the bar, the wind lashes at the side of my face, the wind chill near freezing. Always a cold punishment when I piss her off. Before I go inside, I give myself a minute to come up with a plan. A grand romantic gesture sounds way too cheesy, considering it's Valentine's Day, but I need to show Callie she wasn't wasting her time on me. I fish out my phone and look up the number for anywhere open that sells flowers. I call the closest one.

The wind crackles in the speaker when someone answers.

"Hold on," I say, moving to the side of the building. "I can't hear you with the—oh shit." Around the corner, I freeze with Callie right in front of me. I shove my phone in my pocket. "I've been looking for you."

"I don't care." She pushes past me to the front of the building.

I chase after her because, well, I'm really fucking experienced with it. "Callie, ask me the question again."

"No, Jordan. I'm done playing this game with you. At this point, I'll sleep with you just to make you go away."

She has no choice but to stop when I plant myself in front of her. "Ask me."

She crosses her arms and unleashes one hell of a glare.

"Damn it, you stubborn-ass woman."

Her constant need to challenge me frustrates me to no end, but I can't imagine it any other way. I step toward her, willing to bend since she refuses.

"No," I tell her. "This isn't about having sex with you. On some level, it's always been about more. I have wanted to be with you in some way, shape, or form ever since I hit the damn turn signal to go to the coffee shop."

Once the words leave my mouth, any doubt about them being sincere vanishes. Each time I questioned what the hell I was doing, I decided to be with her. All the time I focused on winning her over made me miss how she was affecting me. For her, I want to show up, to always kiss her before leaving, to call her beautiful every day, for her to trust me, rely on me. With her, responsibility and commitment are worth the effort.

We were never in an alternate world. She just changed mine as she went from intriguing to necessary. None of the rest of the bullshit matters anymore. Unless maybe it does because her face remains unswayed.

Then, after the longest pause imaginable, she shrugs. "Okay."

She has to be kidding.

"Okay?" I ask. "After all that, the only thing you have is *okay*?"

"Okay," she says again. "Now, was that so hard to admit?"

Fuck, this girl is going to kill me.

"You have no idea."

She smiles, and I tug her toward me. I can't get my mouth on hers fast enough, crashing my lips down on hers. She whimpers as my palm moves to her neck, and I use my thumb to pull down on her chin, so her lips part for me. I slip my tongue between them, groaning when I taste her again. Way too fucking long.

Callie glides her hands up the back of my neck and into my hair while my other one's not sure where it wants to be—her face, her back, her ass. I just know I need more of her. Guiding her to the wall, I pin her against it. She bites my bottom lip, and I grind my erection into her hip.

"You feel so fucking good." I grab the backs of her thighs, hiking her up. "I can't stop."

"Then don't," she breathes.

She locks her legs around me as I dip down to her neck, licking and sucking my way back up. I kiss over her jaw while unbuttoning the red coat that started all this, our eyes connecting before she pulls my mouth back to hers. Her skin's so fucking warm when I push under her shirt.

"Damn, get it, Waters," shouts a dead man.

I growl, my friends as obnoxious as ever. My mouth's still firmly on hers until Callie turns her head to look at them. With a heavy sigh, I lower her and push off the wall behind her. I readjust, so I won't have a zipper imprint on my cock, and her lips turn up.

I duck in to kiss her one more time before linking our fingers and leading her down the sidewalk toward Rusty and Gavin.

Their nicotine fix has officially ruined our moment. Now we're expected to go inside to a bar full of people, destined to spend the rest of the night eye-fucking—

Nah, screw 'em.

"Say, 'Goodbye Callie,'" I tell them once we're closer.

"Goodbye, Callie," they say.

She lets out a surprised yelp as I throw her over my shoulder. I'll spend my birthday how I want, and I want to spend it alone with her. I dart between parked cars and set her down by the passenger door of the Jeep. "Priorities, Callie."

She laughs and climbs in. As I pull out of the parking lot, I drag her hand over, needing to touch her. Now that I can, I might never stop. I bring it to my lips, kissing her fingers and knuckles and inner wrist.

The dorms oddly provide more privacy than the house. But more importantly, they're closer, and right now, the closer, the better. After I park, I jet around to her side and yank her out. She's smiling. I'm smiling. Everyone's fucking smiling because this moment has taken far too long. Unwilling to take my eyes off her, I walk backward to the building. When I hit the door, I hook her around the waist, pulling her to me.

"Still *certain* about me never getting another show?" I ask, seeking a repeat of her performance from after the party, but with a drastically different ending. My face buried between her legs while she comes on my tongue sounds like a pretty good one.

"Well"—she bites her lip, nearly destroying me—"it *is* your birthday."

I overemphasize a nod.

It's so my fucking birthday.

"I'm not stripping for you until we're inside."

The door flies open with more force than necessary, bouncing off the wall. I resume my backward walking and lead her up the stairs. We only make it that far before I have to kiss her, and then my hands stay on her, hers running up my chest when we round the corner to her hall. But once her gaze travels behind me, it never returns.

Her hands fall away as she stops moving. All color washes from her face. Everything that makes her Callie drains from her eyes, her stare fixed somewhere down the corridor.

"Callie, what's wrong?" I touch her pale cheek. Her focus flashes to me and then down the hall again. I check over my shoulder, and in front of her door are two men in sheriff's jackets, waiting, facing away from us. "Cops?"

The men turn around when they hear me. One with a buzz cut and a boxy face wears an expression hard as stone. The other one can't possibly be much older than me. Dark hair hangs over his ears and forehead, and even from a distance, his face is an apology.

When I look back at Callie, she only gives me a second to process a line of red rising up her neck, eyes murderous. Then she explodes past me, one emotion propelling her down the hallway—complete fucking rage.

"You don't have any fucking jurisdiction here, Kevin," Callie yells.

Wait, she knows them? I rush after her, no idea what the fuck else to do.

"Calm down," says the younger officer. He touches her arm when she reaches him. Evidently, it's the wrong thing to do. She uses all the momentum she has built up and rams her palms into his chest. The strike sends him backward and—oh my God, she's lost her damn mind.

Ready to do more damage, she advances.

I grab her by the shoulders and drag her back a few steps. "Callie, stop."

The victim of her fury shuffles a small step over, keeping between her and the buzz cut, almost as a barrier. "Either we came, or Graham was coming," he says.

Her shoulders tense even more. "Screw you, Trey."

"Callista—"

"Callie," she interrupts the buzz cut, who must be Kevin.

"Whatever." Kevin swings his arm out, removing Trey from between them. "Pack a bag."

"You can't make me go with you."

"I'll tell you one more time. Pack. A. Bag."

Her fists clench at her sides. I'm about to intervene, but she doesn't give me a chance. "I have to admit, the sheriff doing Graham's dirty work is a new low. Nothing better to do tonight than help your little brother fuck up my life? The taxpayers must be proud."

Mafia? My Mafia theory? No fucking way.

Kevin stands taller, widening his shoulders as his focus lasers in on her, and he barks, "Damn it, Callista, enough."

"Callie," she shouts back.

"Cal, please." Trey holds up his hands, pleading with her.

My mind struggles to keep up. Each refers to a different name—Callista, Callie, Cal—all appearing to belong to the girl whose shoulders heave beneath my hands while she tries to maintain some semblance of control.

Kevin's eyes dart to me, a malicious look accompanying his smirk when they drag back to her. "You been drinking tonight, *Callie?*" The way he says her name makes me want to beat his face in. He nods at me. "You have ID on you, son?"

"Dad, don't." Trey's eyes stay on Callie, even though he directs his comment toward Kevin.

She twirls around to face me, touching my arm. "Don't show him anything. Don't *say* anything. He can't do anything here."

Kevin steps toward us. "Either you're a minor or you're not. Judging by *Callie's* reaction, you're not. So, if she were to blow anything that registers on a Breathalyzer, smart money says you'd be suspect of furnishing alcohol to a minor."

Callie huffs and turns around. "You couldn't possibly prove that."

"Hard to say," he says. "Local law enforcement would need to investigate such a suspicion."

I'm far from concerned by his idle threat, but Callie shifts, so I move my hands back to her shoulders. She's right; even if she were drunk, which she's not, no one could prove I played any role in it.

"But…" Kevin steps toward us again, holding up his finger like he has a better idea. "Since they're here, I might suggest they search the dorms for contraband. Maybe check Callista's back pocket for her fake ID. You still keep it back there?"

Her shoulders spike when she sucks in air. The piece of shit developed a stronger tactic. Odds favor at least one of those girls keeps alcohol in their room, and unless she found a creative way into the bar, he's right about her having a fake ID. If she defies him, she risks screwing over her friends—not to mention, herself.

Trey lowers his head about the same time Callie takes a deep breath. "I need a few minutes to pack," she says.

Kevin steps out of the way to let us into the suite. Trey attempts to follow me in, but Callie throws all her weight against the door, pushing him back. He doesn't fight it, letting out a sigh as it shuts with him on the other side. I hit the light switch, ready to ask questions—Callista, Mafia, assaulting a cop. But when I turn around, I see her face, heavy and defeated. I fold my arms around her, and she hides her face in my chest, her breathing erratic.

"Are you going to tell me what's going on?"

"Can we talk about it on Monday?" she whispers.

"You're going with them?" I pull away to study her face. "Is that safe? They were just threatening you—and me."

"It's fine," she says dismissively. "My uncle and cousin are harmless."

Enough dots connect to at least partly fill in the picture. Trey's a cousin and calls her Cal, like Cate does. Kevin must use her full name—Callista. A pretty name. I wonder why she doesn't use it.

"Graham's your dad?"

She nods but offers nothing else.

Nothing about this feels right. Not the sleazy uncle authority figure who does her father's bidding. Or the helpless cousin, clearly aware of how fucked up the situation is but going along with it anyway. From the looks of it, out of necessity. Forget about how the ordinarily tenacious girl in front of me looks exhausted and subdued.

But I have to trust her.

Right?

Callie interrupts my internal conflict when she drags her finger over my bottom lip. "Rain check on the floor show?"

Her smile reaches her eyes, teeth denting her bottom lip, and I can't help but smile back—whatever she wants. Then she kisses me as if nothing happened. We came around the corner, down the hallway, into the dorm suite, and two men aren't outside, waiting for her. She slides her hands up over my chest to my neck, and my lips make their way down to hers.

"Cal." Trey knocks.

"I might end up hitting a cop," she says.

I groan into her neck. "That would be incredibly sexy."

"Don't move." She backs all the way to her room and picks up two bags. "I want you to be right there when I get back Sunday night."

I say the only thing I can, "All right, beautiful. I'll be waiting."

***

In the morning, I lie in bed, staring at my ceiling. In the eighties, they used our house as a dormitory for the local cosmetology school. I swear, my new bedroom retains the vague odor of Aqua Net. Six months in here smells more like a life sentence.

The fifth call from Dustin vibrates the blankets. All morning, I've ignored his calls and texts, not even bothering to read them. Annoyed by his persistence, I fish around in the comforter to locate my phone.

"Dude, take a hint." I hit the speaker button and balance it on my forehead.

"Yeah, Jordan," he says enthusiastically. "I'm good. Thank you, brother. How are you this morning?"

"What's wrong with you? Does someone have a gun to your balls?"

"That's great." He chuckles and repeats, "That's great."

"Dude, seriously, are you in danger?" I ask.

"I can't wait to hear all about it. I was calling to let you know that we're about ten minutes out."

I sit up, and the phone drops onto my lap. "Oh shit."

"Yes, Mom and Dad are very excited to see you, too."

I roll to my feet and dig through my drawer for a pair of khakis. "Stall," I tell him, bouncing around on one leg, sliding the other through the hole.

"They've been looking forward to it since last month."

The light-blue polo shirt from Nana hangs in my closet, but my belt—where the fuck is my belt?

"It was great of you to invite us for the day."

Brown Dr. Martens wait in their original box under my bed along with a pair of dress socks but no belt.

"Maybe we can swing by that coffee place you like and pick you up something."

I poke my head in from the hallway. "Yes, please, Dustin. Earn me a few extra minutes."

In the bathroom—*oh fuck, the bathroom*—I squeeze toothpaste onto my toothbrush and multitask. The towels on the floor go in the hamper. I wipe out the sink, run an antibacterial wipe around the rim of the toilet, wash my hands, and spit.

"…with two sugars?" Dustin says as I return to my room.

"Text me updates." I end the call. He'll pretend to say goodbye.

Shit. Great idea to invite the family down the day after my birthday.

Sliding down the hall, I pound on Gavin's door. "Mr. and Mrs. Waters touch down in T-minus ten minutes. Clean up Rusty."

"Oh fuck."

The door jerks open, and he tears past me in his boxers to wake up Rusty in the basement. Everyone knows ten minutes affords little leeway to make our place presentable—well, at least to my parents' unattainable standards.

I barge into Benji's room. He groans and mutters while I rummage through the closet. My belt. Success.

"Benj. Up. My parents will be here in ten."

He straightens up in bed like an electrical current shot through his dick. "Someone came home with Rusty last night."

Of course they did.

"Gavin's on it," I tell him. "Nice clothes. Clean up."

The guys won't screw around with tidying up and presenting themselves well. My parents hold the lease and pay our utilities as part of the deal for me attending law school after graduation. They're under the impression everyone pays me for living here. Not so much. I see no need for my friends to hand over their hard-earned cash since a summer job with one of my father's lawyer friends guarantees me more than enough for the school year.

I launch myself down the stairs and pick up in the living room. I fan out the magazines on the coffee table like frickin' Martha Stewart and add fresh smelly stuff to the thing on the other table where the smelly stuff resides. Coming around the corner from the living room, holding the cellophane bag of dried, scented flowers, I slam straight into … Jess? Her eyes do a down-up, and she giggles. Apparently, she can't recognize a sense of style.

Rusty comes up from the basement behind her. He lets out a, "*Fuck*," when he sees me and drags his hands through his hair.

I weigh the pros and cons of killing him, but then I'd need to change and clean more.

"Rustin, get upstairs and find something to wear in either my closet or Gavin's." He keeps his head down on his way by, and I return my attention to Jess. "How are you getting home?"

"I either need a ride or have to wait for Felicia to come and get me."

"Oh God. You're going to meet my parents."

Aware of what's coming, I give her a once over. She's wearing last night's makeup and has wrinkles in her clothes from them lying on the floor all night, and her being at the house at nine-thirty on a Saturday morning seems suspect on its own.

"There's an iron in my room and clean washcloths in the hall closet." I usher her to the stairs. "You're Rusty's cousin. Tell the guys."

My phone vibrates at the same time a car pulls up outside. Showtime.

I swing open the front door with a huge-ass grin. "You made it."

Down the steps I go to hug my mother. She kisses my cheek and wipes pink lipstick away before her eyes flit to my hair. Damn, I forgot about my hair. My hands quickly sweep through it in the usual left-back-forward pattern. A firm handshake with my father turns into a hug with a pat on the back. Affection in my family is only acceptable during greetings and farewells.

Dustin throws his arm around my neck and cracks his hard skull against the side of mine. "You got more warning than I did. Dad knocked, and I shoved a naked chick under the bed."

Ever the gentleman my brother.

"We should really write this shit down," I say.

He agrees, dragging me toward the house.

"Carol! Ray!" Gavin meets them on the steps, a cheesy smile accompanying his enthusiastic greeting.

He wraps his arms around my mother. He's her favorite of the guys, always kissing her ass. My father prefers Benji, and Dustin pairs best with Rusty. Everyone settles into the clean, odor-free living room where Ray presents me with cigars and a twenty-one-year-old bottle of scotch. No one dares say no to his request to share a glass with him. I toss my terrible coffee—two sugars—and switch to a single malt at ten in the morning.

Jess reappears as we finish our drinks. I introduce her as Rusty's cousin to my family. She looks impressively put together, considering how rough she looked earlier, but my mother becomes rigid the second she walks into the room. Internal sigh at the impossible-to-please Carol Waters.

Jess nudges me and leans in. "My phone's dead. I need to call Felicia."

I hand her mine, wondering how I can escape long enough to talk to Felicia when she gets here. My trusty sidekick and I have some investigating to do. I want to learn more about Callie, and waiting until she comes back sounds like an impossible undertaking. Outside of the small amount of information she gave me, everything I know comes from a six-year-old. Unless Callie owns two unicorns and teaches children how to make wishes, my source isn't the most reliable.

Dustin ducks closer, his eyes following Jess out of the room. "Is that the girl?" he asks in a hushed voice.

I lower my eyebrows at him in response.

"It'd better not be," he says. "Do you know how fast Mom will run off a girl she hasn't handpicked for you? She's already looking at her like she's planning out how to ruin her life."

The only experience I have with my mother's distaste for women is from the ones Dustin has brought home. Of course, none of them have been the type you should bring home to your mother; latex is never a great choice when meeting the parents.

In high school, I would only date girls for a few weeks before moving on to the next. Once I figured out they put out without the title, girlfriends became a thing of the past. Even so, I have no concerns about my mother's opinion on it. My parents might end up getting law school out of me, but an arranged relationship will never happen. Regardless of the offer they put on the table.

Jess returns and gives me my phone. "She'll be here in a bit. She was still sleeping."

I offer her my spot on the couch. My mother scowls at the use of the manners she taught me.

Oh, Mother.

"I think we need to celebrate with these cigars." My father holds up the case.

Right, and leave poor Jess to the shark who detects blood in the water?

"You go ahead, Dad. I usually wait until at least noon."

He cocks a dark brow. "You are no son of mine."

"Only a blood test can confirm," I reply.

He and the rest of the men refill their scotch glasses and retire to the smoking garage.

As soon as they leave, Carol announces, "I'm just going to use the powder room."

An attempted smile in Jess's direction almost injures her and ends up as more of a sneer.

I wait for her to disappear down the hallway before sliding onto the couch with Jess. "She's going to snoop."

Jess laughs and relaxes, the air returning to the room.

Shortly after my mother returns from a twenty-minute search for evidence of my unsatisfactory living conditions, Felicia pulls up to the house. I stand to walk Jess out, and Carol clears her throat. I give her a wink on my way by and go anyway.

Felicia hangs out her window. "Hey, how did last night go?"

Jess and I exchange glances, unsure of which of us she's asking, so she points to Jess. "Not you. Gross. Rusty?" Then she points at me. "You, go. I missed Callie before she left this morning."

"She left last night. But we're good. I did you proud."

She grins. "I always knew you would."

"Can I come by later?" I ask.

"I'll be around," she says, dipping back in the car.

I wave as they back out of the drive and head inside where my mother is waiting with a concerned half-smile that comes off condescending.

"We need to talk, honey."

Oh, great, a heart-to-heart between the displeased mother and her disappointing son. My morning can't possibly get any better.

She pulls her leg up between us on the couch and angles herself toward me. For someone who wants to talk, she stares for a long time. With the silence growing uncomfortably awkward, I chance a guess at our topic of conversation. "You don't like my girlfriend, Jess?"

She sighs, face dropping into her hand. "I was afraid of this." She looks back up. "I had hoped, with as eager as you were for these four years, you wouldn't squander them on *some girl*."

It's almost too easy, and I have to focus on keeping a straight face. "Don't you want me to be happy and in love?"

On the last word, an unbridled expression of disgust pinches her face. "We'll find you someone more suitable." She pats my leg. "After law school."

"Oh, Mother." I shake my head. "No, you won't. I'm going to marry that girl. In fact, I plan to ask Nana for the ring she promised me. A June wedding maybe? Unless you think fall is more fitting."

Her eyes close, her skin turning white. In the mood for a celebratory cigar over my impending fake engagement, I leave her on the couch to needlessly panic.

Point for the disappointing son.

After three glasses of scotch, my body believes it is time for bed, but it's only one o'clock in the afternoon. I stretch out on the floor in Felicia and Jess's room and check my phone. Still no word from Callie. On my way in, I noticed her car in the parking lot, so someone must plan on bringing her back tomorrow.

Felicia joins me with her laptop. "So, you think if we search Callista instead of Callie?"

"Did you know her full name?"

"No. I looked all over social media for her the first couple of weeks of school but gave up when I couldn't find her. That must be why." She runs a search for Callista Henders and shakes her head. "Nothing. I think I found her brother's profile though."

I recognize Connor from the picture in her room as Felicia pulls it up and starts scrolling. Intermingled with snapshots of basketball games and his friends, we see glimpses of the closeness between Callie and her siblings. Even through the computer screen, the bond is evident. I keep an eye out for anyone who could be her father, mostly to debunk my Mafia theory once and for all. But except for a basketball coach, everyone is younger.

The account only goes back a few years, so I think we're ready to move on until Felicia says, "It says he lives in Waymore, but a lot of these were taken somewhere else." She stops on one where a sign in the background reads *Sutterville*.

What I consider an insignificant detail sends her into a clicking frenzy. Detective Felicia does not come to play. She maneuvers back and forth from one account to the next until she ninjas her way to a profile for someone named Shayna.

"That's why we can't find her," she says. "Callie disabled her account. See?" She points to a post on the screen. "It's her name but in a regular font, so you can't click it. This must be a friend who tagged her in pictures before, so her name still shows up."

I have no idea what she's talking about, but images of Callie fill the screen in front of us. We see her at prom, graduation, and camping. Felicia even spots some of her with blonde hair and laughs.

"Hold on." I scroll back up to the most recent picture Shayna has of Callie. Felicia clicks it, making it larger, and goes through them from there. They start in May of last year, slowly rewinding.

"I don't think I've ever seen her smile this much," Felicia says.

She's right, but the further back in time we travel, the less this girl resembles Callie. Her eyes lose their spark, and the vibrancy of her smile fades away. Felicia and I stop talking and stop recognizing the person on the screen.

In the pictures from two years ago, she wears way less clothes and poses with a number of guys. I wouldn't normally care about either, but the more I look, the more I see beneath the surface, unease twisting through me.

The dudes with her appear to be random since they only show up once or twice. Each one stakes their claim—arms around her, mouths pressed against her shoulder or neck, hands on her in different yet equally possessive ways. In several, she looks ready to lose consciousness. Worse are the ones where she already has.

Even further back, three or four years ago, a too-thin blonde's empty eyes are bloodshot with dilated pupils. In the videos and pictures, she chugs out of liquor bottles, stands on top of a moving car, hangs off the ladder at the top of a water tower, laughs as Kevin handcuffs her, jumps over a fire, and lies in a snowdrift, wearing nothing more than a tank top and gym shorts.

A few of the same faces show up in the background most of the time. I slide the laptop closer and sift through the photos again, concentrating on these faces. Most of the time, they're blurry and out of focus, but once I recognize him, my eyes quickly identify him over and over—Trey.

I try to call Callie.

No answer.

Again.

I close the laptop, my jaw clenching. I never should have let her leave.

Instead of writing a song, I tap the pen on my knee, thinking about Callie because that's all my mind does now. Nine-thirty on Sunday night, and still no word from her since she walked out the door on Friday.

"She'll be here soon." Felicia's attempt at reassurance falls flat, considering she looks as worried as I feel.

None of it feels right—even without the pictures.

Someone knocks, and my heart almost flies out of my chest. But Callie wouldn't knock. I relax back on the cushions while Felicia goes to answer.

"I am so sorry about this," a guy says.

"Jordan?"

The panic in Felicia's voice has me on my feet. In staggers Trey with Callie. He's supporting most of her weight, and when she laughs, her knees buckle. I race to catch her other arm before she topples them both over.

"I told you to wait over there." She motions at a spot behind me.

Damn, she's drunk—adorable, but trashed.

Felicia leads us into Callie's bedroom, and we lay her down. Her eyes shut the second she hits the pillow, but Felicia pries them open again. "How much has she had to drink?"

Trey hovers nervously by the doorway in jeans and a T-shirt. "I lost track around seven o'clock. But she only blew a point-one-five on the Breathalyzer in my truck a few minutes ago, so she's come down a lot from earlier."

"Only?" I say. "That's almost double the legal limit. How drunk was she earlier?"

Felicia cocks her head to the side. "How was she still drinking at seven? Isn't the trip here three hours?"

Trey rubs the back of his neck. "I lost track at seven this morning."

I almost lose my shit, my temper narrowly in check as I shoulder past him out of the room. I'm not sure of the consequences for punching an off-duty sheriff's deputy, but I'll find out if he keeps talking.

He's there when I turn around, hands up in defense. "This is not my fault."

Fuck it. I stalk toward him, no longer giving a shit what happens. He already has an excellent black eye going that I can add to. Or maybe I can bust back open the cut on his cheek someone already left him.

I halt mid-stride, Callie's words from the other night resurfacing. "Did Callie hit you?"

"She almost broke my nose." He gestures to his eye and cheek. "These beauts came from her elbow blow."

It might have been a joke, but I do find her hitting him incredibly sexy. I scrub my hands over my face and give myself a few deep breaths to calm down. She doesn't need me to fight this battle for her. Plus, Trey looks miserable enough without help. He hangs his head, watching his feet.

"I'll never be able to apologize enough to her," he says.

"Want to fill me in?" I drop onto the couch, and he joins me.

"We've been drinking together since she was fourteen, so I know Cal will remember everything up until around two this morning. That's about when we went to our friend Pete's grandparents' farm. Highlights after that include her falling out of a tree, smashing mailboxes, and crashing a four-wheeler into a barn. I stopped her from doing anything too wild."

"None of that's too wild?"

He shakes his head. "She sobered up a little this morning, and I made her eat. But then I turned my back for two seconds, and she dumped vodka into her orange juice and started all over again."

"Who the hell is this girl?" I mumble the thought to myself, but Trey volunteers an answer.

"Someone who's sick of everyone else dictating how she lives her life. She hasn't been this determined to forget in a long time, though. Graham might have finally broken her.

The same unease from yesterday settles in the pit of my stomach. I have no clue about Callie's life. Not with the long talk from the other night or what I saw yesterday.

"I'm guessing this is all new information," he says.

I nod.

"That's not surprising. Cal's wanted to get away since we were kids. This was supposed to be her chance." He pauses, looking down at his hands. "It fucking kills me that I had anything to do with ruining it for her."

I start to ask what specifically she's trying to escape, but Felicia comes out. "She's asleep."

Trey gets to his feet. "Good news is if she hasn't puked by now, she's not going to. The bad news, she's not down for the night. Expect a short rally in a few hours."

Felicia and I exchange glances. Drunk Callie sounds like quite an undertaking, especially if someone who apparently knows her much better than us has such trouble handling her.

Not giving me a chance for follow-up questions, Trey grabs her bags from his truck and hands over her phone and keys. Halfway out the door, he turns around. "Tell her…" His eyebrows draw in as he focuses on Callie's room. "I know she's still mad at me but tell her to call me. She needs someone to fill in the holes for her, and I'd rather it be me." He hesitates a second longer before leaving, his face so fucking sad.

"Are you staying?" Felicia asks, closing the door.

"I'm staying."

"I'll be on the couch then if you need me."

It's late when Callie's hand runs through my hair. She licks a line up my neck and then over my jawline. That's all it takes for me to pull her against me. Her leg hooks over my hip, and I cup her ass, grinding her down on my hardening cock.

She pushes me onto my back, climbing up and straddling me. My mouth finds hers, fingers tangling in her hair. I groan as her tongue teases mine. She playfully bites down, and holy fuck, it's hot. Her hand slides between us and grabs my dick through my jeans—*shit*.

She's drunk.

I roll her onto the mattress.

"Come back," she says as I get up.

Her breathy voice does nothing to ease my erection. I sit on Cam's bed, still in a daze from the unexpected wake-up call. Callie moves in the dark and crawls onto my lap. Her hands hold my face, and her lips are on mine again. I know we need to stop, but my recent stint of only fucking my fist works overtime against me. Her mouth travels to my neck as she pushes up the bottom of my shirt.

"Callie," I grind out, "you're drunk."

"I don't care." She kisses me again, rolling her hips.

The outer limits of my self-control somehow stretch further, and I draw back, bringing my hand to her neck. "We can't do this."

She stops. "You're kidding." She pushes off me and turns on the lamp by her bed. "You've been trying to fuck me for two weeks."

She's mad at me for *not* taking advantage of her? "Not when you're drunk."

Callie rolls her eyes and returns to her bed. "I suppose the plan to screw me and never talk to me again gives you the moral high ground."

I have no response. She can't possibly think the two situations compare. She needs to sleep it off.

"Callie—"

"Just go."

My head jerks back in disbelief. "You're kicking me out because I won't fuck you when you're drunk?"

She crosses her arms and sets her jaw. Either I comply or argue, and there's no point in arguing with her right now.

I stand up, intending to kiss her on the forehead. "All right—"

"Leave," she says.

I sigh on my way out. "Whatever."

Using the light from the TV, I find my coat and bag. Felicia wakes up and asks what happened, but I don't answer. Only one person knows, and she's probably passed out again. The parking lot feels eerie this time of night—even later than the last time. Once in the Jeep, I turn on the defrost and blow into my hands while waiting for the engine to warm.

Callie coming back was supposed to end all the bullshit, not start a whole new set of issues. Now I'm dealing with a version of her that reminds me of the chicks Dustin brings home. Someone I smile at from the stage and forget about the next day.

Every time I replay the last several hours, starting with her stumbling through the door, a blonde girl with vacant eyes replaces her in my mind.

Every. Single. Time.

I want Callie, not her—not this empty girl.

The limit for Callie avoiding me: two days.

My fist hammers on the door. Felicia finally answers, her perma-smile absent.

"It's Wednesday, Gibson. She's sent me three texts since she kicked me out on Monday morning. You said to give her some time. I did."

She shrugs. A fucking shrug? Everyone in the damn suite is apparently involved in a pact to drive me mad. Well, I'm done letting them.

"I want to see her," I tell her.

"Jordan, you can't come in."

"Felicia, I don't care." I duck my way past her.

"Jordan." She tugs on my arm, so I haul her scrawny ass across the common area with me.

The bedroom door swings open and bangs against the wall as I come through with an angry Felicia on my heels. Callie rips a blanket off her head, and she pulls out an earbud, her eyes widening as she watches the two of us from her bed.

"I told him he couldn't come in here, Callie."

"And I told her I didn't care, *Callie*."

"Stop acting like a child, Jordan," Felicia fires back.

"Oh, that's cute, coming from someone who cries during *Bambi*."

Her mouth falls open, and she shoves me in the chest. "Shut up!"

"I have a better idea." I pick her up and set her down over the threshold. She struggles, but the door closes with her on the other side. I flip the lock before returning my attention to Callie. "She's almost as frustrating as you are."

Callie removes the other earbud and repositions to sit against the wall. I'm about to give her hell and demand a long, overdue explanation. Two days have given me more than enough time to perfect a speech involving a multitude of rewrites. But one look at her leg completely derails me. A purple-and-black monstrosity covers a majority of the side of her upper thigh, disappearing under her fabric shorts.

"What the fuck?" I rush over and gently run my thumb over the bruise. My mind races, pissed off over who did this to her, but then I remember all the shit Trey said. "Is this from the tree or four-wheeler?" I ask.

"What?" She winces when she leans back on a large white bandage covering her shoulder blade.

Another one? How high is her pain tolerance?

"Trey said you fell out of a tree and wrecked a four-wheeler."

"I wrecked into a barn door?" she asks.

I shrug. "He just said a barn."

"Tree and barn would correlate to hip and shoulder then." She nods as if I solved some great mystery and places an ice pack on her hip.

I climb onto the mattress next to her. As I toss the blanket over her legs, I see a thin, two-inch-long burn on her forearm. The branded skin shines a dark red. Yeah, Trey and I differ vastly in our definitions of the word *wild*. I never want to know what he does think fits in the category.

"What happened here?" I touch her arm.

Callie shrugs with her uninjured shoulder, staring at her fingers in her lap. All my irritation toward her settles. I just want to know what happened and why and if she needs anything from me. I want to make it better for her.

"What's going on with you?" I reach for her hand, but she pulls away, drawing in a deep breath.

"I don't think we should see each other anymore."

What the actual fuck?

Her eyes dart to mine, once again impossible to read. "I meant what I said about not being able to handle anything else right now. I never wanted anything serious, Jordan."

Gravity increases as I push off the bed. Each body part threatens to drag me down, but I need to move. I need to process what just left her mouth because it's not making sense. Six steps carry me from one end of the room to the other as I pace.

"Let me get this straight," I say, talking it out to see if it makes more sense out loud. "On Friday, you were adamant I admit to wanting more, which I did. I *do*. Then you didn't answer your phone all weekend and drank so much that you blacked out. You kicked me out because I wouldn't fuck you when you were drunk. Which, okay, whatever. Sorry I'm not a creep like those other guys. Now, after avoiding me, you don't want to see each other anymore?"

She rushes off the bed, her brows slanted in. "Other guys?"

Shit. I didn't mean to say that. It's possibly the worst time to bring up the pictures.

My feet move me in the other direction. "Never mind."

"No, what *other* guys, Jordan?" She stands in my way when I turn around, not letting me complete my circuit.

I stop in front of her and rake a hand through my hair, the images playing on a loop. Screw it. I have nothing to lose. "Felicia and I found pictures your friend Shayna posted from high school."

Her eyes shut for a second, and she whispers, "Fuck." She looks at me again. "You saw those?"

There's not nearly enough shock in her voice for my liking. As if it were bound to happen.

"I more than saw them," I say in response to her understatement. "They're all seared into my mind. You half-naked and passed out with different dudes and their hands all over you."

Her gaze flits away. "She said she took them down."

"Well, she didn't. And after seeing what you were like back then, your striptease makes perfect sense." I cringe as soon as the asshole comment falls out of my mouth. "Shit, I'm so sorry, Callie. I didn't mean that."

She blinks a few times, hurt evident in her eyes.

Fuck, Waters. Way too far.

I step toward her, but she jerks her hands up to stop me. "You see pictures from a few years ago and have it all figured out?"

"I'm sorry," I say, desperate to rewind the past twenty seconds.

Her stare goes cold, all the walls back in place when she looks at me. "I'm just some slut, right? But … if I'm so fucking easy and you still haven't screwed me, what does that say about you?"

She punctuates with a head tilt, and I mirror it with mine, but the reason different.

"You know I don't think—"

Callie cuts me off. "I think it says you should go back to banging groupies and anyone else stupid enough to fall for your pathetic bullshit."

My jaw clenches at her retaliatory attack. Warranted or not, we aren't getting anywhere.

"Is that out of your system now?" I ask, my voice harsh.

Her eyes narrow. "I don't know. Are you finished disappointing everyone now?"

Knife. Gut. Twist. Whatever buttons she wanted to press, she hit them all at once. A fucking bullseye with ammo I supplied.

"How do you want me to respond to that, Callie?" I'm really asking because I have no idea. I never have when it comes to her, but now I'm even more in the dark.

She bites her lip for a second before her face returns to an expressionless void. "Walk away."

"You want me to walk away?"

Our gaze meets, and I wait for any sign of the person who smiled on her way out of my life on Friday. Some evidence of the girl who, up until now, was making my world a more sensible place. But it looks like she's not here anymore, and whoever is standing in front of me nods.

I place my hands on the back of my head, unable to stop everything between us from imploding. "If I walk away, I'm done," I tell her. "I'm not chasing you anymore."

"I never wanted you to." Her voice is quiet but resolute. "I told you from the beginning that I wasn't worth wasting your time."

An unfamiliar ache cuts through me when I say, "You were worth everything."

She averts her gaze and steps around me to open the door. Her mind was already made up when I arrived. Hell, she'd probably known long before this, and she only now has let me in on it.

The ache intensifies as I do what she asked, what I was always supposed to do. I walk away. Distracted by how wrong it feels, I nearly knock into Felicia on my way out. A drive home occurs, but the only thing that registers is the sensation of my chest compressing and ripping to pieces all at once. It expands a little more with each passing minute, further tormenting me.

Benji stops me in the living room. "You okay, man?"

"Callie ended things." Reality hits as I say the words out loud, and the unfamiliar pain earns a name. "I'm pretty sure the girl broke my fucking heart."

Rusty misses the downbeat for the third time. Maybe if he were concentrating on the song instead of whatever girl he's sexing up off-stage, we wouldn't sound like complete amateurs. I narrow my eyes at him, warning him to knock off his shit. He smirks, but his eyes stay on the drum kit for the remainder of the set.

Once we've packed up and loaded Gavin's van, I sit down at the bar where the bartender pours me a shot of whatever they're charging a buck for and a beer. Day eight post-Callie progresses the same as day one. Shitty. Any minor detail around me at any given moment sends thoughts of her racing through my brain. I go on with no explanation or insight of what happened to cause her drastic change of mind about us—about me. With little experience in actually caring about a girl, it leaves me wondering how long something like this lasts. Soon enough, the length of time without her will surpass the time with her. Hell, we never even dated, but it hurts all the same.

Rusty lands on the stool next to mine. "Two more," tells the bartender.

I take my shot. "Shouldn't you be in the restroom with a brunette?"

"Already was," he says, proud of his record-setting hook-up.

I'm about to ask if she even got a chance to come in that amount of time, but Gavin shows up and orders the next round as we finish the last. "Better make tonight count. Next week's midterms will cut into my drinking time."

Rusty and I both groan in response.

The night continues on around me. People come and go. Shots and beer appear in front of me, and I drink them. A well-placed chuckle here and a nod there appease my friends. They appreciate the facade after the week of hell I've doled out. Each of them has shown far more patience than my fuck-off attitude deserves. The least I can do in return is to not make everyone around me completely miserable for one night.

Another shot slides in front of me, and I toss it back.

"You good, man?" Benji asks.

Absolutely not, but I nod. "I'm good and drunk, a winning combination."

He slaps a hand on my shoulder. "When do you meet with your dad's friend?"

I shrug, not wanting to talk about it. Stan Hansen, senior partner at Hansen, Bullshit, and Bullshit—the man to impress for a solid recommendation for law school. Initially, I set up the meeting to keep the parental unit off my ass, but at this point, I have nothing better to do with my future than live someone else's dream.

A tap on my shoulder sends my stool spinning. Even after it stops, the room continues to move. Two blurry girls take their sweet time morphing into one short blonde wearing a pink sweater with a white collar. The outfit reminds me of something my mother would wear.

"You're Carol's son, right?" she says.

A laugh chokes out. She dresses like my mother because she *knows* my mother.

"Her least favorite one," I reply.

Straight white teeth between symmetrical lips with a flawless application of soft pink lipstick smile at me. "I'm Terrance Newhouse. We used to play together at the country club."

A hazy memory of hitting golf balls at a little girl with a much broader nose surfaces. "You still cry a lot?"

Her confidence falters. "What?"

"I remember you cried all the time."

"Only when mean little boys hurt my feelings."

I nod. "Fair warning: I'm still an asshole."

Her hand displays a perfect manicure as she flips long, straight hair over her shoulder. "I can handle it."

She keeps talking, but my attention travels to a woman near the entrance. Her brunette hair cascades down her back. It's not even the right color or length for Callie, but the way her top exposes a sliver of skin above her jeans ends up enough to engage me in a best-of-Callie torture session. *Yeah, I need to get a grip.*

I'm half-conscious of Terrance taking over Gavin's seat next to me and fully aware of her hand on my thigh. My feet push the stool around where two shots and a beer await me on the bar. I empty both shot glasses, and I drink my beer, already forgetting about the hand once again on my leg.

"Your mom said I should check out your band," she says. "You guys are awesome."

The corners of my mouth perk up. Mr. and Mrs. Raymond Waters proudly announce the awkward and unwelcome setup of their son Jordan Jensen Waters and Terrance Probably-Marie Newhouse. Sure, I'll play.

"What kind of music do you like?" I ask.

Her hand inches higher. "Oh, I like everything."

Game over. She fails. No one likes everything. No one.

"Well then, which do you like better—post-industrial grindcore or neoclassical dark wave?"

When I look over, she tips her head to the side and nervously giggles. "What?"

"Katy Perry or Taylor Swift?"

Either she doesn't notice my sarcastic smile or doesn't care. "Oh, Taylor, definitely."

The right answer, but I'm still uninterested in continuing a polite conversation. I turn back around and return my gaze to the hair that bears a minor resemblance to Callie's. But on the way, it sweeps over familiar red hair, and I refocus on Felicia.

Holy shit. My heart pounds, chest suddenly tightening. I bump Taylor Swift Fan Thirteen as I jump off the stool and lock on to my target. She stops near a pool table on the other side of the bar. Unsure of whether or not I want to spot Callie, I scan the area.

With my first step, a hand latches on to mine.

"Where are you going?" Terrance asks.

"I…" I realize Callie's not with her, and disappointment and relief battle for top spot. "I need to go talk to someone."

"I'll come with you."

Damn, is my mother paying her to keep me occupied? All jokes aside, I would not be the least bit surprised.

"I appreciate your concern, but I'll manage on my own."

She releases her hold and calls after me, "Find me later."

I haven't seen Felicia since I almost ran her over, trying to get out of their dorm suite. Our interaction leading up to that wasn't much better. She leans a hip on the pool table, holding a stick, eyes wary when she spots me. "You look drunk," she says over the music.

I flash her a grin and stop beside her. "I am."

She nods, unimpressed with my current state.

"Oh, don't be like that, Gibson. I'm much more tolerable this way."

"I somehow doubt that." A small smile develops as my buddy warms to me.

"Where's Callie?" I blurt out. Maybe she's with my filter.

Felicia fidgets. "I think she's studying."

Seeing no reason not to go for broke, I ask, "How is she?"

"Uh…" She drops her gaze. "She's fine."

I stare, willing her to continue. Desperate fails to describe me right now. I know nothing other than what Rusty and Benji have reported over the past week. Rusty saw her when he hung out with Jess at the dorms. Callie smiled at him as she went to her room, not saying anything. A more detailed account came from Benji after he ran into her at a party the same night. He said she was talking to a guy whose intentions were obvious from across the room. Being my best friend, he took it upon himself to drag her off to a secluded area away from anything testosterone-driven. A valiant effort, but she gave him the slip within a few minutes.

"Jordan, I shouldn't talk about her with you."

"Come on, Gibs."

She shakes her head, an apology on her face. "I'm sorry."

My once-trusty sidekick is now on edge around me, which bothers me more than I thought it would. On top of everything else in a life I vaguely recognize as my own, I add losing Felicia to the pile. I take a deep breath and rub my numb face. "Yeah, I'll see ya around."

A sad wave from her brings on an unenthusiastic wave from me.

Terrance hasn't moved from her spot at the bar. Her country club smile greets me. "You're back."

She displays an uncanny resemblance to a picture my father once showed me of my mother in college. That alone gives me enough reason to dodge her. So, I join Benji several stools away, not acknowledging her. Mother's mini-me storms off in response to my disinterest. An unhappy call from Carol will wake me in the morning.

Benji slides a beer toward me and holds out his hand. I set my phone in his palm without further prompting. He shoves it in his pocket, keeping his promise to stop me from texting Callie.

"The two most stubborn people I know, man," he says, shaking his head.

We were both stubborn, but apparently, only one of us is suffering. Callie goes to parties, talks to guys, and carries on as if nothing happened. Meanwhile, I torment anyone who attempts to engage me in human interaction and drink to avoid dealing with the hole she carved out and set on fire in my chest. *What if I actually run into her?* The thought alone threatens to send me spiraling. I need to get away from here—from her—and employ a hard restart.

In the morning, I'll book a plane ticket. Tijuana will host both of the Waters brothers for spring break. Somewhere at the bottom of a tequila bottle or buried beneath a stack of panties, I'll rediscover pre-Callie Jordan. And I really want to find him.

The week after my run-in with Felicia, my future sits in front of me. Both his suit and haircut, no doubt, possess an outrageous price tag. His rigid demeanor matches an uncomfortable pair of loafers. He also wears an all-important air of superiority required of anyone running in the same circle as my parents.

Stan and I discuss sailing—well, he discusses while I feign interest. Our parents insisted both their children learn, preparing us for moments such as these. I dutifully laugh at a corny joke he made about how much port wine is left on the port side or something equally irrelevant.

"Down to business then." Stan sips his brandy and crosses his legs. "When do you plan on completing the LSAT?"

"I'll be taking the test in June, sir."

"Excellent. That will give you plenty of time to study and retake in the fall."

"Oh, I doubt that will be necessary." I smirk, confident in my abilities. If Dustin managed a one-sixty-seven, then anything less on the first try I'll deem unacceptable.

Stan wags his finger. "The Waters' self-assurance. I have yet to see anyone in your family unable to back it up."

"That's because those who do are swiftly locked away, and all records of them are destroyed."

A deep chuckle shakes his entire body. "Your mother warned me about your spirited wit."

Her response to my "spirited wit" was anything but pleasant after I dismissed her attempt to find me a suitable match with Terrance. The look on her face when I dug out an old picture of Terrance Newhouse pre-nose and chin job as proof our children would not be as attractive as she'd claimed still makes me laugh.

"Now," he continues, "Carol's informed me you're only considering schools out of state—Georgetown, Michigan, Northwestern."

Yes, she wants me anywhere that distances me from my fake girlfriend, Jess. If I didn't think her attempts were so damn amusing, I would find them exhausting.

"With my GPA, summer internships, and outstanding recommendations from prestigious men such as yourself, I would hate to limit myself," I say, getting more comfortable in the leather chair. "You attended the University of Pennsylvania if I'm not mistaken."

"They offer a fantastic program," he says, his eyes lighting up. "My wife and I are still very involved alumni."

"Not a school to be discounted from the considerations then."

He tips his glass toward me. "Indeed."

By the time I walk out of the cigar club, I've secured myself work for the summer at his law firm and guaranteed myself an excellent recommendation, regardless of where I choose. I tug to loosen my tie as I start my Jeep. Three missed calls from Carol are already waiting for me. Her voice comes over the speakers as I pull out of the parking lot.

"How did everything go with Stanley?"

"He was quite offended by my antiestablishment tendencies, which led me to spit on his Italian loafers."

She sighs. "Jordan..."

I merge onto the highway to head home. "He will be singing my praises from the rooftops, Mother. I let him know of my interest in local schools since it seems to have slipped your mind."

She stays silent on the other end, carefully choosing her words to keep me from further rebellion. "As long as you keep your mind open to future possibilities."

"Of course I will." I pause long enough for her guard to lower before I add, "I can't forget the possibility of knocking up Jess and marrying her to make sure she understands I will always choose her over my career."

"Ha-ha, very funny," she says. I don't answer, letting her jump to conclusions. "Jordan?" The panic in her voice is undeniable.

"We'll talk later. Bye, Mother—I mean, Grandma."

I end the call and smile at the thought of her face pinching. She really makes it too easy.

Once I return to the house, I spread out my notes in the living room to study for my final midterm. Dr. Miller scheduled our exam on a Friday morning, winning himself zero admirers, but I don't mind. Two hours of diving into the philosophical beliefs of existentialism sounds like a welcome escape.

Benji knocks the notebook out of my hands and plants himself on the coffee table in front of me. We aren't talking at the moment. Technically, I'm not speaking to him, which pisses him off, so he stopped talking to me. It's all very mature, and all over a comment he made a few days ago while we were working on a new song.

"You still mad?" he asks.

I pick up my notebook, ignoring him.

He gives an exasperated groan and unfolds a paper from his wallet. "*Certain of the unsure in a meaningless void. Frantic beauty hides beyond her serene blue eyes. She left as mine and never returned. A scab not yet a scar in a messy, wounded life.*"

"You just carry those around with you now?" I bite, annoyed he grabbed my lyrics out of the trash.

"Come on, man. I'm sorry, but you need to let this go. You wrote shitty lyrics about a broken heart, and I called you out on it. I would expect for you to do the same thing for me."

He's right because he's Benji, and the guy has the most irritating habit of always being right about everything. Also, it takes more energy to stay mad at him than I care to commit to any longer, so I fold.

"Whatever. If I tell you we're good, will you throw them away?"

"Tell me you love me."

"I love you," I say dryly.

"Tell me like you mean it."

I plaster on a grin and talk through clenched teeth. "I love you, Benjamin."

He taps my cheek, triumphant. "I love you too, Jordy."

"Great. So, you'll throw them away?"

"Nope." He refolds the paper and stashes it back in his wallet. "I'm hanging on to them in case you piss me off again."

My glare goes unnoticed as he disappears up the stairs, but I let it go. We both know he won't bring them up again and remind me of Callie. Complete misery mode might have ended, but as the lyrics prove, I'm not as over her, as I'd like. I never realized how empty my life felt until I discovered something that made it better. Then I lost it, and now that I know what I'm missing out on, everything left seems less significant. Along with this bright new view, I've made a glorious return to floating mindlessly through life with the added bonus of not caring what happens. Not even a loss of freedom and locking into a career I have no interest in bothers me anymore.

My new outlook makes me a goddamn delight.

A few pages of notes in, Rusty cruises through the living room, wearing jeans without holes. I do a double take. "Oh God, end times are upon us."

He flips me off. "I'm hitting a party at State tonight. You want to come?"

I gesture to the study materials covering the table and couch cushions on either side of me. "Plus, I need to pack tonight. My flight leaves tomorrow afternoon."

"I assume Dustin's arranged for everyone to get a shot of penicillin on the flight home?"

I chuckle, having asked the same question. "I figure it'll be a good way to get out of whatever *mood* I've been in lately. A full reset, courtesy of an endless supply of booze and girls in bikinis, ready to make poor life choices."

He shakes his head either in disapproval of my methods or doubtful of their chances for success. "Are you going anywhere tonight?"

"No plans," I say. "Why?"

He shoves his hands in his pockets and looks at me through his lashes like he's trying to fucking seduce me. "It's a pity to leave your Jeep in the driveway all night."

Oh. He is trying to seduce me. He owns a motorcycle and frequently borrows my vehicle when it's cold. His ski trip with Gavin will end a few days before I get back, and he's already asked if he can drive it then.

I toss him my keys. "Don't let Benji drive."

"Aye, aye, *capitán*."

Speaking of, Benji comes down the stairs, and Rusty follows him to the kitchen. I go back to my notes, skimming over the existentialist concept of bad faith. At least I am until parts of their conversation travel in, hijacking my concentration.

"…Jess and Felicia are going … leaving soon."

"Does Calico know we … possibly … with him in there?"

I tap a finger, trying to block them out but fail—hard. Callie plans on going to another party. Another party at another college and another night of driving myself insane, thinking about her with another guy.

An hour away from the dorms, she won't be able to rush out to avoid me. I can find her, make her talk to me, maybe figure all of this out. I stand up to tell them I want to go. Then I sit straight back down. Enough people in Callie's life force her to do things from the sound of it. Regardless of how much I want closure, I want my name to stay off that list more.

She's made it clear what she wants, and the time has arrived for me to let her go. I'll stick to the plan. Study tonight, leave tomorrow, and return with a new perspective to a life that doesn't include Callie Henders.

Either my arguments have grown stronger since I ran after her the night of the frat party, or I'm finally ready to accept her not being a part of my life anymore. Whatever the reason, the once-overpowering urge to chase her never emerges. Not even when Benji and Rusty walk out the door to go see her without me.

———

The next morning, Dr. Miller reads a journal article at his desk. I turn in my blue book, and he peers up over the top of his bifocals. "I'm confident you've given me a fascinating read."

"Nonsensical ramblings of a madman, I'm sure," I tell him.

"There's a fine line between the madman and genius, Mr. Waters."

"And I have terrible balance, sir."

He chuckles as I stroll out of the lecture hall.

The closer I get to my flight, the more ready I am for spring break and to wipe the last few weeks from my mind permanently.

A spectacular ass even earns my attention as it passes me in the parking lot. I spin and walk backward to enjoy the view a little longer. The brunette looks over her shoulder. I respond with my, as of late, greatly underutilized *get some* smirk. She blushes and bites her bottom lip.

I drive back to the house and gather anything I don't want in my Jeep over the next week. *Only use in emergencies* to Rusty translates to anytime he damn well pleases. I'll consider myself lucky if she's in one piece when I return. He's in the kitchen, and I toss him the keys on my way through. Already itching to go somewhere, he heads straight out the door. Predictable.

Upstairs, I finish the last bit of packing and zip up my carry-on, securing the luggage tag to the handle. The suitcase bangs on the stairs as I drag it down behind me. I set it by the entryway before heading back up to kill time until the cab arrives. My foot hits the top step as someone knocks.

Rusty left. Benji's on the way to Vermont with his cousin. Gavin is…

"Gavin?"

"What?" his voice answers from down the hall.

"Do you have anyone coming over?"

"Nope." He pops the *p*, which I've never heard him do before.

I turn on my heels and descend the stairs again. When I swing the door open, my world screeches to a halt. Callie's on the porch, holding a box and as gorgeous as ever. Dark hair frames her face, contrasting her brilliant blue eyes. The sight hurls me back to the coffee shop. All my progress vanishes in a span of two seconds, and once again, I'm at a loss for how I'll ever get her out of my head.

"Hey," she says.

A verbal response isn't in the cards. Fuck, breathing is almost unmanageable at the moment. So, my chin rises enough to count as a subtle nod.

Her lips twitch. "I didn't think you'd be here. Your Jeep's gone, and Benji said you had a midterm."

She might as well have karate-chopped me in the throat. She's not here for me. Nothing has changed. I give myself a deep breath to regain my equilibrium the best I can. A run-in with her had to happen at some point. I just wish it had held off for another three to seven years.

"Sorry to disappoint—*again*." My words come out much rougher than intended, courtesy of the giant lump in my throat.

She huffs and rolls her eyes. "Nothing can ever be easy with you." She shoves the box at me and bounces down the steps to her car.

I want to yell after her that she's the one who makes everything difficult and I miss her and I don't want her stupid box and I want her and to never come back and to never leave. Instead, I just stand here, watching her drive away.

After my brain regains control of my body, I kick the front door shut behind me and set the box on the coffee table. A thorough examination from all sides follows while I search for any hint to what my unexpected gift holds. Whatever's inside will surely reopen wounds still struggling to heal.

I pace, attempting to identify the best way of dealing with the box. In less than an hour, a car will show up to take me to the airport to officially remove the irritating woman from my life once and for all. Yet, in true Callie form, she showed up just in time to crawl under my skin again.

Careful, Waters. The situation requires me to tread lightly—*get out*—unlike all the other times I decided to walk away, and she reeled me back in with a comment or her tits. I need to react differently this time. Prove my growth by making better choices.

A creak on the stairs sends me spinning.

Gavin tromps down, his eyes on his phone. "Are you pacing down here?"

"I'm thinking," I snap.

"What's in the box?" He collapses on the couch and watches, amused. "Gwyneth Paltrow's head?"

Ignoring him and his movie reference, I tug at my bottom lip before picking it up. It's almost weightless, and I shake it around. Nothing shifts inside, so I put it down and resume my back-and-forth. What would she drop off for me? *Is it for me?* Technically, she never said.

Gavin enters my line of vision, aiming his phone at me.

"Are you recording my misery?" I ask.

"You're acting insane. This is documentation in case we need to have you committed."

Damn it, he's right. A stupid box, more than likely containing an inconsequential item I forgot in Callie's room, holds power over my sanity.

I sit and flip the flaps open. Green packing peanuts spill over the top as I dig but come up empty-handed. Everything dumps out when I tip it over. I sort through the packing materials. Once, twice, three times.

"Nothing?" I'm on my feet. "She got in my head over *nothing?*"

All the buried anger and frustration from the last few weeks claws its way to the surface. I storm through the living room and grab my coat. Callie's finally succeeded in making me lose my shit, and she deserves to fucking know.

The back door slams, and I stomp down the steps toward—an empty space.

Rusty took my Jeep.

My head drops back as I unleash a colorful combination of words. Some I direct at Rusty for not owning a real fucking vehicle for northeastern winters. A few I aim at myself for once again putting myself in a position of chasing after the girl. But most of my choice vocabulary goes out to Callie Henders, the most infuriating human being on the planet, and her ability to reduce me to a neurotic mess with minimal effort.

I rub the back of my hair, taking a second to collect myself. But it's a complete waste of time, because as soon as I turn around, my composure scatters all fucking over the place. At the bottom of the stairs is Callie, coffee in hand.

"Good afternoon, beautiful," she says.

Every feeling for her slams into my chest at once, leaving ones I didn't even know existed in a free-for-all inside me. My gaze locks on her chest. Not on her tits, but on the picture of me in a towel, hat, and scarf that decorates the front of her white T-shirt. She twists around and swipes her hair to the side, showing me the back where *Mission Tell Jordan Sorry* is sprawled along the width of her shoulders. This time, she not only stole my move and line, but she also ripped off my shirt idea.

Over the past few weeks, I've played out dozens of scenarios of our next encounter. A majority of them involved wildly improbable situations. In one, we met at a dog park even though neither of us owns a dog. For another, a hostage situation broke out at a sea park we both went to on the same day. None came close to her standing outside my house while holding a cup of coffee, wearing my face, and calling me beautiful.

But it's so much fucking better.

Even if I wanted to hold on to the irritation that had driven me out here after her, it seems pointless, because despite the serious explanation she owes for putting me through hell, she amazes me. She amazes me and she's here and, for now, that's enough.

She's guarded, trying to gauge my reaction as I walk toward the house.

"For future reference," I say, stopping in front of her, "everything at once is overkill."

She visibly relaxes and sips my coffee. "You know, I was a little worried about that."

"Pro tip—spread it out over a couple of hours."

She flips up her wrist, checking the time on a nonexistent watch. "Sorry, but I'm working under rather restrictive time constraints since someone plans on fleeing the country."

I step closer, so she has to tip her chin up, and I grasp the sides of her neck, not chancing her going anywhere this time.

"Let's fast-forward then, shall we?"

I drop my mouth onto hers. It's what I've been desperate for, the feel of her lips. Soft and warm and kissing me back until she starts using them to apologize. Well, she tries to, but I won't stop long enough to let her.

"So sorry … deserved better … didn't mean anything … explain everything."

I pull back, my eyes bouncing between hers. "Your apology is distracting me from forgiving you."

She smiles, and the world snaps back into focus, making sense again. All Callie in her eyes, no sign of the empty girl. God, I've missed her. Unless I distract myself, I'll rip her clothes off and make up for lost time on the lawn. She's not wearing a coat, so I kiss her again before removing the cup from her hand and leading her to the house.

"So, the box?"

"A decoy," she says. Her hand fits perfectly in mine. "The idea was for you to chase after me. Full circle and all."

I hold the door for her, shaking my head. My irrational response to the situation ended up predictable. "What if it didn't work?"

"Gavin was going to get you all riled up over it until you did." She turns, walking past me. "Your friends are not loyal to you in the least, by the way."

I finish my apology coffee and throw it away in the kitchen. On our way into the living room, Gavin grins and tosses one final packing peanut back in the box. In the short amount of time since I went outside, he's changed clothes, now also wearing a *Mission Tell Jordan Sorry* T-shirt.

I glare at Callie. "Oh, come on."

"What? They were cheaper to order by the dozen." She winks.

Gavin heads up the stairs. "Face it, Waters. You've met your match."

A more accurate statement has never been made.

Callie wanders farther away from me, checking her phone. I'm ready to carry her upstairs to my closet of a bedroom, but the alarm on *my* phone goes off.

Shit, my flight.

I return to the kitchen and cancel the car. Mexico's original purpose of distracting me from missing Callie no longer applies. Plus, staying allows me to bail Dustin's ass out if he gets in trouble. I send him a heads-up.

> *I'm not coming. Hate me all you want, just wear a condom while doing it.*

Callie's still on her phone when I come back. I snake my arms around her from behind and kiss her neck, immersing myself in the scent of coconut and Callie that's been noticeably absent from my life. Instantly soothing.

"Does this mean you aren't going to Tijuana to bang chicks?"

I tug the neck of her shirt over and brush my lips over the exposed skin on her shoulder. "Not unless you want to come bang chicks with me."

She reaches up and tugs at the back of my hair, and fuck, I've missed that too.

"I have another idea," she says.

Hopefully, her suggestion involves her naked and the two of us not leaving the soon to be an empty house for the next several days. Except maybe to eat at some point.

"Go on."

"How do you feel about road trips?" She spins around and rests her hands on my biceps. "I have to go home for the weekend and want you to come with me." The apprehension must read on my face because her gaze lowers. "Sorry. I shouldn't have—"

"I'll go." The words fly out of my mouth, and her eyes dart to mine, a surprised look in them.

Most people would question the decision to travel across the state with the woman who broke my heart and bailed without an explanation. But after finally getting her back, there's no way in hell I'm ready to let her go again.

Plus ... I'm already packed.

***

I scan over the bags hanging in front of me at the gas station. *Teriyaki or hot? Teriyaki or hot?* I grab both types of beef jerky and return to the counter, tossing them on top of the obscene amount of candy already there. I forgot sour gummy worms, so I return to the candy aisle and get them, adding them to my collection. Oh. We need those peach things.

Callie catches my arm when I turn. "Three hours, Jordan. The trip is three hours, not three days."

"Fine." I take out my wallet. "But if we have to stop again, it's on you."

On our way to Callie's car, I dig through the bag to find the licorice. She pulls out on the highway as I chew on a piece and hook up my phone to the Bluetooth.

"Help me pick appropriate background music."

She raises her eyebrows and glances over. "We need a soundtrack for this?"

"Well, I don't want the music contradicting the tone. I mean, we can't have you talking about a traumatic life event with Bieber playing. What about a happy story with Nine Inch Nails? That would be pure lunacy, Callie."

She rolls her eyes, probably regretting the invite to her mother's house.

Without any help from her, I start a playlist full of pop punk bands everyone forgot about years ago. The first song makes her smile, so I must have chosen well. I pass her some licorice before turning the volume down to barely audible. The enigma of Callie Henders is about to unravel in front of me. I don't want any distractions.

She bites off a piece. "Are you ready now?"

More than ready, I sink back into the seat and nod.

"So, I've never had a stable or healthy relationship with my parents," she says. "Graham and Lara were sixteen when they had me and got married. It only took me until five to realize they hated each other, and by seven, Graham made it clear I was to blame for everything wrong in his life. That's also when they started daily screaming matches and throwing things. It escalated until I was sixteen, and she finally filed for divorce after he threatened to lock her in the house and set it on fire."

Damn. I shift in my seat and ask the first question that pops into my head, "How do you know he blames you?"

Her lips press together as she hesitates and then, "His exact words were, 'I should have just left you in a dumpster to die so I wouldn't have ended up stuck with this cheap whore.'"

"Fuck, Callie. What did your mom say?"

She snorts. "Lara slapped him for calling her cheap."

"You were seven?" I hardly get the words out, an ache clenching in my chest. At that age, I worried about my parents buying me the right scooter, not whether they regretted my existence.

"Pretty great parenting, huh?" She glances over when I don't answer. "Trust me. They've only gotten better with time. Lara's borderline neglectful now, and Graham … we'll get back to him."

She sounds so detached from what she's saying, the facts of her life tiresome. I've been an idiot, thinking one happy photo in her dorm room told me shit about her family. If anything, unstable and unhealthy are understatements.

"I'm sorry." I reach over and push her hair back.

"Before they split, when they had Cate, I couldn't wrap my head around how they could bring another kid into so much toxicity. By that point, I had so much anger and resentment toward them. I was miserable and shut everyone out other than Connor, Trey, and Pete."

"Your first boyfriend Pete?"

She nods. "His grandparents sent him to camp the summer I turned fourteen. That's when Trey and I met Brock—the second worst thing ever to happen to me."

"What was the first?" I ask.

"Graham," she says, a hint of sadness breaking through. "Brock was my solution to all of it. He was every red flag imaginable. He taught me to drink and get high to forget the rage eating me alive on the inside. For two years, we were so fucking toxic to each other and everyone around us. We were my parents."

My gaze trails out the window while I piece together what she's saying with what I already know, fitting the timeline together. "The pictures of you as a blonde we saw were from when you dated Brock?"

"Most of them, probably. Trey did what he could to keep me relatively safe. All my friends from back then got dragged along for my spiral of self-destruction. Even Pete after I dumped him. I wish they wouldn't have, but…" Her eyebrows pull together, the disconnect she showed lessening.

"Two years," I say, tapping the licorice on my leg. "You broke up when you were sixteen, so when your parents divorced."

"Yeah. Lara took out a restraining order and moved us to the next town over. The towns' high schools were combined, and without a reason to go to Sutterville anymore, Brock and I stopped seeing each other. It seemed to solve a lot of problems at first. But then my parents realized they could use the divorce to control one another. It made a bad situation so much worse. Shayna's pictures tell you more about the next several months than I can even remember."

I reach over, locking my fingers with hers on her thigh. "I was such a fucking dick for bringing up the pictures the way I did, Callie. It was out of line."

"I blindsided you, and you reacted," she says. "I'm the one who used what you'd said about your parents against you. Out of everyone, I should know better, and I'm so, so sorry."

"Forgiven," I tell her without hesitation. "So, so forgiven."

She glances over and gives me a soft smile. It fades when she looks back at the road, and I drag my thumb over hers.

"Connor's actually the one who saved me from myself. He gave me a calendar counting down to my eighteenth birthday when I wouldn't have to follow the custody agreement anymore. It's silly but crossing out the numbers changed everything. Each day closer to freedom, the less power they held over me. I stopped partying and avoided anyone who might start it back up again, including my friends. I spent the summer working my ass off on Pete's grandparents' farm to save money. The plan was to leave for school and never go back. All the bad memories would be hours away, and Graham would just be someone I survived."

"But now, you have a countdown calendar to nineteen and drive back on the weekends."

"Enter Graham's desperate need for control." She blows out a deep breath, the indifference fading even more. "Thanks to an amendment in their divorce agreement, he pays child support until we're nineteen. In his mind, he owns us until then, but I turned eighteen and refused to see him. That's when the stream of texts and calls started. When those didn't work, he withheld my mail, used Cate and Connor to get to me, canceled my insurance, reported my car as stolen."

"The piece of shit said you stole it?"

"Twice," she says. "He tried whatever he could think of until he found what worked."

"What's that?" I ask.

"He stopped making support payments. Not just for me, but for Cate and Connor, too. Lara blamed me the first month her money didn't show up. Since I caused the problem, she expected me to fix it."

My head falls onto the headrest, jaw tightening. "So, you agreed to visit him."

"Every other weekend until I'm nineteen. If I don't, he resorts to his alternatives." She turns off onto another highway, one without a car in sight.

For the first time, I see the entire picture. It gives Trey's words about other people dictating how she lives her life a whole new meaning. No wonder she wanted to escape.

"You were supposed to be there the night of my birthday."

"Yeah," she says. "I told Graham I'd be home Saturday morning, and he showed up at the dorms to inform me otherwise. It pissed me off, and everything started to domino. Uncle Kev showed up and made me leave my car. Then Graham took away my phone when I got there. I felt isolated and trapped, and I couldn't take it anymore."

Callie pulls over on the shoulder, her hand pulling from mine to shift into park. She turns toward me but stares at the console between us. I tuck her hand right back into mine and shut off the music. Whatever song's playing, she might forever associate with whatever she's thinking and feeling right now, and I can't stand the thought of anything bringing her back because she looks so damn hurt.

"When I woke up that Monday, I only remembered out-of-order pieces from the weekend. Without context, everything was pretty damning, so when Brock texted and lied about something happening between us, I believed him. For the first time in a long time, I felt like Callista, the girl with a less-than-stellar reputation who lets the worst part of her life ruin the rest of it. I didn't want you dealing with the fallout."

I run her knuckles over my lips. "You should have just told me."

"I know, and I'm sorry." She finally looks at me. Her eyes offer just as much of an apology. "I wasn't ready for you to know what a mess my life is. I'm still not entirely sure I am, but I'm sick of missing out on things because of it. And it really is a disaster, Jordan," she says fast. "Seriously, you should run right now."

Without looking, she hits the button on the door behind her, flipping the locks to unlocked.

I curl my fingers around the back of her neck, then I pull her closer and lean in until my forehead presses into hers. "I'm not going anywhere, Callie. I don't care how messy your life is. Messy, complicated, unpredictable—I want it all if it means I can have you." Doubt lingers in her eyes, so I kiss her. "I can handle it," I say, my lips brushing hers. "I'm *certain*."

There aren't many things in my life I'm sure of, but I am about this. Her mouth turns up, the doubt disappearing, and I kiss her until it vanishes altogether. Then I kiss her one more time because we still have a long drive ahead of us, and I won't get another chance for a while.

When I drag myself away, I relax back in my seat. She reaches for the gearshift but pauses and twists back to me. "One more thing … Rusty almost got into a fight with Lara's boyfriend last night."

My eyebrows lower. "He was at a State party?"

"Tyler's only twenty-two," she says. "I try not to talk to him, so I didn't even think about him going there until I saw him."

At first, picturing someone my mother's age dating someone my age throws me, but then I remember Lara's only around thirty-four.

"So, why exactly was Rusty going to fight him?"

She chews on her lip, her gaze lowering, her voice quiet when she says, "He got a little aggressive with me in a hallway."

My entire body tenses, a weight hitting the pit of my stomach. "He fucking what?"

The question comes out harsh, and her eyes dart to mine.

"Don't worry about it. He was just drunker and more persistent than usual."

"Than usual?" My voice hits a new octave, rage building. "Shit like this has happened before?"

"Nothing serious," she says dismissively. "Until last night, he's always backed off after a few comments or grabbing my ass. For whatever reason, he pushed it further, but Rusty rode in on his white horse and pulled him off."

"Fuck, Callie." It's all I can say to her.

A man put his hands on her without her consent, and she's sitting next to me, unfazed. But why would she be? Apparently, the people in her life act in abhorrent ways without any fear of repercussion.

I let my head roll, so I can look out the window, my mind in an actual fucking spin. Thoughts run wild with what would have happened to her if not for Rusty. If he had to *pull the guy off* of her, then him showing up even a minute later could have drastically altered everything.

"It's okay, Jordan," she says. Then she touches my arm as if *she* needs to fucking console *me*.

I can't take it anymore. I throw off my seat belt and fling open the door. When I get around the car, I drag her out and into my arms.

"Fuck, I'm sorry, baby," I tell her.

She locks her arms around my waist, face buried in my shirt through my open coat. I press my lips into her hair, wanting to shelter her from all these selfish forces in her life. They hurt her or try to hurt her, and she accepts it as a part of her world, her reality.

We stand on the side of an abandoned highway, grass blowing in the ditch beside us, until she pulls back. She stares up with those wide blue eyes. "Can we maybe listen to Bieber now?"

I nod. "Absolutely."

If I have any say about it, nothing but a happy soundtrack will play for her from now on.

Waymore's population of 1,358 residents redefines my definition of a small town. A flashing red light on top of a stop sign is the closest thing they have to a stoplight. Each person we drive by waves and smiles like they're greeting an old pal. I find the whole thing either charming or unnerving; the jury continues their deliberations.

We stop in front of a yellow ranch-style home surrounded by trees and an old wooden fence. Callie shuts off the engine and watches me take in our surroundings. "Do you feel like I've brought you to the middle of nowhere to kill you?"

"The idea has crossed my mind," I mumble, not joking in the least.

"Just stay out of the woodshed out back." She winks, climbing out of the car.

And this is how I'll die.

I follow her up the sidewalk with our bags. For the first time in years, I prepare to meet a girl's family. She assures me her mother won't be here for the weekend, which is probably in everyone's best interest. Even though Lara fails to compare to Graham, neither of them deserves anything other than an ass-beating for their treatment of Callie and her siblings. My parents will receive a lovely edible bouquet, solely for not being her parents.

She leads me through a living room decorated in blue and white. An enormous flat screen is the focal point across from a wraparound sectional much too large for the space. The only artwork on the walls is a giant Eagles banner.

"Tyler likes to watch *the game* when he's here," she says on our way through.

Another person on the list of people in her life who deserves everything Karma offers. God, if only Rusty had unleashed on him. I've seen him fight, and if he knew the dude put his hands on Callie more than once, the guys and I would have bailed him out of jail. Happily.

We go down a short hall to a bedroom that no doubt belongs to Callie. I drop our bags on the floor when a wall covered in pictures draws me in like a moth to a flame. I point to one where she could pass for her little sister.

"How old are you in this one?"

She examines the picture and takes my coat. "Seven? That's Trey on the left, and Connor's on the right."

Only happy moments exist in her collage. Her hair's dark and her eyes alive. Callie fishes, goes to carnivals, visits the zoo, and lives the life she deserves in each image. A few of her and Trey with a familiar backdrop stand out.

"Is that the science building on campus?"

"Last October, Trey drove me to Easton for a tour." Callie hangs our coats behind the door and comes back over. "We snuck off on our own and ran into a group of girls. He made up a ridiculous story about being an oil heir named Bradford. They pointed out his name tag said Trey, so he hunted down a marker. After he changed his name, he asked who I wanted to be while we were there."

She removes the pin holding one picture up and flips it over. Stuck on the back is one of those *Hello, My Name Is* stickers. Callista's been scribbled out with red marker, Callie written in underneath.

"You were Callie," I say.

"I have been ever since."

I turn it over and point at a spot to the left of her and Trey. "Right there, Callie met Jordan."

She smiles, returning the photo to its rightful place.

I stay facing the wall, but my eyes roam all over her, standing next to me. She's still in her white T-shirt with my face on it. Rather tired of looking at myself, I tug at the hem. "The shirt has to go, beautiful."

She shrugs and lifts her arms. Compliant Callie emerges for the first time, and man, do I throw her shirt on the floor fast. Her mouth's on mine when I grasp her hips, grazing the smooth skin above her jeans. She pushes up my shirt then, so I reach back, tugging it off. Her eyes scan down, stopping on my abs. She licks her lips, and I pull her to me.

"You guys have met, right?"

I flatten her palm low on my torso, but it doesn't stay there long. Fingers glide over my skin, and I kiss her before moving down her neck and over her collarbone.

But when I push her hair over her shoulder, my attention's held hostage by a deep purple bruise below it. Then I see the indentations, slightly curved and set in an arch.

Teeth.

"Jordan."

I look up, my jaw so tight it might snap, and Callie touches the side of my face, careful like maybe she shouldn't.

"It's fine," she says, dismissively.

My eyebrows draw in, and I can't tell if I'm more pissed she's saying it's fine or that her life experiences have taught her it is.

"The bastard bit you?" I grind out, the answer right in front of me. My fingertips graze over the swollen mark as Callie blinks up at me.

"I…" she starts and never finishes, shaking her head slightly.

The emotions swirling behind those baby blues plead with me to not force her to relive what happened with her mother's boyfriend. So I won't. Not now anyway.

Swallowing the anger, I push my hand into her hair, pulling her mouth to mine. She breathes out in relief and kisses me harder. It all disappears for a little while. Like neither of us is willing to let it between us.

Callie pushes me back until the bed stops me, and when I drop down, she crawls onto my lap. I lie back, bringing her with me. Her hair falls around us, and she stares down at me, fucking gorgeous. My hands run up her thighs and then up her back, one coming around to cup her jaw. She feels phenomenal, the scent of her shampoo surrounding me, and I want to tick through the rest of my senses.

"Pretend I said something funny," I tell her.

She drags her hands through my hair and can continue doing it for the rest of my damn life. "What?"

"The blood supply to my brain is lacking, but I want to hear you laugh right now. So pretend I made a hilariously witty comment about pheasants or acorns or anything as long as you find it funny."

"Acorns?" Her entire face lights up as she laughs, confirming my new favorite tree nut.

"Fucking acorns, beautiful."

I pull her face to mine before she takes over. Her lips, her tongue, her hands, her breath on my jaw, my neck, my ear, my chest. She grinds against my erection, and I grab two handfuls of her ass, pressing her down harder. The whimper she makes as her clit drags over my dick drives me insane.

"You finally going to let me play with this pussy, Callie?" I flex my hips, and she nods, holding my face and kissing me.

But then her movements slow.

No.

She stops altogether.

No. No.

She straightens up, touching her lips where mine belong.

"No. No. No."

"Terrible timing," she says, an apology in her eyes.

And because everyone has conspired for me never to have sex again, she swings her leg over and climbs off me and the bed. My shirt lands on my face a second later.

"Think about baseball or a car accident or—"

"Nana Waters," I supply, sitting up.

She bends over, unzipping her bag, and I squeeze my aching cock through my jeans. "Think about Nana Waters then. The monster descends upon us."

Once she no longer distracts me with her ass in the air and pulls a top on, I yank on my shirt. But Nana Waters does nothing to lessen the Callie Henders effect.

A thumping starts quiet but quickly grows louder. Callie opens her bedroom door just in time for a squealing blur of dark hair to hurtle toward me. A Callie clone scrambles onto my lap, succeeding where Nana failed. Miniature hands smash my face between them. She knees me, readjusting in order to kiss my forehead, and then Cate sits on her heels, staring me down. "Hi," she says.

"Hi," I say back.

She giggles and leans back, gripping my shirt for support. "Can we keep him, Cal?"

Callie's in the doorway, pressing her lips together in an attempt not to laugh. The boy towering next to her employs the same technique. He rests against the doorframe with his arms crossed and shakes the hair out of his eyes. "Come on, Monster. You left your coat on the floor."

Cate clambers down and dances her way out of the room.

As he kicks off the doorframe, Connor nods in my direction. "Nice to finally meet you, Lover Boy."

Callie bats at him, but he swats her hand away.

"Pizza for supper?" she asks.

"Whatever," he says over his shoulder.

She rolls her eyes and brings our bags to the bed. Her first mistake is being irresistible. Her second is coming within arm's reach. I snag ahold of her, and in one quick movement, I have her pinned beneath me.

"Lover Boy, huh?" I dip my head down to kiss her when she smiles. "Small children go to bed at, like, seven, right?"

Her fingers tease their way up my jawline. "She needs fed, bathed, and read to. After that, I'm all yours."

"That's the sexiest thing I've ever heard, if I disregard everything but the last three words." Before I lose all willpower, I jump up and drag her off the bed. "Let's go play house."

"Jordan?"

"Yes," I answer.

"Are you sitting by the door?" Cate asks.

"Yes."

"Do you still have on your tiara?"

"Yes."

"I don't believe him, Cal. Check."

The bathroom door cracks open next to me. Callie pokes her head out and looks down. She eyes the pink, sparkly princess crown in my hands instead of on my head. We smile at each other before she returns to Cate. "He's right where you left him," she says. "Tiara and all."

My head drops against the wall behind me. A few hours with Cate have exhausted me. Other than when I was a child, I've never spent much time around kids, but I don't remember them being nearly as demanding as the little girl in the bathtub. I let my eyes fall shut and await further orders.

I almost stab myself in the eye, returning the tiara to my head, when the door flies open. Out she comes with her hands on her hips, wearing a nightgown covered in pictures of princesses. "Oh," Cate says, the disappointment obvious. "You are wearing it."

On her way out of the bathroom, Callie scoops up Cate. "Bedtime, my monster queen."

"Jordan has to read to me." She reaches down for me.

Callie spins around, her back to me. "Jordan doesn't know how to read."

"He doesn't?"

"No, and he's very sad about it. But I bet if you read to him, it would make him feel better." Callie carries her down the hall to her room.

My illiterate ass gets off the floor, and I follow because— might as well admit it—I'm nothing more than a puppy dog when it comes to either of them.

After three different renditions of the same book, Cate's eyes close. In stealth mode, I move about a centimeter at a time and dislodge from the grasp of her tiny hands, holding my breath until I escape to the hallway.

When I get to the living room Callie and Connor are on the couch, watching something bloody and gory on the unreasonably large TV. She lets me under her blanket and cuddles into me.

A cliché scene comes on where a woman walks downstairs to a basement instead of getting the hell out of the house. The ghost or demon or guy in costume leaps out at her from behind a furnace. Callie jolts and hides her face in my chest, gripping my shirt.

Thank you, jump scare.

As she recovers, her fingers slowly sweep down my stomach, redirecting my attention from the screen. She slips them under my shirt and trails over my abs and then lower to the button on my jeans. Now, this is how you watch a movie.

Even in the low light from the screen, I see her suppress a smile when I readjust, so she'll have all the access she needs. I have my arm around her and move my hand, sliding it under the top of her sweatpants. She stalls out on my zipper as I stroke up her outer thigh until I reach lace. Her eyes meet mine, a challenge in them. So, my fingers follow the curve inward before I push the rest of the way between her thighs. Callie suck in a breath, her hips shifting.

Connor groans from the other side of her. "Come on, guys. Your room is literally a thirty-second walk away."

Upset she got caught, she wrinkles her nose—but it was clearly her own fault.

"Watch your movie, Con," she says.

"Seriously, no one moves that much under a blanket unless they're getting some action."

She straightens up, jerking her head toward him. "What the hell do you know about getting action?"

He grins and shakes the mop of hair out of his eyes. "Dude, I'm almost sixteen. Don't for a second think you're the first girl to be felt up on this couch."

Her jaw falls open, shocked by his confession. I laugh at her reaction and slowly pull my hand out of her sweats. Connor puts his fist up over her head where I give him a well-deserved bump.

She snaps her attention back to me. "Do not encourage him."

Shit.

An eyebrow quirks as he lifts his fist again, daring me to risk her wrath. I'm not sure if a reflection gives him away or she's just that in tune with her sibling, but Callie whirls around and pounces on him.

Given his size, he could effortlessly overthrow her attack. Instead, he laughs and raises his hands in defeat. "Okay. Okay. No more feeling up girls on the couch." He pauses a beat until she relaxes. "Full-on sex or nothing. Cal's orders." Before she can react, he shoves her toward me and bolts out of the room.

She collapses back in my arms and sighs. "He stresses me out."

"Want me to help you relax?"

She nods, and I stand with her in my arms before she changes her mind. Connor's entertaining himself. Cate's asleep in her bed. After a night of kick-ass parenting, we've earned alone time. But when I let her down in her bedroom, she heads right back out. "I'm going to take a quick shower." She pauses in the doorway, looking back. "Be in bed when I get back."

Yes, ma'am.

I strip out of my shirt and jeans and pull on a pair of sweatpants. The wall diverts my attention as I put my clothes in my bag. A prom picture shows Callie in a low-cut red dress with the same date as the one Felicia and I saw from a different prom.

The light-brown-haired, all-American-looking boy stares at her like she makes his world stop.

"I feel you, guy."

I switch out the overhead light in favor of a lamp and check my phone, in bed, per Callie's command. Messages from Dustin become more vulgar, the later it gets. Then I reach the picture messages. Even though I had every intention of seeing the tits in person twelve hours ago, I release my phone as if merely witnessing topless girls endangers my life.

Callie and I haven't discussed our status, but I have no plans of letting her get the wrong idea about what I want—her and only her. I pick up my phone and send him a message.

Cool it, bro. Keep the tits in Mexico.

He answers fast.

You're missing out though.

I have no need for a bimbo. Let it go.

Dude. No. Tell me it ain't so.

Falling hard like I got vertigo.

But relationships be like a tornado.

She makes my heart beat allegro.

Oh. Whoa.

I know.

The last photo deletes as the knob turns. The door creaks open a little and stops. Another inch of movement, and it stands still again. A giggle comes through the crack seconds before Cate bounds in. She doesn't hesitate to climb right into bed with me.

"Ew, Jordan. Put a shirt on."

I lean over and retrieve one from my bag. "Why aren't you asleep in your room?"

"Cal lets me sleep in here when she's home."

I narrow my eyes, doubting her story. She squints back, daring me to challenge her. Stubbornness runs in Callie's genes. I put my shirt on, and Cate beams, proud to win. She makes herself comfortable and wraps her little arms around one of mine.

"Goodnight."

Within two minutes, she's sideways on the other side of the bed, snoring. I continue playing on my phone until Callie returns. She shakes her head on the way over. "Sorry. I'll move her. Just prepare yourself because she's going to scream."

I get up and catch her hand, yanking her toward me. "I can sleep on the floor."

"Jordan, you don't have to do that."

I kiss her, tucking her wet hair behind her ear. "There's nothing in the world I would rather do."

One of my eyes peeks open.

"Hi," Cate says, her nose almost touching mine. She brings a finger to her mouth. "Shh. Cal's asleep."

I scrunch my eyes shut and reach up above me, knocking my phone off the nightstand. Seven. I roll over onto my back and stretch, yawning. Oh, the familiar ache in my back from sleeping on a floor. One day, I'll sleep in a bed with Callie.

One day. I hope.

"I'm bored," she whispers louder than necessary. She flops down next to me and puts her hands behind her head.

"Well, what should we do?" I whisper back.

She sits right back up, her eyes huge. "Make breakfast."

Cate jumps to her feet. I fold up the blankets and stack them with the pillows at the end of the bed. Callie's asleep on her side, her hair a tangled mess over her face. I brush it away and kiss her cheek before I track down Cate.

By make breakfast, she means play dress-up and pretend to eat food. An old blue bathrobe, a giant pair of wire-rimmed glasses, and a smoking pipe make up my costume. She chooses to wear her pink robe but can't find another pair of glasses. To avoid a meltdown, I suggest a pair of swim goggles.

In the hunt for appropriate reading material, she stumbles across a photo album. Connor helped her with it after she tried to build a wall like Callie's, using gum to stick up the pictures. Out of all the photos, not a single one in her book includes their parents. Birthdays, holidays, all the other special occasions, they never once appear. I wonder whether they weren't there or were purposely left out.

From what I gather, Lara's absence is a frequent occurrence. She parties with people her daughter's age while her daughter cares for her children. If not for Callie sacrificing her free weekends, Connor would watch Cate all the time, unable to do much of anything else.

All dressed up, I brew coffee. Cate disappears for a while, and upon her return, she insists we sit down to enjoy the home-cooked meal she spent her morning slaving away over at the stove. Naturally, I read the paper and smoke my pipe. She looks through her comic book, and we have a polite conversation as if we were straight out of a fifties' sitcom.

I shake out my month-old newspaper. "Well, my dear, Sport and Kitten should be down for breakfast soon."

She giggles. "They'd better hurry, or they'll be late for school."

"Would you like me to drop them off on my way to the office?"

"That would be nice." She sighs, resting her chin on her hand. "I need to mop the floors again."

"Very well," I say, pushing a pretend plate toward her. "Would you like more ham?"

From the kitchen doorway, Callie laughs, and I glance over.

"What the hell, Cate?" Connor elbows his way past her into the room. "You can't just strip away a guy's dignity as soon as he walks through the door. You have to build up to embarrassing him like this."

I toss down my pipe and fold up the newspaper. "I'm not wearing a pink ballerina tutu, holding a doll and watching *Swan Lake*, so I'm going to say I'm ahead in the dignity department."

Connor glares. "Cate showed you the photo album?"

"First thing this morning. Now, sit down and eat, Sport." I set my glasses on top of the newspaper on the table.

Cate giggles, and I wink at her.

I pour a cup of coffee for Callie and take it over. "Good morning, beautiful."

Cate growls at me from behind for breaking character.

"I mean, good morning, Kitten." I check over my shoulder where she nods and goes back to her reading. A distraction I fully intend to take advantage of. I steal the mug back from Callie and put it down. "Honey, Kitten needs help with her science homework before I drop her off at school."

"That's nice, dear," she says, disinterested and flipping a page.

I snake my arms around Callie and back her into the living room, all the way to the couch. I lower us down on the cushions. She laughs when I pull the blanket over us to gain privacy for our study session.

"Anatomy, right?" I brace on my arm beneath her head and kiss my way up her jawline. "The strongest muscle in the body is in the jaw."

"Is that so?"

"Mmhmm. And this is the longest bone in the human body." My hand drags up her outer thigh.

"The smallest is in the ear," she says.

Not about to argue with that, I graze my teeth over her earlobe. Her sigh attracts the attention of another piece of my anatomy. I skim her fingertips over the scruff on my jaw and then brush my thumb over her bottom lip. "The lips are hundreds of times more sensitive to touch than the fingertips."

She stares up at me, breathy when she asks, "Any other facts I should know?"

I press her hand flat against my chest and then place mine on hers. "Kissing raises the pulse to over one hundred beats per minute."

Under my palm, her heart races as I slowly bring my face closer to hers. Her gaze drops to my mouth, but I stop just shy of kissing her, hovering above her until Callie grabs the back of my neck and pulls me the rest of the way. I groan and move my hand lower to cup her breast through her shirt.

She arches into it, an airy sigh escaping. "Jordan."

I'm done. I have to keep fucking touching her.

"Mmm, you want one more fact, Callie?" I ask against her lips.

I glide my hand lower, under the top of her sweatpants, and she gasps when my fingers slip into her panties and parts her thighs for me.

"Right here…" I stroke through her wet pussy and then stop over her clit, causing her to whimper. "This," I tell her, "is how I make you come."

I roll over her clit, and Callie sucks in a sharp breath.

"Fuck," she hisses.

She grasps my bicep while I add more pressure, her chest rising and falling in ragged breaths. My cock's already rock hard as she digs her nails into my skin.

Then I stop.

She casts her eyes up, and I smirk.

"This concludes our tutoring session for today, but I am available for…"

I trail off when Callie's hand joins mine inside her panties. Her heavy-lidded gaze locks onto mine, and she presses down on my fingers, lifting her hips and dragging her clit against my fingers.

So fucking sexy—lips parted and cheeks pink while she uses my hand to get herself off. I take over again, having planned to make her come all along. Her hold moves to my wrist, and I slide lower, easily dipping a finger inside her.

"Be quiet for me, beautiful."

"Yes," she breathes, grinding against my palm.

I thrust in a second and then seal my mouth over hers just in time to muffle her moan. She tightens her grip, her pussy clenching as she comes. I pump slowly while she comes down. Her hold on me goes slack, and she watches me suck the taste of her off my glistening fingers.

"Best student I've ever had," I tell her. She schools a smile, and I rub her puffy bottom lip. "If you enjoyed my tutoring services, please recommend me to a friend."

Callie squints at me. "You want me to recruit competition now? Between Felicia and my sister, I don't already have enough?"

I swipe her hand and softly kiss her inner wrist. "Competition implies anyone else would stand a chance. We've been beyond that since the first time you increased my heart rate to over one hundred beats per minute."

She stares up at me, eyes bouncing between mine. "You should be careful, saying things like that."

"Why?" I ask.

"It could make a girl feel things."

"Good." I drop my mouth onto hers and kiss her hard before I get up, taking the blanket with me. I toss it back over her. "My mission is to make you fall in love with me."

I leave her all wide-eyed and head into the kitchen for seconds of some imaginary breakfast.

Cate's refusal to remove her goggles inspires Callie to take her swimming after lunch. We pile into her car and drive about ten minutes to an old stone-faced structure she worked at during high school. She explains the county originally built a fitness center to generate revenue, but a YMCA moved in down the road two months later. Since then, this place has been a hidden *gym*.

Cate runs inside the creepy building with Connor on her tail. Still partially convinced of my demise on this trip, I secure Callie's hand on our way up the sidewalk. I hold the door for her, watching the top of Connor's head disappear down a set of steps inside.

The blonde sitting at a desk behind the counter lights up when she sees us. Shayna looks exactly like her pictures, except she now has blue streaks in her hair. She jumps up on the counter and swings her legs around. "Thank God it's you, Henders. I thought I might actually have to do some work."

"Anybody come in today?" Callie asks.

Shayna laughs and picks at something on her jeans. "Not a soul. I fell asleep while reading a bit ago."

"A normal Saturday afternoon then." Callie picks up a pen and starts writing on a sign-in sheet without giving me an introduction. I nudge her, and she glances up. "Sorry. Jordan, this is Shayna. Shayna, Jordan."

"*The* Jordan?" Shayna says, eyebrows raised.

Oh, the girl has talked about the Jordan.

"She's mentioned me?" I look at Callie, but she doesn't notice because she's giving a death glare to her friend.

"She might have said your name once." Shayna's attempt to hide a smile suggests the number's plenty higher, but she quickly redirects. "Is Cate taking swim lessons? They start in about a month."

"What are they charging for Saturday classes?" Callie asks. "You know Lara won't bring her during the week."

Shayna rolls her eyes, familiar with the song and dance of shitty parenting. "Regular costs forty-five for six lessons and…" She leans back to look at something. "Damn, the bitch charges double for the weekends."

Callie thinks for a second and shrugs. "We'll see."

Shayna nods. "I'll put her name down to keep a spot open."

"Thanks, Shay." Callie turns toward me. "You ready to be assaulted by a six-year-old in swim floats?"

"Absolutely." I follow her to the stairs, but a nagging feeling in my chest keeps me from going any farther. "I forgot my phone in the car. Meet you down there?"

She hands me the keys, and I go outside. I wait until she and Shayna finish a quick exchange. Once she descends the steps, I head in again.

"That was fast." Shayna sits back in her chair behind the desk.

I lean on the counter. "What are the chances their parents pay the extra for weekend lessons?"

She snorts. "None. She or Connor will end up paying the difference, if not all of it. They always do."

Of course they do. I fish out my wallet to pay for Cate's swim lessons, succeeding at what Graham nor Lara seems capable of—giving a shit.

"Well, aren't you a knight in shining armor? Not that she needs one or anything. Henders can handle herself." Her eyebrow arches. "Me, on the other hand…"

I shake my head and walk away while she laughs.

The stairway brings me out in the middle of a hallway. At one end, I find the men's locker room. Connor sits on a bench in his swim trunks. Without looking up from his phone, he tosses me the backpack with mine in it. I hurry up and change, and when we're ready, he leads the way.

One door on each end allows for easy access from both locker rooms to the pool area. A standard-sized pool with lap ropes fills most of the space with a hot tub and a plastic table and chairs on the same wall as the doors. Far from the pool at the country club.

Connor throws our towels on the table and steps behind a corner near the door closest to the women's locker room. He motions for me to join him. I step out of sight as Cate marches in, wearing her goggles and arm floats with her towel and flip-flops on. Connor lunges at her, and she shrieks. He hands off her stuff to Callie before dangling her at arm's length over the water, and a strange mixture of screams and giggles echo around the room.

Callie goes to put their stuff down without seeing me, but holy shit, Callie Henders in a two-piece will be my undoing. Memories pale in comparison to the real deal in front of me. All flawless skin and the freckle on her shoulder and those legs, and this will become a problem for me the moment she turns around.

I steal a page from Connor's book and sneak up behind her. Cate warns her with a screeched version of her name, but she's too late. Callie turns just in time to see me before I grab her up and launch us both into the pool.

We surface, and I smile at her. "Sorry, but to keep it PG, you need to stay submerged from the neck down."

I swim in a circle around her like a shark, ready to attack if she defies me.

She wipes the wet hair away from her face. "Were you one of those boys who pushed girls they liked in the pool?"

"I wasn't until right now," I say, splashing her.

"Jordan has to race Connor." Cate taps her foot on the pool deck.

Securing Callie around the waist, I drag her through the water with me. "I will win this race in your honor."

She laughs, and I deposit her before shaking hands with my competitor. Cate counts us down from ten. She repeats four twice, causing confusion about when to go, but we figure it out and push off the wall. Once I surface, I quickly remember Rusty, Gavin, and I have fallen out of our workout routine the past few months.

I hit the wall and flip around, and there's fucking Callie up on the ledge at the opposite end. Each time I take a breath, my eyes want to search for her perfect cleavage.

When I reach them, instead of starting my second lap, I stand up and glare. "Do you want me to lose? Get in the damn water and stop distracting me."

Her eyes roll as she hops down. I kiss her—because why wouldn't I?—and resume my race. Connor's pulled ahead, but by the fourth and final lap, I close the distance and slap the wall first. Cate crowns me the winner while my chest heaves, and my lungs burn. We need to start hitting cardio again but not for a few weeks. I'll require at least that long to recover from this.

Connor and I shake hands again per the request of a bossy six-year-old.

I lean back on the wall next to my prize. "I won. No thanks to you." I pull her closer to my side, my skin craving contact with her. "Connor, you're no joke," I say.

He offers Cate a hand to steady herself on her way down the steps into the water. "Same, man. You play sports?"

"Lacrosse when I was younger."

"A sport for those who can't keep up in basketball." Connor pushes Cate through the water, sending her gliding over to us. "Why did you stop?"

I let go of Callie to catch her.

"I wasn't playing for the right reasons."

He and I keep passing Cate back and forth, talking about different sports. He plays a lot of them but considering the way his face lights up at the mention of basketball, he's discovered his passion. We trade jabs over the weaknesses of the other's game until Cate tells us to stop being so boring.

We all bow to her, following her orders to do handstands, hold our breath, and throw her around. After a while, she kicks Callie and Connor out of the pool and sends them to the hot tub. She has me swim a few laps with her holding on to my neck, and then I spend a solid two minutes spinning her around.

When I look over at the hot tub, Callie's climbing out. She tortures me with the water dripping off her body until she goes out into the hallway. About ten minutes later, she comes back, wearing a towel—thank God. She crouches down by the edge of the pool, and I walk over with Cate on my shoulders.

"Rinse off," she says. "I'll meet you in the steam room."

A knee hits my face while Cate scrambles onto the side. She cannonballs into the hot tub with Connor catching her.

I climb out and catch up with Callie in the hallway, snagging her hand. "Steam room?"

She shrugs and steps into the locker room. "No one under the age of sixteen is allowed. It's against policy."

One of the most useful policies I've ever heard.

I wash off the chlorine and follow a sign hanging from the ceiling to a cross hall. A small window shows a basketball court on one side with two other doors, one marked *Maintenance* and *Janitorial* on the other. At the end of the hall, I step into an off-white tiled room filled with steam. Two levels of seating run around three walls, and a pile of towels waits by the door.

I spread one out on the lower level and lean back to rest my elbows on the seat behind me. My lower jaw aches from Cate's earlier assault. How anyone keeps up with her on a daily basis, I can't imagine. Less than twenty-four hours with her, and I feel like an eighty-year-old.

All thoughts of anyone other than Callie disappear when she comes in, a towel around her waist. Watching her walking through a wall of steam has blood pumping straight to my cock.

"Hello, beautiful."

She smiles and scoops down to pick up a chain connected to a metal sign that reads *Out of Order.* She hangs it up outside, and the lights dim before she pulls the glass door shut. What's she up to? Next thing I know, she MacGyver's the shit out of the door with a broom angled just right and braced against the wall. The glass has already steamed over when she jerks the handle forward and back to demonstrate her makeshift lock.

"What if there's a fire?" I ask.

She gestures around the room. "In the case of a fire, I think we'll be safe."

I chuckle at her point well made and waste no time in getting from point A to point B. My lips reach their destination as my arms encircle her waist. Once again, her hands in my hair confuse my senses, exhilarating and relaxing. Her tongue slides against mine, but she breaks away far too soon—as in ever.

She squints. "Did you and Cate eat those fruit snacks after I told her no?"

All I can do is grin, because of course we ate them. They were fucking fruit snacks, and they were delicious. She sighs and guides me back to the bench with a hand on my chest. I sit on my towel as hers falls to the floor. No kids. No towel. No hesitation to pull her onto my lap. She places a knee on each side and stares down at me.

"What are you doing to me, beautiful?"

Kissing me—that's what she's doing. My lips, my jaw, my neck, and then—*fuck*—her teeth tug at my ear. I groan and fist my hand in her hair, bringing her mouth back to mine. Her palms glide up my chest while my lips travel down to hers.

On the way, I gently press my lips to the mark, swearing to myself that I'll cover it with my own once it isn't so tender. I lick and suck my way lower and cup her breast through the swim top, and her back arches into me. She circles her hips, mine flexing to give her the friction she wants while I drag my teeth over her pebbled nipple through the material.

The steam on our skin makes an already-heated situation all the hotter. As much as I want to fuck her, I need to slow this down.

I sit back against the seat behind me and squeeze her thighs. "You're one hip thrust away from passing the outer realm of my restraint."

"Yeah?" She leans in to bite my lower lip and then grinds down on my cock.

My hands slide around to her ass, thin fabric the only thing keeping me from sinking into her tight cunt. Except every condom in my possession is in a bag in her room.

Fuck.

Dropping my head back, I shut my eyes as tight as possible while she continues to test my resolve. Every move she makes, I counter with a thought to avoid pinning her against the wall.

But when her tongue slowly drags from the base of my neck up over my throat, I growl, losing the battle.

I can't move.

"Jordan," she says.

My name out of her mouth makes my dick throb.

"Jordan?"

I lift my head but keep my eyes closed. Any visual will only send me over the edge, and I don't think I could even eat her pussy right now without ending up balls deep inside her.

Callie grabs one of my hands and places something in my palm. I trace my thumb over a familiar square package. My eyes open, meeting hers, and she smiles.

Thank fuck.

My mouth crashes into hers, frantic and desperate for her. She pulls at the back of my head, forcing me closer even though no space remains between us.

I shove up her top, making her breath hitch. My new favorite sound. I break away to drag the fabric over her head and toss it aside. When I look at her, all thoughts leave my head. Water vapor beads on her skin. Hair spills over her shoulders to frame the curves of her breasts. A soft pink paints her cheeks. Her lips are parted. Everything about her is...

"Perfect."

My hands slide up her smooth back, bringing her toward me. Her bare skin against mine feels better than I ever imagined, nipples dragging against my chest. Everywhere on her body my hands touch, my mouth follows—kissing, sucking, nibbling, exploring. Slow and meticulous to savor the moment along with her.

Callie moans when I scrape my teeth over her nipple and press down on her clit. So, I move her bottoms to the side to get another one and groan, feeling how soaked she is for me.

"Tell me we have enough time for you to come on my face," I mumble before looking up.

She shakes her head. "No time." She kisses me. "Fuck me, Jordan." She kisses me again. "Please, fuck me."

This time *I* kiss *her*. Then I stand her up to push my trunks down. I give my cock a few strokes, watching Callie wiggle out of her bottoms, and then I'm hooking her around the waist.

"Fuck, I need to be inside you."

A thigh lands on each side of mine, her slick pussy a tease against me. Callie holds the condom wrapper to my mouth. With a snarl, I bite the corner for her to rip it open. Her laugh's infectious, her forehead presses to mine, and those eyes gaze at me. In this moment, I have no doubt that I'll fall in love with the ever-challenging girl in a red coat.

Our lips meet as she reaches between us. Her fingers wrap around my shaft, gliding up and down and driving me mad before she rolls on the condom. I grasp her hips, urging her up onto her knees, and then she sinks down, excruciatingly slow.

Worth every fucking second of the wait.

Once I've watched her take every inch of me, I almost lose it. "So fucking good," I tell her with a hard thrust.

She whimpers and braces on my shoulders, graceful as she slides up and back down. I speed us up, guiding her hips and pumping into her.

Steam settles on her skin, and I chase it with my tongue. It almost tastes as good as the preview I got of her pussy earlier. I slam into her at the reminder, causing Callie to clench around me.

After a month of wanting her, the way she looks spread around my cock, and how incredible it feels, I unleash a deep, guttural groan.

Callie clamps a hand over my mouth. "Echoey halls."

"Don't give a shit," I mumble into her palm.

She never loses her rhythm, replacing it with her mouth and trapping another groan between us. I let my hands roam over her, a need for closeness I've never experienced with anyone else driving me. Every touch, kiss, and gasp from her is not enough to satisfy it.

Our bodies move against one another faster, our panted breaths bouncing off the walls. If she has any interest in me lasting much longer, we need to slow down. Way down.

But Callie has no such interest.

When I try to adjust our pace, she shoves my hands away from her hips and slams down harder.

"Callie…"

I abandon the rest of my warning when she breathes my name. The want and need in her voice destroys any idea of control. I grab a handful of her perky ass, fingers flexing into her skin, and I drop my other hand down to rub her clit.

"This is what you want, right? This right here?"

She bites down on her lip to stay quiet, the sexiest sounds still escaping her. Whether she meant it as a challenge or not, I accept it as one and fuck her harder. It doesn't take long for her to dig her nails into me, her movements bordering on desperate.

I control our rhythm, never letting up even when I bring my lips to her ear. "We both know your cunt's been mine since day one, beautiful. Now I want what's mine to come all over my cock."

"Yes," she rasps. "Fuck, fuck. It's yours, Jordan. I'm yours."

Damn right she is.

I drive into her, and all her concerns for not making noise vanish when her legs start to tremble. She moans and then cries out, her pussy strangling me when she comes, and my breaths struggle in response.

"Fuck, Callie. Just. Like. That."

I thrust deeper until a shudder rips through me. My cock pulses inside her, and I groan, pumping into her before slumping back on the seat.

I pull her against me, inhaling the hot, humid air with her head pressed into my cheek. I'm more content than I thought possible while she traces her fingers up and down my arm. It brings the same sensation as her hands in my hair, her effect on me indescribable. How I ever thought my feelings for her were anything but real is completely beyond me. She makes shit matter.

"My birthday was endgame, and I thought you were lacrosse." I blurt it out and immediately recognize how insane it sounds.

She straightens up, her face showing concern for my well-being.

I need to try that all again. "That's why I didn't want to tell you it was about more than sex."

A solid attempt, but not any clearer on my meaning.

She, unfortunately, climbs off me. "Care to elaborate?"

I take care of the condom, shoving it in the pocket of my swim trunks after pulling them up. "Lacrosse was just a challenge to me," I try to explain. "It ended up just another way for me to beat my brother. After I met my goal, I stopped caring and quit. I was afraid, if I told you I wanted to be with you before my stupid challenge was over, I wouldn't want you anymore."

She, regrettably, puts on her bottoms. "What does that have to do with your birthday?"

"The night I followed you home from the party, I had no intentions of ever seeing you again. But then"—I close the distance between us—"you roped me back."

She rolls her eyes, knowing precisely what I mean as she pulls on her top and kills my view.

I run my hands over her waist, bringing them behind her. "I closed my eyes and pointed to your calendar and gave myself until then to sleep with you. I just so happened to pick my birthday— twice."

"So, you kept trying to put me off until Saturday after the challenge ended." She smiles. "I chose Friday as endgame, too."

My head jerks back. "What?"

"Benji told me he thought you had real feelings for me, so I decided you had until Friday to tell me. Otherwise, I wasn't going to see you when I came back."

"Is that why you showed up at the bar instead of going to Graham's?"

She nods.

What the fuck?

I feel as if someone punched me in the gut and simultaneously ripped out my heart, only to crush it in front of me. The tension forms in my head so fast that I release her to massage it away before it worsens.

"Everything that happened that weekend was because I wouldn't tell you how I felt earlier?" The room allows very little pacing space, but I need to move, so back and forth between the benches I go. "Why would you do something so stupid? Why would I do something so stupid? Damn it, we really are the most stubborn two people."

"Jordan, stop. Everything's fine. We're fine."

"Fine?" I stop and throw my hands in the air because she's lost her fucking mind. Round-the-clock-care kind of lost her mind. Trey needs a new definition for wild. She needs one for fine. Come Christmas time, everyone's getting a dictionary.

"Callie, you went on a bender," I remind her. "We stopped seeing each other because you were acting like a completely different person. You broke my fucking heart, and all I needed to do to prevent it from happening was tell you I wanted to be with you?"

I did. I always wanted her. I just took too long to figure it out and then scared myself out of it like a tool. I rub my temples, pacing again. Nothing in the last few weeks needed to happen. Not her feeling as if she lost control over her life or her blackout or Tyler assaulting her. None of it. By trying not to let her down, I let her down.

The thoughts and emotions flood through me, and I need a way to let her know how I feel without words because I have no more. She jumps at my sudden change in direction. I crash into her, my mouth melding to hers, and everything transfers from me to her. Through my lips, my tongue, my arms holding her tight against me—all of it telling her what my brain fails to convey. Let everyone else in her life care about themselves. I'll put her first.

When my mind slows enough so that I can string together sentences again, I break away from her. She's out of breath, the most adorable, bewildered look on her face.

I cup her cheeks and drop my forehead onto hers. "We're going to start telling each other what we're thinking. And I'm starting right now."

Her eyes widen. "Jordan…"

She sounds utterly terrified, and I can't help myself.

"Callie, I have to say it." I inhale slowly, drawing out her panic. "I'm starving."

———

I'm in free fall—eighty-five percent euphoric and fifteen percent terror-stricken.

In some families, a younger brother falling for a girl receives helpful advice from his big brother. Mine just sent me a picture of a random girl sucking on his big toe. As far as Callie goes, I'm on my own. I tuck my phone in my pocket and shut the locker.

Connor's already dressed, and he hands me the backpack on his way to the door. Unaware of where he's going because of his phone, I grab his shoulder to redirect him seconds before he walks straight into the wall. *Kids.*

In the hallway, Cate waits for us with her arms crossed. "You told her? I can't believe you, Jordan!"

I raise my hands in submission. "Calm down, my dear. I told who, what?"

She marches over and pokes me with her finger. "Cal. Fruit snacks."

Send me to jail and throw away the key because I'm no better than a criminal. "I promise I didn't tell her anything. She's a mind reader."

Cate giggles, and apparently, I've earned forgiveness. She grabs my hand and drags me to the stairs. I snag Connor's shirtsleeve to let him know we're leaving. When we reach the top, I glance around but no Callie.

"Thanks for waiting, everybody," she says, coming up from behind us. Her hair's pulled high into a wet ponytail, skin still flush from our time in the steam room.

How does she expect me to keep my hands off her when she looks so gorgeous?

She dangles her keys. "Connor, go start the car."

With his eyes still fixed on his phone, he swipes them out of her hand. A giddy Cate skips out behind him. Callie's fingers interlace with mine on our way to the desk where Shayna waves a twenty-dollar bill.

"Pay the man," Callie says.

Shayna offers me the money—for what, I have no idea. I accept reluctantly while she gives me a shameless once-over that reminds me of Jess.

"I never got a good look," she whines. "What happened to you showing him off for the cameras before he changed?"

Callie pulls me to safety, heading toward the exit. "Bye, Shayna."

"Pete's birthday's coming up," she shouts after us. "You should come!"

The instant we step outside, I tug Callie around so her chest bumps into mine. "What's the money for?" I ask.

"Consider it the first installment for Cate's swim lessons."

Well, that didn't take long for her to find out about.

"First of all, swim lessons are on me." A quick kiss intended to prevent her from arguing turns out to be a mistake because I want more. "I have a follow-up question then. What was she paying you for?"

Callie presses her lips together, her face turning a hint redder. "We might have won a long-standing bet by having sex in the steam room." She rushes down the sidewalk, away from me.

She amazes me. No, she astounds me.

After I get in the car, I twist around to the backseat passengers. "Who wants to go spend twenty dollars?"

Cate squeals, and Connor looks up from his phone. Callie, well, I feel her glare penetrating my soul.

Sorry, beautiful.

"Can we have blue slushies, Cal?" Cate asks.

The innocent question makes Connor's brows pull together, his eyes darting to Callie. Her head tilts in a conspicuous manner, and they stare at each other. It's like they're engaging in an entire conversation without words until the crease between his eyebrows disappears.

She nods at Cate. "Blue slushies it is."

Turning out of the parking lot, Callie heads in the opposite direction from where we came. She glances over, keeping her voice low when she says, "Sutterville's convenience store has a blue slushie machine."

"Sutterville, as in…" I trail off, not wanting to say much more with Cate listening.

She nods. "We usually try to avoid it since *anyone* could be there."

Anyone meaning Graham. My shoulders tense at the possibility of seeing her father. More often than not, I encourage a peaceful resolution, but I doubt my pacifistic preferences will prevail if I see him. Other than Hitler and those types, he's the first person I've hated without meeting.

Through the rearview mirror, I catch Connor staring out the window. His expression's hard to place. Haunted maybe. The empty eyes remind me of Callie's the week of my birthday. Trey mentioned being scared of Graham breaking her. I've never once stopped to think how the same might apply to Connor.

Fifteen's a hard age in itself between the hormones and wanting to be an adult, but everyone treats you like a child. At that age, Callie found an escape. She drank, smoked, and put herself in danger, all to help her forget the pain and anger inside. What does Connor do? Sports? Maybe basketball's his way of dealing with emotions too heavy for him to cope with on his own.

Our drive only takes a few minutes. Callie slows down to a crawl, pulling in while she and Connor scan the area. With her patience worn thin, Cate jumps out the second we park. Connor grumbles and hurries in after her. Callie meets me at the front of the car. She runs her hand up my arm, and the girl does things to me when she bites her lip. I hold the door and slide my hand over her ass as she walks through.

Bedtime can't come fast enough.

She grins, waving to the lady behind the counter. "Hi, Rhonda."

The middle-aged lady with stringy black hair nods and returns her attention to a magazine.

Straight in, the slushie machine occupies Connor and Cate. After she reaches them, Callie veers left and back to the wall of cooler doors. I wander around the gas station, taking in the small-town life. Sutterville's only a third of the size of Waymore. Hell, we drove in on an unpaved street.

Mostly to annoy Callie, I pick up more fruit snacks before joining her siblings. So Cate can press the button, Connor holds her. She's filling a second forty-ounce cup. I hope she's making one for each of us because that much blue slush in that little of a girl cannot lead anywhere good.

A bell dings as a customer enters. I blame movies for my disappointment when he's not wearing boots or a cowboy hat. Actually, if the other residents look like him, I'm way off base. He wears an unbuttoned plaid shirt over a white T-shirt and black jeans. He slips off his beanie and reveals styled blond hair. A nod and a smirk on his way to the back add to an asshole vibe given off by his eyebrow ring.

"Oh shit," Connor says over his shoulder. He glances between the coolers and the third cup Cate's filling. "Hold this."

Suddenly my hands are full of a six-year-old as he starts down the aisle toward the back.

I step forward, letting Cate continue her mission, and my eyes work their way to Callie. She bends over in front of an open cooler door, grabbing for something off the bottom shelf. The blond stops behind her. And the smack of his hand on her ass cracks through the store like a whip.

Oh. Fuck. No.

I jerk in their direction so fast that I almost drop Cate alongside the fruit snacks. The pulse pounds in my ears as she scrambles for a hold around my neck. I only make it a few steps before Callie rotates and slams her knee into the guy's crotch. He growls out something, doubling over. Connor spins to face us, the breath he blows out puffing his cheeks. When I reach him, I try to set Cate down.

"No! I'm scared." Her grip tightens on me. "Pick me up!"

I pull at her wrists to pry them away, but she buries her face in my shoulder. The next time I attempt to break her hold, she whimpers.

Fuck. I clench my jaw and force myself to straighten up with her in my arms. As badly as I want to destroy this guy, I can't bring myself to frighten her more.

"What the fuck is wrong with you?" the blond chokes out, hands on his knees.

"Can you seriously be asking me that?" Callie shakes her head and tries to walk away.

He grabs her wrist, and Connor and I start toward them, but she doesn't need us. She rips her arm away and shoves him—hard. To keep his balance, he grabs at the shelf next to him and knocks over a selection of cheap gas station liquor. All the plastic bottles bounce, but a glass one shatters, wine spilling over the floor.

"Don't ever fucking touch me again," she hisses. "Better yet, forget you met me." She walks toward us, pausing to take Cate from me and to grab one of the slushie cups. Her lips turn up for a second. "Let's go."

The bell dings as she backs out the door. I'm still where she left me, the temptation of finishing the job she started hard to walk away from. Connor pushes the hair out of his eyes and nudges me back a few steps until I voluntarily turn around. He snags the last two cups as I toss the twenty on the counter for the cashier.

"Three slushies and a bottle of merlot. Sorry for the mess," I say.

The lady shrugs. "Don't worry about it. I'll make Brock clean it up."

Just shy of the door, I stop in my tracks. Callie's ex that fucked with her head. Heat spreads from my extremities to my core at the sound of his name. It might not be Callie's father, but it is someone who's wronged her. Over and over. As expected, I want to beat the living shit out of him—no, I need to see him unconscious on the floor, bleeding.

I charge in the other direction straight into Connor.

"No way." He drives me backward, the bell sounding as he forces me out of the building.

I throw him off, already on my way back in. His hand catches my shirt and slows me down enough that he gets in front of me again, blocking my path. But I have no problem going through him.

"Fucking move, Connor." I step into him, forcing him to retreat a step.

"Or what? You'll fight me too?"

He straightens up, exaggerating his three-inch height advantage, but his hard swallow betrays him. The chance I'll accept his challenge terrifies the kid. I growl and head in the opposite direction of the building. No particular destination in mind, just putting distance between me and the piece of shit inside.

It takes a block to calm down enough until I trust myself to turn around. As soon as I do, it hits me. *Where the hell is Callie?*

Connor strong-armed me right past her car. Not only did she not come and stop us, but I never even saw her. I sprint back, and as I reach the parking lot, Connor's exiting the store with those damn slushie cups.

"Where's Callie?" I ask, rechecking the car.

He glances around, equally panicked. "I have no idea."

I reach for my phone but stop when her infectious laugh floats through the air. A look of concern passes between us before we follow it around the corner of the building. It grows louder along with giggles from Cate. On our way past a weatherworn picnic table, Connor's foot crushes an empty cup, and blue liquid trickles out into the dirt.

Our search ends behind the gas station. In the middle of the gravel road, they spin with their arms outstretched, staring up at a cloudless sky. They pause when they notice us but promptly resume their twirling.

"What the hell is happening right now?" I ask. "Are they frolicking?"

"Probably," Connor says with a grin. "In case you haven't noticed, my sisters are totally cracked."

Cracked or not, he doesn't hesitate to partake, setting down the slushie cups and dashing over to them. He catches Callie around the waist and swings her around and then switches to Cate.

They team up and tackle him to the ground, laughing and smiling the entire time.

The three of them keep playing in the street without concern. The confrontation with Brock, Connor's torment from earlier, all the heaviness from their lives suddenly gone. From what I can tell, it's a rare moment—everything in their world bright and happy and right. And it's a remarkable thing to witness.

Callie. Callie. Callie. Callie. Callie. A million more times, Callie. At the end of the bed, she sits cross-legged, wearing nothing but a black bra and matching thong, playing an acoustic guitar. As unbelievable as she looks, she sounds horrific. Each strum is an insult to every musician everywhere, dead or alive. But I'm lying here, in my boxers, loving every single second of it because, anytime she hits a particularly offensive chord, she peeks up and smiles.

We've taken over Benji's room for the last two days. Sunday night, when we returned from Waymore, we stayed in my janitor-closet-sized room. The next morning, over breakfast, I told her about my deal with Benji to trade for six months. She marched up the stairs, changed the sheets on his bed, and claimed it as her own until his return. If he freaks out at her, I plan on playing the innocent card. But she and Benji seem to share a strange connection, so I doubt he'll get angry.

Callie slides the strap over her head and sets the guitar down by the bed. "When Beta Void finally decides to replace their awful guitarist, I'm auditioning."

Straight for the jugular.

I lunge at her and drag her back on the bed with me. Her surprised giggle is a welcome sound after half an hour of shit guitar.

Dark hair sprawls over my face until she whips around and crawls on top of me. "Are you bored of me yet?"

"Not yet. And when I do tire of you, we just need to have sex, and I'll be good for another few hours."

Her eyes roll. She climbs off to snoop through Benji's vinyl collection. I stay put, perfectly content to lie here, staring at her. The Callie channel—featuring all Callie, all the time—receives no complaints from this avid viewer.

An album catches her attention, and she pulls it out. "Polka?"

Really? Excellent material for holding over Benji's head rarely makes an appearance.

I hop up and snag the sleeve from her hand. My eyes travel over her legs. Certainly, she's a better dancer than a guitarist.

"Come on." I toss the vinyl on top of the others and grab her hand, leading her out of the bedroom.

Downstairs, she watches me like I've gone mad while I push the two couches in the living room farther apart and move the coffee table. Space is a must for my plan.

"What are we doing?" she asks.

I hook up my laptop to the stereo and pick a random polka song off a streaming site. "We're going to polka."

Skeptical, she raises her eyebrows as the whine of an accordion fills the room. "You know how?"

"My grandmother on my mother's side taught me before she died." I throw one of her hands over my shoulder and take her other in mine. I place my free hand on her hip. The bare skin beneath my palm distracts me, but I force myself to focus on teaching her the dance. "All right, beautiful, we start with—"

She steps back with her right foot, following with a shorter left-right.

Of course she already knows how to polka. Why would I expect anything else? I shake my head and one-two-three her— half-naked—around the room. As the song ends, I swing her onto the couch and collapse next to her.

"You could have given me an ego boost and at least pretended to let me teach you."

She sighs. "Don't bother trying with the fox-trot, waltz, or square dancing either. Our gym teacher ran out of sports and taught us how to dance."

"I'm with you all the way to square dancing. I draw a line there." I jump up and search my music. I stop on one I noticed on her playlist over the weekend.

"Shall we fox-trot?" I extend my hands.

"Sex on Fire" by Kings of Leon blares from the speakers. After a head shake at my musical selection, she accepts my offer. I yank her off the couch. She holds up her dance frame, so I equal her professionalism with rigid posture. She knows her steps, keeping up with any challenge I throw out. Around the living room, we slow-slow-quick-quick to a song written about an unforgettable sexual relationship. Grandmother would have been proud of me putting my training to use. Any approval, however, would have ended there.

Mid-promenade, a movement in the doorway catches my eye. The two of us freeze—actually, all four of us do. Rusty drops his bag, eyes open as wide as his mouth, which happens to mirror my expression exactly.

Next to him, Gavin doubles over in hysterics, lowering himself to the floor. "Oh my God."

My attire does nothing to embarrass me, but a spotlight shining on my ballroom dancing skills less than enthuses me. They already have the T-shirts. Now this. Not even Benji's polka collection will spare me from constant ridicule in the coming weeks.

"Dude. Callie." Rusty holds a hand over his eyes in the most gentlemanly display I've ever witnessed from him.

Completely unfazed, Callie retrieves a blanket from the couch and drapes it around herself like a towel. "Hello, boys."

Shit, at this point, I just need to lean in. I pause the music and turn around to face my over-occupied living room. "Disappear, hooligans." I flippantly wave my hand. "We have yet to waltz."

Rusty shakes his head, picking up his bag. "Damn, Waters. If this is you with a girlfriend, I'm terrified for our band's image." He disappears into the basement.

On the way upstairs, Gavin continues to cackle. Even after his bedroom door shuts, we hear him howling. He'll make me extra miserable.

Alone again, my focus returns to the situation at hand. A waltz—a much harder to find song in my repertoire. I scroll through my options, finally settling on Edwin McCain's "I'll Be." Far from my first choice and a little fast, but it will work. I crank up the volume to block out Gavin and any other potential interruptions.

Callie lets the blanket fall as I walk toward her. "Are you taking me to prom in the late nineties?"

I pull her into my arms. "Just dance, you impossible woman."

We do, gliding across the room. As an excuse to watch her move, I spin her more than necessary, her feet never failing to follow my lead. It only takes until the second chorus for me to toss her other arm over my shoulder and clasp my hands behind her. Our choreography becomes nothing more than a slow sway with my forehead resting on hers. I lose myself in her eyes, her scent, her touch, her everything and might have found meaning in an absurd universe.

Dammit.

If I'm saying shit like I've found meaning in an absurd universe, Rusty's right. My sap level needs lowered by a few thousand percent.

I walk my hands down Callie's lower back and slip my thumbs beneath the lace. "I'm bored of you," I whisper.

Without warning, she launches into my arms and wraps her legs around my waist. "We can't have that now, can we?"

I slam the laptop shut, and we're up the stairs and back in Benji's room before the music even stops playing. I drop her onto the bed, landing over her. We bounce, and by the time we still, her thong's down her thighs. She sits up and pushes down my boxers while I unclasp her bra.

She lies back, and I have to take inventory. Her skin, her hair, her breasts, her pussy, her eyes, her mouth.

"Perfect."

My lips only stay on hers a few seconds before I move lower. The breathy whimper she makes when my tongue drags over her nipple shoots down my spine. I grind my erection against her, the sounds doing everything for me.

As I kiss my way down her stomach, she thrusts a hand into my hair and lets out a sexy sigh. Another after I settle between her legs and lick up her inner thigh, and I groan.

"Jesus, baby." I lift my head to see her face. "I'm trying to think of a nice way to say this."

She pushes up onto her elbows, frowning. "A nice way to say what?"

I crawl up and hover over her, holding a serious expression. "If you don't stop making those fucking noises, I'll finish before we even start."

Callie laughs. "Get your shit together, Waters."

She then does nothing to help me get my shit together by grabbing my dick and twisting her hand on the way up. I growl and clench and—"Screw you, Henders."

She blinks up at me with a sexy-as-sin grin. "That's what I'm waiting for."

Fucking. Perfect.

I drop my mouth to the mark below her shoulder and suck hard enough she squeals. *My* mark.

Retracing my steps, I shove my shoulders between her thighs and then shove my face there, too. I lick a line up her pussy, holding her open for me, the taste one I want permanently on my tongue. She arches off the bed when I latch onto her clit.

"Jordan," she almost whispers.

Her hands push into my hair, her hips lifting for more. I slip a finger inside her, easily pumping in and out of her soaking cunt. As I push in another, Callie whimpers. Barely audible.

At first, I think she took my joke about her sexy sounds seriously, but she's still *making* them, just at minimum volume. It takes me about two seconds to figure out the Quiet Game from the steam room has resumed with Tweedle Dee and Tweedle Dickhead in the house.

That is not going to work for me.

So, I bat at her clit a few more times before I push her leg higher, replacing my tongue with my thumb. My fingers slide in and out of her while I kiss along her inner thigh, and on the next soft moan, I lick the tight ring of her ass.

She jolts and cries out, her thighs squeezing together.

"That's better, beautiful. Give me that sexy voice."

After another swipe, I swap with my thumb again. My mouth seals over her, and I rub my spit over her ass, slowly adding pressure. Callie's breaths grow erratic as she rides my fingers toward her release.

"Fuck, Jordan." She moans and tugs at my hair. "I'm so close."

"Allow me, then." I nip at her clit and press against the barrier. It sends her over the edge, her pussy clamping down and a chant of *yes* filling the room.

The only music I ever want to hear from her.

I let her ride out her orgasm before I grab a condom from the box on the floor. My dick's throbbing by the time I roll it on, but Callie's on the same page. She yanks me down and locks her legs around me, trying to get me to sink into her.

"Mmm." I ease in a few inches and drag out, only leaving the tip inside her perfect pussy. "Careful or I might think you're needy for my cock."

"I am," she says, staring up at me. "But not as needy as it is for me."

Then her heels kick into my ass, driving me inside her. I groan and drop my mouth onto hers. I kiss her, slowly drawing back and sinking forward again.

"*God,* you feel incredible," I say against her lips. "You're wrong. All of me is fucking needy for you."

It doesn't matter how much of her I get. It's never enough.

I speed up my thrusts, Callie's hips rising to meet each one. She digs her nails into the muscles on my back. Each scrape and buck does wonders to help me forget the sentimental shit that supported Rusty's comment.

And because rocking in and out of her is the worst fucking moment for me to think about Rusty, I can't stop thinking about him. Specifically, when he called her my girlfriend. Neither of us corrected him even though we've never come close to a conversation about labels. Really, I've never even considered it. I just know I want her—all of her.

Callie pulls me into her faster, and I adjust my angle, thrusting deeper. Our bodies move in sync, aware of what the other wants. Is the same true of our relationship? Are we under some mutual understanding of our status without an actual talk? Am I fine with this? Is she fine with it? Should I ask her? Obviously not now but after she comes? Why are these distracting thoughts only surfacing while I'm in the middle of pounding into her?

She moans out my name, arching off the mattress, and it snaps me back. I flex my hips into her harder and dive down to suck on her tit, bouncing every time I slam into her.

"Let me feel your pussy pulse for me, baby."

I lick up to my mark, and my fingers find her clit while I claim it as mine all over again.

"God, yes," she cries.

That one's loud enough to summon a deep thumping of bass from down the hall—Gavin's room if I had to guess. Their fault for coming back early.

Callie's coming, so she doesn't give a fuck.

I grasp the back of her thigh and pound into her until her body quivers beneath me, her cunt a pulsing vice-grip around my cock. I'm right there with her, all coherent thought gone. A mangled curse and her name escape mid-groan, and my muscles tense as I bury into her as deep as I can. I'm not sure I ever want to leave.

I collapse with most of my weight next to her and lay my head on her chest. It rises fast, her heart pounding away against my cheek. She brushes her fingers over my skin, sending chills through me, and I kiss whatever part of her my lips reach, unwilling to move. The longer we stay here, the better. Just her and me.

My girlfriend. My partner. My significant other. My home skillet. I couldn't care less what she goes by so long as she's my here, my now, and my Callie. And, damn it, she's my beautiful meaning in an absurd universe.

Our uninterrupted week together ends with Callie leaving for Graham's. All the time with her spoiled me, making me forget what I did on the weekends for the previous twenty-one years. Boredom only lasts a few hours though. A stream of texts and a few highly erotic—and essential—video chats occupy my time until she comes back.

After that, we return to our regularly scheduled program for school, but classes aren't the only activity to resume. Every morning, I bring her a coffee, and every morning, she rolls her eyes. The ideal start to my day—caffeine and sass. Each day ends just as excellent—with her in my arms.

But before that can happen on Thursday, I need to survive Date Night. Not under the circumstances I envisioned either.

Armed with a mirror, I engage in an epic battle with a particularly stubborn section of my hair that refuses to blend in with the rest. I rake my hands through the entire thing one last time and go with the results. Seriously, no one will ever notice.

A knock sounds as I walk down the stairs. Callie smiles from the other side of the threshold. I drag her inside, my lips on hers before the door latches. Eventually, I regain control of myself, and I lock my arms around her waist.

"Sorry, beautiful. You can't just show up, looking like that, and think I'm not going to kiss you."

"You saw me wearing the exact same thing a few hours ago."

"I kissed you then, too, if you remember."

The way her lips twitch says she does. "So, what do you have planned for tonight?" she asks.

I graze the tip of her nose with mine, affecting myself more than her. "A movie, followed by coffee."

"What movie?"

My mouth latches on to her neck, and she hums out a sexy sound. To stop myself from throwing her to the ground—poor form and all—I pull back. "Something foreign and terrible with subtitles. The perfect movie to not pay attention to." I grin when her eyes narrow. "What's your plan?"

"Dinner and open mic night."

Damn, her evening sounds much more entertaining than mine.

I lose her attention, her gaze traveling to the table.

"Did you buy flowers?"

"Of course I did. It's Date Night, Callie." I retrieve the bouquet of random flowers someone at the shop recommended for her inspection.

She sniffs them. "For future reference, don't buy me flowers."

I set them back on the table. "Coffee and jewelry only, I promise."

She squeaks as I dip her, kissing her much longer than necessary before bringing her up.

"Get your hands off my date, man," Benji says, coming from the living room. "You have a little redhead waiting for you."

Ah, yes. Felicia. She insisted on calling the two of us hanging out together Date Night and sounded so damn excited that I went with it. The annoying part came when Benji and Callie picked up on the name. Not only did they give me shit about it, but they also decided to enjoy one themselves. My best friend going on a date with her before I do, not unnoticed.

Hell, I still don't even know if she thinks of me as her boyfriend. My revelation that I don't care lasted all of five minutes.

Since then, I refer to her as my girlfriend in my head and panic anytime I almost say it out loud. Lame.

Staking my claim while I can, I make a show of running my hands all over her. "See you later, beautiful."

I kiss her with far too much tongue, and she smiles.

"Don't get any ideas," I say to Benji.

He winks. Quite possibly the first time I've ever witnessed him do so.

I grab the flowers and go pick up Felicia. She gives the reaction they deserve. She gushes, hugs me, and rushes to put them in water.

We drive over to a theater. The marquee holds no words I know or even attempt to pronounce. I simply tell the guy selling tickets, "That one," and point to what she wants.

No matter what movie she chooses, it will be far superior to the animated puppies or the chicken documentary.

Oh, those poor chicks.

A stale bag of popcorn and two sodas later, we settle into our squeaky theater seats.

"You're going to enjoy this," Felicia whispers as the lights dim.

But when the screen lights up, I groan so loudly that the heads in front of us turn. The film not only requires subtitles but is also in black and white. *Jesus*. She misunderstands the word *enjoy*. Another definition-deficient person who needs a dictionary for Christmas. The list continues to grow.

Three years in the future, the French avant-garde film ends, and what the fuck did I just watch? None of it made sense. None of it.

"We should do this every week," she says, climbing in the Jeep.

"Absolutely not, Gibson. I'm not letting you choose the movie ever again."

"Never?"

"Never."

She crosses her arms, pouting. Technically, I owe her for the rest of my life because of her help with Callie, but a future of reading movies and trying to follow an obscure plot sounds unbearable. A few blocks of silence makes me glance at my still-sullen sidekick.

Damn it.

"Maybe, if I pick three in a row, then we go to one you choose."

Her somber expression holds fast.

I sigh. "Switch off every other?"

Just like that, her face brightens. "Callie told me pouting would work."

Great. Devious women have overrun my life.

She stays chipper the rest of the way to Java Quest. We order coffees and sit at a table up front near the windows. In the midst of her explanation of the symbolism of the shadow on the wall during one scene in the movie, Felicia stops talking.

"And then?" I'm almost intrigued now that I understand the basics of the storyline. When she doesn't continue, I look in the general direction she's staring and notice a burly guy wearing a fedora. "A fedora? Really, Gibson?"

"Shut up." Her smile falters when she kicks me under the table, but she glues it right back on. "He's cute, but he probably thinks we're together."

I rotate around, checking out the guy who's checking out my date—extremely rude of him, might I add. His eyes flick from Felicia to me, and his face falls.

"Yeah, he definitely thinks we're together."

She shrugs, gazing forlornly at him over my shoulder. "Oh well."

"Text me when you need a ride," I say, getting up.

Her eyebrow arches. "What?"

"Go flirt your heart out, get the guy, text me, and I'll come pick you up."

"You're sure?"

I nod, pushing in my chair. Just so he's clear of our platonic friendship, I give her a fist bump on my way by. My phone vibrates by the time I get in my Jeep.

Felicia: *Fedoras are hot.*

Agree to disagree.

Thank you.

Anytime, Gibs.

I consider my repayment underway. Now to kill time until she tells me to come back. Luckily, only one place in town hosts an open mic night during the week. I flip on my blinker, turning out of the parking lot. I have a date to crash. One happening between my best friend and my ... Callie.

———

A lot of people showed up for open mic night at the dive bar. I order a beer and scan over the tops of heads for Benji or Callie. A girl with an acoustic guitar wraps up a breakup ballad. An unenthusiastic round of applause follows.

I recognize the guy who hops up onstage from a few different music events around campus. I can't remember his name though. He grabs the mic from the stand.

"Thanks, Savannah." He waits for her to finish shuffling off before continuing, "Anyone familiar with the music scene on campus will know our next performer. He usually has three guys standing behind him. But the lead singer of Beta Void is going solo tonight. Let's hear it for Benji Jones."

Callie hollers from near the middle of the room. Benji climbs the stairs to the stage. He grins, taking the mic, and secures it in the stand by the electric keyboard as he sits down.

In the two-and-a-half years we've known each other, I've never once seen him perform without the band. A night filled with firsts for him. I pay for my beer and lean against the bar, not wanting to distract him by wandering through to find Callie.

"Hey, everybody," he says. "As Mike pointed out, I'm used to having other people to blame a poor performance on, so bear with me." He winks. I presume it's at Callie since he does that sort of thing now. "Uh, this song's called 'Exquisite Twilight,' and it's for you, Calico. Here we go."

On edge, Benji licks his lips and clears his throat. At our gigs, he exudes confidence, but an original song with just him up there

195

seems as good a time as any for nerves. His eyes close as he plays a slow melody in a minor key.

A few measures in, his mouth turns up, and he looks out at the audience, ready for his performance. He leans closer to the microphone.

> *When our world seemed destined to break us,*
> *She searched through the darkness for the stars,*
> *And in spite of all the chaos and destruction in our lives,*
> *She never once lost sight of who we are.*

He sings the words in a lower, raspier voice than usual. It adds to the emotion on his face and those coming through the notes.

> *Each time, she saw the sunshine when it rained,*
> *She knew the lines would soon begin to blur,*
> *And hidden beyond black shadows and all doubts and absolutes,*
> *She'd find what's really beautiful to her.*

Benji smiles, looking off the stage as the melody alters slightly. I anticipate the build that will bring us to the chorus. His eyes shut again.

> *Frantic beauty lies all around,*
> *And sometimes what we seek should not be found.*
> *All our lives, we strive and struggle for our truth*
> *Because of this, we'll always remain bound.*

Frantic beauty? After giving me hell for writing it, he steals it? This guy.

The song slows, becoming more somber.

> *True happiness is for her,*
> *Not for you or me or those*
> *Who choose to sit idly by,*
> *Letting the best parts fade away,*
> *Lost forever deep inside.*

He plays for several measures, the song regaining speed. After two choruses, the notes slow for a final time.

I'll always remain bound,
Bound to you.

The last chord of the song resolves, and he jumps up for a bow. The applause for him is much more genuine than what they gave Guitar Girl. Well deserved, of course. He's a born performer.

Mike reclaims the stage. "Who needs a band with that kind of talent?" He slaps Benji on the shoulder. "Next up, we have Dan Williams."

Benji trots down the steps toward Callie. He picks her up, and she beams at him, her arms tight around his neck. I make my way over. When he spots me, he sets her down. "Hear that, man? That's what it sounds like when no one holds me back."

"Yeah, just remember my writing credit after you make it big." I kiss Callie and sit in the chair beside her.

"Where's Felicia?" she asks.

"She found a more attractive guy."

She juts out her lower lip, feeling bad for me, and I let her.

Benji takes a seat on the other side of her. His foot hooks the leg of her chair, and he drags it closer to him. "My date."

She laughs, shrugging her shoulders. I almost comment about her being more his girlfriend than mine but stop myself. The middle of a crowded bar is not the place to sound like an idiot on the label front.

The kid on the stage with his guitar earns our attention. His song's a little too twangy for my taste. During the chorus, Benji whispers something in Callie's ear. She wrinkles her nose and smiles. Honestly, I'm not sure what to think of their interaction and unsure if it bothers me.

He notices me watching and nods.

Twangy finishes, and Mike announces a short break between performers. When the regular bar music kicks on over the speakers, Callie goes to get another drink and leaves Benji and me at the table. Other than short exchanges coming and going, our last in-depth conversation happened weeks ago. Since returning from spring break, he's given me space with Callie. I figure he's enjoying a vacation after dealing with the mopey ghost of Jordan.

"When did you start working on your own stuff?" I ask.

"A onetime thing, I assure you."

"The one song you write and perform alone is about Callie?"

He takes a swig of his beer. "My song's not about her, man. It's about her struggle."

"Her struggle?"

"Your girl inspired me. She finally figured out how to keep the worst part of her life from ruining the rest of it."

My eyebrows pull together at his choice of phrasing. Callie used the exact same description when talking about Graham.

"You know about her father?"

He nods. "We had a long talk on the drive back from the State party."

"You drove her home that night?"

"She was in no condition to stay after her run-in with that fucking prick. Rusty and Jess rode back with Felicia, and Callie and I took your Jeep."

"But … I saw you after you came home." I stare at him in disbelief. "You knew about her family, her past, the reason she stopped seeing me—everything—and you didn't tell me?"

Rarely do I get angry with Benji, but we're well on our way for the second time in a few weeks. More than anyone, he knew how miserable I was after Callie ended things. He stole the lyrics that prove it. He knew my trip was nothing more than a last-ditch effort to rid myself of my feelings for her, and he was willing to let me go without knowing the truth.

He shrugs, not seeing an issue. "Not my story to tell."

"Which makes it perfectly acceptable for you to keep me in the dark about it all?"

"You don't get to be mad at me for being in the right place at the right time."

"You sure about that?" I challenge.

His eyes darken as he leans forward in his chair, staring me down. "That girl needed someone, and I was there. She trusted me to help her sort through her shit, and I don't take that lightly, so get the fuck over it."

Fuck, he went from chill to intimidating in a nanosecond. As rarely as he makes me mad, he loses his temper even less.

I put my hands up, surrendering. "All right. I'm sorry."

He relaxes back in his chair. "If anything, you should be thanking me."

"Thank you," I say. "You found a way to help her when I couldn't."

"I didn't do it for you; I did it for her. But that's not what I was talking about."

"Then what am I thanking you for?"

Scary Benji's long gone, and his cocky grin appears. "You really think Calico showing up the next day was a coincidence? My hands were all over that reunion, man." He picks a familiar piece of paper out of his wallet and tosses it over. "You can have those back now. They served their purpose."

"You showed her these?"

"You two were always going to find your way back to each other. I just gave a little nudge so you wouldn't screw your way across Tijuana before it happened."

I look down at the lyrics in my hand and then back at him. "You're right, Benj. I definitely owe you."

"We're family," he says. "You don't owe me anything. Unless you fuck it up with her. Then I'm coming for you."

I don't doubt that he would for a second. I stick the lyrics in my pocket to destroy later, and he raises his beer. We're about to have a real bro moment when a body lands in my lap. Blonde hair flicks me in the face. Sugary perfume assaults me.

"Miss me?" Brooke trails a finger down my neck.

"Get the fuck off me," I say, pulling my head back from her.

She laughs. "Someone forgot how to be fun."

Then Callie appears, stopping a few feet away.

Shit. This isn't happening.

Before I can drop Brooke's ass to the floor, Callie sits on Benji's lap. She presses her lips together, and is she trying not to fucking smile?

"Jordan," she says with amusement in her tone, "who's your friend?"

"Not a friend. Brooke, you need to—"

"Wait." Callie looks down at Benji. "This is *Brooke*?"

Fuck. She knows about Brooke? Jesus Christ, how *much* does she know? Uncomfortable fails to describe my kind-of girlfriend knowing anything about a girl I used to screw out of sheer boredom.

Benji smirks in response and sips his beer.

The smile Callie's been fighting slowly spreads, and she says, "I've heard wonderful things about your blowjobs."

Brooke's eyes double in size as my jaw drops open, and Benji spits out his beer.

"Fuck, Calico," he chokes out. Obviously in on the joke, he covers his face with a hand, trying not to laugh.

"The problem is," she continues, "the lap you're sitting on belongs to my boyfriend."

Boyfriend?

"Boyfriend?" Brooke speaks my thought.

More than anyone else, I require a repeat of the word.

"Boyfriend. And I'd really love for you to move."

Whatever Brooke's reaction, I miss it, my eyes locked on Callie. All I know is, she vacates my lap, and the smell of her dissipates.

Callie slips down into her own seat. "I can't take you anywhere."

I grab ahold of the chair and yank her over. "You are fucking incredible, you know that?"

She laughs. I lean in to kiss her, but her mouth becomes a moving target when Benji slides her in the opposite direction.

"My date," he says.

"My girlfriend," I counter. It sounds much better out loud than in my head.

Benji tips his head to the side. "Our girlfriend."

I fully intend to argue until Felicia texts. Duty calls. "Whatever. You and your death trap have our girlfriend home in twenty minutes."

After a quick forehead kiss, I leave the bar with one more girlfriend than I had upon arrival. A short drive back to the coffee shop to pick up Felicia and another to drop her off at the dorms concludes Date Night—a rather positive experience, all in all. Now, maybe someday, I'll experience one with Callie.

I beat them to the house, so I head upstairs for a shower. Shampoo streams directly into my eyes at the sound of someone coming into the bathroom.

"Don't say I never gave you anything," Benji says.

The door shuts. I wipe my eyes and poke my head around the shower curtain. "Uh, hi?"

Callie laughs. "Thank God. He said there was a fifty-fifty shot of it being Gavin in here. Three boyfriends sounded exhausting."

"Get your sexy ass in here, you difficult woman."

She complies with my demand, and we add another perfect way to end the day to the list.

We haven't even crawled out of bed in the morning when Callie's phone goes off. Lara's text says she and the douche-lord, Tyler, plan to go out of town for a few days. The question barely leaves her mouth before I agree to go with her for the weekend.

After our last classes, my bag goes in the car—well, my Jeep due to the superior sound system—and we drive the three hours to Waymore. Following a near catastrophe involving Cate's hair and scissors, we suffer through a movie night with Connor. His choice of genre is always horror. So much carnage. So much gore. He attempts to explain his fascination, but it remains lost on me.

Overnight, Cate miraculously transformed into a dog, so we spend most of Saturday leading her around on a leash. For a demanding little girl, she makes an even more taxing puppy. Supper needs to be eaten out of a bowl but not on the floor because that's, "Ew, Jordan."

Once I've taken our giggly canine on her evening walk, I take a shower. As I finish getting dressed, Callie appears in the doorway. She smiles at me through the mirror, clearly up to something. I drag the towel over my hair once more and drop it in the laundry basket.

"What do you want from me?" I ask.

She hesitates, chewing on her lip. "Pete's birthday party's tonight."

Since it's not a question, I don't answer and direct my full attention to the mirror, perfecting my hair. Her arms wrap around me from behind. The feel of her pressed up against me screws with my ability to think, but the seductress won't fool me.

"Not happening, beautiful. I'm not going to your ex-boyfriend's birthday party."

Her cheek rests on my back, and she walks her fingers down my chest to my stomach. "We can just make an appearance and leave as soon as you want to."

"I already want to leave, so no point in going."

"Don't you want to know more about who I used to be?"

I look up in thought. An all-access pass to Callie's life intrigues me but not enough to deal with her ex. "Nah."

She steps between me and the mirror, her crystal-blue eyes cast upward. I steel myself for her to pout. Now that she's shared her preferred tactic with Felicia, she won't catch me off guard with it anymore.

Only then her gaze drops to my crotch, her hand right behind it. She rubs my dick and peers up through her lashes. "Not even if we fool around in the Jeep on our way?"

Fuck.

Connor goes out with his friends, a neighbor agrees to watch Cate for a few hours, and—to no one's surprise—I drive us from Waymore to Sutterville. The trip takes longer with our pit stop on a gravel road to collect on Callie's promise. Well worth the potential awkwardness of the night.

Back roads weave us the rest of the way to Sutterville. Her left-turn-right-turns lead to a shabby house with a blue truck parked out front. A tightness creeps through my chest when I recognize the rust spot on the rear bumper. The truck from in front of the dorms.

"Is this Graham's house?"

"Cate's lived without her favorite book all week because she forgot it," she says, reaching for the handle.

Without thinking, I grab her hand. "She'll be fine until next weekend."

"In and out. Two minutes, tops."

It takes a second for me to let her go. The unease drops to my stomach the farther away she gets. She promised he's never laid a hand on her, but it doesn't matter. Physically or not, he's hurt her. Probably more than she'll ever admit.

She disappears inside, and I check the time. Two minutes. It's all I'm giving her.

About the minute mark, the screen door flies open and bangs against the side of the house. The outline of a man appears with the lights shining behind him. My fists clench the steering wheel until my knuckles turn white.

Graham. I watch the shadow over his face, wanting a better look at him to see if any of them resemble him. The possibility he shares Callie's eyes or, even worse, her smile, unnerves me.

He refuses to move aside, so Callie shoulders past him to get out. On the steps, she comes to an abrupt stop, her back to him. I roll my window down to spy—no, monitor.

"We're late," she says, not turning around.

"It only takes a minute to introduce me to your boyfriend." He's louder than the situation warrants, his gruff voice carrying a harsh edge. "Tell him to get in here."

"Not tonight."

"I'm not asking," he says.

She ignores him, walking down the steps.

"Callista," he shouts.

Callie flinches and ducks her head but continues across the grass. He backs inside and slams the door, the sound echoing off the surrounding houses. I have the Jeep in gear when she crawls in.

"We good?" I ask, driving off.

"Mission was a success." She tosses Cate's book in the backseat.

"And are *you* good?"

"I'm fine," she says.

At a stop sign, I study her to make sure she's my definition of fine and not hers. She catches me staring.

"Jordan, I'm okay. I promise."

More satisfied with this response, I bring her hand over and kiss her knuckles. "Then tell me where the hell I'm going."

She gives a real Callie smile and directs me toward Main Street, the encounter with Graham already forgotten. As it should be. He's not worth the mental energy.

The town of Sutterville—or village might be more accurate—has more dilapidated business buildings than functioning ones. A bar, grocery store, and post office along with an insurance business slash realtor make up the entirety of the main street. Even the school building sits isolated, long abandoned. That is why, when Callie instructs me to turn into a gravel parking lot near the desolate, three-story brick structure, I remember my fear of dying and no one ever recovering my body.

Callie grins as she pulls the sleeves of my hoodie that she's wearing down over her hands. "Are you up-to-date on your tetanus shot?"

I feign a laugh. "If this turns into one of Connor's horror movies, then we're both dead, considering what you let me do to you in the backseat."

She ignores me and gives me a history lesson. "Sutterville and Waymore consolidated schools a few years ago. The school we went to before sits a mile that way off the highway." She waves off in a general direction. "This place hasn't been used for anything but parties since the nineties."

Our phone flashlights light up a path worn through the grass, leading us around back. We pass a tall metal swing set standing next to a broken-down seesaw and wooden merry-go-round. Dead weeds stick up through the out-of-commission playground equipment. An old fire escape slide connects to the red brick on the third floor. Most of the windows have been boarded up, but a few maintain a pane or two of the original glass. Through one on the second story, a light flickers.

At first, I assume we'll use the metal fire escape stairs until I notice half of them are missing. Callie marches up to a large board, wrinkling her nose as she tugs on it. The gentleman in me bounds over to help my woman break into Murder Academy. Her wrinkled nose is undoubtedly in response to the rotting wood smell. I wonder if anyone brought hand sanitizer.

We move the board far enough to slip through the opening and close the hole behind us. Desks, chalkboards, cabinets, and chairs litter the large open room we step into. Dust, cobwebs, and whatever else nature and rodents have left behind over the years cover everything. I expect a red ball to roll across the floor and a creepy ghost girl to chase after it, laughing, or a tricycle to squeak its way through.

"Are you coming?" Callie asks.

She's too far away from me. So, not wanting to be alone and the first one picked off, I chase her down. She shrieks when I crash into her, making a ghoulish sound. My lips find hers long enough to remind me why I voluntarily entered this forsaken place—I would follow the girl straight into a volcano.

We wander up crumbling concrete steps to the second floor. Gray metal lockers line one side of the hall, gaps left for doorways. On the other side is, what I hope, a nonfunctioning drinking fountain along with the restrooms.

Muffled music floats down the hall, leading us to room two-oh-seven, Mrs. Alcott, fifth grade. Callie secures the handle. "Ready to become a part of Callista's world?" she asks.

I tuck a loose strand from her messy bun behind her ear. "It's all Callie's world to me."

She smiles and throws open the door.

"Henders!"

Some guy with an unmarked bottle barrels toward us. He lowers his shoulder and plows into Callie. He drives her back a few steps before stopping and straightening up. A hand slides over the top of his head, pulling off a black stocking cap to reveal short auburn hair. With a wild grin and glassy eyes, he plucks a cigarette from behind his ear and lights it.

Callie latches on to my arm with both hands. "Jordan, this is Tony."

He blows smoke out of his nose. "Well, he's the guy, huh?"

"I'm starting to get the impression she's talked about me quite a bit," I say, ignoring the death glare from Callie.

Tony laughs. "You have no idea, dude. Welcome." He extends his arms and does a quarter turn. "Everything the light touches is our domain. Fire barrel in the middle for warmth and the burning of shit if you feel so inclined. Beer and an assortment of adult beverages in the red coolers." He rotates around, patting his shirt pocket. "And right here, the green if you're keen."

I nod, catching his drift. "Thanks, man."

Callie shakes her head. "Where's the birthday boy?"

She no more than finishes her question when the dozen or so people standing by the burning barrel part. Shadows from the fire dance on his face, but the closer he comes, the more I recognize him. If I still questioned his identity at all, the light in his eyes when he spots Callie verifies him as the all-American boy from the prom pictures.

His J. Crew smile grows, and he hugs her, lifting her feet off the ground. She hugs his neck, and for the first time, a jealous needle pricks at my skin. Pete—the first of a lot of things.

He sets Callie down, turning his attention on me. The lovey-dovey expression fades, and he rubs the back of his neck. "Sorry. I'm Pete. You must be Jordan."

I shake his hand when he offers it. I don't want to be that guy, but I size him up. At an inch or so shorter than me, he hints at a vague awkwardness in his own skin. Callouses on his hands remind me of both Trey and Callie mentioning a farm his grandparents own.

"Happy birthday," I say.

He perks up again. "Ah, thanks. But really, we're just using it as an excuse to party."

Callie juts her chin toward the coolers. "Anyone splurge for something other than Pabst?"

"Cal," he says, "come on. We're not amateurs."

He calls her Cal. Bring on another stab of discontentment in my gut. It shouldn't affect me this way. Callie handled Brooke with such ease. She lived a life before me, and I one before her. But, damn it, I hate how well he knows her—all of her, from both the past and present.

Callie laces her fingers through mine as all three of us head over to Tony and his mystery bottle. A squealing Shayna pops up from somewhere. She jumps on her way over, her cheeks red and eyes bloodshot. She seizes hold of Callie and sways her from side to side. Then she moves on to me, giving me a more enthusiastic hug than I'm prepared for with no end in sight.

"A little help?"

Callie laughs, prying her off me. "Shay, hands off."

"You shared better when we were kids." She pretends to pout.

Tony passes around his bottle, which only stays a mystery until it burns down my throat. Moonshine. No wonder they all look wrecked. We huddle around the fire, switching to beer after a second circuit of the bottle. Each of them is foaming at the mouth to tell a Callie story.

Tony raises his hands, fingers spread out on the hand not clutching his bottle. "Best Henders story ever is the night we stole—"

"Borrowed," Callie interrupts, clearly knowing where he's going.

He grins. "The night we *borrowed* the tractor from the Davis farm. We woke up twenty feet in the air in the loader, two counties over. We had to scale the motherfucking hydraulic arms to get down. But the worst part was driving the son of a bitch back."

"Hungover," she adds.

He raises his bottle to Callie. "The price we paid for a good time."

"I have one," Shayna says. "We were in my car on a dirt road during a freak rainstorm and slid off in the ditch. After ten minutes of throwing mud everywhere, Henders decided to walk. We took turns carrying each other for over a mile until we found a house. The mud was sucking us in, and my flip-flops broke. Worst drunken experience ever."

"My story tops everyone's." Pete smiles at her. "Trey had a trampoline in the backyard at his dad's. Every time it snowed, Kevin would plow the snow into a pile next to it. Cal—in her infinite drunk wisdom—decided we should jump off the roof onto the trampoline, bounce, and land in the snow pile."

"Pete, please don't." Callie buries her face in my chest.

"Pete, please do." I wrap my arms around her.

She looks up, and I wink, making her eyes narrow. This wild and crazy part of her life fascinates me. Not that I ever want a firsthand experience or anything. I just love learning more about her.

"So," Pete continues, "she insists on going first, and we're all on the roof. Trey's doing his whining thing. '*Caaaal, this isn't saaaafe.*' She grins. Winks. And jumps. She bounces straight over the pile and hits the ground on the other side."

Everyone laughs, except Callie, who's still hiding.

"I thought I broke my ass," she mumbles against my chest.

I kiss the top of her head.

Not all their stories involve her being drunk—a lot but not all. One time, she organized a walkout at the high school when they increased the price on the soda machines. She stole the key for the concession stand candy, forcing the faculty to break into the cabinet, only to find an IOU note. School let out early after she freed an entire petting zoo's worth of animals during an assembly.

By the time she declares story time over, she clearly regrets ever letting them start.

Unlike the others, Callie and I pace ourselves, staying away from the bottle after the first few drinks. But being semi-sober doesn't lessen the shot of panic when a siren blares. The classroom door kicks open. A frenzy of bodies and yelling follows. A flashlight shines in our eyes and temporarily blinds us.

"Everyone's under arrest," a voice blares through a megaphone. "For being a bunch of assholes."

The light shuts off, and groans from every corner greet Trey as he strolls in with a smirk. Tony rushes him, knocking him into a chalkboard hanging on the wall. They wrestle around until Trey rolls his way over to the center of the room. He grabs on to Callie to pull himself up.

"Hey," he says casually. "How's everyone doin' tonight?"

Unimpressed by his entrance, she pushes him away. His arm locks around her head, tucking her face into his armpit. She struggles before he lets her go, and he nods to me. "Good to see you again."

"You too, man."

We engage in a bro half-hug. Now that I know the relation, the resemblance between him and Connor is obvious. A similar set to their eyes and square jaw.

Once their tight-knit inner circle assembles, all others in attendance fade to the outskirts. Years of friendship have built bonds unaffected by Callie's recent absence. Trey, three years older, has been with her since she was born. As I knew, Pete came into the picture in preschool, over the years becoming best friends with Trey. In the fifth grade, Shayna moved to town, and Tony transferred in the next year.

We tour the school with Tony pointing out the more important sights. Most involve the places he hooked up with various girls. Every now and then, Trey and Pete give approving nods or interject their own experiences with the same girls. Small towns lead to a rather shallow dating pool, especially with a class size of twelve until the schools merged.

Fire-breathing moonshine over the barrel entertains everyone for a short time. Then Tony's sleeve catches on fire. Pete pours a beer on him to extinguish the flame.

He examines his singed sweatshirt. "Maybe we should move on to the sword-swallowing portion of the evening."

I laugh at his nonchalance about being on fire. "It might be safer."

"I have a better idea," Trey says.

He retrieves a spotlight from his cruiser and sets it up in the gym. It leads to a basketball game on a warped court with an underinflated kickball. Luckily, neither Pete nor Trey possesses the slightest athletic prowess because a drunk and stoned Tony makes for a shit ball player. My teammate giggles whenever he catches the ball.

At game point, I pivot to take the final shot, but a hand snaps out and knocks the ball away. The other three players are in front of me, so I spin around to see who owns the hand.

"Stick to lacrosse, Lover Boy," Connor says, retrieving the ball.

With a cocky grin, he shoots a three-pointer. His friends near the wooden bleachers cheer. Callie's friends surround him, all excited to see him. Except for Trey, none of them do very often it seems. They act as if he were their long-lost little brother, shaking him around and slapping him on the back. Someone—Tony—even tries to sneak him the moonshine.

Callie swipes away the bottle before it touches his lips. "What the hell do you think you're doing?"

He glances back at his friends. "Not drinking?"

The Cate in her comes out full force. She sets her jaw and places her hands on her hips. "No, Connor."

To keep from smiling, I bite my cheek. Any reaction from me lands me one angry girlfriend, but damn, she's adorable right now.

"Whatever." He heads for the door. "We're leaving anyway. You guys are lame."

A sputter of laughter from the rest of our group almost makes her lose her stern demeanor, but she maintains. "Go home and text me when you get there."

Once he and his friends walk out, most of her friends fall to the floor, cracking up. Trey's the only one brave enough to pop his hip out and mimic her.

She flips him off. "Don't make me kick your ass."

He drops into a wrestler's stance. "I'm ready for you this time."

Pete attacks him from behind and winks at Callie as they roll around on the floor. She slides her arms around me while watching them, and I kiss her temple, soothing another jab of jealousy. I'll never get used to that fucking feeling.

After a while, Connor texts Callie that he picked up Cate. He insists we not hurry home—probably because he has a girl over, but I don't say anything about it to Callie. With both of her siblings taken care of for the night, we agree to venture out to the notorious farm. Each of us grabs a cooler or speaker and slides down the fire escape. The ancient thing should pull away from the building or collapse, but we all land without cuts from rusty bolts or falling to our deaths.

An additional five miles in the middle of nowhere, we turn up a long driveway. An old two-story house with peeling paint sits nestled in the trees. A few outbuildings surround a gravel area where I park next to Trey's cruiser. He climbs out and hooks an arm around Callie's neck.

"Let's get this out of the way right now." He points to an oak by the house. "Don't try to climb that."

He gestures to a red barn in the other direction, but Callie cuts him off, "Let me guess. Don't crash into it."

He laughs and passes her off to me. We meet up with the others down a grassy hill near a small pond. Pete's lighting a bonfire between two tall dirt mounds. A few logs scattered around serve as seats for the rest of us. Callie hides her hands in the sleeves of the sweatshirt again. An excellent excuse to pull her onto my lap to keep her warm.

It doesn't take long for Pete and Tony to disappear. The roar of engines precedes them tearing around the barn on four-wheelers. They take turns ramping the dirt mounds and jumping over the fire. I no longer wonder how Callie wrecked one into the barn. Their group acts invincible when together.

As the night wears on, my guard remains up with Pete around. He stares at Callie as if she holds his world together. But her presence seems significant to each of her friends. At one time, they were all such a big part of each other's lives. They're enjoying a long-awaited reunion of sorts. I can't help but think the guys and I will be the same way in a few years.

Trey straddles a log next to me while I shamelessly watch Callie race Tony back and forth between the fire and barn. Whenever she gains the lead, Tony lunges for her, and she laughs, dodging him.

"She's different," Trey says. When I look, he has a protective look in his eye. "The last time I saw her, she scared me. It was like she'd been fighting this battle inside. I could see her slipping away. But that..."

She throws her arms up in victory, and Tony picks her up, spinning her around.

"That's Cal."

"Callie," I say.

He nods and shoots me a half-smile. "Maybe that's what's different. She's finally found a way to be both." He slaps me on the shoulder before running across the grass and tackling Tony to the ground.

His comment reminds me of the multiple universe theory. What would happen if any of the worlds collided? In a way, that's what happened to Callie. She spent months keeping these worlds separate. Family stayed on one side of the state, school on the other, and anything from her old life she could avoid, she did. It worked until Kevin and Trey walked into the dorms. Then Callista, Cal, and Callie all existed in the same space. All three versions of her struggling with one another and the expectations people held for each. But as Trey pointed out, Callie and Cal appear to have merged and displaced Callista altogether.

Jesus. I'm making my girlfriend sound like she suffers from split personalities. All Callie has done is figure out how to be herself in the midst of everyone's conflicting expectations. Some people work their whole lives to find that balance. Others spend their time in a state of elusion, doing whatever they can to avoid the expectations. I'm firmly in the latter category. For how much longer, I have no idea.

Callie lands in my lap, bringing me out of my philosophical hole. "Oh, hey," she says.

"Hey, beautiful."

She jingles a set of keys between us. "Want to go borrow Trey's cruiser?"

A wicked grin appears, and without giving me a chance to answer, she takes off.

"Shit," Trey shouts, pinpointing her direction. He feels for his keys and sprints off after her. "Caaaal, come on! Not agaaain."

Pete's impersonation of him was dead-on. She beats him to the vehicle. He dives through the open passenger window and pulls his feet in as she flips on the lights. The tires throw gravel behind them, and they speed toward a pasture.

By the time the fire dies out, Tony and Shayna have passed out under a mound of blankets in the rowboat by the pond. Pete is sleeping on a porch swing with his hood pulled over his face. The horizon shows the first signs of dawn, and Trey, Callie, and I climb on top of a hay bale with a perfect view. She sits back between my legs and rests her head on my shoulder. My arms tighten around her. The muted colors gain intensity, and the stars fade away in front of us. The moment eclipses everything prior, and everything in the future faces one hell of a bar to surpass. But with her, I have no doubt something will.

Sometimes, I have great ideas. Other times, they leave something to be desired. Inviting Callie to dinner with my parents without telling them is far from my best. But I figure we should rip off the Band-Aid. We're a month-and-a-half past our temporary setback period, and the more time I spend with her, the more I need. I have no intentions of ever letting her go anywhere.

Wait, then why the fuck am I about to introduce her to Carol? *Oh God.*

I rub my head on the way up the walkway. My other sweaty palm tightly clutches Callie's hand. She's in a sexy black dress that falls mid-thigh, heels, her hair up in a twist. How we made it to my parents' house without me jumping her, I'll never understand.

A smile from her distracts me from my stress-induced anxiety for a second. All warnings about my mother have gone unheeded since she appears way too fucking calm.

"Why aren't you freaking out?" I ask.

"Because they're just parents."

"You should freak out."

She adjusts the collar of my button-down. "I'll get right on that."

"Maybe we should reschedule," I say, foot tapping fiercely. "I mean, with the income tax deadline looming and all."

"Jordan, breathe."

She touches my arm, and I kiss her because I'm not going to not kiss her. But I get carried away, and by the time I ring the bell, I've felt her up enough to add having a semi to the ever-revolving list of problems in my brain.

Greta, the housekeeper, heaves open the heavy door. She hesitates, seeing two of us, but recovers with a smile and ushers us inside. I help Callie out of her coat and hand it to Greta along with mine.

"Your parents are in the sitting room with Dustin. Would you and Jess like a glass of wine?"

Fuck. I completely forgot about Jess.

Callie's eyes widen in shock, and I choke back a laugh. "Greta, this is my girlfriend, Callie. Why my mother would tell you her name was Jess, I have no idea."

Greta forces a smile. Exactly what they pay her to do in awkward situations. "I'm sure I misheard her. Two glasses of wine?"

I nod, and she scurries down the hall. Callie crosses her arms and stares me down until I explain how I've been using Jess to torture my mother.

"No wonder they don't like you," she says.

I smile. She smiles. I feel better.

With that out of the way, we trek through the foyer, down the entrance hallway, hang a right at the kitchen to another hallway, take a water break, veer left at my father's den, and finally arrive at the formal sitting room. No two people need so much square footage, but no one told my parents.

In a final attempt to make her feel as off-balance as I do, I slap Callie's ass on our way in. She never even flinches. The bulging eyes of everyone as we enter the room, however, help me relax. Shock and awe. I'm in my element.

"Guess who I brought to dinner," I announce.

I'm daring my mother to call her Jess, but Carol rises from the sitting couch and glides over. She kisses my cheek. "Jordan, honey, please introduce us to your ... friend."

"Mom, Dad, Dustin, this is my girlfriend, Callie."

Carol's face pinches momentarily. "How lovely." She returns to her seat, flushed when my father struts over.

"Callie, please, join us for a drink." He guides her with a hand on her back to the seat next to Dustin, whose eyes I will gouge out if he doesn't keep them where they belong—i.e., not on my girl.

Callie thanks my father and turns on her charm. Within a minute of us sitting, my mother excuses herself from the room. I doubt we'll see her again until supper. She has the look on her face she usually does when she needs to "lie down."

Ray and Callie cover the basics before Dustin fills us in on his latest goings-on at school. He reminds me how much I missed out on by bailing on spring break. With our present company, he sticks to code words such as *tourists* and *scotch* rather than hookers and blow.

Just as Greta informs us dinner's ready, my mother conveniently resurfaces. We make it most of the way through the main course before she pats her napkin over her mouth and clears her throat. I brace for whatever she's preparing to say.

"Callie, is it?"

My fists clench under the table, but Callie smiles. "Mmhmm."

"We should have your parents over for dinner sometime next week."

"Thank you," she says. "But my parents are divorced and best kept several miles apart."

Ray and Dustin chuckle, and I relax. She knows how to hold her own.

"Separately then," Carol says, her tone shorter than before.

"That won't be necessary. But you and I should get lunch the next time you visit Jordan."

Point to Henders.

Carol laughs condescendingly. "Well, we aren't planning on visiting for a while, so we'll see where you two are by then."

Picking up on the thinly veiled insult about us not lasting, Callie fires back without missing a beat. "Of course. We'll be sure to let you know when we plan our trip before school starts in the fall. I'd hate for us to miss you."

Damn does Carol's face pinch at the sound of a trip invented on the spot.

Callie winks at me, sipping her wine, and that's it. Blow the horns, cue the chorus, and whatever the hell else is supposed to happen at this moment because I fall in love. Well, I finish falling in love. The whole process started months earlier with me in a towel and a thong.

Ray picks up the conversation, educating Callie on sailing. It leaves Carol quiet and provides me ample time to reel over how much I love the girl in a red coat. Needless to say, it also means I overthink the entire situation and talk myself out of telling her until I better gauge the potential reaction. One thing unchanged throughout our relationship is Callie's tendency to respond in the exact opposite way to how I expect.

My distraction proves a massive hindrance when, during dessert, the conversation somehow shifts over to me attending law school.

"Dad, let's go smoke a cigar," I say in a vain attempt to stop a boulder already gaining speed down a fucking mountain.

"We've been talking, honey." Something Carol always says when she's talked, and Ray failed to disagree. "We think you should attend a school out of state."

"Think or decided?"

She gives a soft smile. "We strongly suggest."

My patience for my mother runs out in record time. "What if I strongly suggest I not go to law school at all?"

Dustin chokes on his wine. Honestly, he should refrain from drinking beverages anytime the discussion centers on law school and me. His eyes widen, as he's more than likely urging me to cease and desist.

"What would you do as an alternative?" Ray asks.

Shit. The plan Dustin mentioned that I never thought about again would come in handy right now.

"I'm working on that."

Carol shakes her head. "No."

"Carol," Ray says, "we can talk about this."

"No." She throws her napkin down on her plate. "Jordan will attend law school, and he will do so at a university of our choosing."

Uh, fuck no.

"So now you not only dictate what I do but where I do it?" I don't let them answer. "What's wrong with UPenn? It's good enough for Dustin."

"Dustin shows good judgment."

I scoff. "Wool over the eyes much, Mother?"

"Dude." Dustin straightens up in his chair.

"Sorry," I say. I don't want to set him on fire to save myself.

Ray wipes his mouth, having just finished his cherry torte. "This is a discussion for another time, but I think we would be open to a compromise."

"There will be no discussion. You will choose an out-of-state school or be on your own next year." Carol pushes her chair back. "Now, if you'll excuse me, I need to go lie down."

"Perfect." I toss my napkin on the table to match her dramatics. "Then I'll be on my own."

An exasperated sound accompanies Carol's grand exit. Only now remembering Callie in the room, I glance over. She has set her jaw and won't look at me. Round one with the overbearing mother ends, only for round two with the irritated girlfriend to begin.

Great.

We all sit quietly for a minute before Dustin and Ray begin discussing a story from *The New Yorker*. I excuse us, saying I want to show Callie the rest of the house. Ray tells us to join them when we're finished, and we'll have that cigar I asked about earlier and a brandy.

I lead Callie out the French doors in the sitting room and across the back lawn.

"Where are we going?"

"My room," I say, sorting through my keys for the one to the carriage house.

I hit the lights on our way inside. Callie's eyes dart around, taking in the eclectic mess of High School Jordan. A pile of lacrosse gear still in a corner, a few guitars scattered, a Buddha statue, concert memorabilia, books and books and more books.

When her gaze settles on me, I step toward her. "Why are you mad?"

"Really, I don't want to get into it here."

I gesture around to the most private place we have been in together for quite a while. Other than the car or the rare occasions everyone leaves the house or dorm at the same time, someone is always lurking around a corner.

"If you want to yell at me, this is a prime location."

"Don't be cute," she snaps.

"Impossible," I say. "So, will you please tell me why you're mad?"

"Why won't you consider going to school out of state?"

Oh shit, fight started.

"Why should I have to?"

"Jordan, do you realize how many people would kill to have someone pay for them to go to school? Not only that, but to essentially have a guaranteed high-paying job when they finish?"

"Do *you* realize how many people hate their lives because they're miserable in their careers?"

She narrows her eyes. "Is that *your* reason?"

We're going nowhere, answering questions with more questions, so I concede. "My mother only wants me to go out of state to separate me from you. Well, originally, Jess, but the point remains the same. If I didn't have a girlfriend, she wouldn't care where I went to school."

"What if you didn't have a girlfriend? Would you consider it then?"

I sigh, not liking the direction she's heading. "I don't even want to go to law school, so this entire conversation is irrelevant."

She drops her head back, frustrated. "Fine, ignore the law school aspect. What if your parents offered to pay for grad school for whatever you wanted—music, philosophy, bull riding—the only stipulation being you pick anywhere other than Pennsylvania? What would you say?"

"Would the only reason they want me out of Pennsylvania be to put distance between us?"

"Don't factor me into the decision."

I massage my forehead. What-ifs almost destroyed my chances of being with her once. I'm not letting it happen again. "Callie, this is ridiculous. We're fighting about a made-up scenario."

"I don't want you to base decisions on me and end up trapped with me, Jordan. Even if you decide not to go to law school, you can go anywhere. Do anything. I can't. I'm here for the duration, and I won't be a reason you stay."

"What are you talking about? In a few months, you turn nineteen and then—"

"Then what? Connor and Cate magically stop needing me? My responsibilities miraculously go away?" She almost pauses long enough for me to respond. "The day after my birthday brings the same set of shitty circumstances. My reality stays unaltered. Nothing changes just because of some pointless date circled on a calendar."

"How long will you put your life on hold then, Callie? Do you plan on driving there every weekend for the next twelve years to babysit?"

I immediately regret my choice of words. I have reason to, judging by her reaction.

She laughs, dragging her hands down her face. "Babysit? I forge permission slips and give safe sex talks to teenagers. I call Connor in sick to school when he stays awake all night, worrying about things out of his control. I miss class to comb lice out of Cate's hair because Lara has bailed so that she won't get them. I sell my stuff to buy cleats and book bags and sometimes their food."

"But you shouldn't be doing any of these things. You're their sister, not their parent."

She sighs and folds her arms over her chest. "You don't get it. They don't have parents. They have Lara living out a drunken, sorority-girl fantasy, chained down by the kids she never wanted. And Graham who, on some weekends, refuses to talk to any of us. But others, he screams at Connor for shutting his door too hard. Or at me for looking too much like Lara."

I move closer. "Callie—"

"No." She steps back, maintaining the space between us. "You need to understand what happens behind the curtains. Connor hates Graham more than I do. I'm terrified of what it's doing to him. And what will it do to Cate in a few years? I can't let them go through what I did, let them lose themselves. I just can't."

She chews on her lip, staring up at the ceiling, and I stand here, feeling like a complete asshole as she blinks away tears. Not once have I seen Callie close to crying, and it makes me feel worse than I thought possible.

"This is my life," she continues. "It will be for a long time. I can't escape it or avoid it, and even if I could, I wouldn't. I'm all they have, and I'll never take that away from them." She looks at me again. "But this isn't your life, Jordan, and I don't want it to be, because if you make stupid decisions for me, then one day..." The tears spill over, one after another. "One day, you'll look at me the way Graham does, and the thought of that ever happening kills me."

As if I could ever see her as anything other than the amazing, beautiful, world-changing girl in front of me.

When I start toward her again, she puts her hands up to stop me. "What are you doing?"

"I'm going to kiss you."

She swipes away the tears. "You can't just kiss me to end a fight."

"You can go back to yelling right after, I promise." I inch forward. Maybe she won't notice if I move slow enough.

"I hate when you do that," she says.

"Do what?"

"That thing where you frustrate me and then say or do something..." She takes a deep breath, never finishing her thought. "Promise you won't stay for me, Jordan."

"Don't tell me what to do, Callie."

Only two steps separate us, and I take them both, unable to tolerate the distance any longer. Before she backs up, I pull her into my arms and wipe away the last tear with my thumb. "I'm going to kiss you now, but it's not to end our fight. I'm going to kiss you because I…"

She sucks in a breath, dread filling her eyes. As badly as I want to tell her how in love with her I am, she's not ready to hear it yet. I brush my thumb over her cheek.

"I'm going to kiss you because I'm Jordan, and you're Callie. And that's more than enough reason to kiss you."

She lifts her chin to look at me, resting her hands on my arms. "Frustrating and perfect."

I kiss her forehead and the tip of her nose, and then I press my lips to hers. Her arms wrap around my neck, and I pull back far enough to see her eyes.

"You never have to worry about me, beautiful. All the stupid decisions I make in my life will be no one's fault but my own."

She raises her eyebrows. "Wait, how many do you plan on making?"

"Oh, we're talking about a lot of them." I sway her back and forth. "But the last stupid decision I made turned out pretty great actually."

"What was that one?"

"I chased a girl who wanted nothing to do with me. Now she finds me irresistible and wants me to rail her in my high school bedroom."

She smiles, and just like the last time, I kiss her because I love her and for no other reason. It's just an added benefit that she never resumes her yelling.

After doing exactly what Callie wanted in my room, we track down Dustin and Ray, puffing on their Cubans in the study. As soon as Callie sits on the leather sofa in front of the fire, Dustin makes himself comfortable next to her. With his arm around her, he grins, challenging me to do anything about it. Of course, Callie takes care of that for me when she notices him checking out her tits.

She grasps his chin, rotating it away from her. "Eyes to yourself."

One of his eyebrows shoots up. "If you weren't dating my brother, I'd consider that a challenge."

Been there, done that.

"Well," I tell him, "she is, so don't."

Ray calls me over to show me his newly acquired humidor. He explains at length the importance of humidity control and tobacco, but to me, it remains a fancy box for cigars.

After a few minutes, he stops mid-sentence. "You don't care about this. But I wonder what you'll think about…" He scans his bookshelf with a finger and stops, tapping on the binding of one before pulling it out. "Here."

My jaw drops when he hands me the old book. The binding worn but intact. A gold leaf design decorating the front. "A first edition of *The Gay Science*?"

"He's one of yours, right? Friedrich Nietzsche?"

I nod fervently.

"*'Whither is God?' he cried…*"

"*'I will tell you. We have killed him—you and I,'*" I say, finishing the quote and gently thumbing through the pages. "This is incredible."

"You should see your face right now."

I can imagine. My eyes are drying out from how wide they're stretched, and my mouth refuses to stay shut. Terrified I'll somehow trip over a rug, juggle the book in an attempt to catch it, and land an easy ten grand in the fire on the other side of the room, I hand it back.

"You really have a passion for this," Ray says. "What's so compelling to you?"

"Have you ever found something that just shed light on everything else? It's like all these possibilities and experiences have always existed. You just can't see them until you uncover that one small piece that makes them visible. But, once you do, everything takes on a clearer meaning." I look over when Callie laughs on the couch. "That's kind of how it feels."

He places the book back on the shelf. "What do you say we have dinner next month and discuss alternatives to law school?"

Eyes and mouth gape again. "I would say, does my father know you've been posing as him for the last several minutes, you handsome devil?"

"I might not be so handsome after I tell your mother."

I hate to press my luck with him having bent more in the last thirty seconds than in the past twenty-one-years, but I have to ask, "What about going to school out of state just to complicate my relationship?"

He gives a thoughtful glance to the girl on the couch. "Let's figure out what you want to do and then choose the best place for that to happen."

I surprise both of us when I throw my arms around him, but after a second, he embraces me back.

"Mom looks like she has a wicked uppercut. Be prepared."

He laughs, slapping me on the back. "Good lookin' out, son."

We stay for a glass of brandy, both Ray and Dustin taking a genuine liking to Callie. Who can blame them? She hugs them goodbye as I go upstairs. I knock on my parents' bedroom and let myself in when no one answers.

Mother's in a dramatic pose, sprawled across the bed with her arm draped over her face.

"Callie and I are leaving," I say.

She doesn't respond. I want to tell her how much I love Callie and that she makes me a better person, and if she gives her a chance, she'll understand.

Instead, I sigh and squeeze her shoulder. "Bye, Mom."

Callie and I cross the stone driveway to my Jeep. We only make it halfway before I lift her up and spin her around. She giggles when I set her down. I kiss her and start a list of all the places I want to take her. Because one trip at the end of summer will not be enough.

The weekend ahead of finals, Beta Void plays our last performance for the school year at a small venue twenty minutes away from

State. Over the summer, we'll sprinkle in a few shows, but everyone will work, leaving little time to practice.

My internship with Stan will start mid-June, the week following the LSAT. Until then, a substantial portion of my time will focus on studying for it. Dinner with my parents in the middle of May to discuss my future won't deter me from taking the test to beat Dustin's score. And I will beat Dustin's score.

We finish up our last song and pack up our gear. Gavin walks off the stage with the last of the equipment, leaving Rusty, Benji, and me to decide on a plan for the rest of the night. Either we drive back or hang out until last call and go home in the morning.

Rusty, being Rusty, wants to base his vote on the available females. He and Jess sometimes see each other, but as long as they have an understanding, I don't concern myself.

I help him scope out the talent when a brunette at the bar catches my eye. I squint through the club lights. Even though they're dim and colored and move around a lot, making it difficult to spot all the most defining features of her face, everything about her resembles Callie.

I nudge Benji. "Is that our girlfriend standing by the bar?"

Both he and Rusty look over the mass of people to where she sips her mixed drink through a straw. A tall, built blond with a backward baseball cap secures his arms around her from behind. He nuzzles her neck, and she leans back against his chest. My stomach should sink, or my heart should stop, or my world should shatter, but I just watch it happen because none of this makes sense. Callie knows where we were playing, so what the fuck is she doing?

"Son of a fucking bitch," Rusty says. "It's that motherfucker from the party."

"That's Tyler?"

My eyes dart between Rusty, the dude, and … Lara?

She drags a hand through her hair and tosses it over her shoulder. Something I've never seen Callie do. More than once, she's mentioned she looks as much like her mother as Cate looks like her, but I've never seen her or a picture to confirm. From a distance, the similarities are astounding.

Benji's hand grips the front of my shirt, redirecting my focus to Rusty. He's off the stage, his intentions clear as he practically throws people out of his way on a path leading straight toward Tyler.

Fuck.

We jump down and shove our way through the crowd to intercept him before he reaches the bar. Benji and I manage to get in front of him and bring him to a halt, but with the vein in his forehead visible, I doubt we'll hold him off long.

Gavin catches up with us then, and Benji points out Tyler. He charges forward, and Benji has to stop him as well, pushing him back with a hand on the chest.

Benji glances over his shoulder. "Dude, that's not Calico with him."

"No, it's her fucking mom," I say, trying to keep my cool.

"I don't give a fuck who's with him." Rusty's murderous eyes stay on his target behind me. "He only survived last time because of Callie. I didn't want to scare her more than he already had by pinning her to a fucking wall."

I blow out a breath, all the rage surfacing at the thought of him hurting her. Scaring her. Fuck. *Biting* her.

"He said they were just talking even though Rusty dragged him off her." Benji drops his hand from Gavin's chest. "Her hands were shaking, and she could barely talk. But with all the shit in her life, man, she repeated his words."

Then he shakes his head and aligns himself with the other two, facing the bar. They're all in front of me, ready to defend Callie. To finally show one of these worthless people in her life the consequences of their actions.

"What's the word, Waters?" Gavin asks. "We charging in and taking out this piece of shit?"

"Absolutely not." I turn around and let myself look at Tyler. "We can't charge in because we need to make him swing first."

Rusty slaps a hand on my shoulder, smirking. "All I want is a beer, dude."

Right behind Tyler, where he won't notice them, Rusty and Benji approach the bar. Since he doesn't know us, Gavin and I go to the other side of Lara. I can't focus on him without losing it, so while we wait for the bartender, I study her. I search for every possible difference between her and Callie. The closer I look, the more I find.

Lara's clothes look like she raided Callie's high school wardrobe. A revealing top and giant holes in her jeans expose too much of her skin. Her lips are more unbalanced, a crease appears below each eye, she wears way more makeup, the ends of her hair are split, and a cheap flowery smell wafts off her.

Most importantly, with Callie, I gain a sense of completion, and being around Lara makes me nauseous.

She winks at me. Fucking winks. I almost lose my shit. I want to scream at her and shake some sense into her. How can she think she belongs in this bar, flirting with a college guy? She should be at home with her kids, apologizing to them for the hell she put them through and fixing what she and Graham have done over the years.

My face must give away how close I am to the edge because Gavin's hand grips my shoulder.

"Chill, tiger. Let Rustin work his asshole magic."

On the other side, Benji rubs his chin, his impatience unmissable. He meets my gaze, one eyebrow cocking to confirm my current state. Ready to rip this guy's head off is my response, but before I figure out a gesture to convey this, Rusty flags down the bartender.

He orders us a round and gestures to Tyler and Lara. "And whatever these two are having."

Tyler turns to thank him but never gets that far.

Knowing he recognizes them, Rusty and Benji smirk in unison. They consider a slow buildup a part of the fun in a fight.

"Let's go, babe." Tyler grabs Lara by the elbow.

"No," she says, her voice higher than Callie's. "I want to stay and get to know our new friends."

"Yeah, Tyler," Benji says. "Stay. Get to know us."

"Babe, introduce me." Lara laughs—far from a Callie laugh— and nudges Tyler. "How do you know each other?"

The muscles in his jaw tighten.

Rusty extends a hand to her. "Tyler and I go way back. What was it, almost two months ago, when I pulled you off a girl you were about to rape at that party?"

Lara falls silent, her giddy expression gone as she jerks her hand away. Her eyes dart to Tyler. "Ty?"

He clicks his tongue, peering over at Gavin and me, realizing we're all together. His head turns toward Rusty and Benji and back to us. A smirk forms on his pathetic, drunken face.

Then, he fucking swings.

We wait for Rusty, the last of us they release. He strolls away from the cops, wearing a smug grin despite his split lip. The final car's lights shut off, and they drive away.

Against the side of a brick building, each of us takes an inventory of our injuries. All in all, we walked away fairly unscathed, considering the mayhem after Tyler threw his first punch. State kids don't need a reason to fight. They just want in on the action. The few dozen extra people who involved themselves helped immensely when the cops showed up and had to sort through everyone.

Benji transforms into a mother hen, poking at my eye. "Good thing we don't have any more gigs for a while, man."

"Ow." I pull my head away from him. A sore hand and black eye are well worth the hits I got in on Tyler. Specifically hit jaw. Hell, I could have broken my hand and not cared.

"Ladies dig battle wounds, right?" He winces as his fingers probe at the cut on his cheek.

Rusty wipes the back of his knuckles on his jeans, removing the blood. "Did you see Callie's mom and that asshole screaming at each other a little bit ago?"

"She ran off to her car after slapping him," Benji says.

"What did you say when you had him on the ground, Rusty?" Gavin asks, pinching the bridge of his nose where a random fist landed.

"I told him he needed to find a new girlfriend. From the looks of it, he listened."

Benji bursts out laughing, which sends Gavin off into a giggling fit with Rusty and me not far behind. Of all the times we've shared the last few years, none have made me feel closer to them. The three lads defended the woman I loved without hesitation. They always will. I couldn't ask more than that.

I check the time on my phone. "It's one-thirty. Food?"

Everyone grunts what I assume is a yes. Benji and I take my Jeep and meet the other two with the van at a twenty-four-hour diner. An array of breakfast foods covers our table when Callie's face lights up my phone screen.

I smile and answer, "Hey, beautiful, we might have—"

"Jordan?"

My stomach ties itself into a fucking knot worthy of a Boy Scout's badge. "Connor?" Gavin hits the ground when I shove him out of the booth. I step over him on my way to the door. "What's wrong?"

"Mom just kicked Cal out," Connor says.

"What?" I unlock my Jeep from across the parking lot, ignoring Rusty chasing after me.

"She came home drunk, dragged Cal outside, and took her house key off the key ring before throwing it at her. Then she locked her out. She's rambling about Tyler dumping her and how it's all Cal's fault. Something about her friends—hold on." A rustle comes through the speaker. "You're okay. Come here, my little monster."

"I want Cal." Cate's quiet in the background.

"We'll see her tomorrow," he tells her.

"But what if she doesn't have a blanket?"

"She does. We're all safe."

"Promise?"

"Promise." The speaker crackles again. "Jordan, you still there?"

"What does Callie have other than her keys?" I pull out of the parking lot, not caring that Benji's trying to call me. "Bag? ID? Anything?"

"No. I thought she'd go to Trey's, but he isn't answering his phone. She doesn't have anyone else's number from here saved. I don't know what else to do."

Shit.

She wouldn't go to Graham's under any circumstances. Without ID or money, she wouldn't chance driving back to campus or be able to check into a hotel. She'd find someone who understands her middle-of-the-night eviction.

"I'm a little over an hour away," I say. "I'll find her."

"Did you have something to do with Tyler?"

I hesitate to answer. Lara threw Callie out because of what I had done, but for the life of me, I can't make myself feel guilty. In fact, I'd do it again with a few small tweaks to produce a more favorable outcome.

"I'll call you when I get to Sutterville."

"Jordan," he says, his voice cracking.

"Yeah, man."

Silence, and then he lets out a breath. "Thank you."

I follow Connor's directions to Trey's house on a dead-end road. The only thing on the paved driveway is an oil stain. No lights appear through the windows on either story. Other than a dog behind the fence outside, there are no signs of life.

I make a U-turn and head toward Main Street. As I drive past the gravel parking lot behind the bar, I spot Callie's car. I tell Connor I'll call him back. The rear door sits slightly ajar with light and music streaming out two hours after last call. I walk around a newer extended cab truck parked near the building, the only other vehicle in sight, and go inside.

Empty cardboard boxes litter the floor of a long hallway. I weave around them, pass a dark kitchen, and head through a swinging door. Neither Callie nor Pete notices me at the end of the bar. He stands behind it, across from her on a stool. They laugh and clink shot glasses before knocking them back. She slides her glass toward him, and he fills it again.

"Next?" he asks.

"Summer before freshman year."

Pete's head tilts side to side like he's deliberating. "I didn't go to summer camp, and we stayed at the lake all summer long."

She holds up her glass. "But I still ended up dumping you because you hooked up with Gabby Sinclair behind the boat docks."

His glass stays on the bar. "Seriously, Cal? My first time has to be with Gabby? If I were going to cheat on you, I'd have found someone better than that."

"Fine." Her lips purse. "Tonya White?"

"Acceptable." He lifts his glass.

They clink, and they drink.

The interaction between them cues the jab of insecurity in my gut. I've seen enough of the show and step farther into the room as he pours them another. Wide eyes meet me at first, but then Callie beams and hops off the stool and runs over in shorts, a tank top, and the ugliest brown thermal socks in existence that stretch all the way up to her knees.

"What are you doing here?" She hugs me, and I kiss the top of her head.

"Connor called me on your phone."

"Oh my God, what happened?" She examines the red, not-yet-bruised area decorating my eye.

"Call your brother first, so he stops worrying."

She heads off to a secluded corner across the room with my phone, buying me time before I confess to my evening's activities. I settle on the stool in front of Pete and exchange a head nod with him.

"We're redoing our lives," he says, filling a third glass for me. "Every moment we wish we could change or take back. Then we see how everything would have turned out differently. Once we both agree, we drink."

Ready to play so I can drink, I give a tight-lipped smile. "My fight with Lara's boyfriend tonight didn't result in my girlfriend being kicked out."

He lets out an audible sigh and raises his glass. "But you still fought him, and I was right there with you, throwing punches."

We clink, and we drink.

Callie lands on a stool next to me and tosses back her shot. She sets her jaw and slams the empty glass down, turning to face me. I'm guessing she knows the reason behind her crazy Lara wake-up call. Her glare never wavers as Pete leaves the bottle of whiskey along with a bag of ice on top of the bar. Then, like a smart man, he disappears behind a curtain.

"So, I met Tyler and Lara tonight." At this point, I doubt it will do any good, but I set the ice over my eye anyway. Maybe it'll gain me a little sympathy.

"A bar fight?" she says. "Are you kidding me?"

"He swung first," I say in defense, pouring another shot.

"Unprovoked?"

I shake my head and fail to stop a grin.

"Damn it, Jordan." She covers her face with her hands. "He broke up with her because my friends are too much drama."

"Technically, he broke up with her because Rusty told him to."

She groans behind her hands. "Not any better."

"Sorry, I don't understand how this is a bad thing."

Her hands lower, so she can scowl at me. "She dragged me out of my bed and out of the house in the middle of the night. Cate was screaming, Connor didn't know what the hell he should do, and if Pete had finished cleaning up before I got here, I might still be driving around without socks on."

"How was I supposed to know any of that would happen?"

Since it doesn't help my cause, I toss down the ice. Once more, I attempt to summon guilt over the situation, but a night of drama still seems preferable to the constant worry of him laying his hands on her ever again. All I muster is agitation toward Lara's overreaction—and Callie's.

She stands up. "I can't deal with you right now."

The stool scrapes the floor as I jump up. I grab her arm to stop her from walking away. "What do you want me to do, Callie? Apologize? Because I won't."

"What I want is for you not to get in a fucking bar fight with Tyler in the first place," she shouts.

I stop even trying to hide my frustration. "Ship's already sailed on that one, beautiful. What else?"

"Don't for one second think you get to be upset with me for being mad at you." She rips her arm away from me. "How am I supposed to take care of Connor and Cate if she won't let me in the house?"

Un-fucking-believable.

"That's what you're worried about? This guy tried to sexually assault you. If not for Rusty, he might have…" I can't even say the word. I rake my hands through my hair and walk in a circle. How she puts her safety so far down the totem pole infuriates me. When I face her again, all the niceties have left my system. "He's out of your life, and I couldn't give a fuck about the rest."

Callie holds up her hands, backing away from me, and goes behind the bar. "I'm too angry for this," she says on her way through the curtain.

"Yeah, me too," I say to an empty room.

I sit back down and drain my shot glass, listening to creaking boards and footsteps. Callie's muffled voice starts yelling somewhere above me. It sounds like Pete shouts something back before a door slams. Heavier footsteps, more boards creaking, and the curtain flies open.

Visibly irritated, Pete swipes the whiskey off the bar. He drinks straight from the bottle and wipes his mouth on his arm. "She's gonna sleep upstairs in my apartment tonight."

"She kicked you out?"

"Yep." He takes another swig.

Mad at her or not, I smile. She's a force, and I fucking love her for it.

Pete grabs a beer mug off the counter behind him. "From what Trey said about that guy, you did what was best for Cal tonight."

"Then why am I sitting here with you while my girl's upstairs, pissed off?"

He shrugs and pours a beer. "Because you did what was best for Cal tonight."

"Right," I say. "Thanks for clearing that up."

As he leans against the bar, he slides the full mug over. "In the process of protecting her, you upset Cate and Connor. Twisted Cal logic makes you the bad guy. She thinks, instead of keeping her safe, you should have worried about how it might affect them."

If we're fighting any time I choose her over them, we'll fight a lot, and I might as well get used to it. I vowed to put her first and meant it. Someone in her life has to.

I scrub a hand over my face and yawn.

"If you need a place to crash tonight, I have two cots in the back we can set up."

"Believe it or not, it sounds better than my Jeep."

Pete locks up while I finish my beer. Each of us grabs a cot from the storage room along with a pillow and blanket and set them up on what serves as a dance floor up front, near the jukebox. All the overhead lights turn off, leaving the place lit with neon beer signs hanging on the walls among the animal heads. The shadows cast around the room are a mixture of creepy and cool as I settle in for my slumber party with my girlfriend's ex-boyfriend.

I led such a normal life at one point.

"She's worth the work, you know," Pete says from his cot.

I lock my fingers behind my head and stare up at the glowing purple ceiling. "I really do."

He sighs. "It would be a lot easier to hate you if you didn't."

Not only does Pete not bother me anymore, but I also have to admit that I can see myself liking the guy in the future.

Eventually.

How fucking annoying.

The sizzle and smell of bacon wakes me. In the light of day, the animal heads hanging above me fall solidly in the creepy category. I roll off the army cot and fold up the blanket.

Through the small window behind the bar, Pete's visible, cooking in the kitchen. After I put away my cot and bedding, he emerges through the swinging door.

He hands me a tray of food. "Beer and eggs."

"You work here, live here, cook here. Do you own the place, too?"

"My grandparents do," he says, popping the tops off two bottles. He adds them to the two plates of eggs, bacon, and toast and tosses a set of keys on the tray. "Let your groveling begin."

Goddamn it, he's officially made it impossible not to like him. "Thanks, man."

He shrugs. "She could do worse than you. Now go."

I walk through the curtain and up the stairs to the apartment at the end of the hall. The tray requires a balancing act to unlock the door. In the room, thick curtains block out most of the light, presenting another challenge, but I set everything down without dropping anything.

A giant open area holds the kitchen, living room, and the bedroom with two doors that I assume lead to a bathroom and closet. Callie is sleeping on top of the bed, curled up under a camouflage blanket. I crawl in and curl myself around her, wanting closeness to detract from our fight. She rolls over to face me. We stare at each other, neither of us willing to speak first.

Every road introduces an impasse of some kind. Frequently, I am willing to bend and often meet her more than halfway. Not this time though. She needs to live with the fact that I will choose her over everyone. In all honesty, I don't think I even have the option anymore.

An eternity passes before she sighs. "Pete will never get his place back at this rate."

"I'm sorry, Callie."

I press my lips to hers, then to her cheek, her forehead, and to her lips again. She kisses me back, which makes what I say next all the harder, knowing she will stop.

"But I'm not sorry for what we did."

As expected, she sits up to put distance between us. "Then what exactly are you sorry for?"

Round two commences.

"I'm sorry Lara threw you out because she's incapable of putting you and your safety first."

"You still don't get it, and I'm tired of explaining it to you. Connor and Cate need to come first, not me."

I sit up next to her, running a hand through my hair. "Maybe to you, but for me, it's you. It will always be you. You'll never convince me otherwise, so you might as well stop trying."

"What happens if—"

"No," I say, shaking my head. We aren't traveling down this inane what-if path ever again. "No hypotheticals. No asking what if the three of you are dangling off a cliff, and I can only save two of you. Or what if they need all of your organs for some insane reason that will never happen. We both know you want me to say I would choose them, but I wouldn't. I couldn't. And I don't want to lie to you, so just don't ask."

She stares at me, her expression unreadable.

"You have to tell me what you're thinking, beautiful. Because I feel like a heartless person for having just said that."

Her gaze drops to the comforter between us. "I'm thinking about how, without a doubt, I'd choose them in both scenarios."

Of course she would. I'd expect nothing else from her.

I tilt her chin up so she looks at me. "I won't make you feel guilty for that choice. Don't make me feel guilty for mine."

She sighs, defeated. "We'll never agree on this."

"Probably not."

"So, what do we do?"

I pull her into my arms and kiss her hair. "We go see Cate and Connor because you need to see them."

She settles back against my chest. "And they need to see me."

"And the stars align, and everyone gets what they need," I say with my lips brushing against her cheek. I swallow. "Callie, I—"

"Don't." She twists around to face me with wary eyes. "Not yet and especially not in Pete's bed."

She's right about our less than ideal location. Unless I end up blurting it out—always a possibility with me—I can survive a little while longer without telling her how much I love her.

"I guess that means other activities are off-limits in Pete's bed."

She lifts her eyebrows. "What did you have in mind?"

I whisper in her ear, "Breakfast."

***

Outside of Lara's house, Connor waits for us. Callie no more than climbs out of her car when he seizes hold, crushing her. A grunt encourages him to release her so that she can continue breathing.

He catches my eye and mouths, *Thank you.*

The door to the house flings open, and a screaming banshee in the form of Cate gallops toward us. Both her siblings tense at the sound and rush to quiet her.

"Shh," Callie says, picking her up. "We have to be quiet."

Cate kisses her forehead and holds her around her neck.

"She asleep in the basement?" Callie asks Connor.

"She passed out around five after destroying everything in the house that reminded her of Tyler."

"Everything?" I ask, concerned about the couch and TV.

"I saved anything of actual value." He grins. "Girls dig that couch too much. I couldn't let her take a knife to the cushions."

He watches for my reaction. I hold my hands up and shake my head, not going within a thousand damn feet of that comment. I want to leave with my body intact.

Callie ignores him and sets Cate down. "Well, let's go pack up my shit."

Pack up her shit we do. Still obsessed with everything Callie that I don't already know, I volunteer to deconstruct her photo wall. A distracted Cate spends more time playing dress-up than packing clothes, but it keeps her relatively quiet. A few garment bags from the closet we move to Connor's room for safekeeping. Everything else we place in boxes or a donation pile.

Once we load the Jeep, Callie goes inside one last time to double-check if we missed anything. She leaves me with Connor to coax Cate out of the back end. An awful idea. She keeps burrowing through the boxes. We can't catch her, but a squirrel succeeds where we fail when it darts past the vehicle. The second she vacates to chase after it, I shut all the doors and lock them, not wanting to chase her again.

"Nice shiner," Connor says. "You get any good hits in on Tyler?"

At least someone in this family responds appropriately.

I prop against the side of the Jeep. "Not nearly enough."

"I always wanted to fuck that guy up for the way he looked at Cal." He digs the toe of his shoe into the rocks on the driveway, oblivious to the other reasons he should have wanted to fuck Tyler up. "How mad was she?"

"Nothing I couldn't handle."

"Good." He pushes the rocks into a pile with his foot. "We like having you around, Lover Boy."

"Good," I say. "I plan on being around, kid."

Callie smiles on her way out.

"You ready to go, beautiful?"

She nods and hugs Connor goodbye. "I'll be back next weekend after finals. The rest we'll just have to figure out as we go."

He rolls his eyes. "Wow, Cal, you sure we can manage? We've never had to deal with any of their bullshit before."

She huffs, annoyed by his sarcasm. "Things were going to change anyway. We only have a few weeks until the summer schedule starts."

"Oh, joy. Can't fucking wait." He kicks through the pile of rocks, and they spray across the yard, pelting the house. Then he does it again, almost breaking out a window.

What the fuck is his problem?

"Connor," she shouts. "Knock it off."

I push off the Jeep when she grabs his arm. Something set him off, and given his reaction, she might need a hand.

He jerks away from her. "What do you care? It's not like you live here."

Without another word, he storms inside and slams the door behind him.

Callie's head falls back, and she groans before hiding her face in my chest. I stroke her hair and let her recover from his tantrum.

In all my time around him over the past few months, he's never lost his temper. He talks shit while we play video games and yells at the TV while watching sports, but nothing like this.

"He's becoming impossible," she says, pulling back. "They just keep pushing him. And he has all this anger now."

"I can take your stuff to Trey's if you want to stick around for a while."

Her lips press together as she looks at the house, deliberating. "No, he needs his space."

"Are you sure?"

Her smile doesn't reach her eyes anymore. Connor's not the only one Graham and Lara keep pushing.

"It's fine," she says. "Let's go find the monster."

We track down Cate in the neighbor's backyard. Per usual, she injures me as a going-away present when her teeth knock into my forehead while trying to kiss it. My greatest regret in life will be teaching her that move.

Over at Trey's house, Callie and I meet to unload boxes. Most of them are squished from the evasion attempts of a certain six-year-old. Callie overloads my arms with all the heavy boxes, unaware that Connor and I carried a few out one at a time. Naturally, I can't say anything and risk looking weak in front of my woman, so I persevere.

"What's the summer schedule?" I try sounding casual as my arm muscles strain.

"We spend a week at Lara's and then a week at Graham's. Well, they'll spend a week at Lara's." She opens the door and lets me into Trey's living room. "I guess I'll spend a week here."

I drop the boxes on the floor a few steps in. If she mentions anything about not taking them farther, I will feign ignorance. "You could spend a week with me and then a week at Graham's."

"I could if I didn't need to work this summer and save money."

I cock my head to the side. The schedule she lays out overlooks something I consider somewhat important. "What about us?"

"What do you mean?"

"When do we see each other? On the weekends you aren't at Graham's?"

"It's hard enough to get a summer job around here," she says, picking up a box. "Finding one that doesn't require working every weekend is almost impossible."

"Then when am I going to see you?"

She shrugs, not answering me further. I step in front of her when she tries walking away. I need her to clarify because she talks like, once she leaves after finals, she won't be back.

"Callie, when?"

"What do you want me to say, Jordan? That we won't see each other all summer?"

I almost hear the sound of my heart cracking open in my chest.

"I can't go all summer without you, beautiful."

She starts to respond, but Trey tromps down the stairs.

"Just let yourself in, Cal." On his way past, he slaps me in the chest. "Jordan, you look like she told you she's pregnant." He chuckles at his own joke, not acknowledging the intense stare between Callie and me.

As he grabs the box from her and disappears back upstairs, my mind scrambles to devise a plan because the alternative is not an option. I can take the LSAT in the fall instead of June and decline the internship with Stan.

Shit. Not working for Stan means the guys would need to pay rent next semester. But they'd understand.

A summer in Sutterville sounds like hell. Albeit hell with her still wins out over everything else. I'll need to keep my change in residency from the parental unit. Carol would full-on combust.

A sigh from Callie pulls me from my thoughts, and I refocus on her.

"Are you freaking out?" Her lips twitch, and is she fucking with me? "Pete's grandparents offered me a job at the bar, working during the week with weekends off." She picks up another box. "I planned on telling you last night, but for some reason, I never had the chance."

If I didn't love the girl so much, I would hate her. What happened to the preferred method of payback where she strips her clothes off in front of me? I miss those days.

"Screw you, Henders," I say.

I step toward her to retaliate for the uncalled-for punishment, but a shout from upstairs interrupts me. Trey barrels down the stairs. He shoves me aside and throws the box from Callie's hands to the ground. Clearly out of his mind, he grasps both sides of her face in his hands, his eyes full of dread.

"Fucking Christ, Cal, tell me you're not pregnant."

Even though she's on the pill, I have a moment of panic before I remember her cousin's fucking terrible joke neither of us paid any attention to.

Callie rolls her eyes and laughs. "With twins, Uncle Trey!"

The silence in the garage annoys me to no end. I nod along to the beat of my heart for the third time in the last—I don't know how long because Gavin and Benji removed all the time-keeping devices to help me focus on my practice test for the LSAT. They also confiscated all the cords for the guitars, Rusty's drumsticks and cymbals, everything from the fridge—except a bottle of water—and my shoestrings. The last one was entirely unnecessary, but Benji insisted after the third section of the test when he caught me playing with them.

At the end of week one, I can officially declare that summer sucks. A majority of the time, I spend studying or taking practice tests, during which I mostly space out. The rest, I prepare for dinner with my parents. A few potential plans have come together. None involve law school.

I haven't been in Callie's physical presence for seven days, and Jordan minus Callie times seven equals irritable plus distracted. The texts, phone calls, and video chats only get me so far. To make matters worse, instead of spending her Friday night with me as planned, she decided to attend a party at Felicia and Jess's house.

Who throws a housewarming party for a summer rental?

Frickin' Gibson.

Benji comes in. "Time's up, man."

I stare down at my writing sample, not a word on the page. Oh well, that section doesn't receive an actual score. "Phone?"

He tosses it over.

After ten. Callie promised to only stay at the party until midnight, so I need to occupy myself for another hour or so.

Or not.

"Want to go to Felicia's party?" I ask.

Afraid of my lack of concentration in anticipation of seeing Callie, Benji won't let me drive. Whatever. It means I can ride back with her. Plus, I need to restring my laces.

He parks in front of the house on Monroe Street. I resist the urge to run up to the porch. I even play it cool, letting Benji take the lead and go inside first. My impulse-control issues are a problem from the past I've valiantly overcome.

Jess meets us a few steps in the door. "Jordan?"

"Jess?" I mimic.

Her eyes stay on mine, wide and surprised. "What are you doing here?"

"I was invited?"

Even though she doesn't make me feel like a piece of eye candy for the first time since meeting her, she still needs to work out a few kinks in how she greets people.

"Right." She shakes her head. "Sorry, I just wasn't expecting you. Felicia said you were doing some practice test and weren't coming."

I nod, only half-listening because my fucking chest cavity constricts at the sight of Callie thirty feet away in the living room. A tight top and just as tight jeans and her hair down. She stops her conversation with whoever she's talking to and smiles. Damn, I already hate the thought of saying goodbye to her before I even say hello.

"There's something I've been needing to tell you," Jess says. "But I haven't—"

"Can you hold that thought, Jess?" I walk away without waiting for her response, my eyes never leaving Callie. Whatever she wants can wait while I attend to incredibly urgent business.

We meet in the middle of the room, and Callie leaps into my arms. Her legs lock around my waist, she holds my face in her hands, and her mouth crashes down on mine. Everything Callie floods my senses. Everything is right again.

"Hey," she says.

"Hey, beautiful." I stare into those eyes. A vague memory of a party happening around us surfaces, but no one else matters; they never will as long as she exists. "I kinda missed you," I say.

She kisses me again and not a sweet, I-missed-you-too kiss. The take-me-right-here kind. All tongues and moans, and now we've both forgotten the other people in the room. But man, do we give them a show.

"The two of you are making me nauseous," Benji says, prying Callie off me. He nudges her toward Felicia. "You take yours, and I'll take mine."

Felicia laughs and drags Callie away.

"Bye," she says, giving a longing look over her shoulder.

"Bye, beautiful."

We watch each other until Benji breaks my focus.

"Let's get Calico a drink, man. And maybe we'll have a chat about manners."

Reluctantly, I agree and follow him to the kitchen. He attempts to occupy me with a conversation about a new band he discovered. He's working at a local radio station for the summer and experiencing rock heaven. If he decides not to pursue a career as a professional guru, which has my vote, he can put his mass communications degree to good use as a radio DJ.

Felicia pushes through the swinging door. "Callie's whining, so you can go back in if you behave."

"Thanks, Gibs."

I waste no time in returning to the living room, even neglecting to take our drinks with me. Callie's on the far side, talking to someone. On my way over, I have every intention of acting like a gentleman. But by the time I reach her, my objectives change. My hands slip around her waist, and I bury my face in her neck. She steps back, so I go with her. My mouth is very devoted to making up for lost time.

She giggles, cute as fuck. "Jordan, stop."

Not a chance. In less than forty-one hours, my life will turn back into a pumpkin and stay that way for almost two weeks. I block out the unpleasant thought and move my hands to her ass, holding her tight against me.

"Sorry, Vee," she says to the person who needs to leave me alone with my girl. "My boyfriend's apparently an untrained animal." She presses her hand against my chest. "Jordan, I want you to meet Jess's sister."

I growl into her neck in response to her continued interruptions but stop. Maybe if I get the pleasantries out of the way, she'll let me feel her up. Her gaze meets mine when I straighten up, and I wink to let her know I'll be back.

"Jordan, this is Jess's older sister, Vee."

A fake grin appears on my face, and I turn around to meet … one of the last people I expected. A familiar pair of big brown eyes stares back and matches my level of disbelief.

Fuck.

The expression falls off my face, and I search for Jess. Is this what she was talking about earlier? Her equally big brown eyes watch the whole scene unfolding from across the room.

The eyes. I should have seen it in the eyes.

She grimaces and mouths, *Sorry.*

I could kill her.

"We've met," Vanessa says, bringing my attention back. "A few times actually. Over winter break."

Callie squints for a second, but then her eyes slowly widen. "Oh." It's short and cuts through me.

Then they both look to me. I wish Brooke would land in my lap because at least I know how that awkward situation plays out. This one, however, I can't even fathom. It's bad enough that I ghosted Vanessa when she showed too much interest, but now she just witnessed me maul my girlfriend—the one I swore to her I never wanted.

"Excuse me." Vanessa pushes past me and hurries up the stairs.

I peek at Callie, feeling the scowl hit the side of my face. "I think I need to have a little chat with Jess."

"Yep," she says, storming away.

Perfect.

Jess sees me coming and backs into the kitchen. Like that will save her. The swinging door almost levels Benji when I explode through. I stop a few feet in front of Jess and throw my hands in the air, walking away. Words are not my friend at this particular moment. At least none I feel comfortable sharing with the rest of the class.

"I'm so sorry, Jordan."

My head shakes as I turn around. "How long have you known?"

She shies away from me. "The first time I met you."

"What?" I walk away again.

Benji snares my arm to stop the pacing. It bothers him. "What the fuck's going on?" he asks.

I gesture toward Jess. "Meet Vanessa's sister. Notice the lack of family resemblance that would have come in super handy over the last three-plus months."

A hand covers his mouth to stifle a laugh. He fails.

"Great, yeah, it's hilarious." I rub my face, hoping it erases the entire night from my memory. "Why wouldn't you tell me you knew about what happened over winter break?"

Felicia's mouth falls open. "Oh. My. God. *You're* the guy Vee was hung up on?"

"Welcome to the conversation," I say.

Jess sighs. "I'm sorry. I figured you wouldn't stick around, so why say anything? Then, the longer I waited, the weirder it felt to bring up. I mean, how do I even start that conversation? Remember that chick you ignored until she went away? The one who really liked you but—"

I put my hands on her shoulders and dip my head so we're eye-level. "Yes, that would have worked."

Callie comes in then. I never give her a chance to glare, cross her arms, set her jaw, or anything else. We both know what she expects me to do, so why put off the inevitable?

On my way out of the kitchen, I kiss her forehead. "I'll fix it."

A ghost of a smile forms. "I know," she says.

Of all the things I never thought I'd do, this is easily in the top ten.

Man up, son.

———

Door number one upstairs in the dark hallway of ex-hook-ups reveals nothing but Felicia's belongings. An open bathroom door leaves me with only one other option. I knock. Vanessa is sitting on the floor next to the bed when I go in. The only light comes through curtainless windows, and I can't tell for sure in the dark, but hopefully, no sniffles means no crying. I shut the door behind me and get on the floor next to her.

"Your hair's curly now," I say in a lame attempt at conversation.

A lack of response makes me question whether her hair was always curly, and I, being such an enormous jackass, never noticed. But I am ninety-seven percent positive I am one hundred percent correct in my observation. She has straight brown hair that matches her eyes, a beauty mark on one of her cheeks—or maybe on her chin? She majors in business. No. Biology? Her last name is Ramos, but in all fairness, I'm guessing that one because it's Jess's last name.

Jesus. Since meeting Callie, I've spent precisely thirty seconds of my life thinking about this girl, and that was only after Benji and Rusty brought her up. I avoided her and forgot all about her the second a new distraction came along.

Exactly what I planned on doing to Callie.

The possibility of never being with her sends me spinning. I climb off the floor and pace. I nearly trip over a box but recover and alter my path. Vanessa needs an apology, and a nonsensical mess of an apology she will receive.

"I'm sorry, Vanessa. I should have handled things differently with you. You deserve better. And I meant what I said about not wanting a girlfriend at the time. It sort of just happened, purely on accident. I never even realized it was happening until it was too late. In fact, I'm almost certain I was the last to know. One day, you're just enjoying a morning run without clothes on, and the next, you're chasing a girl—*the* girl—all over campus."

"What?" she asks.

"Never mind. It's not the point."

She fidgets, distracting me for a moment, but I find my way back into my rant.

"As I was saying, the more I think about it, the more I understand that, without her, we wouldn't be having this conversation right now. I would probably still be the pre-Callie version, but then the whole alternate-universe thing happened, and I changed into this Jordan. The one who feels bad about how he treated you. Did I apologize for that yet?"

"Uh," she says, and I take it as a yes.

"Good, because I am sorry. I understand now how it feels to have someone just disappear. During me and the girl's temporary setback period, I was completely miserable until she wore my face on her chest, but that's neither here nor there." I stop and face in her general direction. "Are you still with me?"

"I think so."

"All right, I thought I might have lost you with the face part."

"Yeah, that went in an unexpected direction."

The perfect quote to sum up my life as of late.

Vanessa gets up and turns on a bedside lamp. Clear eyes and a lack of redness verify she hasn't been crying. The light also reveals a beauty mark on her cheek.

Point for Waters.

She sits on the edge of the bed, and it dawns on me that being in a closed bedroom, alone with a woman not named Callie Henders, makes me uncomfortable. I need to move this along.

"So, do you forgive me?" I ask.

She hesitates but then looks up. "Do you promise not to pace anymore if I do?"

"You have my word." I put my hand over my heart, adding a grin for effect.

Her forehead wrinkles, a concerned look in her eye. "Were you always this neurotic?"

I chuckle. If she thinks a micro-ramble and a dozen trips across the room is bad, she really dodged a bullet with me.

"Probably. But I think I used to hide it better. She just brings it out at a higher caliber."

"You really like Callie, huh?"

"I am in love with her beyond all reason," I say. I instantly realize what the fuck I've just done. "Christ. I told you I love Callie before I've told Callie." I bolt out, only making it halfway down the hall before I circle back. "We're good though, right?"

Vanessa starts to nod, and I race out of the room. I tear down the stairs, across the living room, and burst into the kitchen. Four sets of shocked eyes snap to me, but I only care about the blue ones. Callie gasps when I pick her up, not slowing down on my way through. A door off the kitchen leads to a small laundry room, and my foot kicks it shut behind us. I let her down on top of the washing machine. A creepy-ass cartoon nightlight that no doubt belongs to Felicia lights her face.

"Jordan, what the hell are—"

"Don't talk," I say.

I rest my hands on each side of her and stand between her legs, blocking all potential exits. Anytime I come close to saying I love her, she shuts me down. This time, she will hear me out whether she wants to or not. Just as soon as I calm down enough to tell her anyway.

Deep breaths do nothing to help, forcing me to go another route. I kiss her. An irresistible mistake as always, but even more so, given the time away from her. The long-awaited confession slips to the back burner the second her tongue slips into my mouth.

God, I want her.

We're frantic—her shoving the bottom of my shirt up, me reaching between my shoulders to yank it off. Our eyes meet as her top hits the floor, and I have to feel her. I slide her to the edge of the washer. She hooks her legs around me and drags my hips forward over and over.

The desire to be inside her builds until it becomes unmanageable. I find the willpower to stop and grab a stool. I wedge it under the doorknob and rush back to her. My mouth latches on to her neck, tasting the skin I've been starving for. With a palm on my chest, she nudges me back a step, so she can slide off the washer. She unbuttons my jeans and nudges them down, freeing my dick, and then she lowers to her knees in front of me.

I'm already fisting her hair when she fists my shaft and starts pumping, gorgeous eyes on mine. She licks from base to tip before slipping her lips over the head.

"Fuck, beautiful." I groan as she bobs up and down, still looking up at me, lids heavy.

When I push my hips forward, she lets me sink all the way to the back of her throat, and just before I really fuck her mouth, it hits me.

"Damn it, Callie." I ease her off and take a step back so that I can focus. "You're sucking me off to distract me."

She hauls me back by the pockets on my jeans and grips my shaft. Her lips ghost down it until her breath dances over my balls, followed by a swipe of her tongue—*fuck me*.

"Does that mean you want me to stop?" she asks.

Never. I never want her to stop—not challenging me or amazing me or frustrating me. But we're doing things on my terms for once.

"I love you."

And I spook the shit out of her. She straightens up, her eyes wide, and she scrambles to her feet. While I tuck my dick away, she walks toward the door. At first, I think she might walk straight out of it without a shirt on, but she doubles back after slapping

Holy shit, Callie's pacing.

"Take it back," she demands over her shoulder.

"I'm not taking it back."

"Jordan"—she comes toward me—"I'm serious."

"So am I. I love you."

"Stop saying that." Away she goes. "Why do you want to ruin everything between us?"

"Ruin?" I expected resistance, but suggesting I sabotaged our entire relationship seems a little extreme. "I told you I'm in love with you. Explain how it ruins anything."

She stops in front of me and groans. "Just because we love each other doesn't mean we won't destroy each other. I mean, my genetics alone almost guarantee mutual destruction."

Wait…

"Say that all one more time."

Her eyes narrow. "And now you're not listening?"

Oh, I'm listening. But I want her to repeat the part where she admitted she loves me. "Sorry, just say it again."

"Graham and Lara loved each other, too. Then they ended up hating each other and made everyone around them miserable. Fuck, they still do."

Even with her rewording, she still said it.

We. Love. Each. Other. As long as I know that, I can work with the rest of her concerns.

I move toward her, and she backs herself into a wall.

"What are you doing?"

"For starters," I say, sweeping the hair away from her face, "we're nothing like your parents. We never will be."

"How can you say that? We fight all the time."

I shake my head at her exaggeration. "We sometimes bicker and discuss our strong differences in opinion. Which will continue because you challenge me more than anyone I've ever met. It frustrates the hell out of me, but it's also the best damn feeling in the world."

A quick kiss reinforces my words, but I don't linger and risk losing sight of my goal. If I want her to tell me how she feels, she needs to stop comparing us to the worst example of a couple in modern history.

"When we do fight," I continue, "we never scream or throw things or make death threats. If we get too heated, we walk away and come back calmer. Ergo, we are not Graham and Lara."

"Jordan, you—"

"Exactly. I am Jordan, and you are Callie. I can promise you, we will never be anyone else."

She gazes up, relaxing against me. "Promise?"

"Promise." My fingers skim over the bare skin on her collarbone, and her breath falters. Time to make my move before she overthinks everything. "Also, to bring you up to speed, you've said we love each other twice now. As in I love you, and you love me."

Her eyebrows scrunch for a second, but then she laughs and sighs at the same time. "I did, didn't I."

She tries to hide her face with a hand, so I pull it away and brush her knuckles over my lips.

"Now you're going to say the words," I tell her.

"Then what?" The worry returns to both her tone and expression. "We take turns hurting the other until we can't stand the sight of each other?"

"No, baby." I hit the light switch next to her. "Then I'm going to tell you I love you too, and we'll make Gibson regret inviting us to the housewarming party by continuing to traumatize her nightlight."

My vision adjusts to the dim room in time to catch her smile. The perfect smile from the perfect girl who loves me. Now, if she'll only say it. Her fingers twist through my hair, but I pull away when she tries to kiss me.

"Hey. I've laid out a plan for the rest of our night. There's no way I'm letting you skip any of the steps."

She breathes once, twice. "I love you, Jordan."

The world shifts on its axis, and every comet, hurricane, earthquake, and all other natural disasters can feel free to take me out because Callie Henders said the last words I ever want to hear.

"Happy now?"

Immediately followed by sass.

"Oh, I'm fucking ecstatic."

She dodges away when I try to kiss her. "I remember someone being extremely concerned about following a specific agenda."

I frame her cheeks with my hands. "I love you too, Callie. So much it's inappropriate."

She bites her lip, unclasping her bra, and gives me about three seconds of a spectacular view before tossing it over the nightlight in the corner. The room without windows or even a decent strip of light at the bottom of the door darkens even more. The tip of my nose grazes over hers, and then I kiss her, this time slow and deliberate. We have all the time in the world now. Except we don't because of a house full of people on the other side of less than two inches of wood.

I back over at least thirteen objects before I find the counter on the other side of the room. Each time something knocks over, Callie laughs against my mouth. By the time I turn us around, my fingers have dealt with the button on her jeans. I tug them down over her hips along with what feels like a phenomenal pair of panties.

I can just see her from the soft glow escaping from under her bra as I lift her by the waist onto the countertop, but then she cries out when I set her down.

"Shit, what did I do?" I pick her back up, terrified I set her on a cactus. Felicia seems like the type to have random succulent plants spread throughout the house.

"It's cold," she whines.

I laugh at her overreaction. Once upon a time, she refused to smile at me, and I have no one to blame but myself for her being so damn dramatic now.

"I'm sorry, beautiful." I lower her to her feet, and she gasps as I spin her around. "We can't let this sweet ass be cold."

She pushes that sweet ass back against my crotch, looking over her shoulder at me. I growl and shove down my jeans and boxers, and she steps out of the last of her clothes.

Once I step behind her again, my hand comes around to cup her pussy, already slick and ready, and she moans.

"Was it my cock in your throat that has your cunt dripping for me?" I press my erection against her ass, dipping two fingers inside her. "Or did hearing me say I love you do it for you?"

Her head falls back on my chest, legs spreading wider as I stroke in and out. "It's you. All of you."

"Better give you all of me then."

I slide my fingers out and Callie says, "No condom."

Even though she's on birth control and we're both clean, I still ask, "Are you sure?"

She looks back at me, and her mouth curves up. "I'm certain."

"I'm certain you're perfect."

I duck in and kiss her before grasping her hip. Callie leans on the counter while I line up my cock, groaning at the feeling of her bare, and I don't even wait to drive into her. She moans, pushing back for more. I thrust in and out a few times before I yank her up against my chest. Her arm comes up, and she threads her fingers through the back of my hair.

I keep our rhythm slow, savoring each second I have with her. Other than the unsettling nightlight beneath a blue-and-white-striped bra, nothing but the girl and I remain. Every obstacle between us has finally fallen away, and now we can just be together. It's another moment that tops so many irreplaceable memories that came before. And the only thing ruined is my ability to live a life without her.

Dinner with my parents on Saturday at seven means sitting in their driveway at six-fifty, debating whether or not to go inside. Thanks to day six of Callie withdrawals, my nerves are even more keyed up than usual. A twenty-four-hour study break to see her tomorrow is becoming more and more of a probability—no, a necessity.

Her gorgeous face lights up my phone. She couldn't have better timing to tear me out of a cycle of repeatedly opening and closing the door of my Jeep.

"Hello, beautiful."

"Ew, Jordan," Cate says.

I take a second, switching from Callie to Cate mode. "I'm sorry, my dear. How were swim lessons?"

"I passed the backstroke and swimming in the deep end."

"Both in one night? You'll be a fish in no time."

"I want to be a mermaid," she tells me.

"Fine, a mermaid in no time."

"Would you be a mermaid or a fish?"

"Let's get one thing straight: I would be a merman. But if given a choice between merman and fish?" I have to think it over, considering no one's asked me such an important question before.

"My biggest concern with being a merman is, how will you transfer me from one place to another if we need to go somewhere?"

"Mine is, which parts of you stay human and which turn fish?" Callie says.

I laugh, realizing Cate abandoned me mid-conversation. A frequent occurrence. "Hey, beautiful. If you mean my godlike hair and genius mind, they'll stay as they are."

"Nope. Those aren't the parts I'm concerned about."

She sounds less stressed than when we talked yesterday. They started their summer schedule with Graham. With Connor being increasingly on edge over anything to do with their father, she's been dreading an entire week at his house. The two of them were fighting within a few minutes of their arrival, justifying her concerns.

"Did she really pass the backstroke?" I ask.

"Her instructor questioned the legitimacy of her kicking style but gave in to her whining."

The same thing happened the previous weekend when Shayna took her.

"That's my girl."

Callie sighs. "Well, the sea monster beckons me. Good luck with dinner."

My turn to sigh. "We'll see how open they actually are to my alternatives. Dustin promised our dear, sweet mother is coming in willing to negotiate. I think the night will more than likely end with, *Hello, real world and crippling student loan debt.*"

"With an optimistic outlook like that, you can't fail." Her car door dings, and a shrieked, "Callista," follows. "Oh. My. God. Catelynn Renee, stop it."

"Everything all right over there?"

Sounding ready to unleash hell on Cate, the tension-free Callie of earlier fades away as she groans. "I won't survive an entire week here, Jordan. She's being extra Cate-like, so I took her swimming early to let her burn off some energy. Now she's screaming on the steps."

"And Connor?"

"Graham started in on him again first thing this morning about absolutely nothing. He went to basketball this afternoon, so hopefully, he worked off some aggression, but I don't know. I haven't seen him since he left." She grows quiet, and I picture her eyes closed as she presses her lips together to regain her composure. "I don't know how much longer I can keep up with all the fires before they blaze out of fucking control."

I hate her dealing with everything alone. She's admitted to Graham's opinions being more aggressive and outspoken lately. But, as always with Callie, I worry she downplays the situation to prevent me from worrying. Obviously, it doesn't work.

"Want me to come and help tomorrow?" I ask.

"Yes," she says. "Please save me. I'll love you forever."

"Your sexy ass is already going to love me forever."

She laughs, and the sound alone relieves my anxiety. Whatever happens tonight, I will still have her.

"You're right. I will." She groans again, beyond annoyed. "Cate's screaming again. I'll talk to you later."

"Bye, beautiful."

I miss whatever she yells, but if I were Cate, I'd be running my ass off.

Before the calming effects of Callie wear off and I change my mind, I climb out. Greta greets me and ushers me into the foyer. As I set off on my journey to the sitting room, she wishes me luck, like she knows I need it. Not a positive sign when the housekeeper shows concern.

On the way past the kitchen, Dustin snags my arm. "Cutting it close, bro."

"Why are you even here?"

"I'm here as backup in case you need me to go toe-to-toe with Mom." He smiles, smug. "Given I'm the sensible one, she'll listen to me."

I fear my eye roll will never end. "Are you hoping this means I won't take the LSAT? Because I'll beat your score regardless of what we decide tonight."

He chuckles. "You won't beat me. But no, this is about my little brother, who's always wanted to find his own way. You shouldn't have someone else's dreams forced on you."

Terrified of what happened to make him say such a supportive-brother statement, I jerk my head back. "What?"

"I mean it. You have far too much passion to settle on a career someone else picked for you. We all deserve the opportunity to find what makes us ridiculously happy."

"Thanks, Dustin," I say cautiously.

He slaps me on the back, harder than necessary. "Well, it's only fair you follow your dreams since you'll never be smarter or more good-looking than me."

There's my real brother.

"Neither of those is true," I say. "Especially not you being better-looking. I'm devastatingly handsome, and you, my fine fellow, are sexy at best."

We both grin, and he messes up my hair, which, in all honesty, doesn't alter the appearance much at all. Before we go any further, I give him my phone and keys so that nothing in my pockets distracts me.

It's time for battle.

Another seven hundred and thirty-six steps later, we reach the sitting room. My mother stares at her watch, so we must be at least ten seconds late. Ray greets me with the usual handshake that turns into a one-armed hug. I bend over and kiss Carol on the cheek. She keeps her eyes straight ahead, confirming Dustin exaggerated the truth about her being open to this conversation.

Across from them, Dustin and I sit on the couch. Small talk ensues over a glass of scotch. We quickly cycle through the easy topics, so I dive straight in without any more pleasantries.

"I have three different ideas I want to run by you. The first—"

Carol holds up a hand to stop me. "Do any involve you upholding your end of our arrangement?"

And we're off.

"Carol, let the boy talk," Ray says.

I take a deep breath to avoid laying into my mother. "No, none involve me attending law school."

For the first time in my life, I witness my mother roll her eyes. The single gesture speaks volumes of my defeat before I truly begin.

I glance at Dustin for support, but he jumps up and steps out of the room. There goes my self-proclaimed second line of defense. Our new solidarity must not have extended over the threshold.

Thanks, brother.

"Do any put your future ahead of a silly relationship?" Carol continues.

Ray pinches the bridge of his nose and sinks back on the couch. "We agreed not to discuss any of this until after he told us what he'd come up with."

She purses her lips, waiting for my response, and I gladly fucking deliver.

"What exactly did you want me to come in here and say, Mother? That I decided to break up with my girlfriend to appease you? Because I thought we were here to discuss what I wanted to do with the rest of my life, not what I can do to win your approval."

Her mouth transforms into a hard line. "We rarely ask anything of you. But we do expect you to honor your commitments."

Thinking about my twelve-year-old self with a stress-ulcer, ready to pull my hair out, I smile. Long before I agreed to go to law school, I made a promise to him, and damn it, I will keep it. "I don't give a shit what you expect."

Carol's hand flies to her mouth, her eyes wide when she looks to my father for his reaction to my indefensible behavior. The corners of his mouth slightly curl up until he clears his throat.

"Let's watch our language, son," he says.

My hands go up in apology. "Of course."

We wouldn't want our conversation to become overly emotional. Not in this family.

"Let's start over and hear what you've come up with." Ray winks.

I wait on my mother, who sips her chardonnay, unhurried.

Eventually, she runs out of wine and crosses her legs. "I'm listening."

And we begin again.

"So, I've been doing research on the philosophy department in Pittsburgh. The latest numbers show—"

"Jordan"—Dustin's in the doorway—"you need to take this."

At first, I'm annoyed with the interruption, but then I notice his expression. Eyebrows drawn together and lips parted. His chest moves erratically, and he holds a phone against it. My phone.

"They can call back," Carol says. "Especially if it's that *girl.*"

My eyes stay on Dustin; his never leave me.

"It's Callie." He says it in a way that makes me uneasy. Like there is more he's not saying, or the words mean something else entirely.

I'm on my feet.

Carol scoffs. "You need to prioritize, or we'll never be able to trust you to make the right decision."

My attention drags from Dustin to her. "The girl is my priority. She is the right decision. You can like it or not, be a part of my life or don't. Go ahead and choose, but as far as what I do after graduation and who I do it with, that choice is mine."

Not the least bit interested in Carol's reaction, I cross the room to Dustin. He pulls me out to the hallway and shuts the door behind us. The concern in his eyes and his hand staying on my shoulder amplify the anxiety buzzing through me.

Something is wrong. Really. Fucking. Wrong.

By the time he hands me the phone, I no longer expect Callie's voice to answer me, but, *Christ,* I need it to be her.

"Hello?"

"It's all my fault, Jordan," he cries. "I'm so sorry."

A sledgehammer hits my chest, the panic radiating from the point of impact. In the background, Cate bawls, and it makes it even harder for me to concentrate.

"Connor, what happened?" The voice sounds like someone else's, and for a second, I think Dustin has spoken my thoughts. Except he's in front of me, eyes locked on my face, mouth not moving. No, the strained, unrecognizable voice came from me.

"Connor, what the *fuck* happened?"

He only says one word, but it's the only one I need.

"Graham."

"Jordan?" It's Trey now. "Are you there?"

I nod, the air too heavy, suffocating me.

"Jordan?"

The phone is pulled away from my ear, and Dustin puts it on speaker. "Yeah," he answers for me.

"We're on our way to the hospital. She was awake for a few minutes before the ambulance arrived, but—" He chokes off. "She's in pretty bad shape."

My eyes shut, the light too fucking bright, blinding me.

"What happened?" Dustin asks.

"I'm having trouble getting Connor calmed down enough to talk to me. He called and said Graham had Cal in the house and that I needed to get over there. She called a minute later, fucking terrified. Thank God I made it when I did. The son of a bitch was on top of her with his hands around her neck…"

Trey's recount of what happened after he arrived continues. Crying and yelling from Connor and Cate bleed in from the background. The door next to me opens, my parents stepping into the hall. All these things happen around me, but none of them happen *to* me. The world hurtles forward at lightning speed. Maybe I only notice how fast it moves now because I've stopped. Dustin grasps my shoulders, shaking me, willing me to do something—to move. But I just stand here. The chances of keeping up with everything seem impossible, the reason to even try lost on me.

Everyone's voices and words bounce off me, swirling around with nowhere to land. None of them make sense until two break through.

"Jordan, please."

Connor's distress matches my own and acts as a much-needed slap in the face, forcing me away from the abyss of self-pity I was circling. The rest roars back into focus, and why the fuck am I still here? I grab the phone, not having any choice but to keep up.

"Connor, you have to calm down so Cate will stop crying." I snag my keys from Dustin, not even acknowledging him or my parents before running out of the house. "Tell me you heard me, Con."

He sniffs a few times. "Yeah," he croaks out. "Just hurry."

———

Understaffed and unprepared, the hospital in Waymore transfers Callie to a larger one, cutting time off my drive. Even with a shorter distance and heavy foot, my trip takes eons. Anytime where I am heading or why infiltrates my thoughts, I roll down the window and turn up the music. Distractions and avoidance are necessary tools in keeping me from losing my mind right now.

I park next to Pete's truck in the parking lot and pass Trey's cruiser at the curb in front of the building. My shoes squeak across the floors on every turn as I race through the hallways, following the directions Trey gave me. Left through the automatic doors, down a long hallway, taking the first right, a left, another right, do the hokey-fucking-pokey. I glimpse Cate through the window of a door.

When I burst in, everyone looks up. She runs across the room and jumps into my arms. Right behind her comes Connor. He wipes his eyes with the back of a bandaged hand. Unsure of what the hell else to do, I put my free arm around him. The kid latches on to me like I'm his fucking lifeline, and at this moment, I probably am.

She squeezes too tight, he cries, and I let them.

Over the top of Cate's head, I spot Pete in a chair, reading a magazine.

"Where's Trey?" I ask.

"Vending machines. Down the hall, turn right, third door."

I hand Cate off to Connor.

"Wait, let me go with you," he begs.

Pete must read my mind on my way by and cuts Connor off from following me. "He'll be right back."

"Jordan, no—" Connor starts a protest, but I'm already gone.

Down the hall, turn right, third door brings me to a dark, empty room. Through the fourth doorway, however, I find a line of vending machines. Trey stands in full uniform with his forehead pressed against a wall, staring down at the blue carpet. The stance alone answers all my immediate questions.

Nothing has changed.

I slump back beside him. "She's not awake."

He straightens up and winces, a hand reaching for his right side. The other rubs over his face, careful not to hit a cut over his eyelid. "Something about the combination of a concussion and her losing consciousness from the strangulation..." He stops when my head drops onto the wall.

The word makes my stomach wrench, and I feel absolutely helpless. Graham strangled Callie. While I drank scotch with my father and laughed about sailing, hers beat the shit out of her and had his hands around her throat.

Graham strangled Callie. I roll the words around in my head, waiting for them to become easier to understand, but they remain surreal. *Graham strangled Callie.*

Trey's hand on my shoulder reels me back. I kick off the wall and feed quarters to an ancient coffee machine. "Sorry, you were saying?"

"They set her broken wrist, and her ribs will heal in six weeks. When she does wake up, they'll more than likely keep her sedated with pain meds to keep her calm and comfortable." He rolls his eyes. "I have a fucking pamphlet for family members of a strangulation survivor if you want some light reading."

"What happened to Connor's hand?" I ask, needing a change of subject.

"Ten stitches across his knuckles and four in his palm, and he won't tell me why. So, who the fuck knows." He examines the contents of a vending machine. "This is such a fucking disaster. Lara won't answer her phone. Dad won't leave the jail."

He slaps at the buttons without putting money in. Then the heel of his hand slams into them harder. Once more. Now he hits it with a fist. And again. All composure gone, he's teetering at the edge of the same abyss I narrowly escaped earlier.

I catch his arm before he lands another punch. "If you don't stop, you'll need stitches next."

It takes a few seconds, but he unclenches his fist. I release my hold, and he walks away.

His hands drag through his hair and stop on the back of his neck. "A nurse asked how I was doing with everything earlier. I should have answered her like that."

Jesus. Even with my tendency to say the wrong thing at the worst time, I wouldn't have asked that question. A simple blink in his direction could answer—dark circles under his eyes, hardly any color in his face, his movements rigid.

"How *did* you answer her?"

He turns around, laughing without humor. "I looked her dead in the eye and said, 'I'm twenty-one and making serious medical decisions for my eighteen-year-old cousin because no one else gives a shit. I'm fan-fucking-tastic, lady. How the fuck are you?'"

"Very subtle," I say.

"Yeah, well, the uniform typically excuses any lack of tact."

A deep breath makes him grab his side. This time, I doubt Callie did the damage, so I gesture to his eye. "What happened to—"

Pete smacks the doorframe as he rushes in. "Doctor's looking for you."

My untouched coffee lands in the trash on my way out of the room. The three of us haul ass down the hallway to the waiting room. A doctor stands outside when we round the corner. Trey and I bombard him with different versions of the same question.

"Is she awake?"

"Did she wake up?"

His eyes warm in response. "We haven't seen any change yet and are waiting on a few scans. Everyone's body responds differently to trauma. Some take longer to recover, but we have her set up in a room."

"You'll let us see her?" Sheriff's Deputy Henders conveys more of a statement than a question as he straightens up taller and scratches a conveniently placed itch next to his badge.

The doctor offers a small smile. "If you keep the visits to ten minutes, we'll let the three of you see her, one at a time."

"Thank you," Trey says.

Pete and I repeat.

Looking at Trey's eye, the doctor squints. "You should get a stitch or two in that."

"Maybe." Nothing about Trey's answer indicates he will.

He gives a nod and heads down the hall. "A nurse will be out shortly to take one of you back."

All of us blow out a synchronized exhale. Instead of the shallow breaths sustaining me since my parents' house, the air refills my lungs, and I breathe easier.

Shit. Connor.

"Can her brother see her, too?" I call down the hall.

The doctor spins but keeps backing up. "How old is he?"

"Fifteen."

His head tilts side to side while he deliberates. "That should be fine, but someone should accompany him." He turns in time to swipe his badge and pushes through a set of double doors.

I follow the other two into the waiting room. Cate looks up from the floor where she's coloring and sticks her tongue out at me before returning to her masterpiece. Whatever Connor told her to calm her down has worked wonders—or she's forgotten what scared her in the first place.

Wait. My head jerks around the room. "Where's Connor?"

Pete glances up from the stack of magazines he was sifting through. "He went to use the phone charger in my truck."

I drop into the chair next to him and massage my forehead with the heels of my hands. Tension there, across my shoulders, and in my neck persists but barely registers at this point. I consider the tight muscles my new state of being for at least the next several hours, if not longer. Maybe Cate will jump around on my back if I ask.

A nurse walks in, and I shoot out of my chair. Already standing, Trey beats me to her.

Her eyes dart back and forth between us. "Who's going first?"

By the look on Trey's face, I know he plans on pulling rank. He clears his throat to make sure I pay attention to the hand slowly moving to rest on his gun. A dick move, but I don't blame him for using it to his advantage in this situation.

"Whatever. I'll take Connor with me then."

A strategic move. The kid's sanity depends on seeing Callie as much as mine does. Once in her room, he'll help me devise a plan so they can't make us leave. Maybe after we barricade ourselves in, he will tell me what the hell happened.

Trey glances back with a smirk as he follows the nurse. I flip him off.

Ten minutes. I only need to wait ten more minutes. To keep from pacing, I go to bring Connor in from Pete's truck. The last few hours have been absolute torment, but the fresh night air helps lessen my anxiety. All signs point to Callie waking up. That thought alone almost makes me smile. Cate and Connor have calmed down and are safe. According to Trey, Graham is rotting in a jail cell where he belongs. As crazy as it sounds, at the end of all this, everyone will be all right.

It's a nice thought but short-lived.

I stand in the now-empty parking spot next to my Jeep.

Pete's truck is nowhere in sight.

Fuck.

Fuck.

Fuck.

Fuck.

My thoughts stay rather consistent the entire way back to the waiting room.

"He's gone," I say, charging through the door. "Connor's fucking gone."

The magazine slips from Pete's lap as he hits his feet. "Fuck."

Covered that already. Several times.

Both of us look at Cate, humming on the floor. Connor wouldn't leave her without telling her something. Maybe not anything specific, but enough that we might be able to figure out where he went.

When I lower down beside her, she beams up at me. "Hi."

"Hi." I smile back the best I can. "Do you know where Connor went?"

She puts her index finger on her chin, tapping. "Hmm. Let. Me. Think."

"Or where he might go?" I ask, trying to prompt an answer. "When he's upset or sad, does he go play basketball or go to a friend's house?"

Her eyes widen. "He goes to get a blanket."

I stare at her, unable to piece together any information from her off-the-wall comment. "Why would he get a blanket?"

Impatient, she huffs. "Because nothing bad can happen under the blankets, Jordan."

She says it as if it were the truest statement ever made, and a sick feeling creeps into my gut.

"Fuck," Pete says, pulling his hair. "He went to Graham's. Right, Cate? He went to Cal's room to get a blanket?"

She nods and returns to her coloring.

I crawl off the floor, even more confused. "What are you two talking about?"

Pete grabs at the back of his neck. "Cal has a blanket fort in her room from when we were kids. Whenever her parents got into one of their death matches, she'd hide in it with Connor. She promised him they'd always be safe there because nothing bad could ever happen under the blankets."

Screw the sledgehammer from earlier. This time, a Mack Truck of realization obliterates me. Callie told me that the night she built the fort in her dorm room. She told me, but I didn't understand. We were hiding under the pile of blankets so she could feel safe.

From him.

All the anger and annoyance, she uses it to mask how he really makes her feel—scared. She has been scared of him the entire time. And I fucking missed it. *What if I could have prevented all of this?* My vision clouds at the thought, every part of me burning. Anger. Sadness. Hatred. All clawing away inside me. I latch on to the closest thing to me—a magazine rack—and I hurl it across the room. Magazines spill over the floor before it crashes into a row of chairs on the other side.

"Jordan!" Cate jumps onto her knees and throws a red crayon at me. "Don't. Throw. Things."

Her gaze locks with mine, her jaw set in a warning for me to knock off my shit. Exactly what I need, apparently, because the self-control comes rushing back.

What the fuck, Waters?

"Shit." I pull at my hair and rush to clean up my mess, pissed at myself for losing it in front of Cate.

I straighten up the chairs and set back the magazine rack. Pete kneels down to pick up the magazines. He shoots me a sympathetic look, letting me off the hook for my meltdown. I appreciate the understanding, but I need someone else's forgiveness far more.

I go over and roll the crayon toward her with my shoe. "I'm sorry, Cate."

She snatches it up and pokes me in the shin with it. "Just don't let it happen again."

"I promise it never will," I say, and I mean more than just my temper tantrum.

Sure, I might have been able to do something to stop all this from happening if I'd noticed the signs sooner. But the facts are inescapable: I didn't notice, it did happen, and no matter how much guilt and regret I feel or how many objects I throw, I can't change any of it now. But I can make sure it never fucking happens again.

As Pete sets the last of the magazines in the rack, Trey walks in. One look at our faces, and he stops dead in his tracks. "Oh God, now what?"

"Connor stole my truck," Pete says. "We think he went back to Graham's."

Trey ages ten years in front of us. His eyes close, and his chin lowers to his chest. Each forced breath heaves his shoulders, a weight holding them down. When he looks up, his lips press together. A familiar habit that enhances the resemblance between him and his cousins.

"Okay," he breathes out. "Here's the plan." He wipes a hand over his face, and the in-charge demeanor slowly returns. "Jordan, go see Cal. Pete, stay with Cate. I'll hunt down Connor."

If he has anything more to say, I'll never hear it because I'm gone. He follows me into the hall, and we head in opposite directions.

The nurse smiles, walking me toward the double doors. She stops before opening them and checks down the hallway behind me. "Did her brother not want to come?"

I struggle for a less alarming response than the truth—Connor stole a truck to return to the house where his father beat his sister for a blanket in an attempt to regain a sense of security as his world crumbles around him. In the end, I settle for shaking my head.

She swipes her badge, the locks click open, and she pushes open one of the metal doors. "There you go, hon." She holds it, waiting for me to walk through.

But I don't move, my body frozen in place.

Callie's only a few hundred feet away. I can see her face, hold her hand, tell her I love her, kiss her forehead, feel her heartbeat, and hear her breathe. Everything I need to do to keep my world from further falling apart. Yet, for the life of me, I can't take another step because she would choose Connor. Callie wants *me* to choose Connor.

That's when it all changes for me, and my perspective shifts. Not when I decided to chase the girl with the smile and the bluest eyes. Or when she challenged me to trust in myself regardless of the past. But right now, when the what-ifs have become a reality and despite everything I thought and said and want and need, I turn around.

Somehow, I fucking turn around.

My feet show no problems in sprinting my ass the other way down the hall.

"Trey," I call after him. He stops and waits for me to catch up, but I have no plans on slowing down. "I'll find Connor. You stay in case anything changes."

"You sure?" he asks as I pass him. "You don't want to see her first?"

I round the corner without answering him. I can't. Given a chance, I might change my mind.

A few calls to both Callie's and Connor's phones go unanswered before I stop trying. Searching for a distraction on the drive, I call Benji. Of course, when he answers, I remember he has no idea what happened. I consider hanging up but need his company, so I give him an overview, avoiding the S-word. My mind continues to grapple with that particular word. He responds much like I did, which is to say not at all. For several minutes, nothing comes from the speakers.

"You still with me, Benj?"

"I'm here, man," he says, barely audible. "What do you need from us?"

"Can someone go over to tell Felicia? Gibson will be a fucking wreck. I want someone with her."

"I'll take care of her. You call the minute Calico wakes up."

I agree as a call from Dustin beeps through. I switch to him. He wants an update, and we talk the last bit of my drive. Our shared ability to prattle on about nonsense at length finally finds a use. I let him go when I pull into Sutterville just before midnight.

Since the weekend bartender is sitting in a hospital waiting room, they closed the bar. It makes the town appear even more abandoned than usual, not a single car on Main Street.

Even though I drive in on a different road, I easily locate Graham's house again. Next to Callie's car sits Pete's truck with the driver's door ajar. The incessant dinging stops when I pull the keys and shut the door, but the silence that follows bothers me more.

I climb the steps to the open door. Ripped down crime-scene tape blows in the light breeze. My stomach tightens with a dizzying nausea brought on by the sight. The house will be in the same condition as when Trey arrived to find Graham with his hands pressed into Callie's throat.

Graham strangled Callie.

Nope. The thought still seems ridiculous.

When I step through the screen door, a thick wave of tension clouds the kitchen. Heavy, as if the walls were holding on to all the anger through the years. Every hurtful, hate-filled moment lingers, waiting to add the next. The place puts me on edge, and I want to find Connor and get the hell out.

Straight out of the kitchen is the living room. I only intend to do a quick scan to check for him, but as my gaze travels over the room, my entire body numbs. I wish I'd never left the hospital. I want to go back to the state of doubt I lived in until a second ago. I'll never be able to go back to it though. Because everything just became undeniably real.

The hole in the drywall is the same height as Callie. A lamp and coffee table both lie on their sides, knocked over. Blood stains the beige carpet—a few drops here and there and then a larger area where I imagine her lying. Where Trey would have found her. Found them. Where he would have pulled Graham off her to stop him from cutting off her airway. The same spot she woke up in, and he lay with her, trying to keep her awake by talking about a trip they had gone on to an amusement park before she'd left for Easton. Even with one eye swollen, he swears she rolled her eyes at him.

I've stopped breathing, and the need for air brings me back from internal torture. Only the air does little to ease the ache inside, more overwhelming by the second. I need to leave this fucking house and never think about any of this again.

"Connor!" I shout, backing out of the room.

No answer.

Off the kitchen is a hallway. I check the rooms as I go. A princess bedspread covers the bed in the first. The book Cate always reads before bed waits for her on the pillow. Across the hall, a pair of gym shorts lies on the floor, a promising sign I am in Connor's room. When I flip the light on, though, other than half of a torn-down LeBron James poster on the wall, nothing in here reminds me of Connor. Even after years of not playing lacrosse, I still have gear, but not even a gym bag or basketball sits in his room. I shut the door on my way out and move farther down the hall.

I almost bypass the next room completely when I see the door kicked in, a dent in the wood from a foot, and the frame is splintered where the lock and the latch ripped away. Being a masochist, I step in anyway. Blankets and pillows are scattered all over. The remnants of a blanket fort. My eyes sting as I realize he probably found Callie in there. Hiding. I pull the door as closed as possible, filing it away with all the other images to forget.

Other than a bathroom at the end of the hall, only one room remains. I walk into a disaster. A TV lies on the floor, ripped from the wall mount, the screen shattered. The bare mattress balances halfway off the box spring with a smear of red on one corner. Drawers hang open with the contents strewed over the floor. Glass covers the top of the dresser from a broken mirror with more blood in the shards.

An unsettling mess but no Connor and nowhere else to search.

Where the fuck is he?

I race through the house and out the front door, not bothering to shut it behind me. The moment I get outside, I gasp for air, a heaviness leaving my body. How anyone could stay in there for more than a few minutes confounds me. Memories haunt that house, and they carry more negative energy than any ghosts.

Still anxious, I pull out my phone to call Trey. He should have come because I have no clue where to look next. I start across the yard, my eyes landing on the three vehicles parked in front of the house. Callie's car, Pete's truck, my Jeep. Then it hits me—there should be four.

I shove my phone in my pocket and bolt to the Jeep.

All the places I've gone with Callie—Trey's house, the bar, the school, the gas station—are a bust for Graham's truck. I end up driving random streets and somehow even get lost. As I attempt to figure out where I am, a familiar Guns N' Roses song starts playing. I slam the knob to kill the sound. All the stress of the night settles over me at once when I think of her. I throw the shifter into park, roll down the window for some air, and admit defeat.

The kid wins. Life wins. The fucking cold bitch of a universe wins.

A fast-asleep town and the soft hum of the idling engine leave everything too quiet. The lack of noise chips away at already-raw nerves more than some stupid song, so I slap the volume knob for music. If I drove something more akin to Benji's piece-of-shit station wagon, I wouldn't have this problem. That thing roars loud enough that we receive a warning of his arrival from several blocks away.

Risking wearing out the volume control, I push it off again and bring back the near silence. What are the chances Graham's crappy blue pickup makes the same racket?

Worth a try at least.

Windows down, music off, I drive each street from one end to the other. On every turn, I slow down and listen for the faintest hint of an exhaust pipe. A sound that never comes. Soon, I start running out of roads to travel in the small town. One of the last ones takes me out of town to the middle of nothing, fields on all sides. I need both a new long-shot plan and a place to turn around.

Or neither.

My headlights land on Graham's truck, the rust spot unmissable on the bumper. I jerk the steering wheel and slam on the brakes, skidding to a stop on the side of the gravel road.

Oh no, Connor. No. No. No.

Everything loses definition, a dreamlike fuzziness spreading. It makes me wonder how we ever know for sure when we're dreaming. Some people claim they remain lucid and control what happens in their dreams. If that's possible, I need to be one of those people right now. And this needs to be a nightmare I can navigate into a sweet, sweet dream.

I climb out, not taking my keys and leaving the door wide open. Over and over, I try swallowing. Between the lump in my throat and the dryness in my mouth, the whole affair proves futile. Each step is a little slower than the last, but I make it to the passenger side of the cab.

"Hey," I say through the rolled-down window, my voice gravelly.

Connor stares blankly ahead on the other side.

After a successful swallow, I try again. "Hate to tell you this, but you overshot the waiting room by about fifty miles." I shove my hands in my pockets and feel Pete's truck keys. My fingertips drag over the jagged edges. Each scrape helps me believe more and more that what I'm experiencing is real.

He stays unmoving, the ignition next to his knee empty.

I check through his window off into the distance and then peer over my shoulder, doing the same, relieved to see the tracks dark and empty in both directions.

"Where are the keys, Con? We should probably move the truck before a train comes."

He lifts his hand to examine the bandage wrapped around his knuckles. "It's all my fault."

At least he's talking. I can work with that.

"Want to tell me what happened?"

His hand drops to his lap, and his gaze returns straight ahead. "Graham burned my basketball gear, so I trashed his room."

The shattered mirror, the blood on the mattress, his hand. All the result of a boy at his breaking point. Now the pieces of the broken boy sit in front of me. I can only think of one person who knows how to put him back together, and it sure as hell isn't me.

"We were heading to the ER when he came home drunk," he continues, shifting a little. "But Cal forgot her keys, and he followed her inside. I should have gone after her, but she told me to stay with Cate. She made it out the door before…" He wipes his face with his uninjured hand. "We were going to leave and never come back. I was going to make her promise that we would never go back."

The picture that forms in my mind along with what I saw at the house overwhelms me. I have to concentrate on the basics of breathing, eyes directed at the stars until I block everything out. Once I can respond without fear of choking on my own words, I refocus on him.

"You won't have to go back to him, Connor. None of you will. Graham's going to be in a hell of a lot of trouble for what he did. When Callie wakes up, she—"

"Stop," he says. He finally looks at me, the tears streaming down his face. "You don't know that. Everyone says that because it's what we're supposed to say. She'll wake up. He'll go to jail. Our mom will have an epiphany and want to be a mom and learn how to love us." His head falls back against the seat, and his hands cover most of his face. "What in my life would make me think any of that will happen? Why should I believe anything good will ever happen?"

"Because it's just as absurd to think only bad things will ever happen," I say, fighting the urge to go into a full-on philosophical rant. "The universe spits everything out at random. It doesn't differentiate between bad and good. That's our job. Then we take each hit as it comes and search for something that makes it mean something more. Something that helps make the rest worthwhile. It's up to us to find our own meaning in a random, uncaring, and relentless universe."

Connor's quiet for a minute, digesting what probably wasn't the most helpful speech. "What if—"

A chilling tone slices through the crisp night air. His head lifts off the seat and turns toward me. Only, instead of looking at me, he looks past me. Even though I already know, I follow his gaze over my shoulder to the spot of light down the tracks. The train's horn blows a second time, and the dreamlike fuzziness returns full force.

It can't be real, but the bite in my palm as a fist forms around Pete's truck key says otherwise. My eyes close, and I try to keep my mind clear to maintain my composure.

I summon the most authoritative voice I can produce. "Connor, we need to go."

Again, he sits as still as a statue, facing forward. He shows no signs of budging.

"Connor."

Not even a blink.

Nothing equips me to talk a fifteen-year-old off the train tracks. Not the sailing lessons or the piano or all the prep courses. But it doesn't really matter because I need to do it anyway.

When I warned Callie about the stupid decisions I would make in my life, I meant the purchase of the occasional sports car or an impulsive move to Guam. Not one that carries the potential of keeping me from making any type of future decisions. It's my fault for not being more specific, I suppose.

I open the passenger door and climb in, pulling it shut behind me.

Connor's head whips toward me, alarmed that I'm suddenly sitting next to him.

Yeah, me too, kid.

"Jordan, what are you doing?" His voice shakes.

"There's no chance in hell I'm telling Callie I left you here by yourself." I check the train, and sure enough, it keeps on rolling toward us, the spot of light growing. "What are we doing here, Connor?"

He tips his face up to the roof of the cab, eyes shut tight. "I need to make it all stop."

"Everything?" I ask, trying to get him talking again.

No answer.

"That sounds like an awful lot to put on yourself."

His face shows the agony tearing him apart inside. All his unhappiness has surfaced at once, and he's desperate for a way to escape it. Desperation can play tricks on the mind, blocking out the alternatives one by one until it feels like nothing's left. If we were in a dream and I could control it, I'd say something profound that would help him break through it. But we're not, and I can't, so I just start talking.

"It's absolutely terrifying how most of our life is completely out of our hands. Especially when people do terrible things.

Senseless, violent, inexcusable things we can't stop. Eventually, I think we have to make a choice. We keep fighting against everything out of our control and let it consume us. Or we stop blaming ourselves for what we can't change and focus on finding what makes our life worth living. The beauty that makes the rest hurt less."

He opens his eyes, staring at the gray fabric above him. "Neither of those sounds very hopeful."

The train's warning sounds much louder than the last time, and the light shines through the open window, lighting up the side of Connor's face. Panic sets in along with my own desperation to get this kid out of the fucking truck.

"Then screw hope," I say.

His eyebrows pull together, two lines forming between them. He's probably questioning where I'm headed with this. Honestly, I am wondering myself, but I ramble on.

"Hope gives us an excuse to wait for something good to happen and a reason to feel disappointed if it never does. We should seize the fucking day, man. Do what we can. Accept what we can't. We have so little control over what happens to us, so why give up more?"

Another blow from the horn.

Fuck.

"I think that's why Callie lost her shit when she was younger."

His head lowers at the mention of her name, and his gaze shifts to the bench seat between us. "What do you mean?"

"She couldn't control Graham and Lara, but she could control what she did. The drinking and the partying were like a giant *fuck you* anytime they made her mad. Except she ended up giving them even more control. Because she let them control her emotions, her reactions. Now you're doing the exact same thing."

Tears streak down his face again, but he won't look at me. I need him to look at me.

"Think about it, Con. Right now, Graham has more control over you than ever. You're in his truck, upset over what he did, and willing to give up your life to get away from him. But he's not worth it."

I check out my window. The vibrations in the seat match the rumble of the train barreling toward us. Lights on the railroad crossing sign blink. Ringing fills the cab of the truck.

We're out of time.

"Don't let him control you anymore, Connor," I shout over the crossing. "Don't let him decide this for you. Say, *Fuck you*. Say it, and we'll go find something beautiful that makes all the shit worthwhile because it's out there, and we'll find it. I promise."

His eyes snap to mine, and I have no idea what I said, but he's right here with me now.

"Promise?"

Eyes blurring and heart hammering, I nod. "Promise."

Then he nods back, slow at first but becoming more certain until he grabs for the handle. The piercing horn drowns out my command to go as I chase him through the cab and shove him out the door. My feet land on the tracks, ready to run, but Connor loses his balance. I clutch at his shirt, dragging him over the rails. We only run a few seconds before a deafening boom shoots shockwaves through me. I throw us both to the ground.

The collision reverberates through the empty fields around us. Metal shrieks and crunches and scrapes. The shrill noises shred at my insides. I feel them grating everywhere, gnawing at my nerve endings and preventing all rational thought.

Then it stops. Chimes of the crossing and brakes of the train are all that remain.

Neither of us attempts to move. It never even occurs to me. We lie flat on the rocks, on our stomachs, in the dark, under the stars, alive and breathing. Sporadic, ragged, and shallow. But breathing.

When my body responds again, I push myself up and pull Connor to his feet. He stumbles on his first steps, so I help him to the Jeep, not so much as glancing behind us. He sits sideways in the passenger seat, and I frantically check him over. Small scratches on his cheek and chin, eyes puffy, skin pale, but he's in one fucking piece.

His lip trembles before his entire body starts shaking. He gasps for air, panic flooding his eyes.

"You're safe," I say, grabbing on to him. "I promise."

He clings to me, anchoring on like he has nothing else to hold him here. I've never felt so utterly responsible for another person in my entire life, and why he always comes first suddenly makes complete sense. He just does.

After he calms down enough to let go, I head around the back of the vehicle. My eyes refuse to stray from my feet, but I stop before getting in and force them up. A trail of wreckage leads from the crossing to the remains of Graham's truck, overturned in the ditch about a hundred feet down the tracks. The truck bed is partially ripped away from the force of impact. Separate sides of the cab no longer exist, passenger side smashed all the way through to the driver's door.

A cold weakness shoots through my muscles, and I have to brace against the side of the vehicle. Fear and adrenaline wreak havoc as the truth of what almost happened slashes through me. Hot tears burn with each breath more strenuous than the last. Most of tonight, I already wanted to forget, to purge all the unwelcome memories. But erasing this moment, the one when I realize how close we came to not escaping the truck, is fucking crucial to my well-being.

A sense of stability returns, and my muscles loosen enough so that I can straighten up. I wipe my eyes and climb in, and without another look, we leave the nightmare behind.

We ride through town to Graham's house in silence. Personally, I need the quiet reflection time after a night of one chaotic event after another. When we pull up, Tony is waiting next to Pete's truck. A little hesitant to leave the joyrider alone with my keys, I take them and tell Connor to stay put.

Tony stretches out his arms and lets them drop to his sides. "Where the hell have you guys been?"

I explain our little detour and the destruction of a technically stolen truck. He almost appears jealous of missing the action and graciously offers to call Trey about the situation. I let him. I need a longer break.

As Tony handles that business, I fetch a few blankets from Callie's room and a sweatshirt for Connor. He leans against the front of the vehicle and reaches out when I bring them over. Before I forget, I toss Pete's truck keys on the seat. I calculate the odds of two people stealing his truck in one night as low. The guy can't have that bad of luck.

Tony tucks his phone away. "Trey said he'll take care of everything. Whatever that means."

"Did he say anything else?" Connor asks.

He shakes his head. "Sorry, kid."

Connor holds the blankets tight against his chest and presses his nose into the material. I want a little coconut time myself but prefer to experience the real deal.

"We'd better get going."

"I'll drive Pete's truck back later," Tony says. "If I can ever find the keys."

"On the seat," I reply, distracted.

A streetlight reflects off something in the grass in the middle of the yard. I lean down and retrieve a different set of keys— Callie's.

"That must be what she threw before Graham pulled her back inside." Connor swipes them from my hand. He examines them before looking up, confused. "Why would she do that?"

I rough up his hair on my way to the Jeep. "Because she wouldn't leave you dangling off a cliff, Connor."

Neither of us would.

***

Even though every part of me wants to haul ass to the hospital, I know Callie will hold me accountable for Connor not eating. A questionable roadside diner with abnormally high grease content suffices. Torn pleather booth seats, a weird stickiness covering the checkered table. Seems legit.

I also figure I should unearth a little more information on why I almost sacrificed myself to the train gods. If I can get Connor to talk. He's twirling a fork between his fingers and staring at the table to avoid eye contact. He hasn't touched his chocolate milkshake by the time his burger arrives.

"Fork." I hold out my hand.

He relinquishes the utensil and sighs. "You want me to talk about what happened."

"Only seems fair, considering."

His crease appears between his eyebrows, and he sinks against the back of the booth. "Graham showed up at practice, acting like father of the year. Telling the coach how he'd been telling me to dedicate more time to practice. Complete bullshit." A saltshaker gains his attention, and he unscrews the top. "I was so pissed off and distracted that I missed a layup. One fucking layup. Forget the hundreds I've made because he saw me miss one."

"That's why he burned your gear?"

"Not exactly." He switches to the pepper, fingers twisting the lid. "When I got home, he started in on me like he always does. I'm worthless. His money would have been better spent on an abortion."

"Jesus fucking Christ." I shake my head in disbelief. Each time I think this man can't possibly disgust me more, surprise. "Sorry, continue."

"I couldn't take it anymore, and we started yelling at each other. He stomped off and came back with a garbage bag and grabbed my gym bag off the floor." Connor sniffs, rubbing his face with his sweatshirt sleeve. "When I got outside, he put it in a pile along with stuff he'd taken from my room. I tried to grab things, but he must have already put lighter fluid on it because he threw the match, and I had to jump back. Then he just left while I sat there, watching it all burn."

"I'm so sorry, Connor," I say.

He swipes a finger under his eye. "I went to a friend's and got a little buzzed. I thought Cal would be home when I got back, but she wasn't. I went into my room and ... he'd gotten everything— my jerseys, balls, the new shoes Cal had bought me." He shrugs, setting the shakers back. "I decided to return the favor."

"Is that when Callie came home?"

"She found me after I busted open my hand."

A nervous shift occurs, both of us knowing where the story goes from here. Not something I want to hear again or for him to relive. I try to imagine how Graham justifies any of his actions, but

I can't. No decent human being could. Only we're not talking about someone who exists in a realm anywhere decent adjacent. We're discussing an angry, selfish piece of trash, who somehow retains the right to destroy his children every other weekend slash every other week during the summer. Are people that easily fooled, or do they just not care enough to see what's really going on?

"Did you go inside after Trey got there?" I ask, skipping ahead.

He shakes his head. "He put us in the back of his cruiser, so I couldn't get out. But I saw him bring Graham out in handcuffs. He passed him off to another cop and ran back in for Cal." His face crumples when he says her name, on the verge of tears. "If I ever thought for one second he would—" He looks up at the waitress approaching.

"How we doin' over here?" she asks, beaming at us.

I nod, my politeness on the fritz.

She nudges Connor's shoulder. "Not liking the burger, sweetie?"

Other than his red eyes, he gives no indication of his life falling into disarray. He shakes his head and delivers a boyish grin. "Everything's fine. I'm just about to dig in."

"You let me know if you need some pie later."

"Will do," he says.

She winks at him, stepping to her next table. The second she leaves his line of sight, his expression dissolves back to one of misery. No longer needing to put on a performance, I guess.

We don't talk about what happened anymore. I make him eat a few bites and drink half his shake before I agree to leave. He goes to wait outside while I pay. Our server meets me at the counter, next to the cash register. She attempts small talk, and I manage a tight-lipped smile but never reply.

As I turn to leave, she says, "Hope you both enjoy your night."

I shake my head—not only at her use of the word *hope*, but the entire statement. If only she knew where we'd been or where we were going. But then, for a split second, I catch a glimpse of Connor through the large glass windows and see him as she would.

A teenage boy propped next to a Jeep, looking perfectly capable of enjoying his night. Based on her interaction with him, why would she think anything different? All signs of everything wrong in his life are easily missed or dismissed. The evidence of his pain he can make invisible to people not privy to Graham or Lara or what happens behind closed doors. The smile, the "everything's fine"—his entire act is flawless. Just like Callie's.

Once I step outside though, the picture refocuses. The now-dirty bandage covers the fresh stitches across his knuckles. Experience tells me the blank expression on his face accompanies empty eyes. His shoulders slump. He hangs his head. In place of the normally sarcastic and cocky teenager waits a scared and lost little boy.

Before, I wanted to make everything better for Callie. Now, seeing Connor like this, I want to remove all the suffering for him. But I can't, and I hate not having the power to fix things for them.

That's why people invest so much in hope; feeling helpless hurts too damn much. It is easier to hope our problems will solve themselves, to hope our destiny makes itself known eventually. Except that would require the universe to not only give a shit about what happens to us, but also grant us a favor. Not a very promising scenario.

No, we are responsible for ourselves. Our actions, our choices, our beliefs—those things we can control in spite of everything else in our lives that we can't. So, the more time we spend waiting, hoping, and floating, the less time we give ourselves to search for the beauty, the meaning, and the reason.

The first two, I've already found. Callie's the beauty worth living for, and she makes life more meaningful to me. And as I walk toward the broken boy doing all he can to hold himself together, I gain a little insight on the last one. I mean, I wouldn't say I come to grips with the entire reason for my existence in a parking lot, but I sure as hell discover a purpose in one.

Passed out on the floor of the waiting room, Cate snores with her hair a mess over her face. She doesn't even stir when Connor covers her up with the blankets we brought. He settles in beside her and rests his hand on her head.

Pete's shoulders visibly relax when I collapse in the chair next to him. I roll my head toward him. "Connor never stole your truck and tried to get us smashed to smithereens by a coal train."

He raises an imaginary shot. "We never tell Cal about it. *Ever.*"

I nod, eyes wide. "Fucking cheers to that, brother."

We mentally clink and mentally drink.

The door flies open, Trey's eyes seeking out Connor on his way in. He rushes over and drags him off the floor, and his arms engulf him. Connor grips the back of his brown uniform shirt, knuckles white.

"I'm sorry," he says.

Trey steps back and grabs his face. "Don't you ever scare me like that again. We don't do that shit to each other."

Connor nods, and his head crashes down on Trey's shoulder.

Holding on to him, Trey glances over. "Get the fuck over here, man."

I reluctantly do as the officer said. He pulls me in with Connor and holds us both. Before long, his arm shifts enough to make room as Pete forces his way in. We are four dudes in a group hug when someone walks in. All of us scatter to different sides of the room as a doctor with a large yellow envelope warily eyes us. Trey steps toward her. I missed the stitches in the cut above his eye until he cocks his head to the side.

"Here to see me?"

"Your X-rays are back," she says. "You were right—two ribs cracked on your right side."

"Told you I know my body." His mouth turns up.

Good God. He needs to find a better time to pick up women.

"You did." She flirts back. "I also have the report written up."

He fishes around in his wallet and hands her a business card. "District Attorney's information is on there. Send everything you've got."

"Do you need the pictures of your injuries sent separately from hers?"

"No, but can I get physical copies of everything? Scans, injury reports, intake photos?"

"Of course." She backs out the door. "I'll tell the nurse. You let me know if you need anything for the ribs."

"Sure thing." He shoves his hands in his pockets and bites his lip in the most blatant attempt at flirting I've ever witnessed. Once the future mother of his children vacates the room, he returns his attention to us. "DA's already decided on charges for Graham."

Connor sits forward in a chair. "What does that mean?"

"Even if Dad wanted to protect him, he wouldn't be able to get him out of this one."

I want to ask what the fuck Kevin has gotten Graham out of in the past but decide on a less heated question for now. "What are they charging him with?"

"Three counts of aggravated assault," he says.

"Three?"

"Cal, obviously." He holds up a finger. "He attacked me when I showed up." He puts up another as he counts them off. "Then, when my backup arrived, he spit in her face." He waves three fingers around. "Breaking an officer's ribs and exposing another to bodily fluids? No way she wasn't going to file charges."

Connor slumps in the chair as if relaxing for the first time in his life. Only he stiffens right back up. "What about the truck?"

Oh shit, I completely forgot about the truck.

Trey smirks and shrugs. "I took care of it."

As much as the cloak-and-dagger comment intrigues me, I want—no, need to see Callie. Immediately. No more waiting. No distractions. With no hint of where I'm heading, Connor and Trey follow me to the nurses' station. Day seven of Callie withdrawals kicks in while I wait for a nurse to finish doing something I can't imagine is more important than me seeing my girl.

"All she has in now is an IV," Trey tells Connor. "But she still looks pretty rough, okay?"

I assume Connor nods, but I wouldn't know because my gaze continues to bore into the back of the nurse's head. Like a cat, I slowly push a box of tissues off the edge of the desk. It startles her, and she spins around in her chair.

"Hi, can we go now?"

She glowers at us. "I'm only supposed to let you back one at a time."

"Except for her underage brother, who needs someone with him," Trey says. "Doctor's orders."

Probably just eager to get rid of us, she concedes. The reason doesn't matter as long as I get through those doors. With a swipe of her badge, the lock clicks. This time, my feet have no problems, and we follow her through.

Having completed her task, the nurse leaves us in front of the room. Connor pauses, so I wait for him. He takes a deep breath and walks in, and then it's my turn to hesitate. Not for long though. The pain on his face when he reaches the foot of the bed forces me into the room. I round the curtain, and I forget how to breathe, how to think, how to be.

Callie lies abnormally still, her chest slowly rising and falling. Her bottom lip is split open. Both her left eye and cheek are swollen and bruised. In a cast, her left wrist rests on a pillow. A faint redness covers her neck, darker toward the center from his grip.

All the injuries he gave her, I can handle. My brain sorts through them, categorizes, processes. But what I never in my life could have prepared enough for, what destroys me … the claw marks. Distinct lines streak down her neck where her nails dug in, breaking her own skin. Frantic attempts to gain leverage under his fingers and palms as they pressed against her throat. They're the proof of how hard she fought for life against him, to survive.

There's not enough air in the room. Connor sinks to his knees on the floor. He bends forward until his forehead touches the white linoleum, and a sob bursts out of him. I drop down next to him, vaguely aware of my own tears as a numbness creeps through my body. I rest my hand on his back and provide what little comfort I can. His cries calm, only for the pain to rip through him again, sounding more agonizing than the last time. Even after the waves stop, we stay there, neither of us moving or making a sound.

Suddenly, he sits up, face red and eyes bloodshot. "I need to see Cate."

"Okay," I say, fighting out of a daze.

I get to my feet, and my gaze falls on Callie. The sight shatters me a little less on the second go-around. Connor also appears more in control of himself. He goes to the side of the bed and kisses her temple. His hand lingers on her arm for a second before he turns to leave.

On his way by, I stop him with a hand on the chest. "If you ever feel anywhere close to how you felt tonight, talk to someone. Callie, Trey, me. Hell, go have a tea party with Cate. Just promise you won't let it get that bad without asking for help."

He looks down, but his eyes come right back to mine. "I won't. I promise."

The confidence he lacked earlier reappears and reassures me. I drop my hand. "Also, don't expect me as backup when you tell your sister. In fact, I want a heads-up so that I'm out of the country."

One side of his mouth perks up. "You got it, Lover Boy." He glances at Callie once more before heading for the door.

The moment he disappears around the corner, I am at Callie's side. All the things I needed hours earlier are essential to my future survival. I lace my fingers through hers, kiss her forehead, and tell her I love her. My eyes pore over her face, finding all my favorite features that make her Callie. A hand presses against her chest, feeling her heartbeat under my palm. I even stick my ear in her face and listen to the barely audible air entering and exiting her lungs.

I sit down in the chair next to her bed, keeping her hand in mine, and continue my examination of every inch of her face. Even unconscious, she soothes me on a level no one else reaches, and I just need to be near her.

For the next few hours, each time someone walks by in the hallway, I think they'll try to kick me out. A battle I will fight. But no one disturbs us until around five in the morning. Trey knocks on his way in with the nurse behind him. I straighten up in the chair, staring him down just in case.

He puts his hands up. "Easy, killer. You can stay."

My newly acquired nemesis—the nurse—purses her lips. Trey must not have cleared this with her. Rather than argue, though, she checks Callie's vitals and hits a few buttons controlling the IV. "The doctor will be in shortly."

I relax in the chair as she leaves. "What's going on?"

"Just rounds. He'll give us an update." Trey stands at the end of the bed, his hands on Callie's feet through the blanket. "Pete's going out of his mind in the waiting room. Be prepared 'cause the minute visiting hours start, he'll be in here."

"Great," I say, the sarcasm dripping.

"It's Cal's fault. He had an accident when we were kids, and she spent three entire days in his hospital room. She refused to leave. They even let her sleep in there."

I half-smile, unsurprised. "Sounds exactly like her."

The doctor walks in, whistling and much too chipper for my liking. "Good morning."

If not for the jet-black hair with the deep side part, I wouldn't know him. Honestly, I could have met Jesus last night and not remembered his face.

"I see everyone adhered to my *one at a time and ten minutes each* rule." He takes a flashlight from his pocket and clicks it on. Carefully lifting Callie's swollen eyelid, he shines the light in her eye. He switches to her other side and chuckles. "She's trying to shut her eye on me."

Trey and I exchange glances, cautiously optimistic.

"Callista—"

"Callie," we say in unison.

"My apologies." He clicks off his light. "Callie doesn't seem to like me shining a bright light in her eye."

"So, she's…" Not normally one for being superstitious, I'm terrified I'll jinx myself if I say the rest out loud before a medical professional offers his opinion.

"She should open her eyes on her own anytime now."

A collective sigh escapes both of us, and the doubt tucked away in a deep, dark corner of my mind about her not waking up evaporates.

"Everything appears normal on her scans," the doctor continues. "But with oxygen cut off long enough for a loss of consciousness and a concussion, we never want to guess." He taps away at a tablet. "The pain medications could also be making it harder for her to wake up. With her ribs and neck, though, I want to keep the meds where they are for now."

Trey lets out another sigh. A deep one, loud enough to gain the doctor's attention. He pats a hand on Trey's shoulder on his way out.

"Get your ass up." Trey closes in on me. "We're hugging."

I shake my head, releasing Callie's hand as I stand up. "I can't wait for you to be out of that uniform, so I don't feel like I have to listen to you."

He wraps me in his, by now, familiar arms. "Shut up and hold me."

Unfortunately, I do.

The police-ordered affection lasts an uncomfortable amount of time before he switches into update mode and runs out into the hall. I return to my residency in the chair, taking Callie's hand back in mine because I'm not going to *not* hold her hand. I yawn, and my eyes grow heavy. I don't even try to fight it, letting them close.

The flutter against my palm registers since I never completely fell asleep. I consider my state more of a groggy twilight—awareness not quite lost. Another twitch goes without a proper response because, well, groggy twilight.

Callie's hand jerks from mine, and my eyes fly open.

She frantically grabs at her neck. She scans the room, her chest heaving as she gasps for air.

"You're safe, Callie." I secure her hand. "You're okay."

Our eyes meet, hers full of fear until they clamp closed again. Tears escape from the corners, and I wipe them away with my free hand. She tips her head back on the pillow and regains control of her breathing.

"I'll go get someone," I say.

The grip on my hand tightens, her eyes on mine again, pleading.

All right, plan B then.

I press the button for the nurse and return my hand to her face. My thumb grazes over her uninjured cheek, and she turns into my touch. Except when she winces, trying to swallow, her gaze never strays from me. I stare into those gorgeous eyes, disregarding the pink hue staining the whites of them. Just like that, my world reassembles around me.

The nurse comes in and orders me to leave. I don't acknowledge her until Callie slowly nods. I force myself out to the hallway, pulling out my phone. An older man scowls at me, but I have more important business at hand than pleasing my elders.

When Benji answers, loud music makes me yank the phone away from my ear.

"Where the fuck are you?" I ask.

All the noise stops at once.

"Oh, uh … a movie."

"At six in the morning?"

"Yeah. I mean, no, man. Watching one at the house."

If anyone ever accuses Benji of being a good liar, they're the one who can lie. I don't have time for whatever nonsense he has going on. "All right, well, girlfriend is awake. Updates to follow."

I throw open the door to the waiting room and receive a standing ovation. Of course, my dramatic entrance has everyone thinking something is terribly wrong until I extend my arms.

"This is the last time I'm ever offering a loving embrace to anyone in this room other than Cate."

A light returns to Connor. "She's awake."

Trey trips over Pete, asleep on the floor, as he barrels across the room and picks me up like we're in the goddamn *Notebook*. He drops me to my feet and fastens his arms around me. Connor follows, my arms stretching over Trey to reach him. And, never one to be left out of the group hug, Pete joins in without fully waking up.

"Why are we hugging this time?" he asks.

We all laugh, none of us answering him.

"Uh, hello?" Cate says from the chair she's standing on. "What about me?"

Her giggle fills the room when Connor picks her up and dances her around. Wanting to talk to the doctor, Trey rushes out to the hall to track someone down, and Pete calls Tony. Meanwhile, I collapse into a chair, the tension from my neck, shoulders, and forehead releasing after a stressful eleven hours.

Jesus.

It's only been eleven hours.

Callie's doctor comes in with Trey. The rest of us hit our feet, waiting for whatever news he prepares to deliver, while Trey takes a seat, straightening out his legs.

"She's shaken up," the doctor says, "but her neuro tests are good. She has pain and tightness in her neck and throat, and her voice is hoarse. My suggestion of her whispering or not talking did not go over well."

Connor snorts out a laugh, covering his mouth.

"I want to keep her through today to watch the swelling in her throat from the strangulation. We'll also have someone talk to her about the potential symptoms of PTSD."

An eerie silence falls over the room with the reminder of the exact circumstances that led to us being with this doctor in this room in this hospital. Connor's eyes close in response. I hold my breath, waiting for them to open again.

They do.

I exhale.

"When do visiting hours start?" Pete asks.

My glare goes unnoticed.

The doctor checks his watch. "An hour or so, but something tells me I'll see most of you wandering my halls before that." He turns to leave but stops in the doorway. "She didn't like the light shining in her eyes because someone used to make her go fishing?"

Trey smirks, putting his hands behind his head. "She was a pain in the ass to get out of bed at four in the morning. A flashlight in the eyes pissed her off but saved me time."

The doctor smiles on his way out. I chance missing out on yet another four-dude cuddle session and follow him. He scans his badge and steps through the doors with me right behind him. The extra set of footsteps must clue him in on his shadow because he chuckles, turning a corner.

"That didn't take long at all."

The same peach of a nurse from earlier stares in disapproval when she sees me stride into Callie's room. She moves a large glass of water to the side of the bed with my chair. "Encourage small sips." She pulls the door most of the way shut behind her.

Callie shifts, uncomfortable as she turns her head toward me. The fear from earlier has dissipated, and all her injuries fade into background noise I hardly notice.

"Hey," she whispers, her voice raspy.

One word has never meant more in my damn life. "Hey, beautiful."

"Cate and Connor?"

I groan and drop my head onto her shoulder. "I knew we forgot something."

A small smile greets me when I lift my head. "So frustrating."

"You love it," I whisper back.

Her eyes close.

"Want me to leave so you can sleep?" I ask, getting comfortable in the chair. Regardless of her answer, I have no plans on moving from this spot.

"No," she says.

"Good. My presence is nonnegotiable."

When she opens her eyes, her hand eases up to her neck. Her fingers trace over the claw marks. The rise and fall of her chest speeds the longer she explores the damaged skin. I am anxious watching, so I can't imagine how she feels. I reach for her hand and kiss each of her knuckles until her breathing evens out.

"It was getting worse, but I never thought…" She swallows, pain evident on her face. "He snapped."

"He'll never fucking touch you again." I press my lips to her inner wrist. "Don't even think about him."

The door creaks after a soft knock. She draws in a ragged breath, her eyebrows pulling together at the sight of Trey. They stare at each other for a second before he speeds across the room. He cradles her head against his chest, and her hand withdraws from mine to hold on to him.

"Never again, Cal." His cheek rests on the top of her head. "You are never putting me through anything like this ever again."

"And you're never talking about roller coasters again."

He chokes out a sad laugh, his eyes tight. "I think I can manage that." He moves to the end of the bed, clearing his throat.

"Our waiting room's getting a little crowded. You know three guys and a redhead?"

Ah, the mystery of Benji's "movie" solved. The merry band of misfits and Felicia must have already been on their way here. Why would I expect anything less from them?

"Those belong to me," I say, noting the side-eye from Callie. "Well, they belong to us."

Movement in the hallway snags my attention. Connor hovers in the hall with a torn expression. I leave my post long enough to hook my arm around his neck and pull him into the room. When Callie spots him, her face lights up as much as it can. He hurries around the bed and lays his head on her shoulder, trying to touch as little of her as possible.

"I'm so sorry." He pulls back, his eyes glassy.

She sweeps the hair away from his forehead and rasps, "None of this is your fault. Do you hear me?"

He nods, and for the first time, he appears to believe it.

The population of Callie's room encroaches on that of Sutterville when Pete slides through the door. A chair scrapes all the way across the floor behind him. He drops it off near the window before coming to squeeze Callie's hand. "I'll be over there if you need me."

So much for him waiting until visiting hours to set up shop. My not-so-subtle sigh of annoyance makes Trey laugh. Callie tries to clear her throat, so I hand her the water glass. Once she finishes a few sips, I set it down and return to my chair.

Wait.

My head jerks around in Pete's direction. "Where the hell's Cate?"

He never looks up from his phone. "In the waiting room. She was playing with the spiky hair on some guy named Rusty."

I laugh at the thought of such a badass being tamed by a bossy little girl.

"We should go save him, Connor," Trey says. "We'll track down breakfast while we're at it."

Each of them hugs Callie one more time before shuffling out to the hallway.

Finally, I have her to myself. Almost. Maybe I can stuff Pete in a broom closet for a few hours. He pretends to ignore my glare, but I see the smirk. Whatever. I can think of worse people to share the space with for the day.

When I look at Callie, she's smiling. But not at me. No, her heartfelt expression goes to Benji, waltzing in. He shoves around me and crawls right into the bed with her. His arm slides around her, she rests her head on his shoulder, and why the hell didn't I think of that?

"Thanks for taking care of my Calico, man."

"How the hell did you even get back here?" I ask.

"I'm a charming son of a bitch."

About then, my biggest fan—the nurse—walks in. She beams at him and carries a cup of coffee to him.

"Thank you, Sandy," he says with a wink.

She blushes, checking Callie's vitals, and tosses me a scowl before leaving.

Unbelievable.

It doesn't take long for Benji and Callie to double-team me. They insist I catch up to Trey and Connor for something to eat. I hold my own for a while, but the worried looks from Callie cause me to cave. Strategically digging an elbow into Benji's solar plexus, I lean over him and kiss her forehead. He plants an unwelcome kiss on my cheek in retaliation, but her breathy laugh makes the whole affair worthwhile.

I check the waiting room for Trey and Connor. The second I walk in, Felicia flings herself at me. I catch her with a grunt. "Jesus, Gibs."

All signs point to her not letting go soon, so I go the rest of the way across the room with her still clinging on. I release one arm and greet Gavin and Tony with slaps on the back. They're deep in conversation. About what, I never ask. It's safer that way. Shayna squeezes my arm on my way by to nudge Rusty with my foot. He's sitting on the floor, surrounded by crayons, and wearing the familiar face of exhaustion brought on by a specific six-year-old. The same six-year-old who locks a jealous stare on the redhead attached to my chest. Once Felicia remembers how to disengage her python grip, Cate scrambles into my arms, securing her place.

Demanding women have overrun my life. I love it.

Over breakfast, a meeting of the minds, Trey, Connor, and I agree to hold off on telling Callie about Connor versus the train. The last thing we need is her further injuring herself by trying to chase him down.

"I need to leave for a few hours to take care of some Graham business and other stuff," Trey says.

Connor perks up. "The truck?"

He nods, chewing his cafeteria mystery breakfast sandwich.

"What do you plan on doing with it?" Connor feigns disinterest, pushing food around on his plate.

"Don't worry about it." Trey shoves his chair back, leaving us with the question still unanswered.

By the time Connor and I dump our trays, visiting hours are in full swing. I bring him and Cate to Callie's room with me. We host a short question-and-answer session for Cate, most responses vague and filled with half-truths.

"What happened there?" she asks.

"An accident," Callie says.

"And there?"

"Another accident."

"You need to be more careful, Cal."

"I will be. I promise."

"Was Daddy in an accident, too?"

Callie forces a small smile. "Yes."

"Do I have to visit him?"

"No."

"Good."

Pacified, she switches into nurse mode. Cast in the role of the patient is none other than an unsuspecting Rusty when he steps through the door. Within a few minutes, it's clear that being around real medical equipment will lead to him needing an actual nurse, so for his safety, he returns to the waiting room with her in tow. As he carries her out of the room, I can't help myself.

"If this is what you're like around a kid, I'm terrified for our band's image."

He turns around, flipping me off.

Cate covers up his middle finger. "No, Rusty."

"Sorry," he says, disappearing around the corner.

The poor guy never stood a chance against her.

Everyone rotates in and out of the room, Pete and I the constant fixtures. Callie sleeps on and off at first. She always wakes up gasping, searching the room, and reaching for her neck. I grab her hand, and once I say her name, her panicked eyes settle on me, and she calms down.

"Sorry," she says after the third time.

"Nothing to be sorry for, beautiful." I brush my thumb over the hand once again relaxed in mine.

She won't shut her eyes anymore after that, avoiding the onslaught of memories waiting in her dreams. A counselor visits a while later and talks to her about the symptoms of PTSD. She listens, unresponsive until they tell her the nightmares could persist for some time.

"A going-away present from Graham," she whispers, glancing over.

I smile because she means it as a joke, and I'm supposed to, but my fingers tighten on the arm of the chair. She points out a harsh truth. We both know it.

The doctor swings through late in the morning and increases her pain medications to help her swallow easier. The swelling in her throat has stayed consistent, which he considers a net positive. He sounds optimistic she can leave tomorrow—the news she wants. She hates other people taking care of her, but if she thinks it will stop after she comes home, she's mistaken. My ass plans on not letting her lift a fucking finger for the foreseeable future.

She will need to deal with it.

On my way back from a forced lunch break—again ganged up on by the best friend and girl—I bump into Trey, rounding a corner. Out of uniform, he's accompanied by another officer. He evicts Pete and me so that they can record statements from Callie and Connor. Kevin shows up while we wait in the hallway and lets himself in. According to Callie, he apologized and promised to earn their forgiveness for the part he'd played over the years.

"What are the chances of him following through?" I ask, reclaiming my chair next to her.

She conveys her answer through an eye roll that roughly translates to, not very likely.

The door revolves all afternoon. One person out and another in.

When I fell asleep, I'm not sure, but I open my eyes to Gavin tucking me the fuck in with a blanket. He giggles and dodges out of the way as I kick at him.

Supper time rolls around, and the whole group assembles to go out and eat. They are all going a little stir-crazy and need a break from the confines of the waiting room, especially Cate. Of course, I stay behind, not letting Callie out of reach any more than necessary. Pete sticks around, too, glued to his chair by the window, not paying any attention to us.

"Privacy with my girlfriend would be nice at some point," I say from my dueling chair.

He hops up and drags the pink curtain suspended from the ceiling across the room. It blocks me from seeing him. His head pops around the side long enough to smirk. "I solved your problem, sugar plum."

My eyes narrow at Callie and her airy laugh. I blame her for the strange relationship developing between us.

"Want me to kick him out?" she asks, her voice still hoarse.

I shake my head, not all that bothered by him. Visiting hours will end, and he'll leave with his decade-old debt repaid. We aren't going to do anything actually requiring privacy anyway.

Nurse Susie Sunshine joins us. She completes one last check of Callie's throat before her shift ends. She and I share a bitter final exchange of facial expressions. Whether or not she wants to admit it, she will definitely miss me.

Almost alone again, I crawl into the bed. Callie lays her head on my shoulder, and I stroke her hair. The longer we lie here together, the more the previous twenty-four hours fade away.

"I love you, beautiful."

She makes a satisfied humming sound, nuzzling against me. "I love you."

I pick at the cast on her wrist, draped over my stomach. "Should I be offended you haven't asked me about dinner with my parents?"

"How rude am I to make everything about me?" she deadpans.

"Very, but I'll forgive you if we can fool around later."

She tilts her chin up to properly glare at me. "How was dinner?"

I groan. "Terrible. I don't want to talk about it."

A laugh and a smile before she cuddles into my shoulder. "So, you still don't know what you're doing next year."

"Oh, I do. The decision's made."

She lifts her head again, intrigued. "Well? Philosophy in Pittsburgh? Music at Berklee? Or what was the third?"

"Pot farmer. I never expected them to let me make it to my third suggestion, so I didn't put much thought into it."

"Clearly," she says. "So? Option one or two—or else Tony will never leave you alone."

"Pete, can you provide us with a drumroll, please?"

Nothing.

I try again, much louder. "Pete. Drumroll."

A weird sputter comes from the other side of the curtain. Both Callie and I make a face at the sad attempt.

"I requested a drumroll, not a guy who spits a lot."

He stops. "Asshole."

Callie grows impatient with my drawn-out announcement. "Just tell me."

I pause for effect and predict her reaction before I say, "I'm going to attend law school at UPenn."

Eyes widen. "You're kidding." Eyebrows pull together. "After everything?" Mouth falls open when I don't answer. "You're doing exactly what your parents expected all along?"

Doubt, shock, confusion—precisely as I expected for once.

"Technically," I say, "but I'm not doing it for them. Or the financial support they'll provide. Or the outrageous amount of money I can earn, working for one of my father's connections."

"Then why?"

"Because you, Callie Henders, are my muse."

She rolls her eyes. "Smooth answer."

"Real answer." I kiss her, careful of her bottom lip. "You helped me discover what I want to do with my life. My passion, if you will."

"Corporate law?" She guesses way off base. "Mergers and acquisitions?" Even further.

"Absolutely not," I say. "I'm more interested in child advocacy. Custody agreements, termination of parental rights, neglect and abuse cases. You'd be amazed at the shit people get away with regarding their children. Someone needs to give them a voice. Who knows? I might even pursue a judgeship one day. I'd hate to limit my future options. I mean—"

Her mouth cuts me off.

I gently kiss her back before pulling away. "Seriously, beautiful, you can't just kiss me to end the long-winded and at times overly wordy speech I've..."

She smiles, distracting me, and rather than finish, I return my lips to hers. There's really nothing better than being derailed by the girl in a red coat. The girl with the smile and the bluest eyes. The girl who has changed my world. The girl who has changed me.

And, damn it, the girl who is my beautiful meaning in an absurd universe.

Two months later…

"See, this is why I have no choice but to become a lawyer," I say.

Callie rolls her eyes, climbing out of the red Mazda. She's in cutoff jean shorts, a low-cut tank top, her hair in a high ponytail, and why she insists on torturing me, I will never understand. Only a week into July, and while I can't prove anything, I've developed a theory that she chooses outfits specifically with my mental suffering in mind. I either want summer to last forever or end right fucking now to spare me from those legs.

"You're being dramatic," she says.

"Me?" I dramatically grab my chest. "I've never been dramatic a single second of my entire life."

As we cross the street, she leans into me and interlaces our fingers. The wrist brace they gave her after removing her cast a few days ago is on my dresser—unsurprisingly.

"Every cop in a fifteen-mile radius will be here, so we don't need to worry about being busted."

"You misunderstand, beautiful. The fact that every cop in a fifteen-mile radius will be here is the exact reason I need to be a lawyer. You and your friends and your family—"

"My friends? My family? Convenient how when you're trying to make a point, they all belong to me and not us."

"Like I was saying…" I lift my arm up and twirl her around for a better view of the shorts. "You and your friends and your family insist on making these questionable decisions and skirting around the law. I'm going to spend more of my time sorting out their legal issues than practicing in my chosen field."

"First off," she says, "you just took the LSAT and don't start law school for a year."

"Thirteen months," I correct.

She ignores me. "Second, our friends and our family have survived this long without you and your pseudo law degree."

"Barely," I add.

She sighs, stopping at the front of the building. "Third, all I did was parallel park."

"Yes, Callie." I gesture to the car on the opposite side of the street. "But you parallel parked across three horizontal parking spaces."

"Jordan," she says, ready to end the conversation, "we're throwing a sixteen-year-old's birthday party in a bar. Let the legality of the parking job go."

She defeats my argument by proving my point.

Incredible.

She absentmindedly reaches for her neck. It's a lingering habit even though nothing except flawless skin exists, any hint of claw marks gone. I intercept her hand and brush the knuckles over my lips. She smiles up at me, and I kiss her because I'm not going to *not* kiss her. But then I want more and kiss down to her neck. My hands slide to her ass, and she lets out an incredibly sexy sound in my ear. At this point, the bar full of people can wait a little while longer. Hell, they can throw the whole damn party without us. I back her against the building and press into her.

"Jordan," she says in the put-the-brakes-on kind of way instead of the ravish-me one I prefer.

I groan, detaching myself, and hold open the door. "Hurry. I'm weak."

She purposely bites her lip as she passes, adding to my theory. *Torture.*

When we step inside, Cate tears across the building in our direction. From about five feet away, she jumps with her arms forward and legs back. I race to catch her before she face-plants on the floor. At least a potential trip to the emergency room acts as an instant mood killer.

"Hi," she says, smiling.

"Hi." I smile back, setting her down.

She skips off to the Cate Entertainment Table someone set up for her. It's covered with crayons, dolls, and what looks to be a rawhide dog bone. Experience warns me not to ask.

Trey pauses his conversation with Benji when we get to the bar and sticks out his hand. "Keys?"

Callie hands off the car key and takes over the stool on the other side of Benji. He slides her a beer and eyes me as he pulls her stool closer. "My girlfriend."

"Great. You can pay her parking tickets."

She wrinkles her nose, and I wink.

A few stools down from them, I join Gavin. He supervises Pete pouring a tray's worth of shots. Each time he reaches for one, Pete slaps his hand away. The distraction allows me to snag the full beer from in front of him. I finish half before he even notices it's missing.

Yellow balloons and black streamers intermingle with the animal heads on the walls, and stacks of similar-colored plates wait at the end of the bar. The Decorating Committee consists of Felicia and newly recruited Rusty. They're working on hanging Connor's birthday banner. A task made much more difficult by letting Cate instruct them on which end needs adjustment.

"Higher on the right," she says for the second time.

Felicia struggles on top of a stool, pushing up on her tiptoes. "Better?"

"Higher."

I watch the banner become more and more lopsided. "Hey, Cate, show Gibs your right hand."

She immediately holds up her left.

Felicia's head falls forward, defeated by Cate's unwavering confidence. The gentleman I am saves the day and helps Rusty even it out. Both Felicia and Cate coach us, giving conflicting orders. Once we ignore them, we manage to successfully hang the banner.

Returning to the bar, I snake an arm around Callie and reclaim her from Benji. She leans against my side. "Oh, you want me now?"

"Always, beautiful." I kiss the top of her head.

"Shit." Pete dashes over and shoves Callie's beer in front of me. "Hey, Sheriff."

My eyes dart to the mirror on the wall behind the bar. Sure enough, Kevin's on his way over. I spin around and sip the beer now belonging to me.

"You the one who parked like an asshole?" he asks, pointing a blue envelope in my direction.

Without hesitation, I give up the gorgeous girl next to me. "All her, sir."

Callie glares up at me.

"Not surprised by that." He tosses the envelope on the bar in front of her. "Connor's birthday card."

She rotates her stool, knocking into my leg on the way. "He'll be here soon if you want to stick around."

"Nah, I, uh…" Kevin's gaze drops to his shoes.

A tension builds in the air around us, and no one speaks for what stretches on for an eternity. It's the silence used in place of Graham's name. Every Sunday afternoon, without fail, Kevin visits him. But the last few times, Graham refused to see him, mad about Kevin's first step toward making amends with Callie.

Since Graham immediately signed a plea deal for three counts of aggravated assault and a bonus charge of emotional child abuse of Connor, he faces several years in prison. He signed over power of his finances and property to his brother. Well, Kevin turned around and sold the house within a week, gifting the money to Callie. It healed one relationship, only to create a rift in another. Not that I care about Graham in the least, but Kevin's not so bad now that he's not blindly protecting his brother.

"We'll bring some cake by the house later." Callie swipes the beer from my hand and brings it to her lips. "Now, leave before you see something you shouldn't."

She's perfect.

Kevin wags a finger at me, still intimidating as shit. "Can't you get a handle on her?"

"Not at all," I say, pulling her closer. "I've stopped even trying."

He chuckles on his way to the door, only looking back long enough to wave.

As soon as he steps outside, Pete throws his rag at Callie. "Damn it, Cal."

She laughs and tosses it right back.

The alarm on my phone goes off, warning us that the time has arrived. Everyone gathers on the dance floor so we can keep an eye on the swinging door leading to the rear entrance. Pete distributes the shot glasses, providing a special princess cup filled with juice for Cate. Both Trey and Gavin drink theirs immediately, so he makes a second round. Shayna charges through the door first, grinning like a madwoman. She links an arm with Felicia, both of them bouncing around. A few seconds later, Tony swings open the door, and Connor steps through.

"Surprise," we say at varying levels of enthusiasm, Felicia and Shayna by far the loudest.

He covers his face but can't hide his grin. We wait for Tony to get his glass, and we toast to Connor, forcing him to watch us all take our shots.

His embarrassed act continues while everyone fusses over him, hugging him, slapping him on the back, reminiscing about the weird things he said or did as a kid. Or a week earlier in Callie's case. He takes it all in stride with a genuine smile that never fades. All of his smiles lately have been authentic. The good finally outweighs the bad in his eyes.

Pete turns on some background music, which Gavin and Benji quickly change to something more their style. I go to the kitchen and help him carry out the food.

We all congregate around the bar to eat. Everyone picks over the trays of fried food. Loud voices all talk over one another, multiple conversations going on at once.

A food fight almost breaks out when Trey throws a handful of fries at Callie. Given how quickly Pete snatches ahold of the soda gun from behind the bar, it's happened a time or two before. In the process of stopping her attempt to retaliate with the mustard bottle, I wind up getting bit. Not in a hot way, but it does the trick anyway.

After Gavin and Tony disappear into the kitchen, the overhead lights turn off. A hell of a lot of yelling and cussing ensues, but no one volunteers to investigate. They reappear with sixteen sparklers, left over from the Fourth of July, all shoved into and lit on the cake. If you disregard the risk of us ingesting chemicals and metal shavings, it looks cool as shit.

Once the sparklers burn themselves out, Callie steps in front of the cake. "Before we eat your possibly toxic cake"—she narrows her eyes at the guilty parties, who look at the floor to avoid her—"we have a birthday gift for you."

Connor's lines form between his eyebrows. "We?"

Her gaze darts over to Trey and me, our cue to herd him outside. Everyone follows us out to the sidewalk in front of the building. For no other reason than our personal entertainment, we spin him around in circles. We stop once he wobbles, nice and disoriented, and Trey tosses the car keys up in the air.

Connor's eyes bulge as he catches them. "No way. A car?" He hits the button, making the illegally parked red Mazda beep. "Holy shit."

Halfway across the street, he changes directions, running back. I receive the fastest hug of my life and then Trey.

He picks up Callie and swings her around. "Thank you. Thank you. Thank you."

When he sets her down, she grips his arm to keep him from darting off. "Hold on, there's more."

A huge grin spreads across his face. "I'm good with the car."

"Trust me," I say. "You want the second part."

Trey backs me up. "The man speaks the truth."

"Anyone but Pete"—I glance over, and he flips me off—"drumroll, please?"

Various noises occur, none of them very authentic. In fact, I worry no one knows what a drum sounds like at all.

"Everyone, shut up." Rusty stretches his arms and cracks his neck in preparation. "Let a professional handle this." Pantomime and all, he gives one hell of a drumroll.

Callie slides the folded-up papers, neatly tied with a blue ribbon, from my back pocket.

Connor unties and unfolds and scans them. His eyes bounce between her and the papers, confused. "So, he…"

"Graham's parental rights are officially terminated," she tells him. "He'll never be our problem again."

The papers fall to the ground when he grabs her, smashing her face into his chest. "So much better than a fucking car, Cal."

She grunts and mumbles a response, but he only squeezes her tighter. Watching them, I put my arm around Felicia, the happy crier blubbering away next to me. I don't blame her, though. All of us have worked so hard to leave that night behind us. To let it fade into distant memories. The chance to move on from Graham and close this chapter of their lives permanently makes the task a little less daunting. Callie said that, one day, Graham would just be someone she survived. The papers scattered at her feet represent how right she was.

They both wipe tears from their eyes after Connor releases her. He stares at her a second longer before he snatches up Cate and sprints across the street to check out his new car. The rest of our ragtag collection of chosen family members follow them, shouting over one another in their usual obnoxious fashion.

Alone with my girl, I slide my arms around her. "When are you going to tell Connor about petitioning for guardianship?" A topic we've been discussing a lot lately.

Her hands clasp behind my neck. "Not until I meet with Lara next week."

I resist the urge to roll my eyes at the mention of her mother. Lara continues her party-girl lifestyle and shows little interest in her kids. Now that she has them full-time, she wants someone else to take care of them. Someone being Callie. Nothing like returning to school from summer break with two kids. But the potential alternatives aren't an option. For either of us.

"She still wants to go through with it?" I ask. "Send them with you and write a check every month?"

She nods, a worried look in her eyes. "She wants to pay child support and see them every other weekend rather than be their mother. How do I tell them that?"

I rest my forehead on hers. "We'll role-play later."

Her eyebrows shoot up as she seriously misinterprets my comment.

"For how to tell them," I say, grinning. "Jesus, Cal ... unless you want to play student again?"

She laughs, turning her attention toward the commotion across the street. Cate squeals while riding around on Rusty's shoulders and using his hair as reins. Not wanting anyone to show them up, Tony squats down for Trey to crawl up on his shoulders. After a touch-and-go moment when he stands up, Tony takes off running. They don't go far before Trey dives off and tackles Gavin to the ground. The entire group piles on top of them. It creates a mess of arms and legs and laughter in the middle of the road with Cate on the edge, ordering them to stop.

"I would like to make a formal request we get new friends. Less weird ones preferably." I bury my face in her neck, her skin warm from the sun.

"What were you and Connor whispering about earlier?" She pulls away to study my face, looking for clues.

"You'll find out soon enough."

"In sixteen days?"

I shrug, not giving anything up. Surprising Callie requires a hell of a lot of stealth. And I will surprise her.

"I told you," she says, a hint of irritation in her tone, "I don't want you to do anything special for my birthday."

"And I told you, we're already past that. Mission Callie Turns Nineteen has commenced."

"I thought we were done with missions."

"Oh no, beautiful. We have plenty of them left." I press my lips to hers. "Mission Second Grade Cate, Mission Connor Gets Bacne, Mission Let's Have Babies, Mission—"

"Whoa, hold on." The adorable, bewildered expression of a spooked Callie appears. "Mission Let's Have Babies comes after Mission Jordan Marries Callie, and I'm certain that one's not happening anytime soon."

I tilt my head to the side. "You're *certain?*"

She realizes her mistake and shakes her head. "Jordan. No."

I smile. *Far too late, beautiful.*

"Don't even think about say—"

"I accept your challenge."

ACKNOWLEDGMENTS

Throwing a thank you out to the irreplaceable people who helped, supported, rolled their eyes at, and somehow tolerated me through this should be the easy part, right?

Joe (yes, I'm using Joe), you are more patient than I give you credit for. You also shred like a badass, which is pretty sweet.

Emmily, we both know every word of this would have been deleted a hundred times over if not for you. You loved Jordan when I wasn't sure I even liked him.

Cindee, Kara, and Christy Ann, all read Elusion so early on and offered so much encouragement. You ladies should read it again. It's, like, a real book now.

Jovana, thank you for making me appear to know how sentences work. Wording don't go good, sometimes. (Not an actual representation of my work before Jovana.)

Madison, for catching what I missed. And for having such an awesome wedding song.

Murphy Rae: I appreciate you not blocking my email address. Without you, the cover would be … hell, I have no idea, which is why I'm truly grateful for you dealing with me.

A huge shout out to everyone who hyped up the book, shared it, talked about it. You're all amazing, and I can't thank you enough.

Loads of credit to my mom for not judging me all those times she asked what I was doing, and I answered nothing because I didn't want to tell her what I was really doing. See, I wasn't just sitting around watching my stories.

And finally, Andrea, Christy, William, Drew, and Blake. The five of you have turned into incredible human beings and share so much love with each other. I'm proud of you for becoming all you have in spite of the example you were given. You are the reason this book exists. You and your ability to survive your Graham.

Go Team Platipi!

CG Blaine writes unapologetically messy and emotional romance novels. She loves her characters complicated, the connections intense, and rip-your-heart-out feels.

She is obsessed with her vicious cat and aggressively cute bunny. Her favorite stories hit with the hurt and then apologize oh-so well.

Never miss a thing!
Join my reader group: CG's Cool Kids
Instagram: @cgblaine
Facebook Author Page: @cgblaineauthor
Website: cgblaine.com

Be sure to stay in the loop and sign up for CG's newsletter. You'll also snag a **FREE** short story.

Sign up at https://www.cgblaine.com